WAY OF THE WILD

FRANCESCA MCMAHON

Cover Illustration by Arthur Bowling III
Cover Typography by MiblArt
Interior Design by AB Book Services
Editing by Carly Catt

ISBN: 978-1-7398853-4-2 (eBook edition)
ISBN: 978-1-7398853-5-9 (Paperback edition)

DEDICATION

Wolves are beautiful creatures. They deserve to be protected.
Support their protection by going to relistwolves.org now.

WOLF-TO-HUMAN LANGUAGE

Den – Home
False wolves – Dogs
Suns/Moons – Days
Moon cycle – One month
Mother Wolf – "God"/Mother Nature/Spirit
Season – One year
Shadow pass – Hour
Smoking sticks – Guns
Span's distance – A mile
Stolen sunrise – Fire pit
Sun pass – One day
Sun's fall – Sunset
Sun's fever – Fire

PART I

THE PAST HAS A WAY

1

JAMIE

The coffee was bitter on her tongue. It always had been, but she'd relied on it during her studies. It had become a rather masochistic need to drink it before a big day. And this was an important day. So, of course, she was running late.

Jamie only lived five minutes away from campus, yet every day, no matter how prepared she was, she always ended up running late. She'd only just managed to fill her coffee thermos with the magical black liquid before running out. Now, as she chugged the drink, ignoring the burning of her tongue, she speed-walked across campus grounds and towards the back building.

Why does his office have to be on the farthest side of the university? Is he trying to make it hard for me to see him? Jamie thought irritably as she ran down the corridor, her trainers squeaking against the floor as she went.

Passing by all the other professors' offices, Jamie eventually came to the last one. Sitting dead centre at the far end of the corridor was the door labelled "Dr W. Gander-Yoon, Head of the Anthrozoology Department." With a breath, she knocked on the door. Instantly she received a somewhat frustrated "you're late" as the sign to enter the room.

The door opened with a creak that had Jamie cringing. Entering and closing the door behind her, she turned towards the occupied desk in the centre of the room. Hunched over an old-fashioned oak table that was in serious need of replacing, with his glasses dangling on the edge of his nose, was Professor Gander-Yoon, who continued to tap away at his computer as she came closer.

Jamie immediately noticed the bags under his eyes and the takeaway boxes in the bin. It looked as if he hadn't slept or eaten properly in days. She could've sworn his hair had even greyed more.

"Dad, you really need to learn the benefit of self-care."

With a glance up to her, he laughed and gestured to the chair in front of his desk. "Says Miss In-the-Library-Till Three-in-the-Morning-All-Weekend."

Jamie laughed too, realising she had forgotten to cover her own bags with makeup that morning.

"You know I've got to get my report in for the end-of-year project." She dropped heavily into the free chair.

He nodded his head in acknowledgement and turned away from his computer. "Is that why you were late today? You know we only have about" – he checked his watch – "twenty minutes left before I have my meeting."

Jamie had to bite back a sigh. Her dad never compromised his time for her. They only managed to get half an hour together every week, and yet each time they got to spend together, it was always with one eye on the clock. Jamie could be neither early or stay late as he always had something impor-tant before and after her. It's why she was still kicking herself for waking up late.

"Yeah, sorry," she said. "I know you're busy. I tried to get here as soon as I could, but Professor Alicaster decided I needed a further email enquiring about my dissertation." She rolled her eyes. "And because of that late-night email, I barely got any sleep trying to come up with something."

Professor Alicaster had had it out for Jamie since she started her undergrad four years ago. And that hadn't changed even as she was coming to the end of her post-graduate course. Jamie still didn't understand why she had an issue with her.

"Did she offer any help with your essay topic?" her dad asked. He was always looking on the bright side of Jamie's mortal enemies' actions.

"She just said to hurry up and figure out what I want to write."

Her father frowned. "You're still struggling with what it is you want to write about?" She averted her eyes in embarrassment. "Why not write about the wolf-girl you met as a child?"

Jamie turned to him, surprised. "What? Artemis?"

He took a bite of a cookie that he had pulled from somewhere and then pointed it at her. "It'd be an interesting focus on the connection between humans and animals. Especially in relation to feral children. That and" – he smiled – "it's probably your most personal story. Professors love personal stories."

Her father passed her a cookie of her own, which she took and immediately began munching on, lost in thought.

Could I write about Artemis? What would I even write? That I met a wild wolf-girl as a child and have been obsessed with her ever since? That I chose this career because of her? She rolled her eyes at herself. *Yeah, because that won't make me sound crazy at all.*

"Or maybe something in the same vein," her father continued, seemingly catching onto her internal conflict. "I'm sure I have my old paper around somewhere if you're in need of some inspiration or guidance."

"Thanks, Dad." Jamie smiled. "I appreciate it, really. But I don't think a paper on human and wolf relations during the medieval era would help me. It's not my area of expertise. As interesting as it was."

Jamie didn't want to admit that reading her dad's research always frustrated her to a degree – seeing the dates and knowing that, when he was writing the piece, he had left her behind somewhere. She may have chosen the same area of study as him, but that didn't mean she was going to follow the same path.

"I understand," he replied. "Why don't you look at the family dynamics of wolves and their young in relation to their domestication?" he said with a shrug before pulling out another cookie. "Whatever you decide, you know I'll support you."

"I know," she said. "Thank you."

After that, the two of them sat and chewed on snacks in comfortable silence. *Seriously, where is he getting all these snacks from?* she thought, smiling as he threw her her favourite treat, Choco Pies. It was her mum, Seon-mi's, favourite. Jamie's heart always felt warm when she ate it, almost as if her mum had given them to her herself.

As she ate, she thought about how the two of them used to sneak these treats before dinnertime and hide in Jamie's poorly made fort at their old house. They'd each have a turn to take a bite, and to make it more fun, they would make a game out of how loud they could get with their eating until her dad would find them.

Jamie's throat got tight, and eventually, she found herself unable to eat any more without thinking about the past. It didn't help that her dad's office was practically a time capsule of her mum.

The room looked more like hers than his. She liked to decorate a lot, and her mark was everywhere. From the plush red sofa by the window and its decorative handmade cushions to the array of family photos on the bookshelf and desk.

The photo that always faced the visitors chair at her dad's

desk was Jamie's favourite. It was just of her mum, wrapped up in a huge winter coat, with mittens, giant boots, and the biggest smile on her face. She looked absolutely freezing, but she was clearly loving every minute of it.

"It's my favourite picture too," her dad's voice broke through her trip down memory lane. "It was the first time we met; did I tell you that?"

"No, you didn't," Jamie lied with a smile.

She watched as her dad lit up when he began telling the story. Jamie was sure he knew that she knew the story by now, but he always told it when she asked. And Jamie always listened.

"Your mother, as you know, had a thing for stirring up trouble with the authorities..." he began as Jamie's gaze was drawn back to her mum's photo.

As she stared at the picture, she couldn't help but pick up the similarities between her and her mum. Same dark hair that framed her face, deep warm brown eyes, and tanned skin that stood out from the snow around her. The both of them were polar opposites of Jamie's dad, but that made them love him more. Even if he worked too hard and rarely saw them for much of Jamie's childhood. Jamie didn't mind it too much when her mum was around. But after her mum died, Jamie was alone.

It had only been a few years since Jamie had lost her mum when she met Artemis for the first time – or was saved by, is what she should say. The old woman, Mrs Hammond, who'd come after her wasn't exactly a danger, but she knew just the right way to hurt a person. And she'd gone right for the jugular.

Not only had Artemis helped Jamie save face by stopping her from crying over Hammond's words, she'd also been the first person to ever stand up for her.

Maybe Dad does have a point on my thesis, she thought as she turned to her dad who was still telling the story.

"She was about ready to start a fight with the mayor when I stepped in to help." Jamie smiled as he waved his hands around as he spoke, like she did when she talked. And just like she'd done when she first met Artemis.

I think I have my angle.

Leaving her dad's office after the allotted time they had together, Jamie headed home to her flat. With a fresh pot of coffee in hand, she sat down at her computer and pulled up her previously blank document.

"Let's see how this goes..." she muttered to herself as she began to type.

2

JAMIE

Ritchie had to drag her out of her room two weeks later.

"Mate, you give your pops a hard time about not seeing the sun enough, and yet here you are doing the same thing."

They'd found their usual spot in the centre of the near-empty university campus grounds. Where they sat, they were surrounded by the old-fashioned redbrick buildings that reflected the hot sun onto them, making it feel hotter than it was. Jamie laid down on the freshly cut grass next to the trees in hopes of gaining some reprieve from the heat. This was the one place on campus they could be in nature, and she wasn't going to give it up. No matter how much the grass tickled her arms and the sun burned her face.

The school was ridiculously old, and unlike most modern campuses, they didn't have many natural beauties around. Beyond this small stretch of grass, which was smaller than her bedroom, there was nothing. Considering the university was known for its environmental studies, it felt horribly ironic that the campus was practically a concrete forest.

Jamie tried to ignore the feel of Ritchie's stare by taking in a deep breath of fresh air. But eventually she couldn't ignore him any longer and turned towards him. He sat cross-legged next to her, his muscular arms folded over his chest and an eyebrow raised in question. He'd gotten a new haircut; his blonde hair had been cut shorter with the sides shaved almost bald. He looked a lot like Dimitri in *Anastasia*. Jamie guessed that was probably his intention. He made her watch that movie at least twice a year with him.

"Sorry, just been getting caught up in all this work. You know how it is, you were the same with your film last month."

"OK, one." He raised a finger. "I never forgot our lunch dates. And two, you completely forgot to be my support lesbian when I had to meet with Professor Dickhead last week." Ritchie ran his fingers through his hair. "And he was, to no one's surprise, a dick." Shaking his head, he frowned at her, concerned. "You've never been this insane with your essays, so now I want answers. And a milkshake."

Jamie laughed. "I'm sorry, just with Alicaster constantly on my arse about the paper, I knew I had to get working to make her back off. And it was so worth it. Did you know that the Swen Forest is one of the oldest surviving natural lands in the Western hemisphere?" Ritchie rested his chin on his hand, silently telling her to go on. "The wolves have apparently been there for centuries, which is so insanely rare and amazing at the same time. They're survivors."

"Why am I not surprised you chose wolves to study?" he said with a cheeky smile. "How far have you gotten into the paper?"

Jamie began plucking the grass at her side with a frown. "Not that far yet; there was a lot more to research than I initially expected." She turned to Ritchie. "Surprisingly, the town I lived in, Matiria, doesn't seem to have much of an online presence, so I can't figure out their involvement with the forest to be able to really dive into the topic of the relationship dynamics. And whenever I look up Swen, the town is never mentioned."

"OK, that's weird," Ritchie said, sitting up straighter. "Do you want some help? You know how good I am with finding stuff that can't be found."

She offered him a smile. "Yeah, that would be great. Though please try to keep it legal this time. We don't want another Edinburgh incident."

"Look, the map said it was a short cut, I didn't know we were trespassing into an endangered cow—"

"Legal."

"Yes, ma'am." He saluted her before going back to leaning his chin on his hands. "So, what do you remember about Matiria? Maybe that'll help us find more about them?"

Jamie moved to lie back down and rested her hands on her stomach nervously. "I know they weren't exactly … welcoming of the wolves after a few incidents with their sheep, but other than that" – she waved a hand into the air before dropping it back to her stomach – "nothing."

"Well not necessarily nothing, right?"

Jamie nodded her head. "OK, that's true. I also have the knowledge of what they did to Artemis and how they tried to train out the wolf behaviour in her. But at the same time, I don't really know *what* they did to her. Just that it made her desperate to get away." She rolled her head to look at him. "Alongside all that, I need to analyse my time with Artemis to understand the feral child aspects about her." She looked back up to the sky. "Which is kind of hard when I haven't seen her in nearly thirteen years."

Ritchie moved to lie down beside her. "OK, I forgive you for abandoning me. I managed to hang out with Darien anyway, so I wasn't alone. Though I do still want the milkshake. Oreo, specifically." He knocked his hand against hers. "But damn, you don't make things easy for yourself, do you?"

"Tell me about it," Jamie said with a sigh. "I don't even know what happened to Artemis after I left, let alone what the town did. I know Dad managed to get a protection order for the forest, but other than that, who knows."

"Well, at least I know why you've burrowed yourself away in the dark for the last two weeks," Ritchie said, turning to look at her. She turned to him also, waiting for him to continue. "The ultimate lesbian pining, writing an essay on your long lost—"

Jamie punched him in the gut. "Shut up."

With a laughing cough, Ritchie pushed her away. "Am I wrong?"

"I will not dignify that with a response," Jamie said, crossing her arms across her chest. She didn't want to admit that he was right. It had been over a decade since she'd last seen Artemis, and yet she still thought about her whenever her mind wandered.

"You may want to if you really want a certain someone to help you out with your research."

Jamie sat up. "You'll ask Darien to help me?"

This time it was Ritchie who was slapping her in the stomach. "No, you dickhead. Me. I'll help you."

"Are you sure?" Jamie asked. She knew he'd already said he'd help, but she didn't know if he meant it. She was never sure if the people in her life meant the things they said. Jamie definitely owed him that milkshake.

"What are best friends for?" He smiled, his grin slowly turning goofy. "Besides, you need to have fun while you work." He raised his voice, "And having fun isn't hard…"

"IF YOU'VE GOT A LIBRARY CARD!" the two of them sang out, followed by delirious laughter.

"All right, I'll get you that milkshake and meet you at the library. Two minds are better than one, even if one of those brains is soon to be sugar-filled with milkshakes."

One sugary excursion later, Jamie met Ritchie in the library with two Oreo milkshakes in hand and a brain ready for researching.

As she headed towards her designated spot near the back of the library, Jamie found herself pausing every so often to browse the shelves. She loved the library, with its muted walls of dark brown, wooden spiral staircases, and warm light that hung from the ceiling. The whole building reminded her of the woods she would explore as a kid. Even the shelves were made from a well-worn oak. Jamie found herself leaning closer to the wood, and though she knew it was crazy, as she inhaled, she was sure she could still smell the forest the wood had come from. The whole place felt like a secret building. A place only a select few could be allowed to venture into. Especially now at the end of term.

The library was always quiet, but with most of the students having finished for the year and gone home, it felt even more so. There was no quiet hum of chatter in the air. No smell of freshly made coffee or tea. It was just quiet.

"Over here!" Ritchie shouted.

Almost quiet.

Holding back a laugh, Jamie made her way over to her usual desk space and sat down beside her best friend. He'd set everything up for them already, which surprised Jamie, but she appreciated it all the same. She handed over his milkshake the moment she sat down as a reward for his hard work.

They got to work almost immediately. The only sounds to accompany them was the slurping of the milkshakes and Ritchie's tapping foot. They were only about forty minutes in before the complaining started. Jamie was surprised he had lasted this long.

"You know I suck at studying; it's why I chose film." Ritchie groaned as she handed him another book. "I'll be more of a problem than actually able to help," he said as he opened a *Forests of the North* book, frowning. "I mean, can't we just Google this? Or I could find some videos on it? You know I'm way better at digital media than" – he flicked a page of his book with a grimace – "books."

Jamie rolled her eyes. "Read the book, Ritchie, it won't kill you."

"Are you sure about that?" Ritchie asked, staring dubiously at the book in front of him. Jamie raised an eyebrow at him, and he raised his hands in surrender. "Alright, fine, fine."

It was only a few minutes later before he gave up again.

"Ugh, couldn't you ask your dad about this? Like, he used to live there or somethin', right?"

"I'm not asking him," Jamie said snippily.

When Ritchie didn't respond, Jamie sighed. Turning towards him and taking in his hurt expression, she tucked a piece of hair behind her ear.

"Sorry, it's just…" She pinched the bridge of her nose. "The professors in my department already think I didn't get into this course on my own merit. I don't want to give them any further reason to think that."

Ritchie stared at her for a little while, like he was thinking over her words. He shrugged and turned back to the book. He didn't complain again after that. Or at least, for the next hour.

"My God, does this town even exist?!" He dropped his face into his keyboard in frustration before flipping Jamie off when she shushed him. "There's no one here, Jay. I can yell if I want."

"And they say women are dramatic…" she muttered. Closing one book, she opened another. "It's only been two hours. Get a grip. Please. My future career depends on it."

The sounds of tapping on a keyboard caught Jamie's attention, and she rolled her eyes at his distracted, "Yeah … yeah…"

"I swear, if you're playing games on your computer instead of helping—"

"Hush, I'm still helping. I'm just also uploading my new film to YouTube at the same time." He puffed out his chest. "I can multitask."

"Ah yes, like how you multitasked by burning pasta in our kitchen last week because some boy was messaging you."

Ritchie didn't look up from the computer, his fingers still typing away. "First, he was a man. Second, you know I can't cook and yet you left me unsupervised to do it 'cause you were locked up studying like Gollum."

OK, he's got me there, Jamie thought, deciding it was best not to respond.

"None of the books you've been reading about Swen mention the town, right?"

Jamie nodded. "Not that I've found at least." She turned to another page of her book and frowned. "Admittedly, there aren't many books on Swen as it is. And like I said, it doesn't have much of an online presence."

All Jamie got was a thoughtful hum. At least that meant he was listening.

"What was the name of the town again?" Ritchie asked half an hour later.

"Matiria."

"How are you spelling it?"

Jamie closed her eyes and spelt it out. "Uh, I think it's M-A-T-I-R-I-A."

"You sure it has two I's?"

"I'm pretty sure," she said with a frown. "No, yeah, I'm sure."

"Have you ever seen the name written down?"

Jamie took a breath. She knew she was probably just hungry, the Oreo milkshake not having made much of a dent in her growling stomach, but she swore she was going to scream if Ritchie didn't stop distracting her.

"No."

"Hm, I'll try spelling it a different way."

Scrubbing a hand over her face, Jamie didn't respond. She pulled open her laptop and began searching out papers on feral children. Jamie was getting sick of trying to find information on this town. It's not like it was particularly necessary for her to study, but it could be useful to get an insight into the minds of people who thought they were helping when taking someone from their assumed habitat. She remembered reading the case of Dina Sanichar and feeling sad that a boy who, sure, may not have been where he was meant to be, was taken from all he knew.

Another half hour passed, and Jamie had managed to find some pretty useful articles for her subject that examined the differences between the types of feral children and their development when Ritchie spoke up.

"Jay, I think—"

"I swear if you're going to complain again, I'm never getting you another milkshake."

"Rude, but no." Ritchie spun the laptop towards her. "I was watching this video, which led me to this website—"

"Come on, Ritchie, really? You know you were the one who volunteered—"

"Jamie."

"You didn't have to help me, but you put yourself forward, and all you've done is complain while I worked."

"Jamie."

"God, why can't I find anything about this Goddamn town?!"

"Jamie!"

"What?" She whirled on him in frustration only to find him smiling.

"I found the town." He gestured to his laptop screen. Lit up on the page was a picture of Matiria. It was just as Jamie remembered, if a little more modern with their houses.

"How?!" Jamie moved closer to look at the screen.

"I always told you that you should have been tested for dyslexia," Ritchie said. He reached for his keyboard and scrolled down to the main article. "Materia is spelt with an E, not two I's.

M-A-T-E-R-I-A." He frowned and passed the laptop towards her. "I don't think this is the story you were hoping for though."

Jamie took the laptop from him and set it down in front of her. There in big, bold letters were the words, "Why Deforestation Will Help the Environment". Jamie could feel her blood boiling as she scrolled down further. The webpage was vibrant and spoke in a falsely positive manner, as if everything they were showing and talking about was a good thing. It made her feel sick. Then she read the last paragraph.

> The village of Materia lives on the edge of a local forest, a land infested with overgrown vegetation and wildlife that has damaged the local's welfare and infrastructure. As such, Materia has become one of the first towns to sign up and become involved with the Talbot Pacific Group. Their deforestation measures are intended to begin in the fall of this year.

She had to stop herself from slamming the laptop closed. Ritchie would murder her if she did it any harm. With the article still on screen in front of her, Jamie stayed quiet. She started taking deep breaths to keep her cool. She was grateful for Ritchie's silence as he watched her. It was only when a few minutes passed that he eventually spoke up.

"What do you want to do?"

Leaning back in her chair, she brought her hands to her hair and scraped it back, the pressure of her fingers against her scalp calming her as she pulled the hairband off her wrist. Tying her hair up, she took a breath and turned to her friend.

"I'm going to cause hell."

3

JAMIE

"*P*rofessor Alicaster! Wait!" Jamie shouted as she rushed down the cobbled pathway.

She was out of breath and exhausted, a collection of papers clasped tightly in her hands, but she ran as quickly as she could after her evasive professor. She watched as the woman ducked into the science block building. Jamie charged forward, trying to catch up before the door closed. She'd left her ID badge at her flat and wouldn't be able to get in if it did.

"Mother fu—" Jamie hissed out as the door slammed hard against her knee. "Professor Alicaster, wait!" She gritted out as she awkwardly pulled the door open with her elbow. "I'm sorry I missed our meeting."

Just as she slipped through the doorway and into the warm building hallway, Jamie noticed that Alicaster had stopped and turned towards her. Jamie cringed internally at the disappointed scowl sent her way after she caught up to the woman.

"Unless you have been asleep during my lectures for the last four years, I am sure you are well aware that my meeting hours are set in stone."

"I know, professor, I had—"

"And excuses are unacceptable unless notified prior to the appointment?"

"Yes, but professor—"

"Miss Gander-Yoon, I have been patient with you long enough this semester." Alicaster sighed. "You have come in late with your thesis subject, which I have overlooked, you have not arranged any one-on-one sessions with me."

"But that's because you didn't—"

"And now you have missed the last appointment I give students months before the final assignment is due." She folded her arms across her chest. "Why should I listen now?"

"Because an eco-disaster is about to happen."

That gained the woman's attention. As much as Jamie was loath to admit anything positive about her professor, there was one thing she truly respected about her: her dedication to protecting the environment. Jamie had known this since first year; many of their sessions with Alicaster featured anecdotal commentary on the expeditions she and her team had gone on for research and protection purposes. She often travelled in the summer and winter breaks and would return with photos, video, and even physical artefacts that would be used in class. In fact, she and Jamie's dad were a regular team on these journeys.

"Have a seat, Miss Gander-Yoon," Alicaster said, gesturing to the beanbag chairs by the windows. They weren't exactly ideal for a serious discussion, but it would do. "You have five minutes."

Crap.

"To summarise, I guess" – Jamie laid out her papers on the table in front of them – "Swen Forest has been picked by this Talbot foundation group for deforestation. Obvs awful in general, but it gets worse." She pulled out a sheet with the history of Swen on it. "The forest is one of the oldest in the country, and within it is one of the longest running wolf packs. There are, apparently, three different packs within the eight-thousand-acre forest. But that's not even the best part," Jamie glanced up at the professor, trying not to take the seemingly uninterested expression to heart as she pulled out a sketch. A sketch that Ritchie had made for her in their second year of university. "There's a wolf-girl that lives among the pack."

Professor Alicaster raised an eyebrow in interest and lent forward to pick up the picture. It was a rather crude drawing; Ritchie had admitted as much at the time. He'd even offered to make a better version of it for her, but Jamie couldn't help but want to keep the hand-drawn Artemis with her. The green eyes that popped out of the page were something she could never look away from.

"The girl's name is Artemis, I met her in Materia when I was young. She'd been kidnapped from the forest and was being" – Jamie put the next word in air quotes – "'examined' by a sociopath and her group of supposed doctors in the town until she escaped." She sat back in the beanbag. "This is what I'm studying for my thesis: the connection between wolves and humans, but as you can see, there's something more impo—"

"Jamie," Alicaster interrupted, surprising her with the use of her first name. "As devastating as this is, what does an eco-disaster have to do with this? Let alone with your thesis?"

Time for the dive, Jamie thought as she took a breath.

"We saw what happened to Yellowstone with the reintroduction of the wolves. Imagine what'll happen when a forest that has never existed without wolves and other creatures is cut down." Alicaster opened her mouth to speak, but Jamie spoke faster. "If I can get to the forest and gain evidence of its importance, I can present it to the Environmental Impact Agency in order to gain permanent protective status for the forest and the animals inside." She looked at the drawing of Artemis. "If you sign off on a grant for me to go, I'll try to have the forest listed as a national park to gain protection for Artemis and her pack."

Professor Alicaster stared in silence at the papers Jamie had provided. Jamie had to stop herself from biting at her thumb as she anxiously waited for her to speak again.

"This is an admirable proposal, Miss Gander-Yoon," she began, and Jamie could feel her heart start to sink as she knew a *but* was coming. "But I cannot, in good conscience, recommend a grad student for an expedition."

"I understand it's asking a lot—"

"Miss Gander-Yoon, you and I both know that you do not understand the gravity of what you are asking for." She handed over the research papers. Jamie took it with shaking hands. "Yes, your paper is covering an important subject, but instead of focusing on getting in the field, focus on finishing your dissertation instead." She handed her the drawing of Artemis. "I'm sorry I can't be of more help."

Jamie took the drawing. She barely noticed when Alicaster got up and walked away. Left in the silence of the empty hallway, Jamie stared at the drawing in her hands. Those daring green eyes staring back at her with the intelligence of the girl she'd met all those years ago. With a sigh, she dropped the papers onto the table and fell deeper into the beanbag, closing her eyes in frustration.

What am I going to do now? she thought with a huff.

The rattling of papers had her opening her eyes again. Wind from the open window had sent them scattering onto the floor. Reaching forward to catch them, she grabbed hold of the top page. As she searched for something to hold it in place, she found herself looking down at flight information. She'd looked into the best rates for cost and time like her dad always did when he was planning a trip. Now as she stared at the page that told her the most cost-effective way to fly, a plan began to formulate in Jamie's mind. She now had an answer to her previous internal question:

Probably something stupid.

4

JAMIE

This is such a bad idea, Jamie thought as she tried her best to pack the absolute essentials. She'd never been on an expedition before, though she'd dreamt of going on one with her father since she was young. Now the day was here, and she was spinning out. Of course, most of the panic was from the fact that both her dad and the school had no idea what she was about to do.

"I can feel your anxiety from here," Ritchie said from his position on the bed. He'd taken to lying upside down with a phone in front of his face as Jamie paced around the room. "Maybe you should tell your dad instead of freaking—"

"I don't need to tell him," Jamie said sharply. "I'm paying for my own ticket and taking a holiday." She grabbed her notebook from her bedside table. "Besides, as long as I deliver my thesis on time, they'll never know."

"I'm not talking about your dissertation," Ritchie continued. "Your dad knows this stuff, maybe he could help you out and—"

"I don't need his help," she retorted. "I'm perfectly capable of doing this by myself."

"Never said you weren't. But that doesn't change the fact

that he's the expert and has access to fancy-arse equipment that could be of real use to what you're trying to do."

"That doesn't change anything," Jamie said quietly as she grabbed a book from her shelf.

When Ritchie stayed silent, Jamie knew he'd caught onto her real reasons why she didn't want to ask her dad for help. Her dad may have been the one to recommend she write about Artemis for her final piece, but he'd never fully understood her connection to the wolf-girl. Let alone her connection to girls in general. Their relationship had always been complicated, especially after her mum had died, but it'd felt more fractured ever since she came out at sixteen.

"I get it, I do," Ritchie said quietly. And then, like any best friend, he let it go. "Your thermal hat is in your second-from-the-top drawer, near the back. Pack that instead of the fantasy book in your hand."

Jamie nodded absentmindedly and exchanged the items as she searched around for her notebook.

"You already packed it."

"Right, of course," she murmured. "Can I borrow—"

"I already packed one of my cameras in your bag."

"Thank you." Jamie grabbed two pairs of thick gloves and woolly hats.

"And the other one will go in my bag."

Jamie dropped the items. "I'm sorry, what?"

Ritchie roly-polied off the bed and stood up with a smile. "Didn't you know? I'm coming with you."

She stared at him. "I repeat: *what?*"

"Don't look so shocked," Ritchie said with a laugh. "I know we didn't exactly discuss it, but I have enough in my savings for a flight too." His voice tightened. "And there is no chance in hell I'm letting you travel to that racist town solo."

Jamie remembered when she'd confided in him about how the people of that town had treated her as a kid. He'd been absolutely livid. But just like when she told him some of her professors refused to acknowledge her mother's part of her last name, he knew this wasn't something new for her. It didn't stop him from sticking up for her all the same.

Ritchie took a breath to calm himself and smiled. "Besides, you are shite with a camera, so what better than a filmmaker to come along to document your wolf saviour adventure and the reuniting shot with the love of your life."

Brought back to the present and how annoyingly kind Ritchie could be, all Jamie could do was retort, "But you haven't even packed!"

"I see you didn't deny the love-of-your-life part." Ritchie dropped quickly to the ground to avoid the book that was aimed at his head, but the smile didn't leave; he'd already won. "Besides," he continued, pulling a suitcase out from under his bed, "who said I wasn't packed?"

"You're insane."

"It's what you love about me."

"Maybe," Jamie said with a hint of a smile. "But what about Darien? Wasn't she meant to be helping you with that new movie? I don't want to cause you to lose out on—"

"Jay." Ritchie stepped forward and put his hands on her shoulders, looking her in the eye. "How could I give up the chance of making a lesbian love story documentary?"

Jamie pushed him away with a laugh. "You're a douche."

"Uh-huh, whatcha going to do about it?"

Before Jamie could respond, there was a knock at her door.

"To be continued, Mr Bailey," she said as she left him behind to head to the door.

Their flat was open planned, so she could still hear Ritchie's teasing snigger as she walked past the kitchen. She rolled her eyes but smiled. If Ritchie was coming with her on this trip, she would need to be less transparent about her feelings towards Artemis. He teased her enough as it is.

To this day, it surprised her how much about Artemis she remembered. The feel of her calloused hands against hers as they ran. The baring of her teeth as she tried to smile at her in the dark room of the lab. Even the softness of her hug. There was something so ... loving about Artemis. She wondered if she was still the same after so many years.

Shaking her head to remove the memories, she opened the door and found the smiling face of her dad on the other side.

"Dad!" Jamie cried out in surprise. She heard the tell-tale thump of Ritchie's feet on the floor, and she knew Ritchie recognised her warning. It was her hide-everything-incriminating-fast voice. "What're you doing here?"

He leant in to press a kiss to the top of her hair as he shimmied around her to get through the door. "Thought I'd stop by, maybe make you and Ritchie lunch while I share some exciting news."

A pit grew in Jamie's stomach. She knew that tone of voice. It was the same one he used with her when she was a kid before he learnt to cover it up with a more monotone style. He was going on a new trip.

Jamie knew she had no right to be upset. She was sneaking off to the other side of the country after all, but there was a part of her that was still hurt by it.

"We, er, actually have plans already." Jamie closed the door behind him. "What's the news?"

Her dad frowned but recovered his smile quickly enough as he leant against the kitchen counter. "Professor Alicaster and I have just been approved for a special research trip."

"Oh, that's awesome, Mr GY." Ritchie trotted out of the living room with a smile on his face. Jamie quickly glanced at the now empty room. He'd done a good job of hiding their bags. "How long will you guys be gone for?"

Jamie was surprised by the look of excitement on Ritchie's face. He knew how she felt about her dad not making time for her. It was only when she caught his eye did she see a sneaky gleam in them. They'd communicated silently for years; whether it be to bad-mouth the student union rep without getting in trouble or to argue with each other without causing a scene, they knew each other well. And this look said it all: *If he's gone when you are, he'll never find out.*

"We've been given till the end of summer," her dad continued, drawing their attention. "I'll be back in time for you to upload your thesis."

"That's great, Dad!" Jamie's smile became genuine. That was definitely enough time for her to leave and come back. Moving to sit at the kitchen table, she caught her dad's eye. "It'll be a shame to not have your expertise nearby, of course, but I'm sure you and Pro—"

"Oh, you won't be without it."

Jamie blinked in confusion.

"She what now?" Ritchie asked, speaking when Jamie couldn't.

Her dad looked practically giddy as he vibrated with excitement. "Katie—" He paused. "Professor Alicaster, I mean, she heard everything you said about Swen Forest and took a proposal to the board." He stepped forward and placed a hand on Jamie's shoulder. "She was right that you wouldn't get the funding as a grad student, and I'm sorry about that." Patting her arm, he stepped back. "But she could get funding for two field professors seeking out to implement an environmental protection order on an ancient forest." Her dad's smile broadened, a look of pride on his face. "She even managed to get the funding fast-tracked because her proposal was so impressive."

Finally, Jamie was able to speak. "You're going … where?"

"I had no idea there were three packs in Swen, though I suppose it makes sense. They'd have to have enough diversity in the breeding to have survived as long as they have."

Jamie bit the inside of her cheek. Alicaster had taken her research and used it for her proposal.

"Dad, what's going on?"

"You, me, Alicaster, and if he wishes, Ritchie" – he smiled towards the boy behind her, Jamie didn't need turn to look to feel the enthusiastic thumbs-up being sent her dad's way from her best friend – "we're all flying out in four days to Swen Forest."

"No!"

Her dad frowned at her. "No?"

Jamie came back to herself. "I mean, not *no* as in *no, I don't want to go...* uh, I mean *no* as in *no way!*" She forced a smile on her face.

Letting out a laugh, her dad threw back his head before taking a seat of his own opposite her. "As you kids would say, yes way."

"No one says that, sir," Ritchie chimed in unhelpfully.

When her dad reached his hand out to hers, Jamie met his gaze. "I thought you'd be thrilled about this?" he asked with a tilt of his head. "You'll finally see Artemis again and, hopefully, find a way to keep the forest safe."

She took his hand. "I am excited, Dad, I just— I don't know, it..."

Jamie had no idea how to finish that sentence. She should be thrilled. Her professor, the one she was sure hated her, had found a way to get this expedition funded to help save Artemis and the forest. Sure, it may have been by using her research and claiming it as her own, but she still got the grant. And her dad was finally asking her, his daughter, to join him on one of his trips. Something she had wanted to do since she was a kid. She'd even given him an ultimatum about it not long after he'd returned to take her away from that God-awful town. "It's either take me with you or stay with me," she'd said, though in a far less articulate way seeing as she had only been ten.

But here she was. Reluctant to let him go. Reluctant to go with him. All she could think about was when she found Artemis again and worked to save her and her family from Materia, she wanted it to be something that was *hers*. Not another world-renowned mission of explorer Gander-Yoon. She wanted it to be hers. She wanted her time with Artemis to be hers.

Jesus, Jamie, she thought, *how selfish do you sound right now?*

"Ignore me, Dad," Jamie said with a small smile. "I think I'm just in shock that it's happening." She laughed. "This is amazing. We're going to help save Swen."

And Artemis, she thought.

"Jamie," her dad said in a surprisingly serious tone. "I don't want you to give yourself unrealistic expectations." He let go of her hand and sighed. "While our intention, of course, is to help gain protection over the forest, we may not get it. These things are far more complicated than you think."

This made Jamie frown.

"But you managed it once before," she pointed out, remembering the day her dad showed up in Materia after she'd told him about Artemis with an environmental agent and a no-hunting order in hand. "Why can't we do the same now?"

He scratched at his bearded chin. "Politics make things difficult these days. I managed to pull a favour back then, but now we need an abundance of evidence to even have the forest be considered for protection."

"And we'll get it," Jamie said sharply. "We have Artemis. That's proof enough."

"Jamie-bear, have…" he began cautiously. When his blue eyes fell away from hers, she started to feel nervous. "Have you thought of the possibility that Artemis may not—"

"I'll see you at the airport, Dad." Jamie stood abruptly and walked towards the door to open it. "Tell Alicaster thank you and that we'll meet you at check-in, OK?"

Jamie was being an arse. She knew she was. Her dad was right about everything here, but she couldn't consider the possibility. Not now. Not ever. Artemis was out there. She knew it. She'd prove it.

Her dad didn't argue or push back. He even held back a sigh that she knew he wanted to let out as he stood.

"I'm sure it'll be OK, Jamie," he said as he came to stand by her at the door. "I just don't want … I don't want you to get hurt if…" His blue eyes turned shiny as he swallowed hard.

He was thinking of her mum. He always had this look about him when the memory of Seon-mi came to him. A split between devastation and true love peppered his face. Tears would form in his eyes, but the lilt of a smile would be there as they threatened to fall.

"I know, Dad," she whispered gently. "I— I'll see you at the airport on Friday, bright and early." In a turn that surprised them both, she reached out to hug him. It was brief but nice. "Remember to pack the photo, OK?"

"Of course, my love." As her dad walked out the open door, Jamie went to close it behind him before he turned back with a cheeky smile. "Don't worry about re-packing. I'm sure what's already in your suitcase will suffice for the trip."

And with an all-teeth grin that her mum told her had won her over when they'd first met, he was gone.

5

JAMIE

If she'd known how long ten hours on a plane would feel when stuck next to a professor she had a love-hate relationship with, she'd have refused to board. All their seats had supposedly been assigned at random. Of course, some kind of evil fate caused Jamie to end up sitting next to Alicaster while Ritchie and her dad were blessed with sitting next to strangers.

Jamie had asked her dad if he'd swap seats with Alicaster so they could spend some time together. Unfortunately, her dad refused. He said it'd be a good idea for her to discuss her dissertation with the professor ahead of the trip. The plane had Wi-Fi after all. She could get direct help as she worked. Jamie tried not to feel disappointed. It didn't work.

Ritchie sent her a silent fist pump of support before they took off. She never caught his eye again. He was too focused on editing his newest film. The boy was as bad as her when it came to knowing when to rest and when to work.

Jamie let out a sigh after another failed attempt to get her friend's attention.

"You know, I can ask to swap seats with Mr Bailey if you are this desperate to gain his attention," a sharp voice from beside her chimed in.

"Uh, no, no, it's OK. I just wanted to…" Jamie paused for too long. "…ask him about something?"

Alicaster let out an uninterested hum as she continued reading the papers in front of her. Jamie watched as she tucked a piece of blonde hair behind her ear and lent closer to the aeroplane table in front of her, her intense brown eyes focusing in on the words on the page. If Alicaster hadn't been such a pain in her arse, Jamie probably would have had a crush on her like most of the students in her year.

"It may be best to not read your fellow students' dissertation essays," Alicaster said without looking up. "I would hate to mark you down for attempted cheating."

As if you need a reason to mark me down, Jamie thought irritably.

"I wasn't reading them," Jamie retorted. She hated how petulant she sounded. Turning to look back at her own screen, she stared at the insulting cursor blinking at her. "Besides, we're on this trip for my essay, why would I—"

"No. We're not," Alicaster interrupted. "We're on this expedition for your father's and my research and to report our findings to the Environmental Impact Agency."

Jamie rolled her eyes. "Yes, I'm well aware of your cover—"

"Not a cover." Alicaster put down her pen, clearly over pretending she was working. "Whatever you were planning to do by sneaking out here alone" – *dammit, Dad* – "would never have worked. You have no idea how to run a fact-finding mission like this. Let alone how to survive in a cold and wild environment."

"I have a lot more knowledge than you give me credit for," Jamie snapped back.

A nearby passenger hissed "shh" at her, which made Jamie lower her voice. "Saving the forest and Artemis was my idea. It's my paper and plan. Not yours – as much as you tried to pass it off as such at the board meeting." Alicaster didn't deny it. "Without me, you'll never find Artemis or the pack. Admit it, Katie."

Alicaster's jaw clenched again. She hated when students called her by her first name. "We'll see."

She turned away and back to her papers. For the rest of the journey, she refused to look back up or engage with Jamie. Not like Jamie wanted her to. She was sick of Alicaster's attitude towards her.

With her dad asleep a few rows down and Ritchie with his headphones permanently on as he edited, Jamie was unable to find something to distract her. She could be working on her dissertation. It was laid out in front of her after all. But with Alicaster at her side, she didn't want to risk the snide comments that could come her way as she wrote.

Just don't interact with her unless you have to, she thought as she pulled out the one fiction book she'd allowed herself to bring. Maybe reading about academic murder would make her feel better.

Thankfully, ten hours with a good book helps time pass a little quicker. Sooner than she'd expected, they were out of the airport and in a hired car heading towards Materia.

"Do the townsfolk know we're coming?" Ritchie held up his camcorder towards Jamie. The red blinking made it clear he was getting a head start on his documentary.

"I'd hope not," Alicaster replied from the front of the car. Ritchie turned his camera towards her. "But considering the permits we had to have signed off to camp in the forest, I wouldn't put it past the local government to spread private information as a warning."

"Ugh, politicians," Ritchie groaned.

"Agreed," Jamie said in frustration. "Materia really hasn't changed."

"It may be best to give the locals the benefit of the doubt," Alicaster said. "We don't know if they're aware of what they signed up for. Small towns are easily manipulated by corporations."

Jamie held back a scoff. "Unfortunately, I know this town, and destroying the ecosystem and wildlife? Not out of the ordinary for them."

Alicaster hummed nonchalantly as if she were placating a child's whims. Jamie tensed her jaw to stop herself from responding.

"I hate to be that person…" her father began as he took a right turn, "but I grew up there and … well, sadly, Jamie isn't wrong. The people of Materia are not a friend to nature. They know exactly what they've signed up for."

"Well, then," Alicaster said, surrendering easily to her mentor, "it seems we'll have to keep a close eye on the locals."

Jamie remembered the way the people of the town had reacted to her and Artemis's escape attempt. She shared a look with her dad in the rear-view mirror. He seemed to be having the same thought.

"None of us are to go anywhere alone," he said in response.

The car was quiet after that.

IT WAS when their once smooth journey across the roads changed to being bumpy and uneven that Jamie knew they were coming close. As the lights of the city disappeared behind them, she felt the nerves in her stomach start to twist and turn. The sensation didn't lessen after an hour's worth of aimless driving. When an unnatural light appeared in the distance, Jamie knew they were there. Standing out starkly against the natural wilderness around them was Materia, washed in artificial light and the fiery glow of sunset.

Behind the town, rising higher than the largest skyscraper, was the mountainside of the Swen Forest. As Jamie stared, she couldn't help but notice how the oranges and reds in the sky illuminated the trees in a way that made the land look like it was on fire. She remembered watching the sunset from her window when she lived here and being mesmerised by it. Somehow it looked more beautiful than it had when she was younger.

She's in there somewhere, Jamie thought as her eyes scanned the mountainside.

The town was now fully visible, its log buildings standing out against the light summer snow. Even in the summer, the land here had snow everywhere. From a light dusting on the recently cleared roads to the covered logged roofs. The town was picturesque enough to be on a holiday card. As they came closer, Jamie realised that Materia had expanded. Unlike before, there now lay endless rows of houses, and from the multitude of figures she could make out, all of them were occupied. Behind the buildings lay the farmland she remembered, but instead of one sheep pen, the whole hillside was occupied. With three sheep pens, a cattle paddock, and even a stable, it was clear the people here were trying to make their stamp on their land. That much was obvious with how close to the mountain borders their farmland was.

The car veered to the right. With a frown, Jamie went to ask her dad where they were going when she saw it.

Directly ahead, catching the fading sunlight, a silver fence lined the entrance to Materia. It looked like a fence you'd see in those apocalypse shows where they'd create a barrier to keep anyone they didn't want in out. Stood on the other side of the fence was a man dressed in all black, a thick vest across his chest. He was staring at them with a hand at his waist.

"Dad, what's going on?" Her eyes never left the man at the fence.

He didn't answer straight away, focusing more on sticking as close to the mountains as possible as he drove towards the split in the distance. When he did, Jamie got the feeling that things in Materia truly had changed more than she expected.

"We won't be going into the town," he said with a wavering voice. "We'll be staying exclusively in the forest."

6

———

JAMIE

When they reached the split in the mountains, the sunset had faded to darkness. The air was frigid, and they all wrapped themselves up tightly in layers to keep out the cold. With the car abandoned at the mountain and the quad-bike unloaded, they were ready to head in. Or at least they would have been if both Jamie and Ritchie hadn't been left to follow the tyre tracks after her dad and Alicaster headed off on the bike to search for a camping spot. With their bags on their backs and the message of "walking builds character" from her dad as he smiled, they started their walk – much to Ritchie's annoyance. Thankfully, Jamie knew the perfect way to distract him.

"Here you see the intrepid explorers on a journey into the unknown," she said, putting on her best Attenborough impression as she looked into Ritchie's camera lens. "They first seek shelter from the predators—"

"There are predators?" Ritchie said with a squeak.

"Babes, we're looking for wolves. Wolves are predators." Jamie held back a smile. "But they don't like people, so they'll probably avoid us. It's the bears we'll have to be careful of."

"Bears?" he whisper-shouted, making Jamie laugh.

Radio static appeared at Jamie's hip. "Try not to draw too much attention to yourself, Miss Gander-Yoon," Alicaster's crackly yet stern voice said. "We aren't the only beings out at night. Remember that."

"Man, I hate that woman," Jamie muttered but made sure to keep her laughter to a minimum. She'd always had an almost obnoxiously loud laugh.

"It's all that—"

"If you say anything about enemies-to-lovers, I'll hit you."

Ritchie lowered his camera with a smile. "Hey now, I was just going to say professional jealousy. But let's explore that mo—"

Jamie hit him.

"Ow!"

"Mr Bailey, the noise notice applies to you too." Alicaster's voice appeared again from the walkie talkie. "We've found our resting spot. Walk faster."

"Damn, she is demanding." Ritchie rubbed his arm. "Maybe I should ask her out."

Jamie rolled her eyes and walked off. Ritchie quickly followed her. He definitely wouldn't admit it, but Jamie knew he was becoming less and less of a fan of being in the wilderness.

Following the tracks her dad and Alicaster had made in silence, Jamie watched as Ritchie continued filming. Every so often, they would stop so he could raise his camera to film the landscape for his B-roll. It made their journey to the camp longer, but in the end, that's exactly what Jamie needed. The further in they travelled, the more anxious she started to get. Her hands were sweaty, her heart was racing, and she nearly stumbled off the path as she stared at the forest around them.

Ritchie took her hand, his camera turned off and hanging around his neck, and squeezed it.

"You'll find her. I know it."

She squeezed his hand back.

The two of them had been thinking about going on adventures together since their second year of university. Jamie had told Ritchie all about Artemis. How she spoke, how she looked, and how Jamie had felt when she was with her even if she couldn't understand it at the time. Ritchie had told her about his dreams of being a director and how his family hadn't supported his creative aspirations, and definitely not the people he loved.

The two became closer than ever over their aspirations. They'd talked together for years now about how they'd find Artemis one day and how Ritchie would film it and become an award-winning director. The simple goals for life. But now they were here. They were actually doing it.

It was as they stepped into the clearing that the reality truly hit.

Jamie's dad had found the perfect spot. An open clearing surrounded by a tight group of trees that, from the scuff marks in the summer snow, had made it difficult for the quad bike to get through. They'd already started setting up the camp in the centre of the space which offered them a three-sixty view of the forest around them to help keep an eye out for possible predators. To the right, above the trees, Jamie could make out the split mountain in the distance. To the left, she could see the rock face that spread in both directions further than the eye could see. They'd been placed almost dead centre between the two mountains.

Her dad and Alicaster had already unpacked the essentials to build the camp. Tents, sleeping bags, fire fuel, and flashlights were scattered around the place. With the sun gone and their only light the moon and their torches, they needed to move quickly. It wouldn't be long now before temperatures dropped and predators started their hunts.

The radio crackled at her side again. Instead of the grumpy

voice of her professor, it was the humour-filled tone of her dad. "Come on, you two, the camp isn't going to build itself. Over."

Finally knocked out of their awe, Ritchie and Jamie rushed for the camp. They'd barely come to a stop before her dad was issuing out their marching orders.

"The tents are in the two red bags just underneath the suitcases. They're complicated to build, so Jamie and Katie, you two get working on that." Jamie held back a protest at having to work with the woman again. Her dad turned to Ritchie. "Grab the axe and find a dormant log or tree stump to chop up. Anything that's dry is usable. We need to get a fire going quickly."

Ritchie raised his hands in the air. "No offence, Mr GY, I don't think my hands are made for—" Jamie's dad raised an eyebrow at him. "I'll get to work."

"What do you want me to do once we've finished with the tent, Dad?" Jamie asked. She hoped that they'd have a chance to work together, even if it was something small.

"Katie will tell you," he said distractedly as he focused on unpacking the specialist equipment they'd brought with them. From satellite phones, a dart gun (just in case), heat sensors, and many other things, they were ready for whatever came next.

"Yeah, sure," Jamie whispered in disappointment. Walking over to the red tent bag, she got to work. She knew her dad's brush-off wasn't personal. He was in work mode after all. But that didn't make the feeling any less painful.

It's day one, Jamie thought as she read the tent instructions. *We'll have time to work together. I'm sure.*

IT TOOK them until the moon was high in the sky above them for the camp to be finished. They had two tents sitting on opposing sides of the tables and chairs and fire pit that sat in between them. Around the tents, small devices had been planted in the snow. Her dad had said it was too dangerous to have a fire going all night, so to warn off predators, he'd brought along an animal repellent device and had dotted them around the camp. Ritchie had commented that their neighbour had the same thing to stop cats from pissing in their flowers.

They had parked the quad bikes beside the tents and had flipped the wagon that had carried their belongings upside down so it wouldn't collect snow. Their hope was that surrounding the tents with the foreign items and cat deterrents would keep animals away from them as much as possible.

After they had finished building the camp, Jamie's dad had lit the fire. As the flames warmed her skin, she let out a contented sigh. She was happy to just sit there and fall asleep, but a slice of buttered toast was pushed toward her. It wasn't the usual late-night meal, but for something quick before they slept, it would do.

Jamie thought they may keep the silence until they'd head to sleep as they all happily munched on their food. Of course, she forgot that they had a filmmaker on board.

"Where will we be looking first?" Ritchie directed the camera at her dad just as he was swallowing a particularly large bite of toast. "What's the plan? If there is one, of course."

"As any great explorer would say," her dad began in a deep voice. He'd always been one for dramatics. Of course, the effect was undercut when the light of the fire showed the light sprinkling of butter that covered his bearded chin. "We start at the beginning." He turned to Jamie. "What do you remember about your time with Artemis that could help us figure out where she may be?"

Jamie nearly choked on her toast at the sudden question. Ritchie turned the camera onto her. He wouldn't want to miss out on the blooper reel shot.

"Uhm," she coughed out. "Well, she didn't share too much.

Artemis didn't speak English well. She only knew a few basic phrases at the time."

"How did the two of you communicate then?" Alicaster asked. Jamie was surprised at the earnestness in her question.

"Well, I guess a lot of it was through touch … oh, and body language. Body language was definitely the main way she communicated with me. Lots of listening and reacting. She often guided me to what she wanted to say or what she needed." Jamie put her plate down. "Like, I tried to describe sheep to her once and had to do the physical movements and sounds to help her understand."

"Hmm," Alicaster hummed. "That makes sense for her wolf side. Wolves communicate mainly through body language rather than sound." She rested her hand beneath her chin. "Is there anything distinct about her that could hint about her living environment?"

Jamie frowned, thinking hard on that question.

"Artemis never seemed to get cold much." Jamie frowned. "There were a few moments, but I think that was more due to the fact that she'd been locked up and not able to be out in nature.

"She was quite pale when I saw her, but her arms looked darker, almost like she was tanned. Maybe the pack lived in an open area where she could catch the sun?" Jamie bit her lip lightly. "She had a few scars on her face and arms. Some looked like animal scratches, possibly from play fights with the wolves or maybe from another predator. But some of them looked more like what you'd get from thorns or sharp branches, a little more jagged than straight in their markings."

An image of Artemis came to her mind. She looked older here, standing taller than Jamie, her tanned skin glowing in the moonlight, as the knife Jamie had given her was gripped tightly in her hand. She'd have a few more scars from her time with the wolves, but the kindness in her gaze would be just as strong as it was when they locked eyes as kids.

I have been waiting for you, Artemis would say in her wolf way, and somehow Jamie would know what it would mean.

"And I've been looking for you," Jamie would reply before rushing forward and pulling Artemis into her arms. Their lips—

"Jamie?" her dad's voice said.

Blinking, Jamie came back to the real world and looked around the group to find all eyes on her.

"I'm sorry, what?"

"We were discussing splitting into pairs tomorrow to start tracking the pack," her dad said with a frown. "Would you like to pair with me to venture out?"

"Oh!" Jamie exclaimed in delight. "Yes, I'd love that."

"Lovely," he replied with a smile. He then clapped his hands together and rubbed them. "All right, campers, time for rest. We'll have an early start tomorrow." He stood up from his chair. "Remember to wear at least two layers while you sleep. The nights here can drop to below freezing even in the summer."

The group nodded and set about packing up for the night.

After cleaning their dishes and switching on the animal repellent devices, they were all ready to head to sleep. It was likely close to midnight by now, if not a little after. And they were all feeling it now.

"For logical reasons," her father said with a yawn. He pointed to the navy tent behind him. "The boys tent." He pointed to the red tent behind Jamie. "And the girls tent."

Without a word or a chance for Jamie to offer a rebuttal, her dad had walked towards the boys tent, slipped off his shoes, and stepped inside. Ritchie looked to the tent and then back to Jamie.

"Uh, I better..." He gestured behind him. "Sleep tight." With an awkward smile, he rushed inside and pulled up the zip of the tent.

Jamie didn't blame him. You could cut the tension between her and Alicaster with a knife.

"Best get inside before you freeze," the voice of her nightmares said. Jamie only heard the sound of the tent zipper being undone and the sound of Alicaster stepping inside their tent.

Just grit your teeth and bear it, Jamie, she thought as she shivered and stepped towards the tent.

"Take your shoes off at the door."

Jamie mouthed a biting swear word at the tent door before taking off her shoes and slipping inside.

I'm not going to survive this trip.

JAMIE

Alicaster was trying to kill her.

She was asleep, but there was no doubt in Jamie's mind that that's what she was trying to do. Alicaster was going to drain the very existence and will to live from her with the intensity of her damn snores. It was like a foghorn in Jamie's ears every couple of breaths.

Once she thought the woman had stopped, and Jamie finally snuggled down into her sleeping bag. It turned out that she'd only stopped breathing for a second. Just as Jamie had closed her eyes, she heard Alicaster choke-snort before the foghorn began again. Jamie only briefly wished she hadn't continued breathing. Briefly. Maybe. Definitely.

After dealing with it for more hours than she should have, Jamie let out an exhausted huff and clamoured out of her sleeping bag and put on her thick coat. She'd go join Ritchie and her dad for the night. She and Ritchie had shared a single bed before – a sleeping bag would be fine.

Zipping and unzipping her tent, she slipped on her shoes and headed over to the boys. When she reached their tent, she began tugging at the zipper. It didn't budge. They had put a lock on their entrance from the inside.

"Goddammit." Jamie stomped her foot in the snow. Of course they'd locked it. She couldn't have any luck on this trip.

Sighing, she resigned to having to go back to her tent. She'd not even stepped one foot in its direction when she heard the snoring.

"No, not a chance in hell," Jamie muttered.

Heading quickly to the tent, she leant in to grab her torch and a box of matches before leaving again. She'd just sleep earlier tomorrow instead. A day of hard work on no sleep should be enough to knock her out and not hear the foghorn professor.

The forest was dark and eerie, which according to her watch, made sense as it was after midnight. Rubbing her eyes in frustration and exhaustion, she came to the cold fire pit. Chucking in a few logs, she got to work with starting a fire. If she was going to be stuck out here, she was going to at least keep warm. When the flames slowly crackled to life, Jamie realised it would take some time for the fire to actually be warm enough.

Staring at the rising flames, she wrapped her arms around herself. Her dad hadn't been wrong; the night here was absolutely freezing. Even with her thermal leggings, thick jogging bottoms, three top layers and a coat, she was still shivering. Tucking her gloved hands under her coat-covered armpits, Jamie began to bounce in place. She was sure she looked ridiculous, but that wouldn't matter if it had made a difference in her warmth. It didn't.

She considered heading back into the tent and smothering her head with a pillow to block out the sound of snoring. The only reason she didn't is because she didn't feel like accidentally suffocating herself for just a few hours of sleep.

Letting out a heavy sigh, Jamie turned on her torch and

decided to patrol around the camp. Hopefully a short walk in circles would help warm her up enough until the fire grew. She also hoped that, once she was warm, it would make her feel so tired that even the foghorn of a snore wouldn't keep her from sleeping. She doubted it, but she was irritated enough to give it a shot.

Walking in a forest at night was exactly like what horror films made it out to be. Creepy. While there was a certain beauty about it all, the hoots of the owls echoing in the sky, the creaking of the trees as they bent in the cool wind, it didn't stop her from feeling nervous as the moon's rays left eerie glows across the fallen snow.

To not spook the possible animals among the trees, Jamie kept her torch low to the ground. In an attempt of a patrol, she squinted at the edges of the tree-line but couldn't see much. Even with her glasses on, she was struggling. Jamie couldn't tell if that was just because of her eyesight, the cold fog growing on her lenses, or just that it was too dark to see anything. The latter made the most sense seeing as it was after midnight.

Jamie found herself straying further away from the camp to get a closer look into the bush. She didn't really know why she was attempting to patrol the woods around them, but she kept doing it anyway.

Why am I lying to myself? Jamie thought with a shake of her head.

She couldn't deny to herself that she was searching the woods in hopes of seeing Artemis. Part of her wished that the racket they had made when they came into the forest with their quad bikes, fire pits, and loud conversation would have signalled to the wolves their arrival. And with them, Artemis.

It was a stupid long shot. Wolves could hear for miles; if they had heard them, they'd likely move further away. The bad history between humans and wolves would be enough justification for them to flee at the first sign of humans in their home. Just because it was her here now didn't change anything.

Jamie sighed. She'd been walking around the camp for at least half an hour now and not only was she still cold but she was more tired than she was before.

"No point in dragging this out," she muttered. "I can nap at some point tomorrow."

She took one step toward the camp when she heard it.

A howl.

Jamie stopped in place. For a second, she wondered if she'd imagined it. Night-time could play tricks with a person's mind after all. But then came another.

Turning towards the grove of trees behind her, Jamie stared into the darkness in the hopes of finding answers to where that howl had come from. A wolf's howl could be heard from miles and miles away. It's possible it was an echo. But what if…?

Don't be stupid, Jamie, she thought as she took a single step towards the trees. *Everyone's asleep, and if you get in trouble, you'll—*

Jamie started walking with purpose towards the tree-line – ignoring the voice in her head screaming at her that this was a bad idea.

Keeping her torch low to the ground, just in case, she took a cautious approach into the row of trees. Resting her hand against the solid bark, the roughness scratching against her gloves, she leant her head past a tree trunk.

Unlike the camp, everything here was pitch black, save for the little ground illuminated by the glow of her torch and the moon above. She could only just make out the trees a few metres in front of her, yet even with so little visibility, she stepped further into the forest.

Jamie could hear her dad's voice the moment she did.

"You're as reckless as your mother," he'd say in that quietly angry tone that always had Jamie feeling guilty at scaring him.

Though there was always a hint of pride in his voice whenever he compared her to her mother.

Wolves were her mum's first love, and here Jamie was now, carrying on that adoration for the creatures and with her father at her side. Just like her mum. Jamie hadn't really thought about how this trip could make her feel closer to her mum, but it was. Wolves had always been her connection to Mum. Now she was here to protect them, like her mum would have done. Even if, in her case, it was for one of them in particular. One whose gentle green eyes would come to her in her dreams. One whose hand she had held. One who—

Her foot caught on a tree root and sent Jamie tumbling to the ground, hard. Her torch went flying from her hand.

"Ow," she groaned.

Pushing herself to her feet, she shook free the snow that had stuck to her coat and trousers. Jamie was thankful that she'd listened to Ritchie when packing her thermal trousers. But that didn't stop the snow from slipping down the back of her coat.

"OK, time to go back," she said after a shiver.

Her torch had rolled up against a nearby tree trunk and, not wanting to get in trouble with her dad for losing it, she wrapped her arms tightly around herself and walked toward the light that pointed into the darkness. As she bent to grab it, Jamie thought she saw something ahead of her. When she lifted the torch up for a better look, she couldn't see a thing.

"OK, you're definitely tired…" She rubbed a gloved hand sluggishly over her face. "Time for sleep."

Heaving a sigh, Jamie began to make her way back to the camp. She could see the distant glow of the fire and imagined the warmth against her already when she heard the snap of a twig behind her.

Jamie froze in place. The dumb part of her brain wanted to turn to look and see what was behind her, but she kept deathly still. Jamie knew most animals worked off movement. The less movement you made, the better. She knew how it all worked, but she was still human.

Slowly, she glanced over her shoulder at what was behind her. And immediately wished she hadn't.

About ten strides away, crouched between two tree trunks, stood a golden-eyed cougar. Its sandy-coloured coat blended in against the darkness of the trees, but the white of its teeth caught the light of the moon in a menacing smile. Jamie swallowed.

In a move that could only be described as stalking, the cougar stepped out into the thick of the snow. Jamie knew how fast cougars were. It could reach her in two skilled bounds. And be eating her by the third.

Cougars only kill if antagonised or threatened. Come on, Jamie, you know this. Calm down. As much as she told herself that, her breathing still picked up in panic. *Just stay still and don't run. It'll leave you alone ... eventually. Maybe. Unless this is its den. Then you're dead.*

The cougar kept coming closer. Its eyes solely on Jamie. And Jamie was still standing with her back to it. The worst position she could be in if she had to defend herself.

"Help..." Jamie let out in a strangled whisper. "Someone ... help..."

The cougar charged, and she shut her eyes.

The first day of her first expedition hadn't even started properly, and not only had she broken her dad's rules, she'd managed to get herself killed within a few hours of arrival.

As she heard the snarl of the cougar, she clenched her body to prepare for an impact that never came.

Instead, she only heard the sounds of a scuffle and a set of growls that didn't belong to just one animal. Opening her eyes, she turned fully to find the cougar fighting in the snowy ground with another animal. And losing.

Jamie knew this was her chance to run away. She tried to do

so but only managed an awkward stumble, her legs too much like jelly to work. Her attempt only had her falling to the ground, her torch landing in the snow once again.

She watched in horror as the two creatures fought. It was a blind scuffle of claws, growls, and teeth. The tan-furred creature was underneath the cougar, and yet somehow, it was landing more blows if the kitten-like mewl of pain that kept escaping the cat was anything to go by.

With the force of its legs, the smaller creature kicked the cougar off its body and into the trunk of a nearby tree. The cougar let out a screeching howl of pain as it fell to the ground. Jamie watched as it hissed fiercely at its opponent. The two-legged creature released a snarl that had the cougar run off and Jamie's hair standing on end.

With shaky hands, Jamie reached for her torch. The light shook around them as she held it, but that didn't stop her from turning it toward the creature that had saved her.

The light caught the lean muscles of the creature's back. Jamie had to hold back a grimace at the sight of the bleeding cuts from the cougar's claws that marred its skin. They didn't seem deep, but it must still be painful for the animal. As Jamie slowly moved to stand, the light illuminated the rest of the creature. Their legs were muscular and lanky with its thighs covered by a dark brown cloth that was torn at its edges. Their arms were just as taut with muscle but lay bare of cloth or fur. The only thing that covered the creature's torso were an array of new and old scars. As Jamie stood, a glint of something caught Jamie's eyes, blinding her briefly. Clearing her vision with a few furious blinks, she saw a silver blade that was dripping in blood. It was as the creature glanced at Jamie from over its shoulder that she forgot how to breathe.

With the mix of glow from the moon and light of her torch, she could see the eyes of the creature – no, of the woman – in front of her. Soft, curly brown hair framed her face which, just as she remembered it, was marred with an array of scars. But it was those eyes. Those familiar light forest-green eyes that she knew so well.

Then, without warning, the woman turned and ran. She disappeared so quickly into the darkness of the forest, it was as if she'd never even been there.

Jamie stood there in the silence for a long while, unable to fully comprehend what she'd seen until it all clicked into place.

The wolf pack must still be here, she thought, *because so is Artemis.*

8

ARTEMIS

Artemis knew it was going to be a difficult day the moment the fading light of the red sky woke her up. Starting one's day with a wolf pup's butt in your face and another's claws digging into your stomach was usually a sign. Her suspicions were confirmed when she stepped outside the cave and right into young Kai's vomit.

A growl of irritation grew in her throat, but she quickly smothered it away. *No point in starting the day with anger in one's heart.* That's what Kiba had always said.

She felt the lump in her throat as she thought of her lost brother. It had been many seasons, and she still missed him. At least she knew he was where he needed to be. With Rae.

Artemis yawned loudly and began her walk from the cave's entrance to the nearby stream. It was only a short walk away, but it was refreshing to do so in the chilled air. Once there, she bent down to drink the ice-cold water, hoping to rid the taste of Solar's fur on her tongue. Feeling refreshed, Artemis stretched her limbs and listened for the cracks and clicks that always followed. With that done, she was ready to get started with the day of training. Or she would be if her students weren't still napping.

I will give them half a shadow pass, Artemis thought, perching herself on one of the nearby rocks.

She loved evenings at the Den. From the cool brisk air that would make the thin hair on her skin stand on edge to watching the birds taking flight above as they sought out shelter for their night, her world never lost its beauty. That sentiment was made even more true by the sight of the sky aflame.

In the sky above, the soft oranges and reds illuminated the land around them. Colour touched the tips of trees and reflected in the stream in a way that made Artemis wish she could touch the light. Artemis watched as the colours lit up the cave's entrance and disturbed the pups from their slumber. She bit back a laugh at their whines of complaint.

As she listened to their little grumbles, Artemis surveyed the land. The elders had gone out to hunt earlier, leaving her with the responsibility of the young as she had been since Rae's litter. Their Den here offered great security to the pack, but that didn't stop Artemis from keeping watch.

With the thick trees and branches that were always filled with leaves or snow surrounding them, they were offered season-round protection. This was helped by being near the stream. Vegetation grew at the water's side, which if they were ever struggling in their hunts, would be enough to stave off hunger until they succeeded. It also meant they never had to fear dehydration. Yet being by water could be just as dangerous. Wolves weren't the only creatures that needed water. Which was why the caves were a sanctuary. They never had to worry about predators sneaking up on them. There was only one way in or out, and any who dared, like the cougar who had tried a few suns prior, would be in for a rude awakening.

Speaking of, she thought, getting to her feet.

Up, you fiends, she barked as she headed to the cave's entrance. **I shall give you to the count of three. If you are not out by then, no deer for you.**

Grumbling huffs were muffled against the small bodies of the siblings as, slowly but surely, the fluffballs clambered out of the cave in irritation.

This is not fair, little Solar whined. Her patchy white-grey fur made her stand out from her siblings as she trotted towards Artemis.

Father does not make us get up this early, Rickon, a small black-furred pup, snorted. Artemis watched as he shouldered his sister out of the way. As much as he complained, Rickon liked being by Artemis's side and *always* listened to her.

Artemis laughed and pushed the pup with her back paw. **Do I look like your father to you, young one?**

Kai barked a laugh at her quip. When his siblings scowled at him, he shied away. He was the runt of the three pups, making him most likely to be picked on. Artemis often found herself wondering what Kai would be like if Anja, the would-be runt of their litter, had survived.

The day Anja had been born, she hadn't been the same as the other pups. Yue, their mother, had already birthed her first three – a painful and bloody process. It had taken another two sun passes for Anja to arrive. The pack had been distressed the whole time. None knew what to do to help Yue. Fenris had been beside himself. He had even attacked Artemis when she had tried to come to Yue's aid.

On the day Anja had arrived, Yue collapsed. She had been exhausted, close to death if the rotting smell had been anything to go by, but survived. Anja had not been as lucky. While she was born and took her first breath, she had not survived beyond two sun's passes. The pack had rallied to Yue and Fenris's side in silent and unwavering support. They had mourned the loss of young Anja for a full moon cycle. Ever since that day,

Artemis had been more attentive to the pups. She would do everything in her power to keep her pack from feeling that grief again.

You must learn and be alert at every and any moment, Artemis began. **I start you early so you will be ready sooner. Life waits for no wolf.**

As you well know, Artemis, a familiar voice said.

Before she could get her charges under control, they were already bounding forward away from her and towards a black-and-white-furred wolf. His soft hazel eyes reminded her so much of the ones she had lost, his coat a beautiful mixture of the two. He stood tall and strong, a silent but ever-present power in his stance.

Hello, Father Fenris. Artemis bowed her head in respect. **What brings you and the pack home so early?** As she mentioned the pack, she frowned. The others were not following behind. It was just Fenris.

When she met his gaze, she saw it. The change. It was subtle. So subtle that the pups, thankfully, didn't notice a thing. But Artemis did. The twitch of his ear towards the trees, the pause in his breathing, and the flash of fear in his eyes.

She caught the change. And he knew she did. One look said it all.

Not here.

The elk have moved further out than we expected. We will try again for caribou later instead, he said calmly. **Young ones, how about you show me what you have learnt recently?**

Artemis knew what he was doing, and she was grateful that the pups were always eager to show off their progress to their father. Without pause, they began to showcase their hunting and pouncing practices. Rickon and Solar paired off together, as they often did, and showed their individual styles of attack. Rickon jumped at Solar's side, knocking her over, while Solar charged straight ahead, catching him off guard. Kai watched from the sidelines to learn. He wasn't strong enough yet to engage.

With the pups focused on one another and trying to outdo the other to show off to Fenris, Artemis sat down at his side. Her bottom furs pooled at her haunches, and the knife she had secured in a small pouch within them rubbed against her hip. Artemis took a breath. She was ready to listen.

Yue is with the pack now, he said quietly. **There is a new arrival – Very good, Rickon! Solar, tighten your haunches when you jump – in the Forest.**

What is it? Artemis's gaze never left the pups. **Rickon, I have warned you to be gentle with your brother. Remember or you will go in the stream.**

She listened for Fenris's answer, but it never came. He seemed almost reluctant to continue, which made Artemis more anxious. While she knew the pups were in earshot, it wasn't like Fenris to keep things from her.

By the badger's nest... he said without looking in her direction. It was almost as if he hadn't spoken to her at all.

With a careful nod, she announced to her charges that their father would be taking over for tonight. She smiled to herself when she realised they weren't listening to a word she said.

Slipping away from the Den, she began to walk calmly towards the tree-line. She worked to keep her heartbeat as normal as possible so as to not alert the pups. As she made it through the trees and came to the thinning side of the stream that flowed past their territory, she found her way to the abandoned badger hideout.

There she saw the pack. Their twelve-strong family stood together forming a circle with Yue, Fenris's soul, in the centre. Her white-as-snow fur made her easily distinguishable among the group. Artemis recognised the sign of an elder meeting. They had not had one of these in a while. The last being about the sun's fever that caught the Forest only a few seasons past.

Yue moved around the circle as she spoke. Artemis couldn't hear her clearly from where she stood, but the anger in her yellow eyes could not be ignored. She was an image of strength, at least to those who didn't know her well. In her eyes, past the shroud she used as protection, Artemis could see the fear she tried to hide.

Then those eyes turned to her, and a brief moment of relief appeared in them. Bowing her head in respect, Artemis came closer to join the meeting of wolves. Seiko, a white wolf like his mother, and Taki, a grey wolf, shuffled aside to allow her in.

Mother Yue. Artemis lowered her head once more to honour her title. **What has happened?**

I fear we are once again in danger, Yue said in a wavering voice. It seemed with Artemis's arrival, she was now unable to hide the fear growing within her, and the pack picked up on it. **An old enemy has crossed into our territory.**

Artemis lost the ability to breathe.

She remembered a scenario like this so many seasons ago. Back then, her sister Rae spoke of a danger that threatened them all. And then she was killed by that very danger.

We have not been able to determine how many have arrived. Yue's gaze stayed on Artemis. **Our scouts were only able to sense so much, but one thing is clear.**

Artemis waited for the words she feared were coming to pass Yue's maw. And she prayed to the Mother Wolf that she was wrong.

Humans have returned to the Forest.

Artemis felt the pack's eyes on her the moment those words entered the air. Unlike when she was young, she knew it wasn't out of fear or disgust or even blame. Kiba and even Fenris had made sure that never happened again. Yue became part of that protection squad not long after she joined the pack. Her home in the pack was never in question, but the stares of concern were just as daunting.

It was no secret that Artemis had been taken once by humans. Nor was the fact that she was a wolf-girl. Instead, it was embraced by the pack. This was helped by the fact that with her blade, she was just as capable hunting as the rest of them. It had made her a valuable teaching asset when it came to training the pups in their younger years before they branched out with the others. Yue had always said they were in her debt with her help and guidance.

Yet, even with those positives, the fallout from her capture meant that anything regarding the outside human world was seen as a sore subject for them all. They'd lost Rae and Shadow to the Mother Wolf because of them as well as Artemis for an entire season. The trauma of it all had stayed with them.

Not that everything about that world was terrible... she thought to herself. A flash of oak-coloured eyes came to her mind, but she shook her head to stop the memories from taking over. Now was not the time to wonder how her old friend was, where she had gone, and what she looked like now. There were bigger things to focus on.

Ignoring the stares of the pack around her, she looked to Yue who knew better than to worry about her and tightened her jaw. **What do you need us to do?**

THE LAST THING Artemis expected was for them to move territories.

It had been their home for so long that most of the members of the pack, barring Fenris and Artemis, knew no other home than here. She could barely fathom leaving. It was that thought alone that had Artemis asking something she probably shouldn't have.

Should we not investigate the trespassers first? Artemis asked. **Find out why they are here and study them—**

No, Yue snapped. **We will not risk our family when there is a simple solution.**

The meeting adjourned not long after that, and the pack headed back to the Den already prepared to move out. But Artemis wasn't done yet. She couldn't believe that there was no better option than running. She found Fenris waiting by the tree-line and went to his side.

Is leaving truly the best option, Fenris? she questioned.

Yue has told you— he began, but Artemis wasn't done.

Surely uprooting the entire pack is more complex than a small investigation, she said forcefully. **If you are concerned for the wolves, I could go. They would never suspect—**

Fenris rounded on her with bared teeth. Though she was much taller on her two legs, his nose barely reaching the height of her stomach, his sudden turn sent her tumbling backwards. When he moved closer with a growl in his throat, Artemis lowered her head in shame.

Fenris paused at the motion before letting out a sigh. **I am sorry. That was too far of me.** He came to her side and nudged his head against hers. Artemis rested hers against his in acceptance. He sat down at her side. **I cannot risk you being lost to us once again.**

Artemis looked up in surprise at his words and the emotion behind them.

We did not speak much of what it was like when you were gone; we tried our best to put the memory of it behind us as you know. He looked away from her. **But I remember father's soft cries at night for mother and for you. I remember the blame I felt for not saving you. I remember more than anything the heartbreaking relief at your return.** He turned his golden eyes to her. **I will not risk this pack losing you again.**

Artemis rested her head heavily against him. She raised her paws and placed one against the side of his neck, hoping to express the love and gratitude she felt at what he had shared with her.

I understand... she said gently. It would hurt having to say goodbye to another home, but she understood. **I will not see the humans.**

Fenris pulled back from her and nodded his head in thanks before he moved towards the Den to prepare for what came next. They had to find a new home after all, one far away from the humans. They'd need scouts for that. Artemis followed after them and went to head back to the pups when she overheard something that gained her attention.

The four humans reside not far from the split mountainside in the open thicket, Taki said. He turned to Mai, a black-white-furred wolf. **We observed what appears to be two males and two females if the scents we detected are accurate.**

Fenris nodded. **Thank you both. We may need further scouting before we leave to make sure they do not move.** The wolves bowed their heads. **For now, join Yue and the others.**

Artemis watched as the elder wolves came together at the cave's entrance. It was now her job to distract the pups as they discussed what came next. It was a job she was good at.

Taking the pups to the other side of the stream, she began to guide them through their pouncing methods. As they worked and played, Artemis found her mind slipping away from her and to that open thicket.

Four humans were in the Forest. Two of whom were female.

She remembered so long ago, the last kind words she heard from the one who had saved her from cruelty. Those beautiful oak eyes came to her once more, and this time she did not brush the thoughts away.

"I will come back," she had said. Artemis remembered it as she stared out towards the split mountains. *Did she really keep her promise?*

9

ARTEMIS

*Y*ou have truly lost your mind, she thought as she lay at the edge of the cave looking up at the stars.

Glancing to the right, she took in the sight of her pack resting. It was strange to see them all deeply asleep during the height of the moon. Night was a time of adventure, training, and hunting. Not sleeping. The arrival of the humans had changed them greatly.

Fenris had ordered the pack to sleep only a few shadow passes ago. They would sleep at night just as the humans do and leave in the morning to scout for a new home. Artemis understood the plan. Understood the reasons behind Fenris's decision, but that didn't make it any easier to sleep. Her mind was far too alive with questions.

Why were the humans here? What did they want? Why has it taken them so long? Could it be Oak? Why has she come if it is?

Her lack of sleep wasn't helped by the fact that the human side of her brain struggled to rest easily when she had been asleep not long before. Wolves could sleep whenever, wherever, and however. Artemis was not that lucky. Not in her elder years at least.

Turning to stare back up the night sky, Artemis held back a sigh she wanted to release. She had been planning what to do ever since the last of the wolves had drifted off. When they had, she walked it through her mind once, twice, three times before putting it into action.

Fenris is going to hate me.

With a final glance towards her family, she slowly slipped from the cave. Placing her paws carefully in the already made prints in the ground in the hopes of hiding her tracks, Artemis made her way towards the trees. Reaching the grove's entrance, she turned back to the cave. She couldn't make out her pack through the darkness, but she knew they were still there.

Artemis could only hope they would forgive her for what she had to do. They may not understand it like Kiba did, but maybe they would come to. She had to know what was out there – even if she didn't understand why.

Drawing the knife she'd kept at her side ever since she escaped from that human place, she slipped into the shadows and away from the Den. She only had a few shadow passes until the first of them would stir. She had to make them count.

Her eyesight wasn't as strong as her pack's, but she wasn't as hopeless as she had been as a youngling. She knew their territory like the back of her paw. Pass the willow tree, the centre marker for their territory, cross the stream by badgers, and follow the direction of the split mountains. Though she made sure to stay as far away from there as she could while keeping it in sight.

Artemis had made a promise to Kiba not long after her return that she would never go near that place. He had been afraid of what may happen to her if she did. That promise continued long after his passing out of respect for his fears and wishes. Until now, that was.

Kiba would understand, Artemis justified to herself as she trotted ahead. He knew about Oak after all. She had told him everything about her after her first moon cycle back home.

Though as she thought back on that time now, she remembered the sadness in his eyes when she had finished. Artemis hadn't thought much of it at the time, had barely even noticed it until after he passed. Had Kiba felt the same as Fenris in regard to her fascination with humans? Had he been hurt by the care she'd felt towards Oak? Artemis found herself questioning whether Kiba had understood her after all.

Staring down at the knife in her hands, the glint of silver catching the moon's light, she wondered if he would have allowed her to seek out her answers about the humans. Kiba had always understood her curiosity, but maybe he would not have understood this.

I wish you were here, she said in her mind, hoping that wherever he and Rae existed now, they would hear her. *You would tell me what to do.*

Artemis pictured his handsome face and sparkling golden eyes. He would smile at her in the way that showed that he knew what she was thinking before nudging her with his head towards the reckless action she was about to take. Kiba may not have understood her fascination with Oak or her human side, but that didn't mean he hadn't tried.

She smiled up at the stars above. **Thank you, brother.**

Pushing herself forward and through the thicket, she ran faster. Her time was limited, and she was only a half a shadow's way there with another two to go. She'd have to be quick on her feet if she was going to make it back to the Den without being noticed. Unfortunately for her, the land here was not in the mood to help.

The land by the split mountains had always been unkempt.

Unlike their territory that lay before the willow tree, this land was overgrown and harder to travel through. It was the reason her family rarely travelled to this part of their land. They only returned every two moon cycles to restate their claim to those who may try to infiltrate it.

Artemis found herself having to climb fallen trees, duck beneath overhanging branches, and sidestep the prickle bushes. She'd not expected so much debris to be in her way, but she supposed it had been many seasons since she had been in this part of their land. The world changes fast among the Forest.

Part of her half wished she'd attempted to gain more information from Taki or Mai about what they had seen. If much of the land here had changed, then it was possible that the markers had too. To know she was heading in the right direction she would have to hope that—

A-ha! Artemis cheered internally as she came across the abandoned fox den. The second-to-last marker. There was no denying it was the right one. She'd joined the hunting party four seasons ago when they had gone after the fox for stealing their meal.

This meant she was close.

Determination in her step and her blade in hand, she allowed the calm of the Forest to fill her. Night for a wolf was a time of power. With how the land lay still, its silence only broken by the occasional hooting of the owl's or squeal of a captured mouse by a fox, Artemis could feel her heartbeat slow. Just as any predators would while on the hunt. Each animal of the Forest respected the power of the night.

It was as Artemis caught sight of the grove of oak trees, the border line to the expanse of land within, that something felt off. When she travelled before this moment, the noise of the Forest was clear. Tweets, chirps, howls, scuffling. Everything that made the Forest alive could be heard. But here...

Here, it was silent. And silence was dangerous.

She took a careful step past the first line of trees only to turn away at the bright flicker of light in the distance. Her vision was dazzled, and she quickly blinked and shook her head to regain her sight. Seeing in the dark may not be her strong suit, but seeing *nothing* was far more dangerous for a creature like her.

With the flickers of light no longer trapped in her eyes, she carefully returned her gaze to the direction of the glow but made sure to look no higher than the edges of light. The strange sun's fall colours stretched far into the trees. Artemis was unsure what was creating the light, so she avoided the ground it touched as best she could as she moved forward. The glow was small, like the sun as it fell behind the mountains, but bright enough to keep illuminating the human Den. At least, she assumed it was the human Den. It was strange enough looking that she knew it couldn't be any other creature's. She'd have seen the strange black shapes before now if it was from here. Of course, they had the occasional new arrival among the Forest. Migration meant these things were to be expected, but this was like nothing she had ever seen.

Artemis moved closer. She had to get a better look. Had to know what it was that they were dealing with.

That was when another light caught her attention. One as bright as the moon above. But it was closer.

In panic, Artemis stumbled to hide behind the tree, afraid of being caught. She held her breath and listened intently to the land around her. Not far ahead of her, where the light had come from, she could hear the sound of crunching snow beneath paws. It didn't sound close, but she didn't risk moving until the noise lessened enough that she could no longer hear it. Only then did she lean around the tree to seek out signs of the intruder.

To her surprise, she saw a two-footed creature walking in circles around the strange Den. There were only two kinds of animals that walked on two feet in this Forest. And this creature was too big to be a bird.

It was one of the humans.

Artemis watched closely behind her tree as the human figure moved in circles around its Den. On the fourth rotation, Artemis frowned. *Was this some kind of human practice to protect from predators?* she wondered as she leant out further, fascinated.

Occasionally she would lose sight of the human from her position behind the tree, and wanting to figure out what they were doing, Artemis decided to head to higher ground. Placing her blade within her bottom fur pouch, she used the trunk and branches of her hiding tree to pull herself up into it. With its height and foliage, she could keep out of sight while keeping the humans in hers for observation. She'd done this many times before, especially after she'd become grown. Whether it be reaching the honey hives with ease or being able to climb the tree trunks to scout for her family, it had many benefits. Which is why, from her position in the trees, she was able to see the unmistakable shadow of a human slinking past the entrance of the trees where Artemis hid.

Holding onto the trunk, she leant forward and squinted into the darkness for the human's position. With the light in their paw, it made it easier for Artemis to spot them. Unfortunately, with her eyesight, all she could make out was their vague shape. It would be near impossible to note anything of significance about them at this distance. She could barely figure out if the human she was watching was female or male.

Moving further out onto the branch and using her fine balancing skills to keep herself upright, she hoped to get a better look of the human as they moved closer to her part of the grove.

That was when she heard the howl. She knew that howl.

Her heart thudded in her chest. Fenris knew she was gone. And she knew that he knew what she was doing. He always did.

With a tenseness in her shoulders, Artemis moved back to

the trunk and held on. She was preparing to climb down the tree and run home, a figurative tail between her legs, when a flash of light on the ground beneath her caught her attention.

Artemis froze in place. She knew she should have been trying to make her escape, running far and fast in the hopes of not being caught by the human nor scolded as harshly by Fenris for her disobedience. But she couldn't move.

When the figure stepped into the trees, the light of the moon in their hands, Artemis started to wonder if she'd made the right choice. She was alone here. Trapped now with a human that could be dangerous for all she knew. Fenris had been right. Seeking them out was foolish.

The figure took another step into the trees, its light moving all around as if it were searching for something. Artemis held her breath, praying to the Mother Wolf that she would not be found.

Then she heard the human's voice.

It was only for a moment, no more than a few words before they suddenly fell to the ground. But it was enough. The warm tones of their voice, a lower register than Artemis would expect, especially considering their small stature. It felt … familiar. Similar to the voice of the girl she had once known but different. Artemis tried not to let disappointment fill her at the thought that she was wrong.

A bright light flashed in her face, stunning her for a moment. It was only when it was removed and she'd blinked multiple times that Artemis could see again. She had to hold back an intake of breath in surprise.

Below her, only a few branches away, was the human.

With them closer, Artemis could now make out a little more of what they looked like. Their head fur was long and brown, the brown like the bark of the trees. Their skin, unlike Artemis's pale, was a deep tan that stood out from the snow. They were tall, that much Artemis could tell, but she couldn't make out much else about them.

She should have been worried about how close they were to her, but her curiosity got the better of her. Artemis considered moving down the tree quietly in an attempt to get a closer look when she heard a twig snap.

Both Artemis and the human froze.

Glancing around in the dark, Artemis sought out the new arrival. She hoped against all hope that it wasn't Fenris. He'd already discovered her disappearance, but if he found her here with a human, she feared what that could do to their relationship.

When she finally saw the new arrival, she wished it had been him.

Slinking through two tree trunks behind her was a golden-eyed and tanned-hide cougar. His lips were curled backwards, exposing his saliva-covered teeth, and his claws were extended as he stepped through the trunks.

Artemis felt a growl grow in her throat. The cougars had been causing a lot of problems for the pack recently. Not only did they hate Artemis on principle for being a half-breed, they had been infiltrating their territory and attacking the herd there, causing them to flee further into the mountains. Away from the pack. Suffice to say that the cats and wolves were not on good terms. Which made this situation complicated.

When Artemis realised the cougar wasn't looking at her, she felt relief. It seemed like he didn't even know she was there. She followed his golden eyes to where he stared and found him heading for the human who stood frozen.

Shout at the beast, Artemis begged in her mind. *Make yourself big and scare them.*

The human didn't do that. Standing halfway turned towards the cougar and towards their Den, they didn't move an inch. At least they weren't meeting the cat's eyes, that was a guaranteed death sentence for any creature. But that would only get them so far. Artemis clenched her jaw in frustration. The damn human was going to get themselves killed, and Artemis would have to watch.

The human spoke again, grabbing both Artemis's and the cougar's attention. She could hear the tremble in the words even if she did not understand them. When they spoke again, there was a crack in their tone that sounded so painful and terrified that Artemis knew she had to help. Even if she didn't know why she should.

So, when the cougar pounced, so did Artemis.

Artemis didn't have much time to think about how dangerous this was before she fell from the tree and landed on the cat's back. Her weapon already drawn, she plunged it deep into the cougar's back and held on for dear life. The goal now was to not die.

A claw swung around and caught her side. Letting out an angry hiss, she wrapped her arms around the cougar's neck and flipped them. Landing on her back with the cat now held in a one-arm grip, she began wildly stabbing at the beast's forelegs and stomach. She found herself feeling grateful for the sun-coloured light that lay motionless on them. It gave her the same advantage as the night-seeing cougar. Or at least, a closer one.

A gasp of pain escaped her when the cat caught her hand with its teeth. Her grip loosened enough for the cougar to spin around and lash out at her. As teeth lunged at her face, Artemis flung out her blade hand and sliced the underside of the cat's jaw, eliciting a yowl of pain from the creature.

With the cougar frozen in pain, Artemis used her long legs to propel the cougar backwards and into the nearest tree with a heavy thud. Clamouring to her feet with only a little stumble, Artemis bared her teeth. **Be gone, cat. This land does not belong to you.**

Limping to its feet, the golden eyes of the cougar locked

onto Artemis with a look of disgust and pain as blood ran down its maw and across its stomach. **We will see, half-breed.**

The cougar turned and ran.

Breathing heavily with the blade still drawn and dripping in the cougar's blood, Artemis pulled herself to her full height. She had to make sure the cat wouldn't return anytime soon. She hadn't risked her safety just for the human to get into the same trouble the moment she left.

Only when the sun-coloured light moved did she glance over her shoulder at the human she saved. The light of the moon broke through the trees above them, and for the first time, Artemis could make out more of the human. Their brown hair and tanned brown skin were the same, but now she could see their eyes. Lying behind strange circular covers were a pair of soft honey oak-coloured eyes that never left hers.

Artemis frowned. *Those eyes ... Why do I feel like I know those eyes?*

It was when the human took a small step towards her that Artemis finally reacted like a wolf should. She turned and ran.

10

ARTEMIS

Y**ou deliberately disobeyed me!** Fenris snarled.

Artemis lay at her leader's feet in submission. The slowly rising sun warmed her back in an uncomfortable way as her superficial wounds were being tended to by Ronan's warm tongue.

I am sorry, Fenris, but I had to know who they were. She bit back a hiss of pain as Ronan's tongue danced across her sore ribs. **How can we defend ourselves from this enemy if we do not know them?**

Fenris stepped forward, and Ronan quickly backed away with a slight bow of his head as he did. He moved to join the other wolves who watched as her judgement unfolded. Artemis could hear the worried mutters of the pups, but she had to stop herself from turning to look at them. Fenris's bared teeth appeared in her eye line.

We do not need to know this enemy, he said hardly. **We have seen what they are capable of as you well know.**

Artemis ducked her head. He was right. She knew exactly what they could do.

Fenris, please, I only intended—

I do not care for your intentions, Fenris said. **You are to stay away from the humans if you wish to keep this family safe.**

The silence that followed his words was deafening. Artemis couldn't even lift her head to meet his gaze. Afraid of what she would see there.

Yes, Father Fenris, she replied quietly.

Fenris turned to the wolves behind her and spoke in a commanding voice. **We leave by sun's fall.**

Her friend said nothing else to her. He just walked away, towards the other wolves, as he called for them to begin preparing to leave. Artemis turned her head and saw the pups watching her, conflicted. Kai stepped towards her but was quickly ushered away by Yue, along with his siblings. She had to look away from the disappointment in Yue's eyes.

Only Mai stayed behind.

Mai was a pup from a litter three seasons ago now. She was a beautiful wolf with a mixture of her father's black fur and her mother's white. Just like Rae had been, Mai was being groomed to take over leadership of the pack once her parents' time had passed. Which, considering their current age, many assumed could happen any day now. She was a no-nonsense kind of wolf, which is why Artemis was surprised she'd not shunned her with silence like many of the others.

Artemis winced at the tear in her side from the cougar's claws as she sat up. **I have received enough from your father, Mai. I do not need it from you.**

Mai said nothing. Artemis watched as the she-wolf came to her injured side and tilted her head at her. **May I?**

Artemis was back on her side instantly. When the warm tongue caressed the oozing scratch, she had to hold back a cry. She'd forgotten how painful injuries like this could be. Thankfully the cougar hadn't cut her too deeply or this would be another story.

I was not going to argue with you over your actions, Mai said between presses of her tongue. **I intended to commend you.**

Now that surprised Artemis enough to be distracted from the pain. **Why is that?**

Unlike my father and mother, I do not believe we should be fleeing our home. We do not know why these humans are here, nor have they made any move to head towards us yet. Mai licked another wound. **I know what they did to you and our family in the past, but to act rashly like this may lead to our downfall.**

How? Artemis asked.

It shows weakness, Mai stated matter-of-factly. **Would we do the same to the cougars? The bears? No. We would investigate what they are doing and fight against it. Why should these humans be any different?**

Artemis had to smile at Mai's belief in the power of the wolves. Even if it was misplaced.

I admire your strength, Mai, I do, Artemis began. **But you underestimate these humans. These beasts do nothing except cause pain and death to all who, in their eyes, are not like them. Our leaders are right. It is safer for us to be on the defensive.**

Then why did you go?

She had her there. How could she explain her reasoning without sounding like a fool?

There... Artemis pushed herself up to sit. **There are some who are not like that.**

Artemis could see that Mai wanted more information but she held herself back. Mai always knew when to push and when to stop. It made Artemis smile. She would make a great leader one day. **We should join the others.**

Your wounds—

Will heal on their own eventually, do not worry about me. Artemis smiled. **Come, let us go.**

As Artemis carefully got to her feet, taking in deep breaths with each movement, she found the young wolf staring up at her in thought. She frowned. **What is it?**

I am not sure but... Mai tilted her head. **There is an emptiness in your eyes that I have never seen before.**

Artemis openly gaped at that. Insulted by the comment. Mai did not seem to notice.

It reminds me of the time when my mother was sick. Father had the same look in his eyes when we were unsure if she would make it. Mai huffed and shook her head. **I apologise, elder, I am speaking nonsense.**

Before Artemis could ask what she meant, Mai was trotting away and towards the wolves that had gathered by the stream. Shaking her head in confusion, Artemis went to join them when she found Yue staring at her from the cave's entrance with an unreadable expression. The two held each other's gaze until Artemis couldn't help but look away.

Holding her side, Artemis slowly made her way to her family at the stream. They were discussing the direction to head that would offer the clearest protection. Talk of the river was being had, and though she intended to pay attention and show that she was serious about doing as Fenris had told her, she couldn't help but think of those eyes.

Even in the night, she could feel the warmth in the human's gaze. She wasn't sure how she had determined it, but she was sure the one she had saved was female. There was something in the way she had looked at Artemis that felt distinctly female. Not that Artemis could fully understand how she knew this.

Why do you feel familiar? she found herself wondering as she thought of those honey oak-coloured eyes. *And why do I want to see you again?*

Fenris joined the pack by the stream and issued an order

that Artemis didn't fully hear. All she could think about were those eyes. She could feel her heart pounding in her chest and hoped that her family only thought of it as a sign of anxiety and not what it truly was:

Hope.

I am sorry, Fenris.

11

JAMIE

Jamie never went to sleep that night. She couldn't. So, wrapped up in a blanket, she sat by the roaring fire and stared out into the grove of trees where she'd seen her, hoping. Hoping she hadn't imagined it. Hoping she'd come back. Hoping for a sign. Hoping for something.

She didn't realise how lost in her own thoughts she was until the light of the sunrise illuminated her, making it clear how long she'd been awake for. Her eyes started to droop at the thought before—

"Morning, Corpse Bride, how you doing?"

Jamie nearly leapt out of her chair in surprise. Her heart pounding, she turned to find a wide-smiled Ritchie standing behind her, blonde hair sticking up in all directions and a camera around his neck. He looked very well rested. She hated him.

When Ritchie caught her expression, he frowned. "Hey, you all right?"

Pushing her glasses up her nose, she offered him a shaky smile. "Yeah … yeah, sorry."

Ritchie pulled up a chair and sat down directly next to Jamie.

His usual jokey self seemed to disappear as he leant forward. "What happened?"

He'd always been able to tell when something was up. Didn't matter if she tried to hide it, Ritchie always knew. It was something about their friendship that she both loved and hated at times.

With a half-smile, she went to speak when the zip of a tent sounded. They both turned to find Alicaster stepping out dressed to the nines. She wore a designer winter thermal coat, a fashionable woolly hat, and a pair of insulated cargo trousers. Much to Jamie's annoyance, she managed to look effortlessly beautiful this early in the morning.

Guess that's what happens when you get a good night's rest, Jamie thought bitterly.

"You could have at least started on the food," Alicaster said. "We need to eat a lot before we head out. You should know this by now."

Jamie rolled her eyes. "I do. Kind of hard to make a meal when you're going on little sleep."

Alicaster tutted and walked towards Jamie's dad's tent. "Why don't the two of you cook while your father and I plan our course for the day?"

"Aren't we meant to be planning that together—"

Alicaster completely ignored Jamie and stepped into the tent. Jamie wasn't having any of this and stormed towards the tent, much to Ritchie's protest. "Hey, I was talking—"

Her dad's head popped out the tent door. Unlike Ritchie, her dad had already prepared for the day. His hair and beard had been brushed, and his winter gear was on. He looked like he did in the pictures Jamie used to see of him and her mum when they had gone on their adventures together.

"Sorry, Jamie-bear, Alicaster and I thought it best to plan our route first and then include you two." He offered a smile over her shoulder to Ritchie. "We managed to get a map of the forest from the EIA, that's the Environmental Impact Agency—"

"I know who they are, Dad," Jamie said snippily.

"Right, of course." He offered her a sheepish smile. "Either way, we'll get started and—"

"I saw Artemis last night."

Everything moved quickly after that. Ritchie cooked the food on the fire pit, Jamie sat in the centre of the makeshift chair circle, with her dad and Alicaster sat opposite her, listening intently as she told her story. Their gaze was somewhat unnerving.

"If it weren't for Artemis, I probably would have been cougar food by now."

Her dad and Alicaster sat silently. A few times, they turned to look at each other, communicating without a single word. A knot formed in Jamie's throat. It hurt seeing someone so close to her dad. She knew that no matter how hard she had tried, they'd never be able to know what the other was thinking.

Alicaster was the first to speak. "Do you have proof that she was here?"

Jamie frowned. "I mean, no. I didn't exactly have time to take pictures or something when I was about to be attacked by a cougar."

"Could you show us where you saw her?" Alicaster asked. Her tone was more interrogation than curiosity.

"I think so, but it was dark and late..." Jamie trailed off as Alicaster and her dad shared a look. "I'm not making this up." She looked at Ritchie, hoping he would back her up. When he didn't meet her eyes, Jamie turned to her dad. "I'm not."

"Jamie-bear, is it possible—"

Jamie was out of her chair and storming away from the camp before he could even finish his sentence. She heard them calling after her, but she ignored them. She knew what she'd seen was real. No amount of exhaustion could have led her to imagining it.

She could hear footsteps behind her. It seemed that as much as they didn't believe her, they were interested enough to see if it was true Now all she had to do was remember where it happened.

Everything looks the same in the dark, which now, in the brightness of the morning, meant she couldn't tell where to go. Jamie just needed a sign. Something that made it clear she hadn't been alone out here. Unfortunately for her, the forest wasn't making it easy. Across the snow, more prints and land disturbance could be seen. Evidence of rabbits, foxes, badgers lined the snow with simple prints or droppings. Anything that could have shown her where she'd seen Artemis would be gone by now.

"Jamie..." Her dad's voice was low as he laid a hand on her shoulder. It reminded her of how he sounded when he was about to tell her that he was leaving again. Sad, understanding, and a little guilty. She hated that tone of voice.

"I know she was here." She shrugged him off and moved into the trees. "There has to be—"

Blood.

Standing out starkly in the snow, far enough away that it was easy to miss, was a scattering of blood droplets among a pile of scuffed-up snow.

Jamie rushed forward with her dad closely in tow. The ground was a mess of claw marks, paw prints, and blood. Jamie scanned the area for what she needed. There, past the signs of the fight, were the distinct prints of the cougar. The blood they saw was clearly from the cat as the flecks of blood followed its path away from the fight. But it was the second pair of prints that kept Jamie's attention.

Jamie could feel the stares of the others at her back. Facing them, she pointed a finger to the unmistakable pair of human prints in the snow. She smiled. "Artemis was here."

"I KNOW you said you had found a feral child when you were young," Alicaster said between bites of her breakfast. They had returned to the camp after Jamie had proved them all wrong. The food Ritchie had made for them was slightly burned now but still edible. They had all been in some kind of shock after the reveal. Jamie didn't even consider gloating about being right, too caught up in her memory of Artemis coming to her rescue to try. "Yet, even after your father confirmed it to me, I still thought this had all been some girlish fantasy of yours."

"Fantasy?" Jamie squeaked out. This woman seemed to find every possible way to insult her.

"Jamie," her dad said in warning. "I'm sure Katie didn't mean it in this way. Feral women are, as I'm sure you know, a rarity outside of fictional stories. It is understandable to not think your story was true."

Clenching her jaw, Jamie tried not to take her dad's words personally.

"Besides," he continued, seemingly deciding this was the right time to shove his foot in his mouth. "We didn't know until now if Artemis would still be alive. It is even rarer for a feral child to live into adulthood in the wild."

"But she did. And I saw her." Jamie had to stop herself from crossing her arms like a petulant child. "She fought a cougar to save me. That means she's not afraid of humans after all that happened."

Her dad nodded absentmindedly until he suddenly stopped. It was like the weight of what she'd said caught up to him, and he came rushing to her side so fast Jamie nearly fell out of her chair.

"Did it get you at all? Were you hurt?" His voice was near panic levels as he unzipped her coat to check for any signs that she was hurt. Jamie was so stunned that she could only shake her head no to his questions. "How could you be so damn foolish, Jamie? Why would you go out alone?"

Jamie had a feeling that saying Alicaster's snoring was a problem wouldn't help the sheer panic in his expression.

"I couldn't sleep…" she whispered. "And then I heard a howl and…" Jamie swallowed. "I know it wasn't smart, but there was just something … I don't know, it was like I could feel someone watching me in the trees. I wanted to see—"

"This is why we don't have untrained novices come on excursions like this," Alicaster interrupted. "I should have sought training for them before we came, or at least brought some of our usual crew so we'd have someone competent at our side."

"That's not fair—"

"Please, Miss Gander-Yoon," Alicaster interrupted. *Again*. "You and I both know this trip is more of a chance for you to reconnect with your wild-child youth than an actual environmental mission."

Jamie glanced at her dad, silently asking him to back her up. But he didn't. He stood up and walked away from her and back to his seat in silence. Back in his chair that sat beside Alicaster, he accepted a plate of food from her and thanked her for it. A pang of jealousy and frustration filled Jamie at the sight.

Swallowing her pride, Jamie pushed ahead. "OK, fine. Maybe I did come here selfishly at first, but that doesn't mean I don't care about this forest." She gestured to herself and Ritchie. "We don't know what we're doing. But you two do. You're supposed to be teachers, right? So, teach us."

Her dad and Alicaster shared a look but stayed silent.

"Artemis and her pack are going to be out there somewhere,"

Jamie continued. "They probably already know we're here if she found us so easily, so we've got to move fast, right?"

Alicaster raised a seemingly impressed eyebrow and nodded. "Indeed. If we want to document their existence, and present evidence to the Environmental Impact Agency of a feral woman living and thriving in this forest, we need to find them fast." Alicaster sipped her coffee. "It'll also be good to seek out the other packs to show the biodiversity in animal groups, the impact it has on the forest, and so forth."

"OK, OK." Jamie nodded her head along. "And how do we do that?"

Alicaster smiled at her, and for the first time, it wasn't the patronising one she gave her when she got a question wrong in class.

"This is why you have trained experts at your disposal. Finish your food and then get your things; we leave in twenty."

AFTER A QUICK TRACKING lesson from Alicaster, they decided to split up. Her dad said it'd be better that way; they'd cover more ground in two groups. Of course, when he'd said it, Jamie hoped that meant he'd pair up with her. What was the point of Alicaster bringing up that they had expert trackers in their group if the two newbies were going to be sent out together? It felt like an unfair test.

"I feel like I should be offended that you're this unhappy to be around me," Ritchie said as he jokingly bumped his shoulder against hers.

"Sorry," Jamie said with a small smile. "I am happy to have more time with you, of course." She tapped her hiking pole against the ground as they walked like Alicaster had told her to do so in case of hunter traps. "But you know…"

Ritchie put an arm around her and squeezed her shoulder. "Yeah, I know."

The two walked on in silence through the trees. Jamie loved that they could do that. Their friendship was the kind that meant they could comfortably spend hours with each other in silence and still be connected. They would offer the other a quiet support until they were ready to talk. This time was no different. Ritchie dropped his arm from around her shoulders the moment she started talking.

"I always thought things would be different when Dad stopped being in the field," Jamie began. "But he still works ridiculous hours, you know? Hell, I go to the same university that he works at and only this year did I finally start to get face-to-face time with him after demanding we have regularly scheduled father-daughter meetings.

"When he came and told me about this trip that he and Alicaster had managed to get approved, I'd hoped that meant we would have time to work together and finally get that chance to reconnect. Then he goes and separates himself from me the first moment he can. So much for being worried about my well-being earlier." Jamie sighed. "I just want to show him what I can do."

"Let's show him then," Ritchie said with a smile. "We'll document what we see, get the evidence, find your true love, and prove to your dad that you are definitely a better explorer than him and that he's been missing out on all your awesomeness for too long."

Jamie laughed. "Alright, cameraman, let's do it. Attenborough style."

ARTEMIS

When she passes onto the next life, Artemis knows that Mother Wolf will have many questions as to why she disobeyed Fenris a second time. She would have to think of an answer before that time came because as she hid herself among the bushes to watch the human female from the other night, she was unsure why she was there.

No need to lie to yourself, a voice in her head that sounded a lot like Rae told her. *You know why.*

Her eyes followed the female walking backwards and speaking with a strange voice, one that didn't match hers, to the other human that followed her. That one held an odd silver box up to his muzzle and pointed it at the female as she talked. When that human spoke, their voice deep and vibrating, Artemis assumed they were one of the males that her pack had mentioned.

Artemis focused on the unknown male for a moment. The silver box in his hands concerned her, especially with how he moved it around to point at the Forest. When it came to Artemis's position, she ducked to the ground and held herself there. When nothing happened, Artemis slowly lifted her head to peek above the bushes and found that the two had disappeared from sight.

Biting back a growl at her naivety, she crawled carefully towards a nearby tree. With a cautious glance around, she climbed the trees as fast as her injured side would let her. After she reached the fourth branch up, she stopped and began scanning the land.

At least here I can see where they are—

The female and male appeared directly beneath the tree she was in. Dropping down flat against the tree branch, she bit the inside of her cheek to stop herself from crying out as a sharp twig jabbed against her wounds. She laid silent and still, afraid that any singular movement would alert them.

She could still hear their voices, though they were quieter than before. Artemis wondered if they had moved away. She knew it was risky, but she had to know if she was safe. Artemis leant over the side to peek.

Artemis pulled back the moment she saw them. They hadn't left after all. They were just sitting in the snow, talking quietly. Artemis pricked her ears to pick up on their tone of voice. Maybe if she could sense their attitude, she would finally figure out if they were friend or foe. But she could sense nothing.

Damn human senses, Artemis thought irritably.

Time continued to pass as she lay in the tree, and eventually, Artemis started to get antsy. The voices of the humans below and the uncomfortable scratching of bark against her stinging side was frustrating. She realised too late her reckless decision to shift into a more comfortable position.

Among the branches lay a few resting birds who, when she moved, sprung wildly into the air in surprise. Artemis froze. Heart pounding, she prayed to hear the voices of the humans below, but they had fallen silent. She was in danger.

The voices below her grew louder. Their tone was higher in pitch, like the pups' yips when it was dinnertime. They were excited about something. Excitement from humans, as she remembered, was never a good sign for her.

She stayed unmoving on the branch – barely even breathing in fear of being caught. When nothing beyond the voices found her, she began to believe that maybe she was in the clear. Making sure to not be reckless, she stayed where she was for another beat before finally glancing over the edge of the branch once more.

Beneath her, the male held the silver box to his face and directed it at the honey-oak-eyed female. She spoke in an excitable tone and waved her paws in the air as she did.

Artemis continued to watch them and attempted to understand what they were doing, but she was left clueless. These humans were stranger than any of the ones she had met all those seasons ago. The two shared in laughter and spoke together in open tones of voice as that silver box continued to be held.

When it was eventually lowered from the male's muzzle, he came to the female's side, and they began to bump shoulders in the playful manner of siblings. They did not look connected in the familial way, the girl being of tanned skin and the boy pale, but Artemis could not assume. After all, her own pack was made of those who chose to join them as well as the offspring of their leaders. Wolves choose their family. Maybe these humans had done the same.

It was as the male stepped away from the female and pointed behind him to the direction they had come from that Artemis's heart sank. She knew they were heading back to the thick oak trees of the grove that surrounded the human's Den. When the female nodded and stepped after him, that was all the more confirmation for Artemis. They were leaving.

No, they can't go yet. She pushed herself up from the branch in a reckless move of desperation. *I still do not know—*

THUD.

Artemis's heart dropped to her stomach.

Caught between two tree roots in the snow below lay the golden tip of the weapon Oak had gifted her all those years ago. The weapon that had given her the skills to become just as important as any other wolf within the pack. The weapon that had guaranteed her survival for many seasons. And now it would be her undoing.

As if in slow motion, Artemis watched as the honey-oak-eyed female glanced back at the tree. She paused for a moment, and Artemis desperately hoped that she'd carry on walking. Luck was not on her side today. The human headed towards her blade.

Please, no, Artemis begged in her mind.

She watched as the girl crouched down into the snow and reached for the golden shell. Artemis had to stop herself from leaping down to take it and run. The weapon was all she had. She couldn't lose it.

Her line of sight was blocked by the girl's head, but she could just catch the soft slice of silver against its casing. A shiver rolled down Artemis's spine at the noise. She didn't like hearing the familiar sound coming from another. Holding her breath, Artemis waited for the human to look up. They had to be wondering where it had come from by now. Artemis tucked herself tightly against the branch, hoping for a miracle that she wouldn't be seen.

She heard the soft warm tone of the girl below her. Her voice echoing in the eerily quiet Forest. Artemis cursed herself once more for not attempting to keep up her understanding of the human tongue. If she had, maybe she'd have known what had been said.

That's when a screaming, crackling noise burst out from the girl's hip. The intensity and suddenness of the noise had Artemis starting in surprise, almost making her fall from the tree.

Leaning over, she sought out the noise and found the honey-oak-eyed female speaking into a strange small black box. Once she had finished, she was on her feet again. Both she and the male began running away from the trees and charging in the direction of their Den at a cautious yet desperate speed. The girl used a stick to wave across the ground as they went. Artemis had no idea what that was about.

Only when the sound of running feet disappeared did Artemis climb down, carefully, from the tree. Her wounded side was bleeding again from the rough bark which would guarantee a talking-to from Yue about personal safety. And questions from Fenris of what she was doing.

Landing on the ground, Artemis almost started running when she noticed it. Her blade. It had been sheathed into its golden casing and laid down in the snow where it had fallen. Frowning, Artemis reached down and picked up her weapon. With a slight shake to her hands, she removed the blade from its casing. The dulled silver weapon with its faded inscription of JGY was the same as it always was. There was nothing to worry about.

But why had she left it? Artemis thought as she returned the blade to its case. *Removing my weapon would put them at an advantage if they were here to cause us harm.* Artemis turned in the direction that the pair had run off in. *Unless they are not here to hurt us...*

A howl sounded in the distance. The warning signal from Mai that she needed to return. Quickly.

Today was exciting enough with the humans, there was no need to push her luck anymore. Besides, she didn't want to face the wrath of Fenris again.

Turning to go, Artemis found herself stopping and looking back to the retreating back of the female without thinking.

I will see you soon, Honey-Oak Eyes.

JAMIE

The one time she didn't want to hear from her dad was the time he finally reached out to make contact. She didn't have much choice after his command to return to the camp. Jamie couldn't exactly say, "Sorry, Dad, can't do that right now. I'm trying to pretend I don't know Artemis is above me in a tree so I don't scare her away."

It wasn't his fault, of course; the universe just seemed to have it out for Jamie at the moment.

She had been so close. When Artemis had dropped her weapon, Jamie was sure that could have been their moment. She'd been so surprised to see her old knife after all these years that she couldn't help but unsheathe it. It was a little more battered than when she'd last seen it. Dried blood had permanently stained the metal now. Even her initials had faded from use. Jamie couldn't help but smile knowing that this small gift had been of use to the wolf-girl. She could feel Artemis's presence above her as she held the weapon. It had probably been a bad idea to do so; some wolves shied away from items and places that have been tainted by the smell of humans.

She'd just been warning Ritchie to not move closer or make

it obvious that they knew Artemis was up there when her dad chimed in on the walkie talkie.

Now, feet pounding against the ground, Jamie couldn't help but let the frustration fester as they eventually arrived back at the oak tree-line of the camp.

"Man, I can't believe how close we came to seeing Artemis close up," Ritchie said breathlessly. His pale face had turned red from exhaustion. "Why didn't you call out to her when you found her?"

"I didn't want to risk scaring her." The two had slowed down the moment they reached the edge of the camp. No point running anymore when they were already here. "She was hiding for a reason. Probably trying to figure out if we're here to hurt her or not. Hopefully me leaving her knife behind will be some kind of sign to her."

"Well, we'll be going out again soon so—"

"About that," her dad interrupted, surprising both Ritchie and Jamie with his sudden appearance in front of them. They'd been too lost in conversation to notice that they'd made it to the tents.

"What?" Jamie asked as she headed towards the camp chairs. Her legs ached, and she needed to sit down. She heard the others follow. "Did you find something?"

Flopping down into the chairs, Jamie and Ritchie let out an exhale of relief. It took Jamie a moment to realise that her dad and Alicaster had been here a while. The fire had been restarted, embers crackling as it worked to grow stronger, and water was boiling atop it for a fresh pot of tea. It was already starting to get dark, which was probably the reason why they had been called back to camp.

"Unfortunately, we did," her dad said with a frown.

Or maybe it wasn't. Jamie sat up right. Her dad looked stressed, if the way he kept tugging at his beard was anything to go by. He never tugged at his beard. Unless it was bad. Even

Alicaster looked uncomfortable as she set about making the tea.

"What is it?" Jamie asked.

Alicaster handed out a mug of tea to everyone. Jamie had a feeling she was trying to find the right words if her fiddling with the cup in her hand was anything to go by. When she did speak up, Jamie almost wished she hadn't. "Hunters. From Materia. They were here."

Jamie's heart dropped. "What … what were they doing?"

"That's why we called you both back." Alicaster pressed two fingers against her temple to massage it. "We have no idea."

"How could you have no idea?" Jamie replied in a far snappier tone than she intended.

"We only caught sight of them as they left," her dad chimed in. "All we saw was them leaving on a quad bike with an empty carrier attached to it." Her dad's tone turned darker. Angrier. His hands clenched into fists on the arms of the chair. "Whatever had been inside it is in the forest now."

"What does that mean?" Jamie asked with a frown.

"It means the forest has become more unreliable to travel in." Alicaster took over answering. Jamie tried not to grit her teeth. It was frustrating seeing how well attuned to conversation her dad and Alicaster were. "We'd already considering the risk of traps but now with the fact they have been in here with something…there's just too many variables to put our safety at risk for."

"But Artemis is out there," Jamie said. "And her family. We can't just leave them to whatever the hunters have done." She turned to her dad. "We have to do something, right? That's the whole point of us being here."

Her dad shook his head. "Jamie, you know we can't risk—"

"That's not good enough," she snapped, not letting him finish. They'd barely been here a day, and they were ready to throw in the towel already. "This forest, these animals, Artemis, they need us to protect them. To find out what it is those hunters have done."

Her dad sighed. "Jamie…"

"Three days. Give us three days to figure out what they did, and if we can't figure it out, we go," Jamie said, trying to keep the desperation out of her voice. "If we do and we can solve the problem, we stay."

"There's too—"

"Think about what Mum would do." *Asshole.* "Would she pack up and go at the first hurdle?" *Cruel.* "Or would she at least investigate?" *Worst daughter ever.*

Jamie dug her nails into the palms of her hand to stop herself from looking away from her dad's glistening eyes. She'd hit his soft spot. She knew she had. Anything regarding her mum was a tough subject. But it was nearly always the one that had her dad bending to her will. It was why she hated doing it.

"You get two days."

Her dad didn't wait for her to respond with a thank-you, nor did he say anything further. Instead, he retreated to his tent. Jamie bit the inside of her cheek, ashamed of herself.

"You best make that time worth it," Alicaster said. To Jamie's surprise, there wasn't any bite to her words. "If those hunters are any bit as ruthless as what you and your father made them out to be, I hope we find and stop them in time."

Too stunned to respond, Jamie only nodded. She watched as Alicaster went to her father's tent with papers in hand. At least she knew he wouldn't be alone right now. Work always helped him feel less lost.

"Well," Ritchie's sudden appearance had Jamie jumping in surprise. "That was … intense."

Jamie sheepishly rubbed at her neck. "I … I forgot you were there."

Ritchie shrugged. "You all did. It's the curse of a filmmaker. You're such a silent observer that people forget your existence."

A smile slipped across Jamie's lips. "You? A silent observer? What lies."

"OK, silent observer when I'm watching a drama unfold. Anything else, I'm a commentator." Ritchie winked. "Speaking of, what are you thinking? I mean, two days to figure out what the hunters have done and save Artemis? I know the powers of lesbian wanting go far" – Jamie smacked his arm for that – "but even your abilities aren't that strong."

Jamie sighed and laid back in her chair. Staring up at the darkening sky and the few twinkling stars that were beginning to emerge, she bit her lip. "All I know is that Artemis has to be the key, and no" – she held up a hand to stop Ritchie's incoming commentary – "it's not for lesbian reasons. If anyone can help the wolves understand what is happening, it'll be Artemis. I can communicate with her; I know it. I just need the time to do so."

"And now you have two days," Ritchie pointed out. "And those two days don't even have anything to do with Artemis. How are you going to figure out what the hunters did?"

Jamie rubbed at her weary eyes. If she was honest, she had absolutely no idea.

"Wing it, I guess?" She turned to Ritchie who, worryingly, was smiling a mischievous smile. "What?"

"You're going to do what you do best, of course."

"And what would that be?" Jamie asked with a raised eyebrow.

"You're going to break the rules."

14

ARTEMIS

If Fenris knew she had been sneaking out, he hadn't let on. Whether it was Artemis's ability to hide her emotions or Mai's skills in masking the scent of humans that lingered on her body, she was both thrilled and ashamed at keeping secrets from him. But for now, it was a necessary betrayal. There was something different about these humans. Well, about one of the humans. She was still unsure about the rest.

Honey-Oak Eyes had shown herself to not be out to cause Artemis harm. She had ample chance to disarm her and take away her protection, and she hadn't. Of course, a cynical part of Artemis wondered if it may be a trick to gain her trust. That cynical voice sounded a lot like Fenris.

Move out! said wolf barked. His tone, while gruff, was full of anxiety.

Fenris and Yue had been having more private conversations in the lead-up to the relocation of the pack. Though Artemis was unsure if nonverbal communication counted as a conversation. Artemis had never understood how that worked. She'd seen this nonverbal form in three different soul pairs now, and it still made no sense. How could one speak with no words?

She shook her head and followed after the pack. Artemis would be taking up the rear with Mai to keep an eye on any straggling pups as they journeyed. Taking the rear of the line of wolves was a great responsibility, and Artemis was honoured to have taken on this position. Even if it meant she would use this trust to keep secrets from them.

How did it go? Mai asked when she came to Artemis's side. **Have you learnt enough yet?**

I am not sure, Artemis said honestly. **There are too many things I still do not understand.**

You told me that they did not harm you when they could have. Does that not answer your question about our safety? Mai pushed ahead to turn and look up at her. Artemis knew she wasn't well versed in hiding her emotions. **Or is there something else?**

Mai's tone was suggestive enough for Artemis to understand what she was meaning. She had to stop herself from biting back. Any explosive reaction would confirm whatever she believed already. No matter how wrong it was.

Artemis shook her head. **I do not have enough information to—**

And if the female had come further into the Forest in search of you?

Her heart thudded heavily in her chest at the idea. **I would hide and examine her from afar. Like I would do for any new predator. It is the only way to understand why they are here.**

The lack of reply from Mai was frustrating. *Why ask a question if you won't acknowledge the answer?* she thought irritably. Artemis didn't stay quiet. **I am not—**

Shh!

Artemis came to a stop. Mai was not one to snap at her elders, no matter how close their relationship was. Respect was never forgotten. Turning to the wolf, she noticed Mai's ears twisting and turning, picking up something in the distance. Artemis swallowed hard and went to call out to the pack only to find they were not in sight. She couldn't even hear the pounding of paws and yips of the pups. They'd fallen further behind than she realised. There was a chance that, whatever Mai was hearing, the pack had no idea about it.

What is it? Her eyes searched the thicket behind them for any sign of an incoming enemy. Her paw fell to the concealed weapon in her bottom furs. **Should I call for help?**

No, you cannot tell them about this, Mai said quietly. **But you will owe me for what is about to happen.**

I do not—

Head to the weeping willow tree, Mai interrupted with a smile. **You can thank me with a fresh rabbit later. Enjoy, elder.**

Artemis couldn't even ask what Mai meant before the she-wolf was bounding off after the pack without another word. As quick as a blink, Artemis was alone under the beaming moon with a heartbeat that grew ever faster.

Mai said something about the female searching for me... she thought and turned to look into the darkening distance. *Could it be?*

15

JAMIE

"**D**ad is going to kill me," Jamie muttered to herself as she trekked through the freshly fallen snow. She had her walking poles with her again and was using them as both support against the slippery ground and as protection for whatever the hunters may have lying in wait. "And then he'll bring me back to life just to yell at me for it."

When Ritchie had mentioned breaking rules, it had sounded like such a great idea. At the time, at least. She'd already unintentionally snuck out at night once before and not been found out. Until she told them what happened, of course. She could easily do it again but on purpose. She had eight hours from now until they woke up to find Artemis and the pack to warn them. Though she didn't actually know *how* she was going to do it. That would be a problem for later. For now, she just had to keep her wits about her and—

Her head torch light began to flicker.

"No, no, no, no," Jamie said in a panicky voice. "Come on, no, I just put new batteries in."

Taking off the torch from her head, she switched it off to

preserve whatever life she may have in it before opening it up to check the battery.

"Crap," she muttered as she realised she'd not closed up the case properly. Snow had managed to get inside and melted and refrozen from the cold air. "Of course."

Jamie tried to dry the batteries as best she could, but it was useless. Rubbing her face in frustration, she took out the batteries and put them in her pocket. She hoped that by drying them out, maybe they'd start working again. She doubted it.

With a sigh, Jamie began her trek again. This time she moved cautiously, as without the light of her torch, all she had to rely on was her shoddy eyesight and the moon. And the latter kept being covered by the trees above her.

You really didn't think this through, she chastised herself as she walked on.

Being out in the dark once more was as nerve-wracking as it had been last night. Of course, she'd prepared herself for being out this time around. Not that that meant anything, seeing as she was without her torch. All she had of use to her was the hiking pole, her walkie talkie, and a flare just in case. Jamie hoped she wouldn't have to use the last two, because if she did, she'd be in big trouble.

Part of her wanted to start calling out for Artemis to get this over with quickly. She knew Artemis wouldn't understand a word she was saying, but maybe just hearing someone shouting would draw the pack's attention. But Jamie shook that idea out of her head quickly. She'd made next to no noise last time and had been found by a cougar. No point in drawing any night-time predators to her location. She was reckless, but she wasn't stupid. Most of the time at least. She continued walking, only stopping when she had to remove the newly fallen snow from her glasses.

For the next hour or so, nothing changed. She moved care-fully through the forest, keeping an eye out for any signs of wolf paw prints or scat. Wolves travelled mostly at night, so she hoped that by being out now, there was a higher chance of finding them.

At one point Jamie had come across a pair of tracks near a fox's den that were definitely wolf prints. From the chaos of the prints alongside the smaller paws of the fox, it seemed a fight had broken out. The wolves had likely been defending their territory if the now abandoned den was anything to go by. But those prints weren't fresh. And that was the only sign the wolves had been near here.

Scrubbing a hand against her face in frustration, Jamie kept moving. As she walked, she took in the forest around her. There was something peaceful about the forest at night. Even if it was terrifying in some ways too. From fallen trees that blocked pathways but created habitats for the rabbits and badgers to the flowing streams that ran across her path, everything seemed to feel alive in the darkness.

I get why Artemis wanted to come back, she thought as she passed under a weeping willow tree.

The dangling vine-like vegetation dragged over her shoulders and head as she walked through it. Jamie paused for a beat beneath its shelter. The shade from the branches helped keep the cold air off her. As Jamie tucked her hands into her pockets to warm them up, she found herself wondering about how strange it was to be in summer and yet feel the cold. She knew Materia and the forest weren't always covered in snow, especially in the summer months, but it was never above freezing. Even when you could see the fields of grass and rocky mountains.

She wondered how Artemis coped in the cold. Jamie was here in the summer and was barely coping in two layers of clothes and a coat. She could hardly imagine how Artemis managed. Though, she supposed, growing up here, she had no choice but to.

While under the cover of the willow tree, Jamie pulled off a glove and reached in for the batteries, hoping they were dry. When she stabbed her stick into the ground so she could have both hands free, everything went sideways.

CRUNCH.

Jamie nearly jumped out of her skin at the cracking sound. Thankfully for her, she didn't move out of shock. If she had, who knows what could have happened.

Right in front of her, where she'd placed her hiking stick, was a vicious-looking bear claw trap. A trap that had snapped off the end of her pole in its vice grip.

"Shit."

The first time Jamie had seen a bear trap, she'd been six and her mum had taken her to one of her protests after she'd begged to go. While there, one of the protestors had been holding up a sign of a snow leopard trapped in the metal claw. Its paw was bleeding, and the animal looked to be screaming in pain. Jamie had started crying.

Her mum had taken her to get a treat to calm her down. When she had, she'd asked her mum why someone would do that to the cat.

Seon-mi had sighed and leant back in her chair. "There are too many answers for that question, my love. It could be they think the animals are dangerous to people, that they're doing it for fun, or because they believe they have no choice." Her mum ran her fingers through her hair. "There's no one answer, but it's why I go to these protests to help protect the animals. The more people who try to help, the more we can work to stop those who don't."

Jamie hadn't fully understood what her mum had meant until she met Artemis and saw what happened to her. Seeing the trap laid out in front of her, a horrifying image of Artemis's leg, bloodied and torn, caught between the silver blades, exploded in her mind. Jamie tried to shake the thought away, but it wouldn't go.

The trap sat menacingly in the snow, the silver glinting cruelly, standing out from the nature around it. Like a scar on the land.

Shivering at the sight, Jamie reached down to collect the remaining part of her hiking pole. She turned to face the way she'd come, intending to make her way back home. Her dad had been right. It wasn't safe to be out right now. Jamie glanced down at the ground below and let out a sigh of relief at the distinct footprints there. She'd be able to follow them back to camp. Jamie went to take a step forward but froze. She heard a rustle from the nearby bushes.

Jamie held her breath and stayed deathly still. She knew that hadn't worked with the cougar, but she hoped that the second time was the charm with surviving.

The rustling sounded again. Closer this time. Jamie let out a shaky breath, the condensation spreading around her as she did. Jamie glanced to the side without any sudden movements, hoping to see what was coming. That's when she spotted a pair of bright green eyes watching her from among the vines.

Jamie's heart raced in her chest. She could hear Ritchie's laughter in her mind at her predictable reaction. Though even he couldn't have predicted how she would come face-to-face with the wolf-woman again. Jamie knew he was going to be pissed about not getting it on camera.

When Artemis began pushing through the willow vines, her head coming into full sight, Jamie finally exhaled.

"Wait." She raised her hands towards Artemis. "Stop there. Stop."

Artemis stood still at the tree's entrance. Her face was visible to Jamie, if a little distorted from the darkness. The top of her clavicle was only just being exposed through the willow trees shroud and a hand of hers was raised towards the vines as if she intended to push them aside. The wolf-girl tilted her head like a confused golden retriever and went to step forward.

Knowing she was risking scaring her, Jamie stepped forward, making sure to not step outside of her footprints in the snow. Her movement startled Artemis into stepping backwards. The top of her shoulders disappeared behind the vines once again.

"Stay," Jamie said firmly. "Stay."

A small frown formed on the woman's forehead, but she stayed. Whether it was out of understanding of Jamie's words or confusion, Jamie didn't care. As long as she stood still.

Lowering her hand to her pocket, not taking her eyes off the wolf-woman, Jamie grabbed her walkie talkie and switched it on. Her plan was in hell, but she had no choice, even if it meant her dad not talking to her again.

"Jamie to base, come in," she said, her voice sticking to the same calming tones so as to not worry Artemis. "Jamie to base, come in. Emergency call. Come in."

The walkie talkie crackled, but there was no response.

Artemis had shuffled further back, nearly vanishing from sight. Panicked, Jamie considered stepping forward but knew that could possibly scare her away or put Jamie in harm's way. There were no footprints close to Artemis.

"Stay. You're OK. We're OK." Jamie raised her hands again in a sign of submission. She clicked the walkie's button. "Dad, come in. It's Jamie. I need help. Come in."

An unresponsive crackle appeared again, and Jamie closed her eyes in frustration.

"Jamie?" CRACKLE. "That you?" CRACKLE.

"Ritchie?" she replied. "Ritchie, I need you to wake up my dad."

Artemis didn't move, but a pair of fearful eyes focused on the walkie talkie. She didn't seem to like the noise it was making if the glint of silver between the vines was anything to go by.

CRACKLE. "Jamie, what the hell are you doing out at night?" CRACKLE.

"Look, Dad, you can yell at me later. I need your help."

CRACKLE. "What do you need?"

"I need you to walk me through resetting a bear trap so I can set it off."

16

ARTEMIS

Artemis owed Mai a rabbit. Probably two.

She'd made her way past the abandoned fox den not long ago when a loud snap had gained her attention within the willow tree. Unsure of what the noise was, Artemis had lowered herself to the ground and slowly made her way towards the billowing vines.

Slowing her breathing till it appeared non-existent, just as she would if she were hunting, she slunk towards the entrance of the willow and peered through the gaps of the leaves.

When she did, she almost forgot she was trying to hide herself. Standing still and tall, brown head fur blowing lightly in the wind, was Honey-Oak like Mai had said.

Artemis went to go forward, ready to test her theory that this human wouldn't hurt her, when the glint of something silver caught her eye. Down on the ground beside Honey-Oak, a stick between its thorns, was an odd-shaped silver nest. Artemis frowned. *What in Mother Wolf's name is that?*

Without thinking, she moved forward, exposing her face and the top of her body through the leaf-covered vines. That was when she met the familiar eyes of Honey-Oak. But something was off.

Panic appeared on the woman's face, and in a low tone that read of calm but felt desperate, she called out to her, forcing Artemis to stop in place.

What followed next, Artemis could hardly explain let alone understand. An invisible human spoke into the air around them, startling the birds in the branches and even a nearby hare. Artemis herself would have fled too if the girl hadn't spoken in that same calming tone to her again.

Confused but intrigued, Artemis stayed put. She watched as the girl crouched beside the silver nest, her face creasing in concentration. It would have been silent around them if it weren't for the intermittent crackling of noise from the strange black box at Honey-Oak's side.

Each time it came to life, the girl moved something else on the nest. She lowered it from its upright position. When Honey-Oak sat back to listen for the crackle, Artemis saw the exposed jagged jaws of the nest. Artemis didn't like the look of it, and from the heavy sigh from the girl, neither did she.

Artemis's sense of smell may not be able to pick up the emotional scent of others, but she could always read another's body well. Even with the thickness of Honey-Oak's coat, she could see the tightness in her jaw, the tenseness of her curved back, and even the slight shake in her hands as she moved. She was anxious. Scared even. Artemis watched her closely until she was done.

The silver nest now lay wide open and flat on the ground. While its teeth were unnerving, Artemis couldn't quite understand what it was that frightened Honey-Oak about it.

Is this all she wanted to show me? Artemis wondered with a frown as Honey-Oak reached for a nearby stick. *It does not look particularly—*

Oak eyes met hers, and she plunged the stick into the nest.

Artemis watched in horror as the silver jaws snapped closed on the stick, cracking it in half. Artemis knew the crack wasn't loud, but she could still hear it echoing in her mind.

A trap. A trick. Artemis backed up. *They are my enemy...*

Honey-Oak's voice broke through her rising panic. It was gentle and calm, if a little nervous. Against her better judgement, Artemis turned in her direction and found the woman cautiously making her way towards her. Her steps were slow and cautious, as if she were worried about being hurt.

This makes no sense... Artemis thought as she considered running again. The longer she stayed, the more trouble she could end up in. But she couldn't make herself move.

Instead, she continued to watch as Honey-Oak made her way to the willow's vines. To Artemis's surprise, she didn't come all the way to her, stopping a few strides in front with her paws raised.

This was the first time that they had been this close. While the woman would not be able to see Artemis well, the leaves of the willow making that difficult, Artemis could see her, even in the darkness.

Dark hair framed her face in a way that drew attention to soft oak-coloured eyes which hid behind shining eye protectors. Her lips were a dark red that stood out against her tanned skin. Her breath came out in short sharp bursts, making her lips look wet with the dew she exerted. Artemis couldn't tell if it was fear or aggression that had her breathing so hard. When Artemis's eyes dropped to her raised paws once more, she took in the cut-up and scarred palms. They looked just like Artemis's from when she climbed the trees.

Everything about this woman was a contradiction. Was she friend or foe? Was she working with nature or against it?

It was while examining Honey-Oak's raised paws that Artemis saw it. On her left paw, a small, jagged line of a scar was drawn across the palm. Exactly where Oak had cut herself while helping Artemis escape. It had looked painful then and, though long since healed, it still looked sore now. Her eyes flitted between the scar and those oak-coloured eyes that shone with familiar tenderness.

That's how Artemis knew.

Oak?

But Oak didn't respond. How could she? She didn't understand a word she was saying, and Artemis couldn't understand her either.

That moment of recognition never passed between them. Instead, Oak pointed at the evil contraption behind them and shook her head at Artemis. She said something Artemis didn't understand but, from how tight she held her body and the wobble in her voice, she knew it wasn't good. That was clear from the demonstration alone. Artemis thought of how carefully Oak had walked towards her and realised why the girl hadn't let her move.

These things were in the Forest. And they had no idea of knowing where.

Oak looked at Artemis, her eyes holding hers, almost consuming her. Neither seemed to know how long they stood staring until the crackle of the little black box interrupted them. Artemis jumped in surprise. She really hated that noise.

A soft sigh left Oak as she mumbled something towards the talking box. She offered her a kind smile, though unlike before, there was a warmth missing behind it. She said something to Artemis before walking back to the side of the trap. Artemis watched as Oak followed the footsteps she had left in the ground with cautious movements.

Throwing something onto her back and picking up the talking box, Oak turned back to Artemis. With a smile as warm as the embrace that she had given her the night of the escape, she spoke in a deep and deliberate voice. Artemis wished that the Mother Wolf would bless her in that moment with understanding, but she knew that was too much to ask.

Oak nodded her head and began to leave. Artemis followed her with her eyes as Oak followed the footprints she'd made out of the willow tree and used a strange red stick to pat the ground ahead. Only when she was gone from sight did the reality of what Artemis had seen hit her.

As she followed her own footprints, mimicking Oak in her methods, she hoped she'd get to them in time. Her pack was in danger of these snap traps. And Oak had helped save them.

17

ARTEMIS

Their new home was near the river. It wasn't as well protected as their previous Den, but it would provide enough stability for a migrating pack. They had access to fresh water, fish for hunting, and small mammals that lived by the riverside. The only downside was that, except for the sleeping hole for the pups, all the adults had to sleep out in the cold air.

That's how Artemis found them. The moon was high in the sky above them, its beautiful glow showcasing the tightly curled-up group of wolves. Their fur coats were covered in a thin layer of snow that had collected as they slept, which reflected in the growing light. From the light dusting on their fur, it appeared as if they had not been sleeping for long. Artemis wondered if they'd known she was gone before fading into slumber.

You have returned, a deep voice droned from behind her.

She had her answer.

Fenris came around to face her, his golden eyes locking with hers. She held his gaze as long as she could until she had to look away. His look of disappointment was too much.

The other wolves slowly began to stir. The tension in the air between Artemis and Fenris was hard to ignore. None of them spoke. Only Yue reacted, moving from her position by the sleeping holes to come closer. Her silent presence beside them was comforting, though Artemis was unsure if it was meant for her or Fenris.

Where have you been? Fenris snapped.

I was scouting for the pups when I found something... Artemis paused. She wasn't sure how to explain what she'd seen. **Something I have never seen before.**

What was it, Artemis? Yue asked. The pack watched their leader's movements as she stepped towards her. Her reaction would determine their own.

Humans have laid traps of death in the Forest.

A ripple of panic began to spread through the pack. It was only when Yue growled to silence the commotion did it dissipate, though only slightly. The pulled-back ears and puffed-up fur was enough to know the actions of their leaders were doing little to calm the wolves.

Fenris focused his attention solely on Artemis. **How did you come to see this? We have come across no such monster within our territory.**

Mother Wolf, please forgive me, she told herself as she played out the lie she had practised in her mind.

I am sorry, Fenris, Yue. She bowed her head. **I travelled further than I should have when searching for a practice hunting spot for the pups. I was distracted by memories and, before I realised, I was at the willow tree near the old Den from when I was a youngling.**

Yue stepped forward, and Artemis had to stop herself from flinching. Any sign of her lie, even if it were an increase in her heartbeat, Yue would know. She always had.

What did you see? Yue questioned.

In the snow, half-hidden, was a jaw-shaped trap that had been sprung by a ... rabbit. It had nearly split the rabbit's leg

in half. Artemis looked away. **It seemed to have died of shock afterwards. I did not see it happen, but just by the look of it, the trap's jaws were as sharp and powerful as a bear.**

The wolves were holding onto her every word. Even the pups who, to her shame, had awoken and snuck out from their sleeping holes. From how they ducked their heads Artemis knew they were frightened.

It had to have been the human's, Yue, Artemis said quickly. **It is the only logical explanation.**

Yes, Yue said, pacing. **And if there is one of these bear jaws, there will be others?**

Artemis nodded. **I am sure of it. I followed my paw prints back once I saw it. Just in case.**

A smart plan, Artemis, Yue said with a hint of pride in her voice. **We will have to follow suit.**

Yue turned to the pack who moved to sit to attention, ready for her orders. Yue hadn't always been a natural leader. When Fenris and she had fallen for one another, there had been concern about whether she could lead. The matriarch was the guide to the pack, and that's what they needed from Yue. Here, after so many years at the head, it was a marvel how far she had come.

Yue's white fur glowed in the moon's light, illuminating her as she held her head high. Artemis moved to join the ranks of the wolves and await her own orders from the leaders.

I know we have only just come to rest in this new Den, but, if what Artemis has told us is true, the entirety of this Forest is at risk. We must leave the territory behind. A grumble began among the pack. **The humans who have trespassed into this land have shown themselves as hostile. It is for our own survival that we leave.** Yue bowed her head, and the wolves grew worried. Yue never avoided their eyes. **When the humans arrived, I was sent to meet with the packs beyond the river. If we were at risk, it was possible they**

would be too. It was – she sighed heavily – **it was while there that a deal was brokered with the Lay pack across the river. They remember Father Kiba with pride and understand the circumstances. We have been offered a home among them until the danger passes.**

Mai stood sharply. **They have vied for our land for generations! We would be giving in—**

That is enough, Mai! Yue bared her teeth. **While we have been hostile before, when it comes to mutual survival, petty grievances will be laid to rest.**

Your mother is right. Fenris came to stand at his soul's side, his black fur pressing against her white. The split halves of a half-risen moon. **If the humans within the Forest are as dangerous as they appear, we have no choice.**

I did not say that it was the humans within the Forest doing this, Artemis spoke up. She bit her tongue the moment she had. *Foolish.*

Fenris's tail flicked in annoyance. **Why would you say that? It is the most logical explanation of what you saw. A trap near the old Den which lay not far from where these humans reside.**

They have shown no sign of hostility to me, Artemis stated calmly. **I do not believe it is them.**

Fenris laughed bitterly. **And, of course, you have never been wrong about humans before.**

Father Fenris, that is not fair— Ronan, the grey wolf who had helped soothe her cougar wounds, spoke up. He was an outsider of the pack and had not grown under her guidance, nor was he one to go against their leaders. His outburst surprised her.

Silence, pup, Fenris snapped. **You may be the confidant of Mai, offering you the chance to one day be a leader with her, but for now you will learn your place.**

Ronan stepped back, head bowed, though he tilted enough

towards Artemis to offer her a look of apology. She nodded her thanks.

You are right, Artemis began. **I have been wrong about humans. The very humans who still live beyond the mountains. Who is to say it is not them bringing the traps?**

Why would they, after all these seasons, return now?

Artemis didn't have an answer for that.

I am offering another view, Fenris, Artemis continued. **We could be wrong about the humans here. There is no reason to be suspicious—**

Did you see that human again? Yue interrupted.

Artemis froze. She turned to her pack who looked away from her the moment she caught their eyes. Even Mai, though supporting her journeys to visit the humans, didn't meet her gaze. She was unable to help her now. It was only when she caught the soft golden eyes of Kai at the sleeping hole's entrance did she drop her head. **I just wanted to understand them.**

Yue sighed and turned away. The disappointment rolled off her in waves. **Do you have any idea the risk you are bringing to your family?**

These humans are different, Artemis began. **Oak is—**

Oak? Fenris growled. **You named the human?**

Artemis held her tongue from speaking any further. Anything she said now would make the situation worse. Of course, it seemed the cruelty of fate was willing to prove her wrong on that.

I have had enough of this, Fenris snapped. **Father Kiba may have put up with your human curiosity, but I will not. Not anymore.** Stepping towards her, Fenris held her eyes until she couldn't help but look away in shame. **You are to not leave the pack's side again. You are to stay at the Den at all times under watch.** Fenris's teeth shone as he growled. **You will never see these humans again, do you understand?**

Artemis wanted to argue. Wanted more than anything to

make Fenris or Yue understand. They didn't see what she did. Didn't know this human like she did. But as she glanced at Kai once more, his small frame standing out against his siblings, Artemis knew she couldn't.

I... She bowed her head to Fenris. **I understand.**

18

JAMIE

"**Y**ou could have been killed!"

Jamie flinched at the boom in her dad's voice. She'd never heard him this angry before. And definitely never at her.

It had taken her over an hour to get back to the camp by following her footsteps and using her remaining stick to test the ground ahead of her. When she had made it back, her dad, Alicaster, and Ritchie were all waiting for her. Jamie hadn't even got a word out before her dad started yelling. She couldn't blame him. What she'd done was incredibly stupid.

"Dad, I—"

"To think, I thought you'd learnt the last time when you were nearly attacked by a *cougar* to not go out alone at night and yet" – he gestured wildly in her direction – "here we are. Two in the morning and up worrying whether or not my daughter will make it back alive."

"Come on, Dad," Jamie began a little more petulantly than she had any right to be.

"Don't," he snapped. "You have shown that you are not ready for expeditions like this." He drew a hand through his hair and tugged at the ends in frustration. "You will not leave this camp again unless escorted by myself or Professor Alicaster. Is that understood?"

Jamie lowered her head. She knew she had no right to be upset. She'd brought this on herself after all. But she couldn't help but be disappointed. *God, I'm the worst daughter ever*, Jamie thought, unable to meet her dad's eyes.

"Is. That. Understood?" he repeated.

She finally lifted her head. "Yes."

"Good," he said. "All of you to bed. Now."

No one argued with him. Jamie watched as he stormed back to his tent and entered it without another word. She could see Alicaster shaking her head at her before she too returned to their tent. Only Ritchie stayed, though he looked as if he would pass out any minute.

"I think my advice was bad…" he said quietly.

Jamie offered him a shrug. "I'm the one who did it. It's on me."

Ritchie only nodded. "Maybe it's a good thing we only go out with one of the adult adults." He glanced towards the trees she'd come from. "This place is a little more dangerous than I thought it would be."

He didn't say anything else after that. Only offering her a small wave before heading into his tent too. Jamie had to hold back a sigh as she looked up at the night sky above. She may have helped to warn Artemis, and hopefully had done it well enough that the pack now understood the dangers, but she'd betrayed her dad's trust in doing so.

Good going, Jamie.

IT HAD BEEN THREE DAYS. Three days since Jamie had ruined everything.

Her dad was barely speaking to her. Alicaster was making snide comments whenever she could. Ritchie was having an existential crisis due to not being able to cope with the tension. And Jamie was losing her mind.

Seeing the others go out during the day to set off and destroy the bear traps and document them for the EIA was infuriating. She knew her punishment was necessary. She'd not only broken her dad's trust, again, but she'd put herself in danger. Again. But that didn't stop her feeling left out. She'd been watching Ritchie and a responsible adult (as Alicaster had been calling themselves) head out while being left with the other adult to keep an eye on her and make sure she didn't sneak off. It was humiliating.

"We'll be back around four." Alicaster tightened the straps on her backpack. "We'll be going past the willow tree today, so we'll be gone longer."

Ritchie let out a sigh. He'd told her the night before in confidence that he wasn't made for constant travel. Nor being stuck in the middle.

"Come on, camera boy," she said with a wry smile in an attempt to cheer him up. "You've got to get your documentary filmed somehow."

"It's not a—"

BANG.

All four of them jumped in place.

"What was—" Ritchie started when another BANG ripped through the air.

Jamie turned to her dad who looked at her in return.

"They're here," Jamie whispered.

"Yes, they are," her dad replied. "And they're out hunting."

No one said anything for a moment, seemingly waiting for the next shot, but nothing came. And that was far scarier than the gun.

"We have to go—" Jamie began.

"No."

"But, Dad—"

"They have guns, Jamie," her dad interrupted. "They may not shoot at us, but the threat that they could is enough for me to say we aren't going anywhere." Jamie went to speak. "We both know what the people of that town are capable of. I'm not going to risk—"

"But Artemis is out there!" Jamie snapped, finally losing her cool. "The wolves are out there. Hell, even the cougar who tried to kill me is out there. They need our help, Dad. We can't leave them to these hunters. Not now."

"What do you expect us to do, hm?" Alicaster chimed in. "This isn't fun and games, Jamie. There are protocols we have to follow to find a way to keep this forest and the animals within it safe. Going rogue like you seem to have a penchant for doing will accomplish nothing."

"But it has accomplished something." Jamie retorted before turning to her dad. "I know what I did; going out alone and all that was stupid. I know. But I did warn Artemis, and her family, about the traps they were putting out." She glared at Alicaster. "Have you found any wolves, or hell, any animals in the traps you've been looking for?"

Alicaster didn't answer.

Jamie stepped closer to her dad, searching his eyes for that part of him that loved nature and wolves. "We need to help them."

Her dad watched her. His cool blue eyes looked deep into hers. His eyes had always reminded Jamie of the ocean, calm and serene but with the same hidden wildness. "What do you propose?"

❄

WHEN SHE'D SUGGESTED HEADING OUT and making as much noise as possible to get the hunters to run off, she'd thought that would mean time with Ritchie to then sneak off and find Artemis.

"You know, you could have been working on your dissertation while on camp arrest," her dad said from the path ahead of her, dragging his stick across the ground to check for traps as he moved. "Artemis is alive and well; she's thrived for, what, maybe twenty years since infancy? That's something you could be writing about."

"Yeah," Jamie replied distractedly as she scanned the forest around them. She could feel the camera Ritchie had given her bouncing against her chest as she walked.

"Would be good to have a camera to catch them in the act," he'd said in a wavering voice. He was scared. Probably as he should be with hunters in the forest, but that didn't stop Jamie feeling guilty.

It's why she'd hoped she'd get to travel with Ritchie. Keep his spirits up and bring out the more excited side of him. The more he'd gone out these last few days, the more anxious he seemed to get.

Instead, she was with her dad. Something she'd normally have been grateful for if it hadn't been made explicitly clear that the only reason it was happening was because she'd needed a babysitter.

"Dad, I know we're—"

She didn't get to finish her sentence because a snap of a metal jaw closed itself on the mountain pole in her dad's hand. It would have pulled him over if Jamie hadn't grabbed him.

Blood was pumping so loudly in her ears, she barely heard him say she could let go now. It was only when he prised one of her hands from his bicep that she came out of her stupor. She let him go quickly.

"Are you OK?" His blue eyes searched hers.

"I-I'm OK," she whispered before clearing her throat. "I'm …
uhm, going to film the trap. We need something to show the—"

BANG.

Her dad pulled her into his arms and dropped to the ground,
pulling her down too, as the gunshot echoed around them.
Jamie held her breath in fear as the two of them sat silently and
waited. She wasn't sure what they were waiting for until she
heard the laughter.

Without thinking, Jamie was on her feet and creeping
towards where the laughter was coming from. She could hear
her dad's whispered protests behind her and knew that she
would get a talking-to when they got back to camp. But she
kept going. When she reached a thick tree trunk, she ducked
behind it and peeked around its edge.

In front of her stood two strangers in a pool of bloody snow.
They were both men, and from how similar they looked, they
must have been related. They were tall, muscular, with bright-
blonde hair that stood out from the green and browns of the
woods. One held a smoking gun, laying it casually against his
shoulder, as if it were the most natural thing in the world. Jamie
wanted to be sick.

"Will this kind of trap catch her?" the one with the gun said
in a deep voice, pointing to something behind him Jamie
couldn't see.

"If it doesn't" – the other shrugged – "at least we have a
backup."

Jamie felt a presence at her back and froze. Only when she
heard the barest whisper of "camera" did she relax in realising
her dad had followed her.

Unclipping the camera from her neck, she placed the lens on
the edge of the tree, keeping it out of sight, and began to record.
To not draw further suspicion, she watched the events through
the camera screen. The sight almost made her vomit.

On the ground, blood pooling from its neck, was a dying

grey wolf. She could see its erratic breathing of panic as it lay in the snow, legs twitching as if trying to escape. Jamie couldn't see where in the neck it had been shot, but from the lack of noise from the wolf, she had to assume it went straight through its throat. She had to look away.

"It's a live trap," the gun-owner said, amusement in his tone. "Lassie won't have seen one like this before, and with this" – a thump of a kick reached her ears – "sheep-eating pest here, she'll be drawn in. No doubt."

Jamie glanced back at the screen. The one with the gun stood closest to the wolf, staring down at it with disgust. To his side was the other who leant against a large silver cage that sat in the snow. She frowned, confused as to what the point of the cage was when they had a dying wolf on their hands.

She zoomed in with the camera, hoping to get a better look at the cage itself. It was slightly blurry, but within the solid metal chinks, she could make out a dangling snare inside. It was clearly a trap meant for large game.

They'd said something about live bait... Jamie thought as she stared at the cage. *What animal would be big enough to fit in this cage that would be interested in a dying wolf?* Her heart jumped into her throat. *Not an animal,* she realised. *Artemis ... they're after Artemis.*

It was when a third member of the hunting team came into view that Jamie's worst fears were confirmed.

Jamie watched as they stepped into the camera's view, their long red hair with streaks of grey tied back into a ponytail, exposing their smiling face as they knelt down beside the dying wolf. Her dad gripped her shoulder, tight, as he came to recognise the woman in front of them.

Jamie remembered seeing this redhead forcing a muzzle onto Artemis and dragging her, kicking and screaming, back into what was colloquially known as the lab. Jamie had known it was a place that was a mix of a doctor's surgery, a veterinary clinic, and even a dentist. She had watched the redhead drag Artemis into a building that Jamie had never seen inside of. Then, for the next however many months, she'd seen the effect of what "Dr" Cora was doing to Artemis. She'd seen the bruises, the fear of loud noises, and the nervousness of others' reactions. Jamie herself had even been interrogated by the woman after she'd helped Artemis escape. Cora was unkind and cruel in ways that made it seem like she wasn't. It had been confusing, but Jamie had put on a show to keep Artemis safe.

Though it seemed Cora had never given up.

"Set the cage up, boys, and get this thing inside," Cora said.

"That'll take a lot of time," the gun-holding man said. "Shouldn't we finish—"

Cora glanced towards the man who spoke. Jamie couldn't see her face, but from the way the man cowered a little, she was glad she couldn't.

"My rules were clear, gentlemen," Cora said in a calm and gentle voice. "When you do as you're told and help me get Artemis, you'll get your furs and your money upon her delivery. No more. No less." She pushed herself to stand. "So do it."

The blonde men only nodded and got to work with the cage. As Cora began to survey the area, Jamie pulled the camera behind the tree trunk, just in case. She could feel the light tug on her shoulder from her dad, a sign that he wanted them to leave. But she couldn't. Not yet.

"Once you're done here," Cora said, "meet me back at the lab and set up the livestream on John's computer. Understood?"

"Yes, ma'am," they said.

"Be out before dark." She glanced around the forest in distaste. "You only have so many bullets."

"Yes, ma'am," they said again.

"Now, if you'll excuse me—"

"Ma'am?" the blonde who had the gun stepped forward.

"Yes?" Cora asked in irritation.

"Could … could we maybe have the map?" He rubbed at the back of his neck. "We may be here for a while and, well, we need to know where the traps are so we—"

"Fine."

Without another word, Cora pulled a folded-up piece of paper from her pocket and handed it to the man. Jamie didn't pay attention to what happened after that. She didn't need to. They had the answer to all their concerns right in front of them. Those men had a map of all the traps they'd set in the forest. Now all Jamie needed to do was steal it.

19

JAMIE

Jamie knew she was crazy. Knew that what she was planning would go down in history as the *dumbest* thing she may ever do. And with her dad behind her, a man who trusted her less than ever from her previous stunts, she was practically guaranteed to be forced to stay at the camp until they left. Or even be sent home.

But she did the stupid thing anyway. Or she would have, if her mind hadn't gone blank of ideas.

With her dad silently trying to usher her away from the guys with guns, Jamie's mind wasn't able to work. If he'd give her a minute, she'd be able to figure this out.

She shook off her dad's touch and focused on the men in front of her. She watched how cautiously they set up the snare within the cage and figured they weren't trained in these kinds of things. Which meant they could make a mistake easily. She just needed to distract them to make that happen. Then she could get the map in the chaos.

Could I throw something and get them tangled in their own trap? Jamie thought. *Should I interrupt them and put them on camera to scare them?* She shook her head. *No, they have a gun, that would be stupid.*

Unfortunately, as she planned her course of action, a perfectly terrible distraction walked right into the clearing.

Past the men, right by the hedgerow that circled them, stood a black-white-furred wolf. From its height and size, Jamie assumed it was a female, but she'd have to get closer to know for sure. And for the wolf's sake, she hoped she wouldn't be able to find out.

She must have been drawn to the smell of wolf's blood, Jamie thought in panic. *Their plan could work...*

Jamie had to try and not cry out at the wolf when she saw it step out from behind the bushes. She was right in the hunter's line of sight. To Jamie's relief, the men were too busy arguing about instructions to see the wolf, which meant she still had time to save her.

Jamie looked around for something to scare the wolf off. She couldn't yell, but maybe she could throw something in their direction to make them scatter. Hopefully. Her dad nudged her shoulder, gaining her attention. He didn't say anything, but the look in his eyes asked a simple question.

What do you see?

Mouthing the word *wolf* and nodding to behind her, his eyes went wide in concern. To her surprise, he quickly bent down to the ground, grabbed a stone, and lobbed it in the vague direction Jamie had pointed.

He tugged Jamie tightly behind the tree, and they both stood frozen for a beat.

"Did you hear something?" Jamie heard one of the men say. But nothing happened after that. No retreating of feet. No word about a wolf. Nothing.

Jamie chanced a glance from behind the tree and found the men still working and the wolf still watching.

Why isn't she staying hidden? Jamie wondered to herself. *Wolves have a natural fear of—*

Then it hit her.

A wolf that, though hiding from the humans, wasn't skittish enough to run away from them was almost unheard of. Jamie's heart thudded in her chest. *Could this she-wolf be a member of Artemis's pack? And if she is, could she lead Artemis to this trap?*

She grabbed a stone and threw it.

Her aim was off, always had been. She was a scholar and occasional mechanic, not a sportsperson. It went wide, hitting the soft snow-covered ground with barely a sound. Of course, being a wolf, its ears twitched towards where the stone had fallen. They knew something had happened.

Jamie threw another. This time it hit a nearby tree, which gained the attention of the wolf, sending her skittering backwards. The only problem was, it wasn't just her who heard the stone.

"Wolf!" the taller blonde called out from his spot by the cage.

Smart as most wolves were, she turned and ran at the sound of his voice. The hunters followed quickly behind her. Gun in tow. Jamie could only hope that the wolf would get out of eye line before he aimed.

As the men ran forward, Jamie began scanning their belongings for the one thing she needed. *Please, please, please,* she chanted in her head.

There, flapping in the wind, tucked beneath a dropped backpack, was the map the men had been looking at moments ago. Jamie turned away from it and towards the hunters, waiting for them to disappear from view.

They'd only just rounded the corner when her dad was jumping over the bushes and running towards the map with the camera he'd slipped out of her hands. Jamie blinked in surprise. He was a lot more athletic than she'd realised.

BANG.

Jamie and her dad froze in place. She watched as he turned towards where the hunters had left, and from the drop of his shoulders, she let out a sigh of relief. They hadn't returned. Yet. Quickly, her dad clicked the camera button once, twice, three times. Jamie guessed he must have turned it to photo mode with the clicking. She wanted him to hurry up; the hunters could return at any moment.

BANG.

Her dad ducked to the ground suddenly. The gunshot sounded a lot closer than before. Without another thought, he was turning and running towards her, camera in hand. She didn't have a chance to say anything when he grabbed her hand and they ran.

As they ran, she looked briefly over her shoulder, just catching a look at the dying wolf in its cage. The people of Materia were accelerating their plans.

Now it was time for her to do the same.

"THAT WAS INCREDIBLY FOOLISH."

Jamie winced at the frustration in her dad's voice and curled tighter into her blanket. "I know."

"But", he continued, "you have shortened our time in finding and destroying these traps."

Jamie raised her eyebrows in surprise. "Does that mean I'm off camp arrest?"

Her dad didn't answer that one. But she took his silence on the matter as a win.

"What is it that happened, exactly?" Alicaster asked as she handed out cups of soup to everyone. It had been an hour since their experience with the hunters, and with the frightening experience and the growing night, they were all trying to stay calm. Soup was the key to calm, at least that's what her mum used to say. "Did they give any indication of what their plan was?"

"The traps aren't just for animals," her dad said between slurps of his soup. "Cora, the – excuse my French – bastard woman from the town who decided to experiment on a child, is the one planning it all."

"She's after Artemis still." Jamie's hands were shaking though she tried to still them. After hearing what Cora had said, Jamie hadn't been able to get rid of the image of Artemis locked up in that cage in the makeshift doctor's office when she'd found her. That was when she was a child. Now she's a grown woman. Jamie couldn't stomach the idea of what they may do to her now. "We can't let them get her. This is Artemis's home; she can't be taken from here."

"Well..." Alicaster began cautiously. "Would it really be so bad if she joined our world?"

Jamie could feel the rage bubbling up. "You agree that these monsters should kidnap her?"

Alicaster rolled her eyes. "Of course not, Jamie. They're criminals and murderers, they will never have my support." She took a breath. "But Artemis is human. Maybe it will be good for her, being the grown woman she is, to join the world she's meant to be in."

"This is the world she's meant to be in. It's why I helped her get back to it." Alicaster went to speak again. "End of discussion."

The two stared each other down, but eventually Alicaster lamented, raising her hands in surrender.

"All we need to do is get this forest on the protection list, and then we go, OK?" Jamie stared down the group, waiting for any one of them to argue back. They made the smart decision to keep quiet. It was only when she felt something dripping down her cheek that she realised why they hadn't answered.

She was crying.

"Jamie-bear…" Her dad stepped forward. "We'll make sure Artemis is safe, don't worry." He lifted the camcorder with the photo of the map on and smiled. "This, alongside the footage of the traps and the killed wolf, should be enough to grant Swen protection."

She could only nod in response. Jamie didn't know why her heart felt so heavy, but she didn't have the time nor the patience to examine the reasons. They needed to get things done. "Call them."

It was while her dad, Alicaster, and even Ritchie were distracted with providing evidence to the committee via a satellite video call that Jamie found her chance. She knew her dad would never forgive her for this. She'd pushed him far past the point of understanding already, but she couldn't help herself. They knew why the humans were here now, but the pack didn't.

She grabbed an unused camera, took a photo of the map with her phone, and slipped away from the camp.

Artemis and her family were in danger, and Jamie refused to wait any longer to tell her. She was going to find Artemis and keep her safe. She just hoped she wasn't too late.

ARTEMIS

There was nothing Artemis hated more than being forced to stay in one place. She enjoyed exploring the land and taking the pups out for adventures to help prepare them for their duties in the pack. Now, with Fenris and Yue's orders of no more human contact, she had no choice but to stay put.

Of course, she still had the duty of caring to the pups – something that she loved more than anything. But unlike before, if they were to be taken out to play-hunt, it would be another wolf doing so.

It was hard not to feel hurt by everything happening. She knew that going behind the leader's backs would have consequences; she just never thought it would leave her feeling so … useless.

Whenever the pups were gone, Artemis had to find ways to pass the time. More often than not, that ended up being climbing. At their temporary home by the river, there were far more trees of great height due to the strength of the earth around them from the rushing water and variety in vegetation. Artemis would climb from branch to branch, using the height of the trees to scout far and wide. She may not be able to leave, but it didn't mean she would be cut off from seeing the world.

The only issue was that there were only a few open areas of the Forest that allowed her to see the ground. Artemis had hoped that she would see Oak somehow. As she looked across the tips of treetops that dipped and rose from the uneven hills, she couldn't make out anything of detail. Her inferior eyesight failed her once more.

She is likely a great distance from here. Of course I would not see her, Artemis thought bitterly as she leant back against the tree stump.

BANG.

Artemis nearly fell out of the tree in surprise.

BANG.

She nearly slipped in her haste to climb down, scraping the side of her paw on the tree's bark. When Artemis reached the ground, she drew her weapon. She recognised that noise all too well.

The pups were out with Nova today, an older grey wolf from the first litter of Fenris and Yue. She wouldn't have taken them far, maybe just downriver. Artemis could only hope that she was keeping the pups safe and hidden. The rest of the pack, except Mai and Ronan, had travelled to meet with the Riverside wolves for negotiation. They wouldn't be back for another two moons.

That could mean that Mai or Ronan had stumbled upon something they shouldn't have.

In the harrowing moments that passed, Artemis stood still. Her eyes flickered every which way as she sought out any sign of an intruder. The Forest had fallen quiet since the smoking sticks had sounded. Silence was never good.

A pounding of feet came charging towards her, rustling through the bushes. Artemis raised her weapon to attack when a terrified Mai burst through a thicket of thorns, only stopping when she saw Artemis in a fighting position.

Humans, Mai panted, **humans have killed a wolf.**

The silver blade dropped from Artemis's hand. **Where are the pups? Was it Nova? They have not returned.**

Mai shook her head, which allowed air to return to Artemis's lungs. **It was not her scent.** She glanced over her shoulder. **He may have been a lone wolf; I did not recognise him. Nor did I recognise the humans who killed him.** Mai looked back to Artemis. **Except for one.**

The hairs on the back of Artemis's neck stood up at that. *No ... it cannot be.*

It was the same scent that was with you when you returned from seeing your human, Mai continued. **There is no doubt in that fact.**

But she—

It is as I said, Mai said quietly. **Maybe she is not the human you believed her to be?**

Artemis didn't want to believe that. Not because it would hurt to know that Oak, though having shown her the dangers in the Forest to protect her, was actually working with those who would kill a wolf. No, it would hurt knowing that the girl she had once known had come to hate her kind so much.

She reached down to grab her weapon. **With what she did for me, I do not believe it. But that does not matter now. We must find Nova and the pups. As well as Ronan. They could be anywhere—**

Mai shook her head. **Nova and the pups are downstream. I can hear young Kai's anxious whimpers. They are close enough to the split in the river that, if the situation worsened, they could cross into the next territory.**

A sigh of relief had Artemis dropping down to the ground. She could breathe easier knowing they were safe. Then another thought came to mind. **Where is Ronan?**

Mai's ears flattened, and her tail tucked beneath her. **I … I do not know. We had been patrolling together when Ronan had a foolish idea.** An annoyed growl grew in Mai's throat. **He claims to be the cautious one, and yet he went off alone, claiming he was seeking out answers.**

Where did he go? Artemis asked.

Towards the mountains, Mai replied. **I was going to follow him when…** Her black-white fur stood on end. **…when I smelt the blood.**

Mai dropped to the ground with a sigh. Artemis could see the distress in her golden eyes and moved closer to her. Reaching out a paw, she rested it against Mai's back, hoping her touch could bring her some comfort.

Ronan is resourceful, he always has been. Artemis absent-mindedly scratched behind Mai's ear. **A lone wolf always knows the risks of being without a family. Ronan is not like that. He has us. He has a home. He will be fine. Have faith that Mother Wolf—**

Like you have faith that your human is on our side? Mai snapped.

Artemis bit her tongue to keep from responding. Mai was hurting. Her soul was out there with dangerous humans. She understood that fear and love made wolves do rash things. Artemis had seen the path that finding a soul had on two generations of leaders now. Mai was no different in her anxiety and affection for Ronan.

Yes, I have faith in Mother Wolf that Oak is different. Why would I not? she asked, drawing the wolf's eyes. **She saved my life once. Who would I be if I believed she was capable of such evil when she showed me nothing but kindness without even knowing who or what I was?**

Mai watched her in silence. Her ears twitched towards the river as if she were still listening to the pups and Nova a distance away. With a heavy sigh, Mai came to her side and licked Artemis's cheek. **I admire you, Elder Artemis,** Mai said. **I hope that my assumptions are—**

Freezing, Mai lifted her head high, black ears twitching every which way as her nose wiggled, picking up a scent. Artemis unsheathed her blade and moved to stand. Her own eyes darted this way and that in search of danger. A soft growl of anxiety grew in Mai's throat as she pawed at the ground. **Your human has followed me.**

How? Artemis hissed. **You know as well as I that my senses are not as strong as yours. That means hers cannot be either.**

She glanced in Mai's direction and found the she-wolf staring in the direction in which she had come not long before. Her eyes were narrowed, focused on seeking out their hunter.

Even you know how to track, Artemis. She may be the same. Mai stepped forward. **She is not close enough to find us, but she has travelled further than the hunters that followed me did. She must be the intelligent one of the group,** she mused, sounding almost impressed.

What should we—

Before Artemis could even finish her question, Mai was gone. Artemis watched her disappear into the bush, charging forward to Mother Wolf knows what.

Mai! she yelled and was about to charge forward when she remembered Fenris's order.

Artemis knew that he would be able to tell that she'd left the Den. He always did. If she broke his rules once more, she couldn't imagine what that would do to him. Or to her pack.

But she couldn't leave Mai to go alone.

Gripping the blade tightly in her hand, Artemis took a breath, and with the image of Fenris's disapproving golden eyes pushed to the back of her mind, she loped after Mai.

JAMIE

*S*he could hear Ritchie now. "Love makes us do rash things," he'd say and then gesture at literally every single thing she'd done this last week as evidence of how true that statement is.

Not that she was in love. She was only doing this to protect Artemis and her family. Jamie rolled her eyes at herself. Even she wasn't buying that anymore.

Jamie couldn't exactly fault Ritchie for what she was bound to hear from him when she made it back to the camp. She could already see Alicaster rolling her eyes at hearing it. It was the thought of the expression of disappointment on her dad's face that had her pausing.

She'd broken his trust once already if she didn't count the cougar incident. Three times if she included that and her stupidity with the hunters. After this, she wouldn't be surprised if she was shipped back home. Jamie knew she'd probably deserve it.

This was reckless. Everything she was doing was reckless. Yet she just kept moving.

The sun was fading above her now, its reds and oranges

lighting up the trees in a way that made them appear to be on fire. In the glow of the sunset, she followed the tracks of the wolf she'd saved. She was sure that the black-white wolf must be part of Artemis's pack. It was the only thing that made sense for why she kept coming close to humans. The only problem with following a wolf that had run off hours ago was that they weren't the only animal on the move.

Crouching down to the ground, she hovered her hand over a mishmash of tracks in the snow. Some seemed to come from larger animals, like a cougar, while others were smaller, like rabbits. This wouldn't necessarily be an issue if it weren't for the fact that all these tracks had distorted the ones she needed.

Jamie knew how to track animals; it had been part of her undergraduate training after all. They were taught how to study the tracks to differentiate such things as patterns of behaviour, indicators of health, and basically anything that would help them learn about the animal. Those teachings, frustratingly, weren't helping her now. Her wolf's prints had been trampled so badly from the others that crossed its path that they were completely unreadable.

"Crap," she muttered. Squinting at the crushed prints in the snow, she tried her best to determine the direction the she-wolf could have gone based on the depth and rotation in the snow. It was too disturbed to show anything. "Crap."

After a few moments of umming and arring, she decided to head in the opposite direction of the rabbits' prints. If there were predators nearby, it was a guarantee that the prey would be going the other way. At least, Jamie hoped that was the case.

Using her hiking pole across the snowy ground, a secondary precaution in case the trap map hadn't listed everything, Jamie kept walking. As she went, she paused every so often to check for further tracks as well as occasionally ducking under low-hanging branches.

It was when she glanced at the map on the phone again that she nearly started shouting at her stupidity.

The map, though not the most detailed, laid out specific landmarks within the forest with Xs where the traps were. It still made Jamie's stomach turn at seeing so many Xs across it, but right now it was a benefit.

Wherever there were traps meant there would be no wolves within a ten-mile radius. Their scent would have lingered in those areas making them a no-go zone for the wolves' safety. That ruled out most of the inner woods and the mountain sides. The only place the hunters and Cora hadn't made it to was a larger patch of land marked only as "the river".

Jamie had no idea how far away that was from here; the map didn't exactly offer up information of proportions and distance, but she knew it was north of the weeping willow she had passed some time ago if the map's markers were correct.

"North it is." Jamie tucked her phone into her coat pocket.

With the last of the sun fading behind the split mountain to her left, Jamie knew she only had so long until it would be near impossible to find her way to the river or back to the camp. As she tightened the straps of her backpack and put the hiking pole to the ground, Jamie started walking.

I'm coming, Artemis.

Walking straight in a forest was a lot harder than Jamie realised.

No pathway was without obstacles. Often, Jamie was climbing over bushes, getting caught on thick tree branches or even the occasional thorn. At one point, she heard the tearing of her coat from one particularly rough journey past a thorn bush. She had to keep from swearing in frustration; the sun had faded now, and she didn't want to alert all the nearby predators to her location. All Jamie had to defend her was a hiking stick that had already lost a battle with a bear trap. She didn't fancy her chances against an irritated fox.

She moved forward at a slightly quicker pace than before because of the slowly rising moon, not taking care when it came to placing her footing. She didn't realise her stupidity until she went flying after her foot got caught on a thick tree root.

"Ow..." she groaned.

Pushing herself quickly into sitting, Jamie's eyes teared up from the pain. Like most people, she'd put out her hands to break her fall. Glancing down at her injured hands, she had to bite back a groan as she took in the peeled skin of her palms mixed with the mud and snow from the ground, making it look a bloody mess.

I'm sure they just look worse than they are, Jamie thought as her hands shook in front of her eyes.

She tried to get to her feet, but with her lack of core muscle strength, just trying to use her legs to stand was harder than she thought. Especially with how dizzy she was feeling from the adrenaline that ran through her veins. She made the mistake of placing one of her hands to the ground.

Her cry echoed around her.

Breathing heavily in and out, she tried to calm herself down. *This is no time to become hysterical*, she chastised herself in her mind. *Calm down and try again.*

The dark was closing in around her. Every noise seemed to be heightened by the night. Blood was pumping in her ears and making her more anxious by the second.

Some adventurer I am, she thought in frustration. *I can't even stay calm enough to get a grip.*

Jamie decided that this was probably a good opportunity to try and rest for a moment. She had no clue how far she'd walked by this point, but a small break would probably be a good idea.

As she sat on the cold ground, she thought of something

Ritchie had said. He'd been talking about how important it was to document anything and everything at this stage. The more footage they had of the forest and what was happening, the more they could present to the EIA and the general public with his film. He'd also said it'd help if they had conversational segments to explain what was going on. Jamie figured this was as good a time as any to get working.

Slipping off her backpack, she carefully pulled out Ritchie's camera. She had to bite her tongue as she gripped the device in her aching hands. Jamie placed the camcorder atop the bag, pointed it at herself, and pressed record.

"So, everyone, you'll have seen what the hunters are doing in previous footage." Jamie went to pull out her phone, but with her injured hands, she struggled to keep a hold of it without being in pain. She sighed. "Ritchie, do some editing magic and show the map will you? So, if it's up on screen, you'll see the map of Swen Forest. You'll also see loads of Xs dotted around it. Well, those marks represent animal traps. If you counted, yes, that is over fifty Xs. Take that in. They put in fifty traps for—" A rustle came from the trees. "Uhm ... yeah, fifty traps for the wolves and Artem—"

A snapping of a branch finally made her shut up.

Please don't be a cougar, please don't be a cougar...

Jamie couldn't tell where the noise was coming from. She considered trying to get to her feet again and running when the bushes in front of her started to bend. Holding her breath, trying to make herself invisible by pure will, Jamie watched as a snarling wolf stepped through the bush.

I know I said no cougar, but this isn't any better! she thought bitterly as the black-white wolf stepped out from the shrubbery, eyes focused solely on Jamie.

It looked like the same wolf from earlier. Its fur was distinct, different from the usual coat of a wolf. There was likely a little bit of dog ancestry somewhere in their line. Jamie supposed with a town nearby, crossbreeding was bound to happen. As if the wolf had heard her thoughts, it snapped its jaws in her direction.

Jamie didn't move an inch. If she didn't move, maybe the wolf wouldn't see her as a threat. She even clenched her hands to stop them from shaking. Though she had to hold her breath at how painful it was. No matter how still or quiet she was, the wolf never stopped growling at her. Its ears flattened against its head and tail between its legs.

She's afraid of me…

While it shouldn't have been surprising, wolves were naturally fearful of humans after all. It still hurt to see. The wolf had seemed less nervous before, but after the hunter fiasco, it seemed she saw Jamie as a threat.

Neither of them moved from their positions. Just watched each other. Jamie wondered how long this would go on for when she noticed the ears of the she-wolf twitching towards the trees behind Jamie. In a move that she knew her dad would have classed as reckless, she turned away from the wolf and glanced behind her. When she did, she had to remind herself how to breathe.

There, in the shadow of the trees, stood Artemis.

Jamie didn't even notice the wolf leaving. Her eyes stayed solely on Artemis as she stepped into the light of the moon. It was their third time meeting, but this was the first time she was seeing her unobstructed.

She was as beautiful as Jamie had pictured. Still the same, in some ways, as the girl she'd met when she was a kid. Just less scrawny and scared. She looked stronger. More powerful. Her tanned pale skin was defined by a layer of muscle that, alongside the array of old and new scars on her body, explained how she'd been able to fight off the cougar all those days ago. Her brown tangled hair fell to her shoulders, curling slightly around her face.

Jamie unclenched her hands in surprise, and a wave of pain washed over her. Closing her eyes, she sucked in a breath to stop herself from crying out. She couldn't scare Artemis away. Not now. When she finally calmed herself down enough to open her eyes, she had to stop herself from jumping at how close Artemis had managed to get. Only a few inches of space remained between them. Jamie's heart thudded.

"Uh..."

Unlike Jamie's awkward cross-legged form, Artemis sat resting on her heels, her balance perfect as she did. Artemis watched her intently. Her piercing green eyes were so hypnotic that Jamie had to stop herself from leaning closer. To collect herself, Jamie dropped her gaze. She immediately looked up again in embarrassment.

Just like when they were kids, Artemis wore a material cloth around her waist, covering her private area. But, just like when they were young, she had nothing protecting the top half.

Eye contact, Jamie, she told herself. *Look respectfully.*

Artemis tilted her head at Jamie in confusion. When she glanced down at Jamie's injured hands and then back up to her eyes, she let out a growling bark at her. Jamie had no idea what she was saying, but she got the gist. Hopefully.

"I fell over a tree." Jamie turned and gestured to the tree behind her. In doing so, she noticed the camera still pointing at them, its red light flashing. Jamie spun back to face Artemis quickly, hoping she hadn't seen it. "And I hurt my hands, tore the skin and everything. Typical, right?"

Artemis just blinked at her.

"Right..." Jamie mumbled. Things were different this time around. When they were young, though she knew Artemis hadn't fully understood her, there'd been enough understanding between them so they could communicate well enough. It had been over a decade since Artemis had learnt some English, so now they were starting from less than scratch.

She showed her injured hands and Jamie said, "Hands." She made a noise of pain. "Hurt." Jamie pointed to the tree. "By tree." She showed her hands again and made the pain noise.

A soft whine of sympathy, Jamie assumed from its pitch, slipped past Artemis's lips. Jamie watched as Artemis reached out to her and wrapped a pair of calloused hands around her wrists. Jamie almost forgot how to breathe. She felt more than saw what Artemis was doing, too afraid to glance down and be disrespectful.

Artemis's grip was a little tight but not so much that it was uncomfortable. Her thumb brushed lightly below the sore flesh of her cut-up hands. Jamie watched the woman's' expression as she narrowed her eyes during her examination. Only when a gentle finger brushed against the centre of her left palm, right beside her scar, did Jamie wince.

After Jamie had hissed in pain, Artemis's fingers on her hands had stopped moving and now rested against the scar. The scar she'd given herself when they were kids. Jamie wondered if Artemis knew what it meant, and when she glanced up to the wild-woman, she got her answer.

Her nose brushed against Artemis's who had moved even closer. Less than an inch of air remained between them now. Jamie found herself staring into the soft green eyes who met her gaze head-on. Artemis carefully lifted her hand up and rested it against Jamie's cheek, her thumb brushing her skin so tenderly that she questioned if it had even happened.

A smile slipped across Jamie's face, and just like when they were kids, she leant forward and pressed her forehead against Artemis's. Both of them released a breath that washed over the other, and though she hadn't opened her eyes again, she could feel the smile on Artemis's face.

"I told you I'd come back." Jamie raised a hand and carefully rested it against the one still holding her cheek. "And I never break a promise."

PART II

OF CHANGING HOW YOU SEE LOVE

JAMIE

Having a conversation with someone who didn't understand or speak English was always a little complicated. Beyond Artemis, the only other person she had this experience with was with her halmoni, her mum's mum. She didn't speak English, and Jamie didn't speak Korean - or at least, not well. But whenever she had been with Halmoni, she always felt like she was being listened to.

Artemis was the same.

The two had stayed sitting on the cold ground – though Jamie's frozen butt protested against the idea – and had been talking beneath the moon's light for some time. Or, at least, Jamie was talking.

Jamie was surprised about how natural this still felt considering her silent partner. She thought that with those knowing green eyes focused solely on her, she'd feel a little unnerved. Even her ex-girlfriends hadn't been this focused on her when she spoke. But she didn't feel uncomfortable. Jamie felt … seen. Even if Artemis didn't understand her.

"And then I snuck out of camp and" – she waved her hand around them – "here we are."

Artemis blinked at her and tilted her head.

"I probably didn't need to give all that backstory, did I?" She huffed out a breath. "What I'm trying to tell you about all of this is…" Jamie trailed off, unsure how to continue.

How do I phrase this in a way she'll understand? she thought as she felt Artemis's eyes on her. *I know wolves work with body language and visuals, maybe I can do something with that?*

Hoping she wouldn't look mad, she shuffled backwards from Artemis to begin her demonstration. Leaning down, Jamie placed her hands on the cold ground face up and curled her fingers into a claw-like shape. She glanced up to check that Artemis was watching, and upon confirming, she smacked her hands together and interlocked her fingers. It hurt like hell, but Artemis jumped, as if recognising the motion.

"Trap," Jamie said. She repeated the motion again, though gently this time. "Trap." She unlocked her fingers and gestured around the forest. "Trap everywhere." Jamie pointed in the direction of the split mountain. "They put" – she made the interlocking motion again – "traps everywhere."

Artemis turned to the mountain and then back to Jamie, a frown forming between her eyebrows.

Jamie shuffled back to Artemis and, with only a slight hesitation, reached out for her forearm. When she made the claw motion again, she did so around her arm. Her grip wasn't tight, her injured hands wouldn't allow that, but it was strong enough to make her point.

"Trap for Artemis." Jamie let go with one hand and pointed to the mountain again. "They lay trap for Artemis."

Artemis's frown deepened. She looked from the mountains and to the trap shape around her arm and then to Jamie. She tilted her head in confusion.

"OK, so that's not working…" Jamie muttered to herself.

She thought of the wolf that had met her ahead of Artemis. While she had been gone from sight for some time now, Jamie didn't believe that the wolf had fully left. No wolf left another behind. Especially after everything that had happened earlier today, Jamie wouldn't be surprised if the she-wolf was waiting in the bushes ready to jump her if she stepped out of place.

The wolf... Jamie thought, an idea coming to her head. It could be frightening for Artemis and maybe even the hidden wolf, but if it got her message across...

"Here goes nothing," she said quietly.

Standing up, Jamie raised her arms. One she stretched out in front of her while the other she held up by her face. She was mimicking the motion of holding a gun and pointed it right at where the wolf had come from. Jamie wasn't sure if she was going crazy or not, but she was sure she could hear a growl as she pretended to cock the weapon and—

"BANG," she shouted.

Beside her, Artemis scrambled back in surprise, and the golden eyes of a furious wolf, growling snout and all, appeared among the bushes. Jamie quickly dropped her imaginary gun and pointed to the split mountains.

"Artemis, they're coming for you," she said. "They're coming for the wolves." She pointed to the wolf who snarled at her action. "But they want you." She pointed at Artemis. Jamie made the motion of the trap and followed it up with the shape of a gun and pointed it at Artemis. She didn't pretend to fire it this time. "They're coming for you."

The three of them were silent and unmoving for some time. Jamie swallowed hard as her eyes darted between the two wolves. They could be communicating right now about how to kill her, and she wouldn't even realise until it happened. Her mind was running a mile a minute with worst-case scenarios, so she just barely heard a snap of teeth from Artemis towards the she-wolf.

Jamie caught the literal tail-end of the wolf disappearing back into the shadows as Artemis stood. She reminded herself that the wolf-woman still had a knife and this could be some kind of ploy to lure her into a false sense of security. She'd done the same to Artemis just now after all.

To her confusion, when Artemis came closer, all she did was reach out a calloused hand and place it over her mouth. Jamie did nothing but try to control her erratic breathing. Artemis grunted and nodded her head towards her, reaching up her other hand to touch her own throat. She made the grunting noise again.

Jamie thought of those days when they were kids and how Artemis would do this motion to try and learn words. Quickly understanding, Jamie repeated everything she'd said against the warm hand on her lips. She spoke slowly, then exaggeratedly, then normally. She didn't stop until Artemis removed her hand.

In the silence, Jamie watched as the wolf-woman stared at her palms and carefully moved her lips in the same way Jamie had. A smile that spread across Jamie's lips at the action. It was just like when they were kids.

Artemis looked up at her. And Jamie's heart froze in place. Was she about to hear Artemis speak?

The wolf-woman nodded her head and offered Jamie a baring teeth smile. Jamie gave her one in return, trying to hide her disappointment. It had been over a decade since Artemis had spoken English. Of course she wouldn't speak it now. This wasn't *Tarzan*. At least she seemed to have understood what she meant. Hopefully she and the pack could get themselves to safety because of her warning.

This could be the last time I see her if she understands me, Jamie thought. *What should I do? Or say? I—*

A singular howl interrupted her spiralling mind. She watched as Artemis sprung up like a dog hearing the postman at the door.

The black-white wolf burst through the bushes and rushed to Artemis's side. It didn't sound like they were talking, but from the movement of their bodies, she had to assume they were.

I guess that's how it was for Artemis this whole time with me.

Artemis pushed her head against the wolf's, signalling her away. The wolf turned her golden eyes on Jamie, watching her with an intensity that Jamie didn't dare look away from. With a snort, the wolf turned and disappeared back into the dark of the forest.

Jamie turned back to Artemis and found the wolf-woman hesitating in following her pack member. Her gaze solely on Jamie as she seemingly unconsciously clenched and unclenched her fingers.

"I'll be OK, you can—"

Arms engulfed her in the tightest hug she'd ever had. Jamie stood still in Artemis's embrace for only a moment before she wrapped her arms around the woman too. Artemis smelt like the earth. A natural pine aroma with the smell of snow, which Jamie didn't even think had a scent, yet somehow, with Artemis, it did. Jamie tucked her face into the nape of the wolf-woman's neck.

"I missed you, Artemis," she whispered as she tried to stop the tears from falling.

Jamie knew she couldn't understand her, but when the strong arms that held her tightened, Jamie believed that maybe she could. As quickly as Artemis had embraced her, she was letting go.

Beautiful green eyes locked onto hers as Jamie watched Artemis walk slowly backwards to the bushes behind her. Only when another howl echoed into the air did she finally turn away, leaping into the shadows and disappearing from sight.

Jamie stood staring into the emptiness longer than her freezing body wanted her to, but she couldn't stop herself.

"I'll help save your forest, Artemis," she whispered into the dark. "Even if it means I never see you again."

ARTEMIS

They were both in trouble, that was as clear as the moonlight above them. It was why she didn't call out for Mai to slow down as the wolf sped on ahead with Artemis following as closely as she could behind her. After leaving her Oak behind, Mai had ushered her to run. Artemis hadn't argued; she could feel the rage from that howl just as Mai had.

She had no idea what they were going to say to the one who awaited them. It was only as they rounded the corner and came across Yue in the middle of the Den that Artemis started to feel a rise of panic. Yue had trusted her, relied on her, and believed in her. How could she deceive her? *Could* she even deceive her?

The two of them slowed to a walk as they met the glower from Yue. Artemis stepped forward first and lowered herself into a deep bow.

Yue, Artemis began. **We did not expect you back so soon—**

Where have you been? the she-wolf demanded.

Thankfully for Artemis, she wouldn't have to think of a lie at this moment as Mai stepped in.

Mother, as you know, I was out scouting. The she-wolf came to Artemis's side. **While out, I sensed something strange.**

I thought another pair of eyes, ones that may remember a human creation, would be of help. She turned to Artemis, smiling knowingly. **And they were.**

It was all on Artemis now. Mai had given her the set-up. She just had no idea what would come next.

There is a new trap, Artemis began. **One similar yet different to what I was shown before. It has been laid out with a dead wolf being used as bait.**

Yue's ears flattened against her head.

He was not of our pack, Mai noted quickly. **From his weakened form, I believe he may have been alone for some time.**

A loss for the Forest. Yue bowed her head in solidarity for the fallen wolf for a beat. **What is the significance of this trap?**

The humans have grown bold, Artemis replied. She could feel Mai's attention on her too. Thankfully for them both, she hid her surprise well. **Their traps have spread beyond where I first found one. They are coming close.**

Yue huffed at this. **What is your point, Artemis? My patience is running thin.**

Ronan is still out there. The mountain pack is out there. They do not know of these traps. Do not know of the danger that lies in waiting for them. Artemis bowed her head. **I humbly request your permission to seek them out in warning.**

The white wolf's gaze held Artemis's so intensely that she was sure Yue was trying to make her look away. Force a sign of obedience that would have her surrender and give up on what she must do next. It was not lost on Artemis that the pups and Nova, as well as the rest of the pack, were nowhere to be seen. Yue had returned to have them leave.

I cannot leave yet, Artemis thought. *Not yet.*

What makes you believe that Fenris and I will allow you

to stay here near the humans after all you have done? Yue questioned.

To Artemis's surprise, Mai stepped forward. **Because I am here.**

Yue turned to her daughter, her teeth bared and fur puffing up on her back. **You dare defy—**

The strength of the wolf is that of its pack, Mai interrupted. **That is what you always taught me. Or was it all a lie?**

The young wolf stepped towards her mother, coming close enough that Yue had to step back. Something no leader would ever do, unless a new one was soon to take their place. Artemis watched Mai. Her golden eyes stayed solely on her mother. A challenge in her gaze.

I will stay with Artemis. I will wait for Ronan and warn the other packs. Mai lifted her head until she was level with her mother. **The humans are here for us. I will not let them succeed.**

Yue looked between the two of them, seemingly conflicted with what they had presented to her. She was still the leader of their pack, the matriarch, the rule giver. To have any, even her own pup, go against her was something most would not allow. Yue let out a heavy sigh. Artemis fought back a smile. Yue was, of course, not like most leaders.

You have four sunrises. Yue's eyes fell to Artemis, her nose twitching, sensing something amiss. Artemis held her breath. **That is all I can allow. Use the time well.**

We will, Mother Yue, Artemis said with a bow of her head. **I promise.**

Yue turned to Mai, her bright-golden eyes piercing the younger wolf's. Mai ducked her head. The strength she had to defy her mother had since gone. Without a word, Yue turned and ran, heading towards the river's path. Neither Mai nor Artemis spoke for some time after that.

What did that human tell you?

Artemis didn't answer. She didn't even turn to meet Mai's gaze. This was not something she could drag Mai into. She couldn't do that to Fenris and Yue.

What do you mean? Artemis asked.

Do not play me for a fool, Artemis, Mai snapped. **Everything that human did, the smoking stick, the bear jaw motion, she was telling you something. What is it?**

Artemis tried not to let out a sigh of her own. Mai had always been far too knowledgeable for her own good. She shouldn't have been surprised; Mai had embraced her occasional human movements and even adapted some of them herself such as marking trails. Of course she'd have understood that Oak was showing her something.

I know why the humans have returned, Artemis said quietly.

Why? Mai asked.

She met the pair of golden eyes that watched her. Understanding and anxiety flickered within them as they waited for Artemis to speak.

They want me.

Mai's tail flicked with nervous energy, and she lowered her head enough that she no longer met Artemis's gaze. **That is why you are leaving.**

Artemis blinked in confusion. **Leaving? Why do you think—**

You could not leave her side, Mai interrupted. **I could feel the hurt in you when you walked away from the human. You are going to find her, are you not?**

I— Artemis's voice faltered. She didn't know how to answer that. She didn't even know if Mai was right or not. Except she did. **She could have the answers to help us protect the family.**

She does not speak our tongue nor you hers, Mai pointed out. **How will you learn these answers?**

We communicated enough now for her to warn me that

the humans came from beyond the mountains, Artemis retorted.

And what of this bond you two seemed to share? Mai questioned, coming to stand before Artemis. **I felt something in the air I have only experienced twice before. There is something more there—**

This is for the family, Mai, Artemis snapped. **That is all it is.**

Mai stepped back, giving her space. Artemis could tell she wanted to push further, but Mai knew that there was nothing stronger than a wolf's stubbornness. And Artemis was famous for hers.

I understand, Mai said, bowing her head in respect. **Just ... just be careful. The smallest things can hurt us when it comes from our—** She stopped short.

Our what? Artemis asked.

It does not matter, she said. **We only have four suns. Go find your Oak. I will seek out the mountain pack and warn them.** Mai's ears drooped. **Hopefully I will find Ronan on my journey.**

Call for me when he has returned? Artemis asked.

Return here when you... Mai tilted her head. **Well, when you have your answers, I suppose.**

Artemis smiled and leant forward to nuzzle Mai's side, her smile widening when Mai returned it.

I wish you luck in finding what you need, Elder Artemis.

Part of Artemis wondered what that meant, but she was not ready to question it. So, taking a breath, Artemis looked at the soon-to-be-abandoned Den and turned away, focusing herself on where she was going.

I am coming, Oak, she thought, smiling. *It is time to learn your secrets.*

24

ARTEMIS

*B*eing careful with her steps, as Oak had warned her, made her patience run thin far too quickly. Following paw prints in the snow to the direction of Oak's false Den was tiresome, and Artemis found herself too often considering rushing. The image of the bear jaws snapping closed was enough to stop her.

As she walked, the light of the moon above began to disappear, its light being chased away by the rising sun. Normally, Artemis would allow herself to be swept up in the wonders of the blossoming light, but she had to focus. Her four sun's timeline was already running out; she had no time to waste.

That was, of course, until she saw a snack.

Ahead of her sat a little brown rabbit eating the fresh grass. It did not seem to notice or sense Artemis's presence. Artemis smiled, her teeth baring proudly as she drew her blade.

Stepping carefully towards her prey, she blended into the surrounding vegetation. With each step, Artemis homed in on the animal, licking her lips at the thought of the fresh meat. It had been a while since she'd had rabbit.

The creature went still, its ears rising high in the air,

twitching every which way. Artemis held her breath and never took her eyes off the creature.

As quick as the wind, the rabbit turned and bounded into the bush, disappearing from sight. With a growl, Artemis followed quickly behind, leaping over the bush. When she landed, she kept running, her eyes locked on the loping bunny.

Never lose sight of the prey. Keep atop them and use their lack of size to your advantage, Kiba's voice said in her head, his lessons returning to her. **When you are close, leap.**

It will be mine... she promised herself as she gripped the blade tighter.

As her prey dashed through another line of bushes, Artemis leapt over the top of it. Seeing the creature below her, she brought her weight down atop it, trapping it beneath her as she delivered the final blow.

Thank you for the life you have given to sustain me, Artemis said – a prayer Kiba had taught her to show respect to her fellow animal.

Using her blade, Artemis went to tear open the stomach of her meal when she noticed a strange glow on the snow. It wasn't a reflection of the moon's gaze. No, it was the colour of a rising sun. This wouldn't normally surprise her, if it weren't for the fact that she had another half-shadow pass before the rise.

Looking up from her meal, she found herself in the middle of an open crevice in the Forest, the very one she had been heading to. It was the sight in front of her that had Artemis almost dropping her prey.

Four humans stood frozen in shock in front of strange Dens and beside a glowing shape that flickered and crackled. When one of them stepped forward, the flicking light illuminated the face of Oak. Artemis watched as she raised her hands to show herself as non-threatening before speaking.

Artemis tried not to bite her cheek in irritation at not being able to understand her words. Instead, she focused on the sound of her voice, hoping that a flicker of memory of their nights together would help her.

Oak came closer, her voice soft and warm as it always was. Her words carried a weight of importance whenever she spoke, even if Artemis couldn't understand them. Artemis smiled as Oak approached her, and she held out the rabbit to her.

You must eat. Eating is important to live, she said as she shook the rabbit at Oak. **We will share.** Artemis frowned and looked back to the Forest. **Or maybe I should catch another so we have enough for both of us?**

A paw touched her forearm, making her turn with a growl back to Oak. You never touch a hungry wolf.

Unfazed, Oak offered a smile to Artemis. Her smiles were strange. They made her stomach feel warm and fluttery, like the time she'd eaten some bad berries. Artemis frowned and found herself tilting her head at Oak, confused. Oak tilted her head too and spoke, her forehead wrinkling into an odd shape as she did.

Her eyes were just as beautiful as they were all those seasons ago, but different this close up. Just like how the great oaks of the Forest grew with age, so had Oak's eyes. There was a wisdom there that dazzled among the amber within them. The oak colour had deepened too, just like the bark of the trees, making her eyes seem limitless. Artemis wondered, if she looked long enough would she find herself lost, just as one could be among the trees?

Artemis didn't realise she'd dropped her weapon until she found her free paw reaching out to touch Oak's jaw. As the tips of her fingers touched the cool skin there, Artemis felt Oak take a shaky breath.

You are truly here, Artemis found herself whispering as she allowed herself to trail her fingers across the soft, pale brown skin beneath them. She only stopped when she found herself reaching the edge of the plump, blood-red lips.

She could feel Oak's breath against her fingers and wondered what it would be like to—

A loud voice interrupted her thoughts, and as quickly as Artemis had relaxed at seeing Oak, she returned to her instincts. Letting go of Oak, she grabbed her weapon and prepared to protect herself and Oak.

To her surprise, it was Oak who responded to the interruption by standing. She stepped in front of Artemis, shielding her, and spoke just as loudly and aggressively back to the human who'd ruined their moment. Leaning sideways, Artemis watched the interaction between Oak and the unfamiliar older male and female.

This male was different to the one she had seen with Oak moons ago. He was taller for one, his mud-coloured head fur longer than the others and dotted with white and grey like Fenris's. He was clearly an elder from the signs of age. His blue-sky eyes, like Rae's, showed a wisdom that Artemis could respect. Though each time he spoke, his tone reeking of frustration and disappointment, she could feel Oak tense up. Artemis wasn't sure if she liked him or not.

The unfamiliar female was one that Artemis couldn't quite get a read on. For most of the berating from the elder male, she stood in silence, her forearms tucked close to her chest. The few times she did speak, usually between the breaks of the older male, Artemis could sense the agitation within Oak grow. It was practically vibrating off her.

A soft growl grew in the back of Artemis's throat as she stared at the female. She watched as the human turned to the older male, seemingly seeking their approval on what they had said. She reminded Artemis a little of Nova whenever she was trying to get on Fenris or Yue's good side. She'd turn on her closest companion if it meant getting closer to them.

On the other side of the flickering stolen sunrise, the young male with the strange item within his paws watched Oak and

Artemis. She knew his face from when she had almost been caught and knew he was of no threat. For now, she paid him no mind.

Eventually the older female let out a grunt of anger and stormed off to one of the false Dens and entered it. Artemis could feel the frustration in the air. She focused back on Oak, trying to understand.

Oak spoke calmly to the older male. From the way the muscles in his neck tensed, Artemis could tell he was irritated by whatever had happened. Unlike the female, he offered Oak a small smile before he too turned and disappeared into the other false Den.

Only the younger male was left with them.

He took a step towards them. Artemis knew he was of no threat, and yet she felt her hackles raise. She'd had enough of this group for now.

Just like Oak, he raised his hands and stepped back. With a word to Oak that had her picking up snow to throw at him, he let out a laugh as he followed the elder male into the false Den.

They were alone.

With the possible threat neutralised, she returned her weapon to its hiding place and stood at her full height. Oak, noticing, turned towards her. Those soft eyes dropped to her chest for a moment before quickly looking back up to Artemis's face.

She has done that a few times now, Artemis thought with a tilt of her head. *I wonder why.*

Shaking her head at the unnecessary question, she became aware of the rabbit in her paws. Holding it out to Oak once more, she shook it at her; it was time to eat.

Artemis frowned when Oak shook her head in refusal. She lowered her paw and tried to hide the pain of the rejection as best she could. When a warm paw wrapped in strange white material rested on hers, Artemis guessed she hadn't hidden it well.

The hand wrapped around hers and began to tug her towards the stolen sunrise. The closer they came, the more uneasy Artemis felt. When a heat began to settle against her skin and a tang of bitterness caught in her throat, she started to panic. She knew this feeling. Had felt it once before when the sun's fever had scorched their land, destroying everything in its path.

Danger... Artemis said as she pulled Oak backwards. **Danger.**

Oak frowned at her in confusion. She didn't seem to understand what she had said, but Oak did stop tugging at her. Artemis watched as Oak let go of her paw and stepped towards the fever itself, holding her paws up to the crackling light. Nothing happened except for a soft sigh of relief slipping past Oak's lips.

Artemis found herself enraptured by the glittering glow that filled Oak's eyes. She didn't know how enthralled she was until she found herself at Oak's side and felt the warmth of the sun's fever against her skin. She glanced down at the heat beside her and wondered how this could be.

Unlike the sun's fever she had seen many seasons ago, this one did not move. While the wood she saw beneath it burned and smouldered like the land it had devoured, it could move no further. It was trapped within this tall bird-like nest. It made no sense to Artemis.

The soft tone of Oak's voice reached her ears and drew her attention towards the girl. She stood relaxed by the trapped sunset's side, her muscles loose and a smile on her face. Oak was not afraid. She was safe with this sun's fever. And so was Artemis.

The two of them stood by its warmth for some time. Only when Artemis became uncomfortably warm did she step away.

Thankfully for her, Oak had begun talking at that moment so her uneasy movements went unnoticed.

Artemis watched Oak as she spoke. The stolen sunrise reflected within her dark eyes as the light of the morning rose behind her. Artemis's stomach felt strange again as she stared at the girl speaking. Only when Oak turned towards her did it fade, albeit only mildly. Oak reached a paw out towards her, and Artemis offered hers in return. Just as they had done only a few shadow passes ago, Oak laid them against her mouth once more. There, against her palm, she felt the gentle press of a word to her skin. Unlike before, this word felt … familiar. Like it should mean something.

Artemis began to mime the movement she was feeling with her own mouth. When she did, Oak stopped speaking. She watched Artemis as she worked through the process they both remembered well. Reaching up to her own lips, Artemis laid her paw there and worked through what she had felt.

"Ar…mis." She closed her eyes in concentration. "…rt…ms… Art…ms… Arte…ms."

She moved her paw to rest against her throat. Opening her eyes, she looked at Oak as she sounded out the word again.

"Arte…mis…" **Oh!** Artemis exclaimed in her own tongue. **That is … that is my name. I am** "Arte…mis!"

"Yes!" Oak exclaimed in a word Artemis was coming to understand. "Yes, Arte…mis."

Oak looked ready to celebrate, but Artemis wasn't done yet. There was still one more word she needed to learn. One she knew was important. Moving her hands back to Oak's lips and stared at the girl in silent pleading.

Oak looked confused for a moment. Artemis tried to help her understand by brushing her thumb against the skin of her chin and nodding her head towards her. She wasn't sure if she was making herself clear until she felt Oak's lips moving against her skin once more.

This time she didn't need to process the word as long. It was direct and beautiful. Just like the owner of it.

Moving her paw away from Oak's mouth, she allowed her eyes to continue staring at the soft lips she'd felt against her skin. Reaching up, she brushed her thumb against the bottom one before stretching out her fingers across Oak's cheek, holding her carefully.

"Jamie..."

25

JAMIE

Jamie was sure she was dreaming. It was the only thing that would explain how the wolf-woman that she'd never forgotten about was sleeping curled up at her side in the tent she shared with her nemesis.

It had taken a lot for her to convince Artemis to enter the tent. She didn't seem to like the material nor the noise of the zip. She especially wasn't fond of the snoring professor if the baring of her teeth was anything to go by. That, Jamie didn't blame her for. Alicaster hadn't exactly made a great first impression.

Lying wide awake in the tent with a foghorn to one side and the radiating warmth of the wild-woman she hadn't stopped thinking about since she was ten against her on the other was enough to keep a girl from sleeping. Add in the light of the sun seeping in above her and she had no chance. So, foregoing sleep, she thought about what Alicaster had said.

"If she's come to us willingly, we have to get the environmental team here to see her and document this," she'd said. "It's the only way to convince them that this forest is a special circumstance. They'd never destroy a forest with a human inside."

Of course, Jamie had argued back. She'd seen what people interested in Artemis had done before. She remembered the muzzle they'd put on her for being a "feral child". She'd been ready to tear Alicaster a new one for even suggesting it, until she'd heard the quiet growl from Artemis beside her. Wolves fed off the energy around them, which meant Artemis did too. If Jamie didn't calm down, Artemis wouldn't either. Thankfully, her dad had enough sense to realise this too and agreed to put a pin in the conversation for now. Jamie had been grateful for his support, even if she couldn't forget the look of disappointment in his eyes after she had, once again, disobeyed him.

Jamie was exhausted after everything. Even though she should be catching a few hours of rest before they began for the day, she couldn't. All she could do was hold back her tears as she replayed over and over again the sound of Artemis saying her name for the first time.

Artemis's voice had surprised her with how light and airy it sounded. It had the feel of a musical instrument, like a flute, with how the words flowed from her. It reminded her of the enunciated voices that you would hear in theatre productions. Like every word that was being said was important. When Artemis said her name, it sounded like it was the greatest thing she had ever said. Jamie had no idea how to feel after that, so she made an excuse for them to head to bed. Not that Artemis knew what she had said.

Turning her head to said sleeping woman, Jamie took in the sight of her up close and in the light. Jamie almost wished she hadn't as she found herself staring at the multitude of scars on her back. Some were pinker than others, fresher, and Jamie could only wince at the memory of the cougar that Artemis had fought to protect her from only a week ago. Others were small scratches, which made her wonder if they'd occurred from wolf play fights. Another stretched across the entirety of her shoulder blades, which had Jamie wondering how Artemis had survived such an injury.

Pulling the hand that was not trapped against her side by Artemis's body from her sleeping bag, Jamie reached out to her shoulder. It was clearly years old, but it still looked painful. She only just stopped herself as her bandaged fingertips were about to brush against the scar.

What am I doing? Jamie thought as she pulled her hand away. *She's sleeping, you creep. Human decency number one: Ask permission before doing something like that—*

Jamie's thoughts were cut off as she glanced back to Artemis to find a pair of forest-green eyes watching her from over a shoulder.

"Uh…" was all she could say at being caught. Jamie watched as Artemis dropped her gaze to look down at her scarred shoulder and then back up to Jamie and nodded. Jamie wasn't sure what she meant, so she asked: "What do you need?"

Artemis frowned. Jamie rolled her eyes internally at herself. Asking her won't help. She was trying to figure out how to help Artemis understand when the wolf-woman solved it for her.

Artemis's hand reached out and grabbed hers and pulled it towards her. Artemis brought Jamie close to her body before letting go and turning away. She only glanced over her shoulder for a second and let out a quiet noise from the back of her throat. She looked away after that and didn't move again.

Jamie swallowed hard. She understood now what Artemis wanted.

She laid her fingers, gently, on the rough skin. Even with her hand wrapped in bandage, Jamie could feel the tensing of Artemis's muscles against her touch. Worried about pushing her too fast, she didn't move her fingers until she was sure Artemis was comfortable. She heard Artemis release a breath and felt the muscles beneath her hand relax. Only then did Jamie begin to trace the scars one by one, missing only the recent pinkish ones. She was worried that she could hurt Artemis if she touched them.

As she traced the criss-crossing lines, Jamie found herself creating stories for each of them. She wondered how close her guesses may be. Her finger traced a small dip of a scar that looked a lot like tiny teeth marks. *One of the pups of the litter got a little too into the play fight,* she thought. Her thumb brushed gently across a dip near the edge of her ribs. *You were a little too confident with climbing trees when you shouldn't have been,* Jamie thought with a smile.

It was then, just under the cover of her hair, that Jamie found a scar that had her blood boiling. Jamie could feel the woman tense as her fingers passed over the puncture wound near the nape of her neck. One that felt similar to the shape of a needle.

Jamie didn't explore this scar like she had most of the others. She let the hair fall back in place to cover it once again. Artemis's muscles relaxed the moment she did. It was in feeling this that Jamie did something she never expected herself to do. She rolled over onto her side and moved her hand to Artemis's bicep, squeezing her lightly. "I won't let them take you," she whispered. "Never again."

As the pull of sleep finally reached her, Jamie closed her eyes. Only a second passed before the body in front of her moved. When she felt the warmth of breath on her face, she realised Artemis had turned to face her.

"Jamie…" the wolf-woman whispered as she curled in closer to Jamie. The sleeping bag was the only thing keeping them apart, a fact that Jamie found herself cursing as a cold nose pressed into her neck.

"Artemis," she responded, her fingers resting lightly against the woman's arm as sleep finally took her.

JAMIE

Waking up alone was like a stab to the heart. The last thing Jamie remembered was the feel of soft fingers against her skin and the tickle of pine-smelling hair against her cheek. Now she was completely alone. Not even Alicaster was beside her.

It wasn't a dream, was it? Jamie wondered as she slowly got dressed for the day.

When she had her jumper halfway off, she found herself shivering from a cold draft. Taking it off quickly, she went to grab her clean shirt when she caught sight of Artemis in the tent's entrance.

"Ah!" She grabbed her clean shirt to cover her bare self with. "Close the door, Artemis."

Artemis tilted her head. Jamie internally chastised herself. She kept forgetting Artemis couldn't understand her. Thankfully, on hearing her name, the wild-woman came fully into the tent, letting the flap of material drop behind her.

With her back to Artemis, Jamie set about putting on her bra and shirt as speedily as she could. Which, considering her injured hands, wasn't easy. After snapping herself with the bra strap and punching herself in the head when putting on the shirt, she finally was dressed. Changed, she turned to face Artemis who, to her surprise, was holding up her discarded jumper. Her eyes were curious as she turned it this way and that.

"Would you like to try it on?" Artemis glanced up at her with a frown. "Right … uh, how to do this…"

Crawling forward on her knees, Jamie came to Artemis's side and reached out for the jumper. Artemis gave it to her after a moment's hesitation. With a smile, Jamie held the head hole up to Artemis's face and waited for permission. Artemis bowed her head towards her.

Gently, Jamie slid the jumper over her head, making sure to not move too fast and spook her. Artemis stayed quiet the whole time. Her gaze never left Jamie, those all-seeing green eyes watching as Jamie helped her into the jumper.

Jamie took extra care in tugging the jumper over Artemis's torso. With so much bare skin, she didn't want to accidentally brush anything she shouldn't. A final tug at the hem had the jumper fully in place.

"There," Jamie said with a smile. "You look great."

She raised her fingers up to untuck the hair that was caught beneath the collar. As she did, she finally locked eyes with the woman in front of her, and her fingers froze at the edges of Artemis's hair.

Jamie hadn't realised how close she'd gotten until her nose was brushing the tip of Artemis's. A soft puff of air brushed against her lips as she gazed deeply into the green in front of her, noticing specks of grey within them. A hand came up to rest gently on the fingers that still held the tips of Artemis's hair. The stayed like that until—

"Knock, knock." The two women jumped as the tent entrance opened and a smiling Ritchie appeared. "Hey, breakfast is— Oh."

Jamie moved away from Artemis instantly, but the rise of Ritchie's eyebrow was enough for her to know she would likely be facing some questions later.

"Sorry, sorry, moment ruined." He smiled. "Finish up and come get breakfast."

"Oh, shut up," Jamie said with a roll of her eyes.

Ritchie laughed and disappeared from view.

Shaking her head, Jamie grabbed her coat and hat and turned back to Artemis. She found herself smiling the moment she took in the mismatch of a look she had. Along with her dirt-stained linen loincloth that covered her private area, she now had a knitted thermal jumper that hung loosely around her torso.

"You look cute," Jamie said before covering her mouth. "I mean, you..." Artemis stared at her blankly. "You don't know that I just embarrassed myself. Alright, that'll be useful for now. Come on, Artemis."

Reaching for the girl's hand, she couldn't hold back the stupid grin on her face when Artemis took it without pausing. Even if her still aching hands protested against the tight grip.

Stepping out into the cold air, Jamie shivered a little and quickly zipped up her coat before making her way with Artemis in tow towards the fire.

Everyone was already by the fireside and ready for the day. Brunch was being prepared by Alicaster who, despite sounding like she was sleeping well, looked exhausted. All of them did. From the bags under their eyes to the unkempt hair and caffeine-filled thermoses, Jamie could feel the guilt rising. It was her fault they'd been up late. Even if the reason why had been worth it in the end, it didn't make her feel any better. And nor did the look in her dad's eyes when she found him staring at hers and Artemis's entwined hands.

Letting go quickly, Jamie encouraged her with a soft voice to follow her. When they were at the fireside, Jamie tried to coax

Artemis into one of the chairs that had been laid out for them. Artemis didn't look exactly pleased about sitting in it. She probably was used to sitting on the cold ground. Jamie was about to move the chair so she could sit where she was comfortable when the wolf-woman's attention was stolen by the sight of food.

Jamie made her a plate filled with all kinds of meat and a slice of toast, just to try. When she brought it to her, she had to bite back a smile at the sight of Artemis crouching on the balls of her feet on the seat.

Food in hand and Artemis sat beside her, Jamie was ready to start her day on the right foot.

"As you weren't here when we spoke to the EIA," her dad said in a disappointed tone, "I'll update you now."

Jamie lowered her fork from her mouth. "Dad, I know I didn't—"

"We'll talk about it later," he said with the wave of his hand. When his eyes dropped to Artemis who was stuffing her face with bacon, Jamie realised he meant when she wasn't with someone with an emotional dial turned up to a hundred by her side. "I received a call from the EIA this morning."

That caught everyone's attention. From the rise of an eyebrow from Alicaster, it seemed even she hadn't known about this. It was nice for Jamie to see that it wasn't only her that her dad left out of conversations, not that she had any right to be smug considering the earful she'd got from the two of them when she'd returned to camp last night.

"What did they say?" Jamie asked.

"They have the evidence we've sent them, but they don't think it'll be enough to convince government officials to bring in a permanent protection order." He tugged at his beard. "Even if it was, they don't think it'd be decided before the deforestation team arrives here in a week's time."

"How does that even work?" Jamie asked, slumping back in

her chair. "We've videos of the traps, of what the hunters are doing, and what they're intending to do to…" She looked over at Artemis who was watching Ritchie as he ate, trying to mimic him with her own food. "How can that not be enough?"

"I'm afraid that's how politics work," Alicaster said. "It's coming up to an election year, and politicians are more worried about losing voters than actually making a difference. It's…" She bit off a piece of toast. "It's just poor timing unfortunately."

"So, what? We're just going to give up?" Jamie asked in annoyance

"Of course not," her dad exclaimed, disturbing Artemis from her concentration on Ritchie. Jamie could feel those green eyes on her but tried not to be distracted by it. "We're going to find a way to get them to listen. In fact, Ritchie here has an idea."

All but Artemis turned to Ritchie who was currently struggling to shove an entire piece of toast into his mouth. Quickly swallowing and somehow not choking, he cleared his throat.

"So," he said with a slap to the knees that had Artemis jumping. "Oh, sorry, Artemis. Uh, anyway, so I've been working on editing this video to show what's happening here." He scratched at his neck. "I've pretty much all the footage I need now; I just need to do my voiceover stuff to narrate it."

"What are you hoping this will do?" Jamie's dad asked. "The video we showed the protection agency didn't get much of a reaction. Why would this be any different?"

"Ah, this isn't for them. This is for the people." He smiled. "My YouTube isn't that big, only a couple thousand subs, but I'm hoping that if it finds its right audience, it could lead people to start spreading the word about what's going on here. Social media campaigns have helped change things before, thought this might too." Ritchie shrugged. "Worth a shot at least."

"Well, we have maybe a week to try and convince the Environmental Impact Agency and the government. How long till you can get it out and have it circulating?" Alicaster asked.

"If I can get Jamie in to do an interview section, I can finalise the editing tonight and have it out either by the end of today or tomorrow."

"An interview with me?" Jamie said, surprised. "Why? I'm just a grad student."

"Everyone loves a heart to the story. Besides" – he turned to the two adult adults – "no offence to you two." He looked back at Jamie. "No one will want to watch or listen if it's a couple of middle-aged folks talking."

"I'm thirty!" Alicaster snapped.

"Same diff."

Before Ritchie could offend anyone else, Jamie spoke up. "So, what do you want me to talk about?"

"I think you know what." Ritchie's eyes fell on Artemis who was trying to steal some bacon from Jamie's plate. "Let's get going."

ARTEMIS

There was one thing Artemis was certain of since arriving at Jamie's Den; these humans were not hunters. She wasn't even sure they could be classed as competent humans. Not that she truly knew what one of those would be.

After eating a confusing yet delicious meal provided to her by Jamie, she found herself sitting and watching the array of human activities around her. It was strange for her to be awake during the day and without good reason, but as she watched Jamie laugh at something the male "Reechee" said, Artemis had to admit it wasn't so bad.

There was something freeing about Jamie. Just as there had been all those years ago, there was a peacefulness that filled Artemis as she watched her. Except for one thing, that was.

"...Jamie..." Oak said with a smile into the odd device that Reechee was pointing at her. The two were sitting down opposite one another, the strange black box standing on a pair of twigs in front of the young male.

Artemis held back a grunt of frustration. It was frustrating to not be able to understand what was being said, but she listened all the same.

With how the two of them interacted, Artemis knew there was a bond between them. From their playful nature of pushes and grappling, it was clear that their relationship was like the ones she had with Kiba or even Mai. A companionship. It made Artemis smile knowing Jamie had someone kind to her in her life. She had often wondered through the years if the girl she always saw alone had found her pack. As Oak kicked Reechee in the leg playfully and he did so right back, Artemis smiled knowing now that she had. A part of her ached at the thought of Jamie with her own pack. Artemis couldn't quite understand why, so she chose not to think on it further.

"...Artemis..." Jamie said with a raise of her paw in her direction. She didn't turn toward her, which frustrated Artemis. *Why say a name if you do not look at them?* she thought irritably.

Oak had only returned to her world such a short time ago, and yet Artemis could not stop thinking about her. Now in her presence, Artemis found herself unable to be without her attention.

"Jam...ie..." she said in reply, her human voice barely above a whisper. The girl in question did not turn her way. Her voice was just too quiet to be heard, a fact that was unsurprising considering her struggle to speak in their tongue.

Artemis shook her head. She needed to give Jamie her space to do as she needed. At least for now. To distract herself, she started making her way around what the humans called "camp".

To her side sat the elder humans, discussing something between one another at a strange, raised log. A silver flat rock sat in front of them which, occasionally, one of them would tap at. Frowning, Artemis turned away. They were too strange for her.

She began to walk around the sleeping holes that sat on opposing sides of the now extinguished sun's fever. Nearby the

tents was an all-black four-legged beast that Artemis remembered all too well from childhood. Jamie had called them "kwad
bye-kes" but Artemis knew what they were capable of. It hadn't
hurt her yet, but she didn't trust it. Walking around the "camp"
was more frustrating than Artemis expected. They had many
unfamiliar things within their Den, and yet everything was kept
close within this open space. She supposed it made sense; there
were many scavengers within the Forest. But it still felt odd to
be so compacted in such a large space.

It felt suffocating.

Glancing back at Jamie, she found the girl still talking to
Reechee and his standing black box. Artemis let out a huff of
annoyance. She was bored and wanted to play. Why wasn't
anyone playing?

Scowling, Artemis stomped towards the two humans.
Reechee caught sight of her first and smiled before turning back
to Jamie.

"Jam..ie," she whispered, reaching out a paw to touch the
woman's shoulder.

The dazzling pair of oak-brown eyes turned towards her,
their softness seeking her out instantly and without pause. A
hand was placed on her own as an earnest voice spoke to her.
"...OK?"

Artemis made an assumption on the question being about
her well-being and just nodded, unsure what to do.

With a smile, Jamie turned back to Reechee's pointing object,
but her hand never left Artemis's. Holding onto the hand that
was still wrapped in strange white material, Artemis listened as
Jamie spoke. As she did, a smile tugged at the edge of her mouth.
Her smile only dulled when she noticed Reechee watching her.
He one-eye blinked at her before focusing back on the still
talking Oak.

Whatever they were doing didn't last long after her arrival.
Whether that was because they were done or because Artemis

couldn't stop fidgeting after a few moments of standing still, she didn't care. They were moving again. Artemis loved moving.

They didn't leave the human's Den that day. Instead, Jamie took her around where they were staying and would point things out to Artemis and say what they were. Just like the night before when she had taught her their names.

Nothing sounded quite right in the human tongue. It was as if there was a level of depth and importance for each word missing. Still, Artemis listened to each word carefully. Tonight, she did not try to speak these new words aloud. The struggle to do so was more frustrating than she'd expected. Jamie was just as patient and understanding as she had been when they were pups. She didn't push for Artemis to speak. Didn't react badly when she couldn't.

She was the same as always. But different too. Being together now felt different than when they had been young. Every touch, every glance, every moment felt weighted somehow. When Jamie's finger brushed against Artemis's, it was like she had been hit by storm winds. The fur on her arms lifted into the air, making her shiver. It was strange.

Being around Jamie was strange.

She never wanted to leave.

The two of them continued their walk around the camp. Jamie was pointing up at the stars above them now, telling a story if the way her voice went high and low in tone was anything to go by. Then Artemis saw it. The very thing she needed to learn.

This one! she cried in her native tongue, grabbing Jamie's hand to take her to a tree, pointing at it desperately. **This one I need to know.**

Jamie looked at the tree and then back to Artemis who was nodding furiously. With a smile, Jamie began to speak. The day was starting to fade behind them, shrouding Jamie in an aura of light that had Artemis forgetting she was meant to be paying attention to what she was saying.

Like before, Artemis reached out to lay her hand against Jamie's lips, feeling the word against her skin, shivering slightly when a delicate hand laid itself against her forearm. She lowered her hand to the girl's throat to sense the word's vibrations.

Closing her eyes, Artemis began to mouth the word to herself before lying her other hand against her own throat as she said it aloud.

"Ohk…" she whispered, frowning. "Ohhk."

Opening her eyes, she looked at Jamie who was saying the word again, encouraging her. She stopped when Artemis nodded her head and closed her eyes once more.

"Ohh…k—" Artemis cut herself off with the shake of a head and started again. "Ooak … Oak … Oak."

A squeeze on her arm had her open her eyes to look at the beaming Jamie who was nodding her head enthusiastically. Artemis smiled and said it again and received another large smile from Jamie.

It was as the excitement from her saying the word faded that Artemis remembered why she wanted to learn it. Removing her hand from her throat and Jamie's, she stepped closer to the woman.

Placing a hand against her own chest, Artemis began to speak as clearly as she could manage. "Arte…mis … an…" She reached the same hand towards Jamie's chest, lying it against her beating heart just as she had only a sun ago. "…Jam…ie."

Jamie smiled and went to speak, but Artemis shook her head to silence her. "Oak…" Artemis reached her other hand up to her cheek. "Jam…ie."

A frown formed between Jamie's eyebrows. Artemis knew she didn't understand, so she tried again.

Stepping closer until their bodies were almost flush against the other, she placed both paws now against the girl's cheeks. "Oak." She drew a finger against one side. "Jamie." She repeated the motion on the other.

Jamie's hands came up to hold Artemis's wrists, her soft oak-brown eyes holding hers so intensely that Artemis wondered how she wasn't being lost in them.

"Oak..." Jamie whispered, "is Jamie?"

Artemis nodded with tears in her eyes. There was so much more she wanted to say to her, but she couldn't. Not in a way that Jamie would ever understand, that is.

I have loved Oak for how she saved me. She leant forward to rest her head against Jamie's. **But it is Jamie who has made me feel whole again.**

JAMIE

She was in trouble.

It had been two days since Artemis's arrival. Right now, they were the only ones in the camp. The others had headed out with copies of the map on their devices to start de-trapping the claws. Ritchie had his camera with him ready to get some additional footage in case he needed it for his other film. He'd said to use his other camera if she could to get some shots with Artemis if she was comfortable with it. Jamie had only nodded, part of her hoping he'd say he was staying behind with them so she wouldn't be alone with Artemis for hours.

Jamie knew Artemis had been just as nervous about the others leaving, though for very different reasons. Jamie had never been sure how much Artemis had understood about the traps she'd shown her but with her uneasiness in the others leaving, even though she was still uncomfortable around them, Jamie guessed she'd grasped the severity of the situation. This was only confirmed to her when Artemis kept glancing towards the tree-line every so often after they'd left.

Jamie eventually managed to get her settled in one of the chairs at the makeshift table. Her dad and Alicaster had suggested that, while they were out, she should start working through some learning media on the satellite computer to help Artemis learn English easier. They said that helping her understand English more could help their chances of explaining to her the level of danger that was coming. Showing her the traps was one thing. Explaining deforestation was another problem entirely.

The satellite laptop was sluggish at best. It would often choose to freeze at inconvenient moments that had Jamie wanting to tear her hair out. Her dad told her this is what home computers were like when she was younger. She was almost grateful she'd not had a permanent home after hearing that. Her patience with inanimate objects wasn't her strong suit.

When the laptop had booted up, Jamie began teaching Artemis the alphabet. She hoped that, in getting Artemis to understand the letters, it would help with explaining what was coming if she knew the sounds. Jamie would still have to keep it simplified, of course, but hopefully it'd be better for Artemis.

They'd only gotten to the letter L when she realised that Artemis wasn't paying attention. Instead, Jamie found her staring out into the forest.

"Artemis?" she asked, gaining the wolf-woman's attention.

Intense green eyes returned to hers. With a slight tilt of her head, Artemis's lips twitched as if she wanted to say something. Of course, only being able to say a few words in English meant she couldn't say much.

"Jamie," Artemis said with emphasis and a frown forming across her forehead. She turned to look at the trees, glanced up high behind Jamie's head. After a beat, she came back to stare at Jamie, leaning towards her when she did.

She had no idea how, maybe her degree was actually being of use, or maybe she just knew Artemis so well, but Jamie knew what Artemis was trying to say.

The look to the tree-line was simple enough. That was

where her dad, Ritchie, and Alicaster had gone. Artemis had already shown she was worried about them being out there. It was the glance behind Jamie's head and higher in the air that gave her the inkling. The split mountain peaks that separated the forest and the town were hard to miss; even at night, they towered over the camp. Put those two motions together and add in the leaning towards Jamie herself, and she had her answer.

Artemis had understood her that night when Jamie had told her about the hunters. Or at least, she had understood the simplified version of it. From the way she kept glancing towards the split mountains and back to Jamie with a tilt of her head, she wanted to know more.

Jamie tugged at the ends of her hair. When she'd physically described what the hunters were doing, it had frightened Artemis enough that a member of her pack had come out snarling at Jamie. If Jamie was going to show her exactly what the humans were planning, she couldn't imagine how Artemis would react. Her lack of English was just an added painful complication that had Jamie loading YouTube on the laptop. She could feel Artemis's eyes on her the whole time as she loaded the first video on deforestation.

"Show you," Jamie said as she gestured to the computer that was slowly booting up. "What will happen because of them." She pointed to the mountains.

Artemis blinked at her.

Biting her tongue to hide her frustration, Jamie focused her attention on the screen. She wasn't annoyed that Artemis couldn't understand. How could she be? This wasn't her fault. No, she was disgusted that the people of Materia had put them in this position. Had put her in a place where she would have to show Artemis the horrors to come and hope she could explain it to her afterwards. It felt cruel.

She loaded up the first video.

T‌HE DISTRESS in Artemis's eyes was enough to break Jamie.

Jamie watched as she leant forward on her chair towards the screen, nearly tumbling out of the precariously balanced seat in the process. It was as if Artemis were hypnotised by what she was seeing.

Her jaw clenched and unclenched. Her fingers curled until they were claw-like. If Artemis had fur, she wouldn't be surprised if it was puffed up in fear as she watched the footage unfold.

Bulldozers carried away chain-sawed trees. Men with spades and jackhammers dug up roots. Others burned the ground to stop anything from regrowing. The video even showed birds and other woodland creatures cawing and crying as they ran from the scene.

"I'm sorry, Artemis." Jamie reached over to turn the video off. "I just needed—"

Her voice stuck in her throat as she saw the tears dripping down pale cheeks. Artemis's chest heaved, as if she were struggling to catch her breath. Her mouth opened and closed like she was desperate to say something but couldn't communicate it.

Jamie reached a hand out to Artemis, hoping to comfort her and explain what she had just seen. When the woman jumped from her chair and away from her touch, Jamie was overcome with disgust over what she'd done. She'd taken things too far.

Artemis's hands clenched and unclenched as she looked up towards the mountain behind them. It was like she was waiting for the men with machines to arrive.

When the muscles in her legs tightened, Jamie rushed to her feet and towards Artemis. She was about to bolt and, with the traps still out in the forest, Artemis could run right into danger.

"Artemis, hey, hey, look at me." Jamie lowered herself to the ground and raised her hands into the air. She hoped putting herself in a vulnerable position would appeal to Artemis's wolf instincts. "It's OK. Nothing here is going to hurt you. I won't let them come. I'll keep you safe. I promise."

Quieter than a mouse, a whimper slipped past Artemis's lips as she continued to stare at the distant mountains.

Lowering herself to be non-threatening wasn't going to work. It wasn't Jamie Artemis was afraid of. Jamie didn't think through her next actions. Moving by instinct, she came to stand in front of Artemis and laid her hands on her cheeks. While the girl's eyes didn't meet hers, too focused on the mountains, her hands came to rest on Jamie's wrists. At least that meant she was aware of Jamie's presence.

"Artemis, I'm sorry I showed you this, but you have to know what's happening." Green eyes met hers before looking away again. "Forest in danger. Humans coming. Wolves in danger." Rough hands slid down her arms till they rested at her elbows. "Humans are coming." Jamie's thumb brushed a tear from Artemis's cheek. "Humans coming for Artemis."

They stood like that for God knows how long. Jamie spoke gentle, reassuring words, though she tried her best to stop promising things she couldn't guarantee. As she spoke, Artemis closed her eyes, and her breathing slowly calmed down.

When the sun above them passed overhead towards the long stretch of mountains in front of her, showing how long they had stood like this, Artemis finally opened her eyes.

"Hu…" she began with a shaky voice, "man?"

Jamie let out a breath and nodded. "Yes, human."

Artemis turned to the mountains again. "Here?"

"Yes." Jamie nodded. She pointed to the black-screened laptop. "To do that."

Trusting green eyes met hers, and with a simple nod, Artemis seemed to accept what she had been told. Jamie wanted to reassure her again. Let her know that they would stop them.

But she didn't get the chance. Artemis pulled Jamie's hands away from her face and dropped them.

Jamie watched as the silent woman walked away and towards their tent. Artemis didn't look back when she ducked inside to rest. Wolves weren't daytime creatures after all.

It shouldn't have hurt, seeing her walk away like that. Artemis clearly needed a moment. And it wasn't like she was leaving her behind. She had only gone into their tent to take a moment, but Jamie couldn't help but think that one day she'd have to watch Artemis leave her.

Jamie wasn't sure she could lose her again.

JAMIE

It was as the sun was setting, hours after the events with Artemis and the video, that her dad and the others returned. Jamie and Artemis were by the fireside, the tension of the day still around them, when they heard the arrival of the others.

"This is absolute bullcrap," Alicaster's distinct voice came. "How can they do this?"

Jamie got to her feet with Artemis following suit. The footage may have frightened her and given her reason to be mad at Jamie, but it seemed her ability to forgive was still strong as she slipped a hand onto Jamie's wrist.

"What's going on?" Jamie called out to them.

As the three arrivals stepped into the light of the fire, Jamie caught sight of her dad's expression. His eyebrows were knitted together in frustration, and though his beard covered much of his jaw, she could tell he was clenching hard if the closed fists were anything to go by.

"Dad," Jamie asked. "What happened?"

Blue eyes met hers, and Jamie could feel her heart sink. "They showed up a week early."

Jamie stepped in front of Artemis protectively. "Can … can they do that? What about the law—"

"They don't give a damn about the laws," Alicaster interrupted. "That's why they had no problem with setting those traps. Which we finished removing by the way. Not that it matters now." She rubbed at her temple. "Who's to say they won't start destroying the forest tomorrow? Or even tonight?"

"Surely they can't do that?" Ritchie asked. "That'd be breaking the agreement, right?"

Her dad sighed, sinking into one of the chairs by the table. "The answer to that is … complicated. Technically they've had the legal right to do what they wanted to Swen for two years now. The deforestation team they hired signed a contract saying they wouldn't start till the following Monday, but because the forest has no protection laws, they can technically start when they want to – but also shouldn't based on the contract." He rubbed at his forehead. "It's a grey area. But seeing as the governors haven't reacted to the inhumane trapping, I have a feeling that they won't have an opinion on them coming a week early to destroy a forest." He scoffed. "Bloody politicians."

Jamie was ready to agree and ask what they could do when she felt a hand at her elbow. She glanced at Artemis and found the woman's eyes flitting from person to person. The muscles in her shoulders had hunched up and the tendons in her neck were tensed. She could tell something was wrong. And she was scared.

Opening her mouth to tell her, Jamie paused. She thought back to Artemis's panic attack from a few hours ago over a video of deforestation. How would she react now if she found out they were already here?

"It's OK," Jamie lied. "You're OK."

She placed a hand on top of Artemis's and began to draw circles into the back of it. Jamie hoped the repetitive motion would calm her down. She turned back to the others. "I showed her what would happen to the forest if we didn't stop them," Jamie said with an even and emotionless voice. "She had a panic attack. If she knows they're here now..." she trailed off.

Her dad looked up at the sky, and from the way he breathed in deeply through his nose, she could tell he was holding back a sigh. It was clear he disapproved but knowing now what was around the corner for them, she believed it had been the best thing to do. No matter the pain it had caused Artemis, it was necessary.

I wonder if Cora thought the same, a cruel voice in her head told her. Jamie shook the thought away.

"We need to find the pack," her dad said. "Do you think you could ask Artemis to show us?"

Jamie chewed her lip. "I'll give it a try. The one I saw seemed to be OK around people, but I don't know if Artemis would want to show us where they live."

"You may have to convince her." Her dad stroked his beard. "If we know where they are, we may be able to protect them."

"Really?" Jamie asked in surprise. "I thought there was nothing we could do?" A thought crossed her mind. "Could we trap the wolves humanely ourselves to relocate?"

"We'd need to receive approved permits for that to happen, and that can take weeks," Alicaster interrupted. "Not to mention we have nowhere to take the animals."

"There's sanctuaries across the country, maybe they'd—"

"Again, a lengthy process that we just don't have the time for."

Jamie took a deep breath to stop from yelling at Alicaster. Artemis's eyes were on her; she couldn't let her see. Even if she hated hiding things like this from her. "OK, my ideas won't work. What do you suggest, then?"

Alicaster stayed silent and looked away. "I don't think there is anything we can do..." She tucked her hands into her pockets.

"We need the governor to get behind this and bring in an emergency injunction. But he's already refused to do it."

"Say he did," Jamie began, thinking. "What would happen if an injunction was brought in?"

"The Talbot group would have to stop what they were doing and wait," her dad replied. "We'd then have the time to fight it out in court with the evidence we have and, hopefully, get permanent protection for the forest if we win."

"How would we get the governor's attention?" she asked.

"We'd need a pretty big public outcry or a petition of over ten thousand signatures to get a response from the government. So, really" – Alicaster gestured to Ritchie – "your boy's documentary may be the only thing that makes a difference."

"That's going to do wonders for my anxiety," Ritchie muttered before shaking his head. "I'll go look to see how it's doing, I guess?" Walking towards the tent, Ritchie met Jamie's eyes and gestured with a small nod to follow him.

"Hey, Dad, could you maybe do some teaching with Artemis while I" – she gestured to Ritchie who'd stepped into his tent. "See if you can get her to learn more of the alphabet without me. Maybe if she can, we can ask her where the pack is."

Her dad offered her a small smile before guiding Artemis towards the table. She could see the disappointed look the woman sent her as she went. Jamie managed to catch the start of her dad's lesson with Artemis and couldn't help but smile as he began with a story about the first time he saw a wolf. He always loved telling stories when teaching. She saw Artemis begin to smile and, upon seeing it, ducked into the tent after Ritchie.

"Do you want the good news or bad news?" he asked.

Jamie just gave him a blank look.

"So, the good news is, the video seems to have been taking off. Don't know how or why. I will look into it further. But hopefully that means the petition I made will get some signatures from it. There aren't many so far, but we'll see." He started tapping away at his computer before groaning. "I appreciate your dad finding a way to hook up my laptop to the satellite connection that his computer has, but God is it slow."

"And the bad?" Jamie questioned.

"We don't have any footage of the wolves," Ritchie said.

Jamie frowned and came to sit beside him. "What about the footage of the she-wolf I got?"

"One wolf and one wolf-woman isn't going to offer much to an audience about why they need protection." He pulled up his editing software, which Jamie could never look at unless she wanted a migraine from how complicated it looked. "The footage I do have, while good, isn't helping to focus on the wolves but more on Artemis. Which, like, that's important too, but if we want environmental activists – and, hell, dog lovers – to get involved, we need to know more about the pack and show more about them."

"But you've already uploaded the video—"

"One of them," Ritchie noted.

"There's more than—" Jamie shook her head. "Wait, never mind, this is you. Of course there's more than one version."

Ritchie smiled. "Always the perfectionist me."

"Yeah, yeah, well, we can't work with the perfectionism if I don't even know where the pack is." Jamie paused. Her heart thudded nervously in her chest. "But Artemis does."

"She can guide you," Ritchie continued. "You can take my camera, just like you did when you bumped into her the other night, and film the pack and Artemis together. I'll then smack it together in the final cut and get it uploaded."

"But how can I do that?" Jamie said, pushing herself to her feet in frustration. "I've only had three proper days with her. That's not enough time to build up trust. She may like and remember me, but I don't think she'd let me near her family. Wolves don't like humans on the best of days." Jamie shook her head. "Besides, how would I even be able to communicate why I need to see the pack? She barely understands me as it is."

"Well, now I know you're being ridiculous if you think she doesn't understand you. Have you seen how she looks at you?"

"That's the freaking problem!" Jamie yelled back.

Ritchie stayed surprisingly calm at her outburst. "What is?"

"I … I can't take advantage of her," she whispered. "I can't get her to take me to the wolves when she doesn't understand why." She looked away from Ritchie. "I can't let her know I have feelings for her when she's just mimicking what I'm doing. I can't do that to her."

"Jamie, you can't seriously—"

"My job was to come here to save her and her family," she said. "Once I finish that, she'll go back to them, and I'll go home. That's how it is. No point thinking about anything more, OK?"

Ritchie went to talk again, but Jamie was finished listening. She knew what he'd tell her. Some sappy rom-com sentimentality about following your heart. It's what he always did. But right now, she couldn't hear it.

"I'll see what we can do about the wolf footage," she said quietly.

He didn't respond, which didn't surprise Jamie. Stepping out of the tent and finding Artemis's eyes on her instantly, Jamie had to look away.

She walked up to Alicaster who, to her confusion, had been watching her since she'd left the tent. Jamie came to her side and grabbed one of the backpacks from the ground. "Let's go screw with their plans."

30

ARTEMIS

Jamie's father was an enthusiastic teacher. Artemis knew that to understand this world from the perspective of an elder would be of great benefit. Her mother, Larka, had always said to listen to her elders. It was her long-since-departed mother's words that had kept her from running after Jamie and the angry female.

She'd waited for her Oak to stop talking with Reechee so she could spend time with her, but to her dismay, Jamie had left the camp extraordinarily quickly. And without a glance in Artemis's direction.

Is there something I have done? Artemis wondered as she sunk into her seat. *Did my fear from before frighten her? Or did she finally understand what I had told her that night?*

Artemis was startled from her thoughts by a pat of a hand against hers. Growling, she set her eyes on Elder Will who, thankfully, was not offended by her reaction.

"Jamie…" He pointed at the Forest. "…back." He pointed to the ground at their paws.

The huff of annoyance she let out had him throwing his head back in laughter. Artemis smiled in response. Elder Will was an interesting man. She may not know much about him, but she liked him. She watched as he shook his head in amusement and began to wonder what had caused the rift between him and Jamie.

She may not understand the human tongue well, but body language is readable in all species. There was a distance between the two when they spoke, one that hurt them both. Between the way Jamie never met her father's eyes unless a situation was dire and how Elder Will would watch Jamie as she left, there was much being unsaid between them.

Would it be intrusive to ask this? Artemis wondered as she tapped the man's knee to gain his attention.

The man lent forward, giving her his full attention, and nodded for her to speak. He was a lot like Jamie. It made Artemis smile.

"Jamie…" She pointed to where she had left. "You." She looked at him. Artemis frowned, unsure of the next word. Unlike when she was younger, she struggled to retain the language as she learnt it. Frustrated, she decided to show what she meant. She put her hands together, symbolising Jamie and Elder Will, before moving them apart from each other.

Elder Will sat in silence, staring at her hands. From the way he tugged at his facial fur, Artemis wasn't sure if he was in thought or insulted until he spoke up.

"Yes." He placed his hands together like she had. "We…" He separated his hands as she had done. Elder Will kept his hands in the air and smiled. "But" – he moved one of the hands towards the other – "trying."

Artemis nodded in understanding. When she'd first returned to the pack after being stolen, it was difficult to rebuild the bonds with her family. Many of them had grown up since she'd been gone. She didn't know them, and they didn't know her. It took a long time, but their bonds were restored. Mostly.

Fenris came to her mind. He had never truly understood

why she held onto things from her time in the human world. Unlike his father, Fenris shunned the human side of her. He only saw her as a wolf, and as much as he tried to hide it, she knew he was disappointed when she embraced her human side in hunting and climbing.

Artemis turned towards the Forest in thought. Seeing the way Jamie and her father were with each other struck a chord with Artemis. Right now, Artemis was betraying her promise to Fenris once again. Yue may have given her time, but she was not Fenris. The pup she had helped raise. The pup who had been there with her when she was near death after what the humans had done.

Will he hate me? Artemis wondered. *Will I be welcomed back once I leave Oak behind?*

"Jamie … you, Artemis," Elder Will said, drawing her attention back to him. "Just…" He shrugged and made a strange expression.

Artemis frowned, unsure how to feel about what he said. Things between her and Jamie felt … complicated. Her deadline to return to the pack was up tomorrow, and she'd have to leave Jamie behind all over again. The picture of a sobbing young Oak came to mind, but she quickly shook it away. With everything that had happened since Jamie had come to the Forest and, more than that, what had been happening to Artemis since they'd reconnected, she found herself struggling with the idea of leaving her again.

A gentle wave of a hand from Elder Will in front of her face gave Artemis the chance to distract herself from her thoughts. Looking back to her elder, she smiled in return to his own gentle one.

When he reached out his paws to hers, she gave them to him willingly.

He held up one of her hands. "Jamie." He raised her other. "Artemis." Elder Will brought the two paws together and interlocked her fingers. "Co-nec-ted." He broke apart the lock and separated her hands. "Apart" – he brought them back together again – "but co-nec-ted."

He let go of her paws, leaving them interlocked. Artemis's mind whirled with so many thoughts. She knew in her heart that it wouldn't be as simple as he made it look, but it was worth trying.

As she let herself plan in her mind, she didn't notice the return of Jamie and the angry female until she heard them.

Leaping from her seat, she rushed to Jamie's side, startling her with her speed. Taking Jamie's paw, she pulled her away from the female, making sure to send her the all-important scowl as she did.

Holding onto Jamie, she tugged her out of earshot of the camp and into the trees. Once far enough, she stopped and spun to face Oak. The girl looked confused, but she didn't ask for answers like most others would. She waited for her to speak.

"Hom," Artemis said quickly. "Jamie hom Artemis."

Jamie tilted her head, just like Artemis did when she was confused. Artemis huffed in annoyance at herself. The human tongue was too hard. Taking a breath, she reached for Jamie's paws and interlocked their fingers together like Elder Will had shown her. Artemis stared into Jamie's beautiful oak-coloured eyes and repeated herself.

"Show Jamie Artemis home."

31

JAMIE

Destroying property was a lot more satisfying than Jamie had expected it to be. She knew smash rooms existed, a place where you could pay to break stuff to relieve tension; she just didn't think she'd be the sort of person who found relief in doing so.

When she had gone out with Alicaster, she'd not really had a plan in mind. All she could think about was how frustrated she was about the whole situation. Thankfully for her, Alicaster had an idea.

They'd already removed the bear traps, though they kept using their hiking poles to spread across the ground, just in case. The only thing they hadn't yet removed was the live bait one.

The smell of the now dead and decaying wolf was potent the moment they came across it. They both had to cover their mouths to stop themselves from gagging at the intensity. It reminded her of the food waste bins at the university when they were left out in the hot sun for days on end. Just add in the smell of a dead body and it was practically identical.

"How ... Why did they think this would work?" Jamie

pinched her nose as they stepped closer. "The smell is awful, and we don't even have heightened senses. Why would this work on an animal?"

Alicaster bent down to pick up a rock. "It's because animals have more empathy than humans do." She threw the stone into the cage. "They would want to help as much as they can, even if it was just to get them out of this prison to properly rest in peace." She threw another stone.

"What are you doing?" Jamie asked.

"We'll never be able to get him out without getting caught or hurting ourselves." She pointed to a silver circle at the entrance of the trap. "There's a pressure plate. I'm trying to trip it."

She threw another stone and, this time, it hit its mark. The doors of the trap slammed shut with a sickening metallic clang. Jamie held back a shiver at the noise. "What now?"

Alicaster rolled her shoulders. "Now we get him out and do some damage."

SHE COULD FEEL Alicaster's eyes on her the entire time as she smashed the steel head of the hammer into the cage's side. Jamie had thought it'd be harder to hit with all the gaps, but if it was, she didn't notice. All she could feel was the anger that burned through her veins. All she could think was that these monsters were the ones who hurt Artemis.

Jamie kicked the side of the cage, hard, knocking herself backwards and to the ground. Her vision was blurry with unshed tears. She went to charge back to the cage when a voice called out: "I think that's enough."

She didn't want to stop. Only when the weight of the hammer tugged her arm to the ground did she eventually drop it into the snow.

Blinking, Jamie took in the sight of the battered cage in front of her. Dents covered every side of the device. Its doors were bent in a way that made it unusable, and the trigger plate was damaged beyond repair. Jamie smiled.

"Good work, Miss Gander-Yoon. A-plus for effort," Alicaster said with a smile to her voice. "I would recommend noting this in your dissertation. Emotional investment in these causes can gain you extra points from your assessors."

Jamie scoffed. "Unless it's Professor Whitaker."

"Yes, that man has always been a dick." She smiled. "But you didn't hear that from me."

Stunned by the playfulness Alicaster was showing her, Jamie didn't even protest when she suggested they head back to the camp. The two of them walked back in silence, Jamie still trying to process her feelings on the Alicaster situation but also on what they were going to do for Artemis now. They didn't exactly have a plan C.

The moment they arrived back at camp, it took Jamie longer than it should have to notice Artemis coming her way. When she did, she was too disorientated to even question where the woman was taking her until they were already among the trees.

Her heart fluttered when Artemis interlocked their fingers. And then she heard her speak.

"Show Jamie Artemis home."

Jamie's heart dropped into her stomach.

She knew it was a good thing that Artemis was suggesting this. It meant they could find out where the wolves were to film them, evacuate them if necessary, and see how they could protect them. So, why did she feel hollow inside?

"Now?" Jamie asked, pointing a finger to the forest. Artemis nodded. "OK, I'll— I'll go get my bag." She forced a smile.

Artemis stayed among the trees as she rushed towards the camp where her dad, Ritchie, and now Alicaster sat by the recently reignited fire. Jamie could feel her heart racing as she made her way towards her dad.

"Artemis is taking me to her family's den. How safe do you think that will be for me?" she asked him quietly. Jamie was hoping for – well, she wasn't sure what she was hoping he'd say. Did she want him to let her go with Artemis or to stop her? She had no idea what she was thinking or feeling anymore.

His eyes warmed at her question. "You know the answer, Jamie. You don't need me to decide this for you."

Jamie frowned. "What does that—"

"If you follow and listen to her, you'll be safe." Ritchie never looked up from his laptop. "Now stop being an idiot and go spend time with Artemis by yourself. We're tired of seeing you moping about in your feelings."

"One day I am going to stop being friends with you," Jamie said.

"Nah, you'll ask me to be your best man at the wedding. Just wait." He looked up at her. "C'mon, Jay, this is the chance to see her world. Don't give that up."

Jamie tried to hide a smile that was blooming behind her frowning lips, but eventually she couldn't help it. "You just want to make a movie about us, that's why you're fighting so hard."

"Oh, yeah," Ritchie said with a smile, "me, Will, and Alicaster here are big fans. The original Artemie shippers."

"We'll make T-shirts!" Her dad laughed.

"And you can use the shirts as evidence towards your graduate assessment," Alicaster chimed in.

"OK." Jamie shook her head and looked at the older woman. "When did you become pro me spending time with Artemis?"

Alicaster folded her arms across her chest. "When I realised that the more you're together, the more chance of saving the forest we get."

"But—"

Her dad stood, drawing her attention. "Jamie, I know you're nervous about what comes next, but you've got to give this a shot. For Artemis. For you." He rested a hand on her shoulder.

"Take the flare with you for safety and stick close to Artemis's side. She's a very capable young woman." He smiled at her, his blue eyes turning as light as the sky above. "Just like you are."

Jamie's mouth opened but nothing came out. She had no idea what to say or what to feel. It was the first time her dad had ever said anything like that to her. Her throat tightened, but she couldn't let herself cry. Nodding silently, Jamie stepped away from his grasp. She offered him a gentle smile so as to not make him think she was rejecting his words before she turned away.

Grabbing her backpack from her tent, she went to head towards the still patiently waiting Artemis near the tree-line. It was as she walked past the boys tent that Jamie found herself pausing outside of it, remembering what Ritchie had said the other day.

Quickly, to not second-guess herself, she unzipped the boys tent, grabbed his camera, and slipped it into her backpack. Jamie had no idea what they'd be stumbling upon, but all she could hope was that Artemis wouldn't hate her for what she was going to do.

ARTEMIS

Artemis had to remember that Jamie wasn't as fast as she was. Nor was she accustomed to the cold, if the thick layering of fur that covered her was anything to go by. Jamie looked like a bear with the bulkiness of it all, which made Artemis laugh.

Jamie's differences are what drew Artemis to her – even if right now they were getting on her nerves. Artemis was desperate to go running. She hadn't had the chance in a few days now. Unfortunately, as Jamie had pointed out, there could be more unknown danger within her home, but that didn't stop her thinking about it. The feel of the ice-cold wind against her skin, her paws pounding against solid ground, the thrill of the race. More than that though, she wanted Jamie to experience her world with her. Jamie may have seen her fight a cougar and even run off with a member of her pack, but she'd never *seen* her.

She wanted to show Jamie what she had given her all those years ago.

"Fast." Artemis bounced on her tiptoes trying to stop herself from running off. "Fast."

"I know, I know," Jamie wheezed out. "Trying."

Artemis bowed her head, feeling guilty. She hadn't thought about how difficult this may be for someone as human as Jamie. Especially with all the additional weight on her back.

Without a word, Artemis reached a paw out towards the bags. Jamie caught her doing so and stepped away from her. Though Artemis had noticed Oak's hesitation towards her since that night at the tree, seeing such a reaction to her closeness still hurt. She couldn't blame Jamie for her reactions. How could she? She'd given so much to her already. What had Artemis given her except the burden of learning?

I will change that soon, Artemis thought as she gestured towards Jamie's bag.

Jamie made an O shape with her mouth; a sign of understanding Artemis was coming to learn. Even after realising what Artemis was asking, she didn't remove the bag from her back. She seemed almost reluctant until Artemis waved her paw at the bag, not taking no for an answer.

With a quiet laugh, Jamie slipped the bag off her back and helped Artemis put it on. With a small shake of her body, Artemis began walking. It felt odd to carry something on her back, but to her surprise, it was not as difficult as Jamie had made it appear.

"You ... strong..." Jamie laughed as Artemis started jogging again. "You ... teach me."

"Run lots," Artemis replied.

Jamie laughed again, louder than before. Artemis stopped and waited for her to calm down. As she watched Jamie's tanned skin turn red from her laughter, she found herself smiling. This was the Jamie she knew.

When Jamie's laughter faded, she glanced up at Artemis. Her beautiful oak eyes were shining with joy, and her cheeks were tinted in a rosy colour. She was breath-taking. Artemis reached out for Jamie's hand. A clammy and warm-to-the-touch hand slipped into hers, and Artemis grinned.

"Run."

Their feet slapped hard against the ground. Their chests heaved as they pushed themselves faster and harder. Jamie gripped her hand tighter as they swerved around trees, ducked beneath branches, and jumped over small streams.

Artemis had always loved running alone. But, with Jamie's hand in hers, and the smile on her face that Artemis saw each time she glanced back, Artemis knew that running alone would never be better than this.

They kept going.

It didn't take long for them to reach their destination after that.

Artemis inhaled deeply, taking it all in. The sound of running water from the stream, the smell of lavender in the air, and the masked entrance of their old Den within the mountainside. It may not have been long since she had been home but it felt like it had. The river Den didn't remotely compare to here. She went to step towards the stream when she heard the thud of a body hit the ground.

"Ugh," Jamie groaned.

She glanced down at Jamie who lay down on her side, her hair a tangled mess mixed with melting snowflakes. Her chest heaved up and down as she breathed heavily.

"Water," Jamie whispered in a deep throaty voice.

Artemis took off the bag and dropped it to the floor. She reached down for Jamie's hand and arm and hooked it around her neck as she slipped her arms beneath the girl's body. Jamie let out a yelp of surprise and threw her other forearm around Artemis's neck as she lifted her into the air.

She was heavier than Artemis expected, which had her making adjustments to hold her tighter. **A well-fed wolf is the survivor**, Rae had told her once. **It is the promise of a long life.** Artemis liked that thought.

As she carried Jamie towards the stream, Artemis couldn't help but be aware of the warm breath that brushed against her neck. It made her feel weak somehow, as if she were coming down with a sickness. She gripped Jamie tighter, just in case, and almost sent them both tumbling to the ground when her readjustment of Jamie's body led to a pair of soft lips pressing against her bare skin.

Rushing towards the stream ahead of them, she put Jamie down quickly and gently. Without a glance to the girl, Artemis dunked her head into the water. She drank deeply hoping to cool the flush of heat that spread across her skin at the touch. Eventually she resurfaced with a gasp.

What is wrong with you, Artemis? she thought with the shake of a head.

Turning back to Jamie, she was surprised to find the girl looking as flushed as she had felt. She was tugging lightly at the ends of her hair, unable to meet Artemis's eyes as a tint of red coloured her cheeks. Artemis's eyes dropped to her soft red lips, which had been caught by the edge of her teeth, hiding the bottom lip. She couldn't stop staring at them. Artemis found herself wondering if the gentle press of them against her neck would feel the same against her lips.

"Artemis?"

Just like that, she was pulled from her spiralling thoughts. In doing so, she realised how much closer she had gotten to Jamie without realising. Standing so close, Artemis was able to see the change in her gaze. Her oak-coloured eyes, dark like the trees, seemed to turn the colour of night as its black centre shrunk in size. Jamie's lips lay parted for a moment before she swallowed hard. Artemis had seen this look a few times before, but she just hadn't figured out what it meant yet. Worried she'd somehow overstepped by being close, Artemis pulled back.

"So-ree." She dipped her head as she would to an elder and crouched down beside the river. "Water."

Jamie frowned but said nothing. Reaching down with her hand, she slowly scooped water to herself to drink from. Artemis watched as the drops of water trickled down Jamie's lips and neck. She only turned away when the thudding in her chest began to beat faster than it should.

Artemis had little time to think on what this strange feeling could be when she found herself engulfed in a shadow as Jamie had stood up. Glancing up at her Oak, her back now turned to the river, Artemis took in the look of awe on her face as Jamie finally noticed the mountain Den behind them.

"Wow…" she whispered as she stared towards the cave.

"Come." Artemis took her hand in hers. "I show home."

33

JAMIE

It was everything Jamie could have wished to see and almost more. From the excited glow in Artemis's eyes to the way she held tightly onto Jamie's hand, she couldn't help but smile.

Watching Artemis in her element as she visually told of her adventures with the pups that she cared for had Jamie forgetting all about the fears of getting too close. Sitting there and seeing the way the woman expressed herself, she'd never felt more … well, she didn't know how to describe it.

That's a lie and you know it, a voice inside her head told her.

Jamie couldn't gain all the context of the stories told her by Artemis. She'd always been terrible at charades, and seeing as Artemis communicated almost exclusively with body language and the occasional English word here and there, it was hard. But Jamie listened and watched just as intensely as if she did understand. Just like Artemis did with her.

"Artemis train wolf." A tug at her hand pulled Jamie towards the centre of the land. From the roughed-up mud and scattered paw prints, she assumed this is where the wolves played and trained. This was confirmed when Artemis mimicked a play fight in the ground, rolling over and faux growling before pretending to surrender.

"Strong wolves," Artemis said as she clambered to her feet. "Artemis..." She frowned, unsure of the word. "Make strong wolves."

Jamie offered her a smile. Everything Artemis had shown her had given Jamie an idea of the life she had lived. From the growling match Artemis had acted out to do with – if she understood the raised arms and bellow correctly – a bear, to showing Jamie one of the places Artemis had gained a scar from, it was clear that the girl she had helped save had lived a happy life.

Could she ever live a life like that with me?

Shaking the thought from her head, Jamie allowed Artemis to take her hand once more and pull her towards the cave.

When they reached the entrance, Artemis motioned for her to wait. She drew the knife Jamie had given her all those years ago and disappeared into the darkness. With her out of sight, Jamie looked around the lightly lit entrance of the den.

Like many wolf dens, moss, stripped bark, and leaves lay across the entrance to form a bedding. If Jamie squinted, she could see caught strips of black, white, and grey wolf hair among them. Wolves often did this if they had young pups to make the ground softer for resting on and to keep them warm in the winter months.

Just past the entrance, pressed into an untouched patch of mud, lay a small paw print. At first, she thought it could be from a wolf pup, but at a closer look, she knew it was actually the mark of a fox.

Foxes never approach wolf dens, unless... Jamie desperately searched for signs of fresh wolf prints or droppings.

There were none.

"Crap..." she cursed silently.

If the wolves weren't here, then... She remembered the river on the trap map. It was the one place where nothing had been set out. She'd thought that had been where the pack could be until Artemis found her when she was nowhere nearby. *This was clearly once a wolf den, so could they have—*

"Safe."

Jamie jumped to her feet, worried she'd been caught snooping. Artemis reappeared in the light of the cave, her head turned away from Jamie as she slipped her knife into her bottom cloth pocket. Jamie held back a sigh of relief at not getting caught.

"Come." Artemis reached a hand out to her.

With a nervous smile, Jamie took the hand, and they both stepped into the cave.

It wasn't as dark as it looked from the outside, and didn't go as far into the rockface as Jamie had expected. The small tunnel was thin, only giving enough room for the two women to walk side by side, and with how low the ceiling was, the two had to duck down regularly to avoid—

"Ow!"

Jamie stopped them in place as she ducked her head, rubbing the sore spot on top.

"Sit," Artemis said, laying her hands on her shoulders. "Look."

Sinking down to the ground, Jamie rested her back against the walls and removed her hand from her head. She winced at the speckle of blood on her fingertips. Jamie watched as Artemis pushed up onto her knees and began to gently press her fingers into her hair. Jamie found herself trying to focus on anything but the sensation. Of course, when you're in a dingy cave, there's not much to look at.

Ritchie would have a field day if he heard about this, Jamie thought as the warm fingers continued to curl into her hair.

"Ah, fu—" she cried out when Artemis pressed into the sore spot. Jamie almost pushed the woman away; it was so painful.

"Shh," Artemis said in an annoyed tone. Jamie almost laughed at how similar she sounded to Alicaster.

Artemis pushed herself up higher, her chest almost pushing into Jamie's face. Jamie stopped breathing. Or at least, it felt like she had.

"Hurt." Fingers dug into her scalp. "Help."

Then, the strangest thing happened. Where the pain throbbed, a sudden heat pressed against it. The wet warmth came and went in soft and deliberate movements. Jamie hissed a little from the sensation but eventually that faded with each press of warmth. It took longer than it should have for Jamie to realise it was Artemis's tongue that she was feeling.

Just like a wolf.

A painful silence followed as Artemis, quite literally, licked her wounds until she was satisfied with what she had done. Only then did Artemis move away and lower herself back to the ground. When their eyes met, neither of them said a word.

Artemis was closer now. So close that Jamie could make out a small line of freckles around the bridge of her nose and the small scar at the edge of her lips. Just as closely as she had been watching Artemis, the wolf-woman seemed to have been watching her.

Cautious fingers moved towards Jamie's face. A soft touch grazed across Jamie's cheek, drawing a line from the top of her jaw down to her chin. Artemis's touch was so light, it was almost like Jamie was imagining it all. Her eyes went to the wild-woman's and found her gaze solely on her lips, entranced, as she began to draw her thumb against Jamie's lips. A blush had bloomed across Artemis's cheeks, and her own lips had parted in wonder.

Jamie desperately wanted to do something stupid. "Artemis, I—"

She had no idea how she was going to end that sentence, her ability to think failing when Artemis leant forward. Closing her eyes, Jamie waited for Artemis to make the first step. She felt her warm breath fall against her lips as gentle fingers danced up her cheek once more. Just as she felt the warm touch of Artemis press against her lips, a howl echoed into the air.

Artemis pulled away, forcing Jamie to open her eyes to face the wolf-woman who stared out of the cave in distress. Ignoring her pounding heart, Jamie followed her gaze and found the black-white wolf she had seen days ago at the cave's entrance.

She knew what was to come as the gentle hands that had been holding her fell away from her body. Those eyes turned back to her once again, the lightness that had been there now gone. "I go."

"I—" Jamie began with a shake in her voice. "I can come with you."

Artemis only shook her head. "Stay," she whispered. "No safe. Only I go."

Jamie felt the knot in her throat. A brush of fingers against her lips was the last thing she felt before she watched Artemis charge out from the cave, faster than expected, and run to her sister's side.

As Jamie watched them go, the guilty feeling built within her as she heard the voice in her head tell her what would happen next.

And I will follow.

Tracking Artemis and the wolf with her was not easy. She knew Artemis was fast. She had to be if she was running with wolves. It only now became clear at how much she'd been holding back when they were running together before.

Jamie only knew she was heading in the right direction based on two things. The first was that the river was the safest place for the wolves right now with the lack of traps and their ability to escape across it. The second was the discarded jumper that lay among an array of wolf paw prints, and a pair of human ones alongside them.

Jamie pushed forward, ignoring the protest of her legs. She set a mental reminder to go to the gym more when she got home.

It was as she moved through a thick grove of trees that she slowed down, catching sight of new wolf prints coming from all directions.

They're all heading one way. I must be close...

She kept close to the vegetation, concerned about being spotted. With the camera now hanging around her neck from its strap, she was ready to start filming the moment she caught sight of the pack.

After rounding a corner of trees, Jamie quickly threw herself backwards, ducking into the nearest bushes and switching on the camera.

A distance ahead by a rushing river, Jamie caught sight of the pack. She could only hope that being among the bushes, near the river, and smelling of Artemis would help keep her hidden. She wasn't far enough away for her liking, but that was a worry for later. She directed the camera lens ahead.

At the river's edge, Jamie counted ten wolves, all of different ages and fur colours. In the centre sat Artemis and the black-white wolf that had come to the cave for her, their heads lowered towards the pair at the front of the group. Jamie deduced from the way they held themselves above the rest that they were the leaders of the pack. That meant they were likely the parents of the younger members, if not the older ones also. One was a wolf of pure white and the other of black fur, which as Jamie observed their behaviours, felt fitting with their yin-yang balance.

The white-furred wolf stood above Artemis and the black-white-furred wolf beside her. It looked as if she was chastising them for something if her bared teeth meant anything.

Zooming her camera in, she watched as the white wolf lowered their head towards Artemis. From how far away Jamie was, she couldn't figure out what was passing between them. Was there an angry growl? A motherly yip? She had no idea.

To her surprise, Artemis leapt to her feet. With her height, she now towered over the white wolf who bared her teeth in rage. Jamie watched as Artemis's hands waved around, showing she was just as angry. Her anger had the other wolves, even the black-white at her side, backing away from her. Only the white-furred wolf didn't move.

Wait, Jamie thought as she zoomed the camera out. *Where's the black-furred—*

Jamie cried out in shock as something sharp latched onto her foot. She tried to kick it away, but its grip tightened to the point of pain as she was dragged free from the bushes and made to stare up at the sky above her.

Her foot was released, and Jamie quickly sat up ready to kick or run from whatever had grabbed her when she came face-to-face with the snarling muzzle of the black-furred wolf. His golden eyes stared into hers as he pulled back his lips to show his teeth.

Carefully, Jamie raised her hands in surrender, desperately hoping to show she wasn't a threat to the wolf. "Hey, boy, I— I'm sorry, I just…"

The wolf pounced.

34

ARTEMIS

Ronan is still missing, Fenris said to the pack, his voice holding the weight of what this meant. **We have returned here, the land to which he was born, to say our farewell.**

Artemis turned to Mai who, for much of their journey back from the cave, had kept silent. Her chest moved shakily as if she were holding back a mournful cry. Her head dropped down, unable to keep eye contact with anyone.

I do not believe it, Artemis thought. *Ronan is out there somewhere. I'm sure of it. He probably just cannot return yet. That must be it.*

It has always been our fear that, even when Mai and Artemis struck out to find him, that he had been lost to us. Yue's gaze crossed across all the wolves, her eyes pausing at Artemis for a moment before moving on. **It would be his wish for us to survive as a pack. That is why this is the last time we will return here.**

Artemis's heart froze in her chest. She knew they had intended to go to the land beyond the river while the human threat arose, but to never return? How could that be? They had a life here. Memories here. This had been her mother's territory since as long as Larka's line had existed.

How would Jamie find me if I leave this land? Artemis found herself wondering. The thought of losing her Oak again hurt as much, if not more, as the loss of her family's history.

You disagree, Artemis? Fenris asked, his words dripping in venom.

Lifting her head, she found the eyes of the pack on her as Fenris singled her out. **I just do not believe that, once all has passed with the humans, we cannot return home one day—**

Do not lie to me, Artemis. I can smell that human on you, Fenris snarled. **To think I trusted you to make the right choice and cut off this ... thing with the human.**

Fenris began to step toward her when something caught his attention. He snorted and walked away from Artemis. Yue stepped in front of her.

Bowing her head, she allowed Yue to stand tall above her. She was waiting for the verbal lashing that would come.

I know your feelings for this human have clouded your judgement, it is as clear in your eyes as it is in your scent, Yue said in a gentle voice. **Artemis, I beg of you to consider the safety of your family above all else.**

Mai spoke up in her defence. **Mother, please understand where she is coming from. You have not seen what I have—**

Hush, pup, Yue snapped. **I will speak with you about your treachery later.**

That was when Artemis broke. She could take the harsh words directed at her. She'd deserved as much. But she would not allow Mai – the one wolf who, like Kiba, understood what Jamie meant to her – to be insulted.

Artemis pushed herself to her feet. At her full height, she stood over Yue and scowled down at the she-wolf, uncaring of the sudden anxiety that she could feel among the pack at her actions.

I have long respected you, Mother Yue, and the way you have led this pack, but do not mistake my respect as blind obedience, Artemis snarled. **Mai has been nothing but loyal to this pack and to your leadership. How dare you question that. And how dare you question** *my* **loyalty to this family.** *The strength of the wolf is that of its pack* **is within my very bones. Yet the mere moment I find a bond with one who looks like me, you say I am disloyal?**

You know nothing of what she has done for me. Know nothing of the devotion and... Artemis stumbled on the next word. **...and the love she has shown me. Respectfully, Mother Yue, this is my pack but, maybe** – she swallowed – **maybe so is Oak.**

Yue turned away from her for a moment, Artemis believed she had made her understand.

Then why did she follow you? Yue asked. Artemis followed the wolf's gaze towards the distant bushes where, to the devastation of Artemis, she found Fenris dragging Jamie out from the vegetation.

Heart pounding in her chest, Artemis ran for dear life away from her pack and towards Fenris who, as he let go of Jamie's foot, lowered himself ready to pounce on his prey.

When Fenris leapt at Jamie, so did Artemis. Knocking him off course and to the ground, Artemis felt his teeth latch into her arm. A screaming howl of pain tore from her throat.

Artemis? He let go in surprise before his rage followed. His golden eyes narrowed on her. **How could—**

You will not hurt her, she growled out as she wrapped her limbs around his body and tightened her grip to keep him from moving. Artemis clenched her jaw as he began to thrash beneath her.

As he kicked, bit, scratched, and twisted within her grasp,

Artemis could sense the pack stirring behind her. They seemed unsure what to do if the tenseness in the air was anything to go by.

Turning to Jamie, the ache of betrayal in her chest as she caught sight of the black filming box around her neck, she screamed at her. "LEAVE!"

Jamie didn't move.

"Go!" she shouted.

Slowly and shakily, tears in her eyes, Jamie tried to speak. "Artemis, I— I'm sorr—"

"Go!" Artemis cried out. Her hold on Fenris began to loosen as he thrashed wildly in her grip. "Now!"

"Please … I had—"

Artemis's grip slipped on Fenris. He kicked his way out of her hold and went to charge at Jamie. He jumped at her once more, and Artemis threw herself on top of him, crushing him into the ground, burying his muzzle into the ground. She wrapped her arms around his neck and torso, holding on so tight that she could hear him struggling to catch his breath.

"Run!" she screamed.

Finally, Jamie listened. Running at full speed into the Forest, only looking back once until she disappeared from sight. It is only when she vanished and the rest of the pack appeared, their sights only on Artemis, did she let Fenris go.

You traitor! he choked out.

Artemis stood to her full height and drew her knife, ready to fight if she had to. She stared both Fenris and the rest of the pack down, her chest pounding from exhaustion. She could feel the trickle of blood from Fenris's claws across her body. Jamie may have betrayed her trust, but Artemis would not betray her.

Touch her, she said, enunciating every word, **and I will kill you.**

A heavy silence fell over the pack as they took in what Artemis had said and done. She could see now, for the first time, the mistrust of her humanity building behind their eyes. She couldn't blame them for it. Jamie had followed them because of her after all.

She had told me the humans were coming, a voice in her mind told her, *and had shown me everything that was putting us in danger. So, why would she follow me?* Artemis thought of the camera around her neck, and she wondered if maybe that had always been her purpose to Jamie. To film her and her family for a video – just like the video she had been shown of a destroyed Forest.

Enough. Mai stepped forward from the group and came to stand at Artemis's side. **Enough of this foolishness. We have larger problems to deal with than a ridiculous** – she turned to her father – **and prejudiced argument.**

Mai turned to Artemis, her soft eyes glancing only briefly at the knife in her hands before meeting her gaze. Artemis knew she should lower it, aware of how it looked to the pack, but there was part of her that felt that she couldn't.

We must go, Artemis, Mai said with a sigh. For one so young, she looked as if she had aged years since hearing of Ronan's loss. The she-wolf turned toward the other wolves. **We must all cross the river.**

Stepping towards the pack, Mai began to usher them forward. Any who refused to move faced the snap of her teeth until they did. Fenris was the last to go, his golden eyes glaring at Artemis until he turned away, running ahead to lead the pack.

Artemis watched him leave, only just catching the confused gaze of Yue who took up the rear of the wolves, until she too turned away. When the pack was out of sight, Artemis let her blade fall from her hand into the snow and allowed the burning tears that had formed trickle down her cheeks. She then collapsed to the ground.

Mai came to her side, her voice shaky and her breath coming

in short, sharp bursts. **We...** Her voice cracked. **We have only a moment before we too must go.**

Artemis leant forward and pressed her forehead into Mai's neck. Together, the two of them mourned over their own losses of what could have been.

35

JAMIE

Those heartbroken green eyes wouldn't leave her alone. They followed her as she limped all the way from the river, past the old Den, towards the split mountains, and back to camp. They stayed with her even as she broke down and cried.

Night had fallen by the time she made it into the camp. Only her dad remained outside, the fire roaring beside him as he wrote in his journal. He caught sight of her as she stumbled closer to the campsite. He let out a relieved breath of air before he saw the slight limp and her tears and came running to her side.

"Jamie, what happened?" he asked, his tone soothing in an attempt to calm her down as he looked her over. "Where's Artemis?"

A sob tore at her throat. Just hearing the name brought the thought of Artemis fighting with her pack to save her. Jamie couldn't even imagine what they could do to Artemis for that.

She threw herself into her dad's arms. "I fucked up, Dad."

His arms wrapped around her, and he tugged her close. He

let her sob into his chest as long as she needed. Not speaking until her cries began to peter out.

"Whatever it is that happened, you can fix it. I know you can." Jamie shook her head against his chest. "You came here to save Artemis, and yes, I know it was for the wolves too, but even you can't lie to yourself and say that Artemis wasn't the main priority for you. She always has been." He tugged her away from his chest to look into her eyes. "What reason could there be that would stop you from apologising?"

Jamie swallowed hard and turned away from his gaze. She'd done enough to disappoint him since they'd been here. She could hardly imagine his reaction to her breaking the one rule he'd set out for them. Again. He wanted her to be safe, and Jamie had ignored him every chance she had.

"What's going on?" A voice came from behind them. Both Jamie and her dad turned towards Ritchie who was rubbing the sleep from his eyes outside the tent. Ritchie, seeing the tears on her face, stepped forward in worry. "Hey, are you OK? What—"

"Congratulations." She stomped towards him and shoved the camera into his chest. "You've got the footage you wanted."

Blinking, Ritchie looked down at his camera and then back up at Jamie. "I don't understand." He looked around. "Where's—"

"Artemis is never coming back," Jamie snapped.

He frowned. "What?"

"You told me to film her and the pack." Her hands were shaking. "She had to attack her own family to save me from the leader because they found me filming them."

Ritchie's eyes went wide just as her dad's panicked voice came in to ask: "Did you get hurt?"

"That's not the point!" Jamie shouted. "You told me to film Artemis, and now I've lost her!"

"The hell I did," Ritchie snapped. "I said it'd be good to get footage if you could, but I never said you had to. I never *told* you to do anything."

"You said we needed it if we wanted—"

"No, we're not doing that." Ritchie stepped closer to her, his blazing eyes staring into hers. "Weren't you the one who said it'd be a bad idea? Sure, you may have said you'll see what you can do about it, but *you're* the one who would know what would be best."

"And you knew I knew, so why didn't you stop me taking your camera?" Jamie knew she was just pushing back for the sake of it now. But she couldn't stop herself.

Ritchie rolled his eyes. "Oh yes, because I'm responsible for all of your actions." Stepping away from Jamie, he drew his fingers through his hair in frustration. "I can't believe how ridiculous you're being right now."

"Ridiculous?!" Jamie let out in a borderline shriek.

"Yes, ridiculous!" he shouted back. "Tell me this, Jamie. If you knew even when I mentioned it that going to find the wolves was a bad idea, why did you do it? Did Artemis even know about the camera? Or that you were going to follow her?"

Her mind flashed to Artemis's final words before she'd run off with the wolf at the caves. "Stay," she'd whispered. "No safe. Only I go." And yet Jamie had ignored her. Ignored her knowledge of wolves and fear of people. Ignored her own comments to Ritchie about how it wouldn't be right to Artemis. Had ignored Artemis herself when she told her no.

Jamie had done this to Artemis. She had known the whole time that it would hurt her, but she'd done it anyway.

"She told me not to…" Jamie croaked out. "But I…"

Ritchie pulled her into his arms. She didn't deserve him as a best friend these days. His embrace was warm, gentle, and calming. At his soft touch, everything she'd been holding inside about everything that had happened spilled over the edge.

"I can't let them hurt her." Jamie sobbed into his chest. "I didn't think, I just, I just want to—"

She couldn't finish her sentence. Didn't even know how she would have. Jamie hadn't exactly thought through her decision to film Artemis and her pack. All she had thought about was how, in just two days' time, this whole forest and Artemis could be gone. She couldn't let them hurt her, and yet she'd caused enough hurt on her own.

"No one's going to hurt her," a different voice said. Ritchie and Jamie broke apart in surprise. Stood by the fire was Alicaster, her arms folded across her chest. "No one's going to hurt those wolves."

Alicaster turned to Jamie's dad. From how tall she stood and the intensity of her tone of voice, it was like she had become a drill sergeant overnight. A drill sergeant in pyjamas.

"William, get in contact with the Environmental Impact Agency again. Let them know about Ritchie's film, and have them organise a press release with it."

"I'll see if Professor Johnson is available," her dad said in reply. "He helped us over a decade ago with the first protection order. Maybe he'll have some contacts."

Alicaster nodded at him and turned to Ritchie. "Get that next film edited with this extra footage from Jamie and have it out within the next few hours."

"But that'll—"

A single glare was enough to silence his protests.

"On it."

Ritchie let Jamie go and went into the tent while her dad headed to the satellite phone. Jamie could hear the computer roaring to life inside the tent when Alicaster came towards her.

"There's two things I need from you, Jamie."

"What?" She sniffled.

"First, stop crying and pull yourself together."

Jamie deflated instantly. "Well, that wasn't called—"

"Second," Alicaster interrupted, "the moment the sun is up,

go find Artemis and apologise. I don't care if you have to get on your knees and beg her. When that drama's sorted, you need to convince her to listen to you. If we don't get them somewhere safe soon, they'll never make it out."

"But she—"

"Save me the young adult drama. You went behind her back to spy on her family. That is, without question, a dick move. But that doesn't mean she won't forgive you." She rested a hand on Jamie's shoulder. "Artemis knows you well enough to know that you wouldn't hurt her intentionally. Make your apology genuine, like I know it is, and she'll forgive you." With an about-turn that had Jamie wondering if Alicaster had actually been a sergeant in a previous life, she walked back to the tent. "Get on that tomorrow, and maybe we'll be able to save this place before they step foot on the mountainside."

Jamie nodded. Just as she was about to head to Ritchie's tent to apologise to him, she paused and turned back to Alicaster. "What are you going to do, professor?"

The woman smiled at her from over her shoulder. "Me? Well, I think the government could do with getting an earful. And who better than the Wicked Witch of the Department, hm?"

Alicaster disappeared into the girls tent without another word. Baffled, Jamie shook her head and went to join Ritchie in his tent. If they all worked together, like Alicaster said, maybe, just maybe, they could do something to save the forest.

When she sat by Ritchie's side, she glanced briefly over the footage he was examining. She had to look away at the sight of Artemis as the guilt of what she'd done filled her again. She wondered if what Alicaster had said about Artemis forgiving her was true.

I can only hope, Jamie thought as she watched Ritchie editing together the footage she'd captured, *that I can prove to Artemis that I deserve her forgiveness.*

36

ARTEMIS

Things were tense among the pack. This tension was only increased by their arrival among the Riverside wolves. Their pack may have known of Artemis, but they were not particularly comfortable around her. Hoping to ease their fears, Artemis had placed herself at a distance by resting against a solid oak tree by the riverside.

Did you see what she did to Fenris? she heard Nova growl in disgust.

All over a human, for shame, Taki replied.

Ignore them. Mai curled in closer to her. She was the only wolf who had refused to ice her out. **They will come to understand your reasons soon enough. You know as well as I that the elders are stubborn about change.**

Artemis didn't respond. Turning away from the glares of both the Riversiders and her own family, she stared across the rushing water and to their old land. She kept watching for a sign of brown hair and the sound of her name on Jamie's lips, but nothing came.

She laid her head back against a tree trunk. This side of the river was much denser in terms of its vegetation. Trees interlocked with each other, fighting for dominance to reach the sun, while bushes and vines covered what ground the trees had not taken. Where the pack now rested was filled with fallen trees that had been dug beneath to create sleeping space. This new land wasn't bad, but it wasn't home either.

Resting a hand against Mai's back, she let out a sigh. **I do not believe they ever will, Mai. I betrayed their trust with Oak. Just like Oak did with mine.**

Artemis had no idea how to feel about what happened. Unable to even comprehend the feeling of betrayal, let alone the other complicated feelings mixed with it. She didn't understand why Jamie did what she did. She had told her to stay, so why hadn't she listened?

What is done is done. Artemis closed her eyes. **They have a right to feel as they do.**

Mai snorted in disbelief and lifted her head from the ground. When Artemis didn't open her eyes, Mai scratched at her side with her claws.

Hey! Artemis shouted.

Stop sulking like a pup, Mai snorted. **You are worse than Kai on bath day.**

But—

Artemis. Mai sat up to be eye-level with her. **You have something so precious within your grasp. Yet you have allowed the judgement of this pack to decide what you can and cannot have. Why, if I knew where Ronan was, I would not waste time moping. I would go out and find him.**

But Ronan never betrayed you. Artemis turned towards the river once more. **She followed us to the pack to spy, Mai. How can I trust her?** She scrubbed at her face in frustration. **Besides, you were the one convinced she was working alongside the hunters. Why the sudden change of heart?**

Mai barked a laugh at the question, surprising the other wolves nearby who glanced over at them in confusion. **I believe you know exactly why. **You were there in the cave, were you not? Tell me what I saw there, what I *felt* there, was not exactly what I suspect it to be and I will let this go.**

Artemis went to retort back but found the words stuck in her throat as the memories washed over her. She could feel her heart pounding in her chest, and from the pricking of ears from the pack behind Mai, she knew the pack could hear it too. Even Fenris, who had refused to look at her since they arrived, had twisted his ears towards her.

That was— The memory of the brush of warm, dry lips against her own overwhelmed her. **I was ... it— it was just...**

What you are feeling – Mai lent forward and pressed her nose against Artemis's pounding heart – **is the pull of a soul.** When Mai pulled back, her bright-golden eyes found Artemis's.

Artemis swallowed and turned to the pack. She could see the surprise in each of their eyes as a murmur brewed among them. When she met Fenris's gaze, her worst fear was realised. Within those eyes, she could see the heartbreak at what Mai had just said. Artemis looked away. **You are wrong.**

Mai shook her head. **You know as well as I that I am not. The pull of a soul is one that cannot be stopped.** Her voice grew louder. **Nor should others attempt to stop it. Why do you think I haven't given up on Ronan? We are souls. Just like Larka and Echo or Rae and Kiba. You found your—**

No, Artemis said sharply as she pushed herself to her feet, forcing Mai to step backwards. **You are wrong. I have no soul.**

Every wolf—

I am no true wolf!

A hush fell over the pack. Even the pups who had been playing peacefully with each other stopped.

Yue stepped forward from the wolves and approached Artemis carefully. Her slow movements reminded Artemis of the way the pack would approach a frightened animal. Which, Artemis supposed, she was.

Artemis, collect yourself, Yue said coolly. **I know you are overwhelmed by this, but you are a member of this pack.**

No. She shook her head. **No, I never was.**

Please, listen to me, I— Artemis!

She couldn't take it anymore. She needed to get away from here. Needed to go somewhere alone. Artemis didn't even realise she was running until she felt the splash of the water beneath her as she leapt from one bank to the other, crashing heavily into the ground on the other side.

Breathing hard, she stared back across the river to see her pack on their feet, watching her. Only Mai was moving, making her way to the water's edge to follow after her. Artemis wouldn't stay for her to catch up.

Turning away from her pack, she was on her feet and running. Running as fast as she could. Her feet slapped against the ground in time with her pounding heart as she hoped against all hope that everything she was feeling would leave her.

She had no idea how long she had been running until, eventually, her legs gave out beneath her. As she hit the snow hard, the image of her pouncing atop Fenris, locking him in a vice grip, came back to her. Shaking her head, she tried to make it stop, but more flashes followed.

Fenris scratching and biting her as she held too tight. Jamie's tearful face as she ran away. The disappointment in Yue's eyes. How Jamie tried to explain but Artemis hadn't wanted to hear it. The disgust and anger of the pack. It was overwhelming.

Bent over in the snow, digging her head into the ground, trying to smother the images out of her skull, Artemis found herself unable to breathe.

The strength of the wolf is that of its pack, her mother had told her all those seasons ago, just before she had left to die because a beast that had come for Artemis got her instead.

I am no wolf, Artemis cried. *I do not deserve to be one.*

As her tears began to dry up, Artemis eventually lifted her

head from the ground. With a pitiful sniffle, she stared beyond the trees around her and up to the split mountain in the distance. That was where the monsters who came to hurt her family came from. Where her species belonged.

She took a shaky breath. The humans were here for her. It was time she went to meet them.

37

JAMIE

Jamie was startled awake by a horrifying feeling.

Pushing herself up from the floor, she found Ritchie still working beside her. He had the satellite computer on his work bench and was sharing the now-completed video.

"How long have I been out?"

"Only a few hours," he said distractedly. "You may want to stand up. Pretty sure you'll have a dead leg from sleeping like you did."

Jamie looked down at her crossed legs. She had no idea how she'd managed to comfortably sleep like that. When she untangled them, she felt the tingle in her legs spread all over.

"Did you get any sleep?" she asked him.

Ritchie turned towards her, his blood-shot eyes making his answer clear. "I had to finish the movie."

She made sure to not comment on his appearance. "Well, it's all done now, try and sleep."

"Mmm," he mumbled as he rubbed his eyes. "At least I won't have to hear you talking anymore. I feel sorry for Artemis with how much you talk."

"I don't talk in my—"

Ritchie dropped backwards and onto his sleeping bag. "Shh, Ritchie is sleeping."

With the roll of her eyes, Jamie left him to it. She had wanted to watch the movie, but she knew how Ritchie felt about having his laptop out of his sight. She'd wait till later when he was awake enough to agree.

"Alright, I'll leave you to rest."

Wobbling like Bambi on her numb legs, Jamie stumbled out of the tent and into her boots. Blinking at the sight of the rising sun, she came face-to-face with the sight of Alicaster cooking breakfast and her dad on the satellite phone.

"And I'm telling you the footage is up there." Her dad turned to her, seeking silent confirmation. She nodded. "Look at the page RitchieOnFilm, you'll see the two films there. It's enough evidence for the EIA to use to send out the word of what's coming." He paused as he listened to the person on the other side of the phone. He offered her a smile before focusing back on the call. "Yes, my daughter made contact with the feral woman. Fred, you have to see the severity of all this. A living, breathing feral woman and a thriving pack. We have—" He stopped talking and grit his teeth. Her dad had always hated being cut off. "You've got to be joking. They've seen the traps, haven't they? It's inhumane!"

Jamie watched her dad as he made his case with this Fred on the phone. It seemed like the man on the other end was sympathetic but didn't have the power. That didn't stop her dad from pushing back. Jamie had always loved seeing her dad's passion for his work. This just happened to feel more special because it was something he was doing with her. She was so enthralled that she didn't notice Alicaster beside her until a plate of food was placed in her lap.

"Eat." Alicaster sat down with her own food in the nearby

chair. "You've a long day of searching for that girlfriend of yours. You'll need your energy."

"She's not—"

"If you deny the facts, I will mark you down in my class."

"You already do!" Jamie argued back. Seeing her dad step away from them, she lowered her voice. "You've always marked me harshly in your class."

"No, I mark you fairly. Just as I do all my students. Besides, you still have the highest grade in the class even with my" – she put the next part in quotes – "*harsh* methods."

"Because it's my best subject," Jamie retorted.

"No, it became your best. Your knowledge on the history of human and animal interaction was basic at the start." Alicaster raised a hand when Jamie went to protest. "I admit that you knew more than your classmates, but it was still basic. What you know *now* is at a level - Why are we arguing about this?" Alicaster shook her head. "Eat. Dress. Go find Artemis. That's all you'll have to do."

"And if I can't find her?"

"Then I may have to fail you if you can't track a singular human," Alicaster said with a smile. "Especially one you're so closely bonded to and in a forest where no other people live."

Jamie closed her mouth, unable to think of a comeback. Annoyed, she went about eating her meal. Just as she'd finished her meal, the satellite phone went flying past her vision and into a pile of snow. Jamie turned to her furious-looking father. "What is it?" she asked.

"That was my friend with the EIA." Her dad rubbed at his tired eyes. "He's speaking to the governor. He's hoping that with Ritchie's video making the rounds, with its big viewer numbers will be enough to sway the officials to put in an injunction."

"And the bad news?"

He sighed, dropping his head. "The deforestation team's materials arrived today at the mountainside."

"But they were already a week early for work," Jamie exclaimed. "You said it's a grey area, right? Surely that means they have to wait for permission."

Her dad rubbed a hand down his face in irritation. "Sadly, like I said before, they've legally had the ability to do what they want whenever. Who knows, maybe that damn Cora woman signed a new contract to bring the time forward. We have no idea. All we do know is they're getting ready to work, and the EIA aren't moving fast enough to stop them."

Is Artemis OK? was the first thought that came to her. Artemis was still out there. Along with her pack. They were all in danger and had no idea. She needed to find Artemis, quickly. Even if she refused to listen, Jamie would find a way to get her to. There was no way she was risking the chance of Artemis getting hurt. But where to start? Maybe the cave? Or should she try the river again?

"Go."

Jamie came back to herself and turned to her dad, his keen eyes watching her with a look of understanding and respect. "What?"

"Go find her, Jamie-bear," he said. "I know that's all you can think about."

"Sorry, I didn't mean to—"

"We'll talk later, OK?" He rested his hand on her shoulder. "I think it may be time to have a proper father-daughter talk about your ... feelings." Jamie cringed a little, though she couldn't deny the warmth in her chest at hearing his willingness. They'd never talked about these things before. Sure, he knew she liked women. He just acted like he didn't. "For now though, go warn your girl."

"Dad, she's not—"

"You're as bad as your mother with these things." He smiled ruefully. "Stop arguing and go find her like I know you can." He went to walk away but stopped. "Oh, and take the flare gun with you again, OK? Just in case."

With a smile and a nod, Jamie leant forward and pressed a kiss to her dad's cheek. Her nose wrinkled a little at the scratch of the stubble when she did, but it was nice. "I'll be back soon."

He nodded and let her go. As Jamie headed out of the campgrounds with a pre-made backpack with supplies, courtesy of Alicaster, she could feel her dad's eyes on her as she went. Her dad believed she could find Artemis, and now, so did Jamie.

38

JAMIE

*E*verything was going terribly, and then she fell in a hole.

Jamie knew where to find the wolves this time. Knew exactly how to get there and how long it would take. The sun was beaming down on her from its peak in the sky, meaning it had been more than a few hours since she left camp. And she wasn't even halfway. In fact, she'd stopped moving altogether.

Jamie had stopped when she found herself at the old Den within the mountains. The last place she and Artemis had been before everything went wrong.

Artemis is out there somewhere, Jamie thought as she wiped the sweat from her forehead. *I just have to hope that she'll listen to me when I find her.*

Letting out a sigh, Jamie reached into her bag to grab her water bottle. She wasn't necessarily thirsty, but she was nervous. She hoped that a fresh drink would help her calm down. It was as she took that first sip that she felt it.

The ground beneath Jamie's feet shuddered violently. Pebbles clattered against the solid ground, the ripples within the stream went ballistic, and birds soared into the sky, screaming in warning. A boom of noise echoed around the forest, bouncing off every tree and mountain till it was heard all around.

Jamie felt her heart jump into her throat when she finally saw what had caused the explosion.

In the distance, between the split mountain, right where the grove would be, she could see smoke rising. It was as black as night and billowing into the sky. Even though she was nowhere near the smoke, it was as if she could taste the burning on her tongue. Rage bubbled in her stomach as the smoke spread out into the forest.

Their time was up. And Jamie was nowhere near Artemis and the wolves to tell them to flee and never return.

Turning away from the smoke, Jamie leapt over the stream and started to run. She still wasn't great at it, and there was no wolf-woman pulling her along or holding her backpack, but she kept going. Felt the burn in her calves as she pushed herself forward. All she had to do was go straight from here. If she kept at this pace, she'd get there before it was too late.

And then the ground beneath her gave way.

Jamie crashed, hard, into a muddy wall. She cried out in pain as she landed awkwardly on her foot. After the dust and snow wafted away, she realised the hole was not meant to hold a person. It was small and uncomfortable, which was why she'd managed to twinge the muscle in her foot. But she was able to see over the rim of the hole without issue.

"What the hell?" Jamie threw her backpack up onto the level ground and pulled herself out of the hole. She only fell back in a few times before she eventually rolled out.

Panting, she looked back at the split mountains where smoke was still travelling across the wind. *They couldn't ... surely they...* she thought, her mind running miles per second with theories. Explosions. New traps. Starting early. *They're coming in hot.*

Getting to her feet, Jamie began to speed-walk towards the river again, a little more carefully now. She was too nervous now to go at a full sprint in case she hurt herself more. She only stopped to pull out her hiking stick in case the holes weren't the only new traps in place.

"Couldn't be easy, could it?" Jamie muttered angrily.

It was as she passed a large oak tree that her newest problem arose.

SNAP.

Jamie froze. She couldn't risk another setback. When she didn't hear anything, she cautiously began to walk on, until she heard the whimpers.

"You don't have time, Jamie," she mumbled to herself as she stepped in the direction of the noise. "It could be a trap. Or another cougar who wants to eat you. It's a bad idea..." The whimpers continued. "Yeah, this is a bad idea."

Jamie headed towards the noise. As she got closer, she could hear the shake of metal alongside the groaning growls. She slowed down, not wanting to spook whatever was there.

She had just stepped into a clearing when a snarling wolf leapt at her, sending her toppling backwards and away from it.

"Holy Christ!" Jamie shouted as she rolled away from the creature's teeth.

In front of her, trapped in a metal vice chain attached to its back leg, was a grey-furred wolf with cool yellow eyes. His fur was sticking up on its end, while his tail curled beneath his body. His muzzle was frothing with saliva as he focused on Jamie. A deep, guttural growl came from within him as he paced awkwardly back and forth watching her, his trapped leg limping painfully as he walked.

Jamie could recognise the anxiety in the wolf easily. In an attempt to give him space, she went to slide backwards in the snow. Unfortunately, the slight movement was enough to send him into a frenzy.

The wolf jumped towards her again. To the surprise of them both, the vice on his leg tightened, leading the wolf to cry out in pain and collapse to the ground from the shock.

Tears pricked in Jamie's eyes at the noise. She went to push her hair out of her face but froze in place when that small movement had the wolf getting back to his feet, with a whimper, to growl at her.

"OK, boy, sorry, I'll stop moving." Jamie whispered in a calm and even voice. "How about you do the same, hm? Moving isn't going to make this any less painful."

The grey wolf snorted at her. She watched as he hobbled backwards towards the hook in the ground. His gaze never left her. Jamie noticed that the closer he got to the hook, the less strain on the tie around his leg there was. It just didn't loosen.

"That's good for now," Jamie continued. "I'm sorry you got caught in one of those awful traps. I know the feeling." She frowned. "Well, not the exact feeling. Falling in a hole isn't as bad as this." She met the wolf's eyes, which gained her a healthy growl. She dropped his gaze. "Fair enough. Probably wasn't my smartest idea coming to find you. Not that I'm not glad that I did, hopefully when you're a little calmer, I can help you out. I'm actually here to find someone."

Jamie looked into the wolf's eyes again. He didn't growl this time.

"Alright, progress, that's a good sign," Jamie said with a smile before continuing on. "Anyway, yeah, I'm looking for someone, a woman in particular." She paused. "Wow, if Ritchie was here, he'd definitely say something snarky like 'aren't we all?' but, well, maybe you are, never know. Sorry, back on topic. I'm looking for a woman, though I guess she's more than that. She's a wolf-woman and grew up with one of the packs here. Maybe you know her?"

The wolf said nothing. Probably because it's a wolf and

wolves don't talk. Instead, the ears atop his head flickered slightly, both turning towards Jamie, focusing in on her voice.

"Her name is Artemis, though I suppose her name sounds different in wolf. I really should have asked her to teach me how to say it. I taught her how to say mine in my language after all." Jamie shook her head. *Not the time.* The wolf moved backwards, unnerved by her movement, but he didn't growl. "She's with the pack by the river, previously in the caves. I … well, I royally screwed things up with her. You know how it is."

He snorted, which Jamie took as an agreement. Her talking seemed to be having an effect. His fur wasn't puffed up anymore, nor was his tail tucked between his legs. He still shook slightly from the anxiety, but it was better than before. It was his attention on her as she spoke that reminded Jamie of one of the nights she'd spent with Artemis.

They'd spent the day walking around the camp. Jamie was teaching her everything about their surroundings, and when they paused to sit against a nearby tree, she told Artemis more stories. It was as she told one about her mum meeting the wolves in the arctic that Artemis interjected.

"Curi-oos," she said in that croaky voice of hers.

Jamie frowned. "What do you mean?"

Instead of answering her question, Artemis slipped away from the tree to sit in front of her. She gestured for her to repeat the part of the story she'd just been telling.

"Mum said the wolves were anxious. They kept coming close to her and her team and then running backwards while crouched low to the ground. Each time, they flicked their ears every which way as Mum talked calmly to her team."

In front of her, Artemis mimicked the movement. She skittered backwards on all four legs, lowering her body close to the ground as she looked to and away from Jamie before coming closer to her and then moving away again.

"Curi-oos," she'd repeated. "Not ank-si-oos."

"Show me more," Jamie had asked, fascinated by the way Artemis moved. She'd been aware of how expressive Artemis had been, even when they were kids. There was an openness to how she interacted with the world around her, and Jamie knew that that came from the wolves. "I want to learn."

Artemis had smiled that bright smile and began to show her. That had gone on for hours, the two of them sharing what they knew with each other. They didn't even realise how long it had been until Jamie's dad was on the walkie calling for them to come back.

Maybe I can use this here... she thought, her eyes on the wolf who, the longer the silence went on, the more tense he seemed to get.

"Artemis has always meant a ridiculous amount to me, you know?" she continued on from where she'd finished before. "I met her for the first time when I was a kid and, well, it's been over a decade now and" – *time for the test*, she thought and lifted her hands from the ground to gesture to herself gently – "here I am."

Jamie paused for a moment. Waiting for a reaction. The wolf tensed. His fur puffed up and a small growl grew in his throat. When Jamie didn't move again, he eventually relaxed.

"The forest is in danger. Some bad people are coming to tear it down and take everyone in here down with it. It's why" – Jamie lowered her hands to the ground in front of her – "that trap is there around your leg. Those bad people put it there." Resting her weight onto her palms, she slowly moved to slide her legs beneath her. Her eyes never left the wolf. "It's why I came here, or at least, that's one of the reasons I'm here."

"I've been trying to deny it, you know?" She held herself in this all-fours crouched position. "Deny that the reason I came here was just for Artemis. I mean, of course it wasn't solely for her. A forest being destroyed because some ridiculous people hate wolves on principle just because they killed some of their sheep over a decade ago? Talk about a grudge."

Stretching herself out, Jamie lowered the top half of her body to the ground while raising her bottom half higher, just like Artemis had shown her.

"But I'd be lying still if I didn't admit that Artemis was the reason I looked into the forest. Artemis is the reason I'm here. Always has been. Hell, even if the forest wasn't in danger, I'm pretty sure I'd still have come." Jamie moved the smallest of movements to the side. A growl made her stop. "Things have changed though. Not in a bad way, nothing about Artemis could ever be bad. But the way I think about her … well, it's different from when I was a kid at least, but you don't need to know about this."

She stepped further forward, keeping her head down and, though the wolf hadn't growled at her, she moved herself backwards to show him she was able to respect boundaries.

"Anyway, things started to go further and, well, I wasn't able to deny what I was feeling anymore." Jamie began crawling. She intended to end up on the other side of the wolf to get closer to the trap. "Then I had to go and screw everything up by following her to film her pack. Big mistake."

Jamie moved closer to the wolf, shifting only an inch at a time. She glanced up briefly, only to find the wolf seemingly distracted. One of his ears was pointed towards her which, seeing as she was talking and moving, made sense. But the other was pointing behind him. It was twitching as if he could hear something.

Please God, don't be hunters, she thought. *Not now.* With the risk being an angry wolf or a dead wolf, Jamie pushed ahead with her plan slightly faster.

"I was on my way to find her to tell her that I was sorry and that it was a mistake." Another step. "Of course, those dickheads had to blow up the grove." Another step. "And then I fell in a hole." Another. "Then I found you." She lifted her head and the wolf growled. She lowered it. "Either way, I have to get to Artemis. I need to get her and her family out of here before it's too late." She stepped closer and, to her dismay, she felt the muscle in her calf twinge slightly. Jamie ignored it. "I'll apologise and hope that she can forgive me. But I'll understand if she doesn't. All I want is" – she felt the twinge in her thigh – "to get you all to safety—ahhh."

The muscle in her calf spasmed with a cramp. Hearing the warning snarl from the wolf, Jamie quickly rolled away. At a safe distance, she curled up into a ball as she grunted in pain.

"Sorry, boy," she grumbled as she tried to dispel the cramp. "This is what happens when you don't exercise enough. Sorry."

"Oak."

Jamie froze, the cramping muscle forgotten as she spun around to face the direction of the newcomer. She almost threw herself back into the path of the angry wolf in doing so. Thankfully he wasn't focusing on her anymore.

On the other side of the trapped wolf, emerging from the nearby trees, was Artemis. And she didn't look pleased. Looking from the wolf whose sole focus was now on her and then back to Jamie, those green eyes locked on her.

"Explain."

ARTEMIS

When Artemis had decided to hand herself over to the humans, she had hoped that would give her the chance to save her home and family. If the humans were only doing this because of her, maybe having her in their grasp would stop them. That was before she felt the quake beneath her paws.

Artemis watched as black smoke billowed into the sky, the sight of it reminding her of the terrifying sun's fever that had ravaged the Forest only a few seasons ago. As the smoke flew higher in the sky, she could hear the cries of the foxes, birds, and all other creatures within her home as they began to flee.

She was too late. Their attack had already begun.

Heart pounding in her chest, Artemis increased her speed and ran for the split mountain. She knew her family would have heard and felt the quake by now. If they hadn't already fled, they would have to now.

Artemis kept her steps light, barely brushing against the ground in case the hunters had returned to lay their monstrous traps once more. The few times she couldn't proceed with light steps, she would take to the trees, leaping as carefully as she could from branch to branch.

As she went, she saw the animals of the Forest running past her. Foxes, rabbits, badgers, and more ran in their family groups or alone towards the stretch of mountain to her left. They were all seeking an escape.

When Artemis came across a lone cougar in the trees, the two of them paused. The wolves and cougars had often picked fights within territories. Gold eyes met Artemis's green, and a quiet agreement was formed. They were all in danger, so as the Forest had always wanted, they bowed their heads and continued their own journey to safety.

They may be enemies, but Artemis would help save them too. She would save her home even if it cost her everything. This was the humans' doing. Only going towards them and surrendering would stop this. Maybe when this horror had passed, she could find her family again. Just as she always had.

Just as Jamie always finds you, a voice that sounded a lot like Mai said in her mind.

You're wrong, Artemis thought angrily in reply. *She only found me for her own gain. She is not worth thinking about.*

And yet she is, another voice said. A voice that sounded a lot like Kiba. *You just cannot deal with this fact yet.*

Ignoring the voices, she continued to power forward and towards the split mountains. The sooner she got there, the sooner the danger would stop.

Eventually, the terrain beneath her feet became harder. Small stones dotted the ground from the rockslides of the mountain, a few catching her back paws painfully. The ground also rose and fell unevenly from the shape of the mountain and trees colliding beneath the ground. She wasn't far away from the split now. Soon it would all be over and—

"...deny what I was feeling."

Artemis came to a halt. She knew that voice.

Stepping closer to its source, Artemis looked through a gap in the foliage and had to hold back a gasp at what she saw.

In front of her, his paw tied to a trap that had cut through his foot till it had bled down his fur, was Ronan. His ears twitched towards her, letting her know he knew she was there. All she had to do was get to him. Artemis was ready to burst through the bushes and rush to his side in relief and joy at seeing him alive when she appeared.

She lay crouched on all fours. Her head was held low and below Ronan's as she spoke in calming tones. Her movements were like a wolf while her voice was that of a human. It was strange to see her expressing two different kinds of language. Artemis had never seen Jamie like this before.

Artemis – Ronan turned to face her – **the human is no threat. You can engage.**

Meeting his golden-eyed gaze, she bowed her head and carefully approached them.

I will not attack the human, Ronan, she said quietly, awaiting his judgement. **You are trapped. Only she can help you.**

Can she be trusted? he asked.

It was a simple question, but Artemis wasn't sure how to answer. Thankfully she didn't have to ponder on it for too long when Jamie suddenly cried out in pain and rolled away from Ronan.

Artemis heard the apologies on Jamie's lips as she curled into a ball of pain. She didn't understand this girl. Here she was, helping a wolf she didn't know, and apologising for her mistakes. Yet only yesterday, she was betraying her trust just like all humans had. It didn't make sense. But for now, Artemis would have to ignore that feeling. She may still distrust Jamie, but Ronan needed her help.

We can for now, she said in reply to Ronan's question as she stepped through the bushes.

"Oak," she said aloud in her human tongue, surprising both Jamie and Ronan.

Jamie turned towards her. Her soft oak-coloured eyes were wide with surprise and a glimmer of something that Artemis didn't fully understand. She looked exhausted. Dark circles swallowed her eyes, and she was covered in sweat and grime. Whatever she had been doing had clearly been intense. And yet, she still looked beautiful.

"Explain."

"Artemis, I—" Jamie started to get to her feet. Ronan growled briefly until Artemis signalled him to calm. "I am so so—"

"Explain."

Jamie dropped her gaze, hurt. There was a part inside of Artemis that thought *good*, but it was squashed easily when those oak-coloured eyes looked back to her in earnest as she confirmed Artemis's worst fears.

"Humans are here," she said.

Artemis closed her eyes in dismay. She shouldn't have been surprised; she'd suspected as much after all. Even so, hearing it confirmed was enough to break her heart. Only a sliver of hope remained as she looked at Jamie who had come all this way to warn her.

"More," Artemis said.

"I came … to warn but—" She gestured to the smoke in the sky. "I was … late." Jamie went to move closer to Artemis, but Ronan growled in warning. "You must go. Take … pack and run." Jamie's eyes held hers tightly. "Don't come back."

What is it? Ronan asked, breaking the spell that was forming between her and Jamie.

Dropping Jamie's gaze, she moved to Ronan's side and crouched next to him. She could feel the anxiety pouring off him. **The humans have returned to the Forest,** she said honestly. Artemis couldn't lie to him. **She says we need to run.**

Why are they here? Ronan narrowed his gaze on Jamie. **And why is she here to warn us? Is it a tri—**

No, Artemis said sharply. No matter what Jamie had done to her, she had come to help. She was sure of it. **This human has shown me that she is on our side. Even if she has made mistakes along the way.**

I will take your word on her, elder, he said. **But I still do not know why they have come.**

Artemis, of course, knew that answer. She half questioned if she should tell Ronan. They'd never been close. He only seemingly tolerated her for the sake of Mai. He knew not to get on her bad side by being distant with Artemis.

Because they are after me. Artemis stared into his bright amber eyes. **They are after us because of me.**

Ronan was silent for a painfully long moment. Artemis was ready to take it all back when he spoke up. **We must get you and the pack to safety. We need to leave, now—** He let out a yelp of pain after he stepped forward.

Do not move, Artemis exclaimed, **I will get you—**

"Let me help."

Both Artemis and Ronan turned towards Jamie. She had lowered herself to the ground and held her hands up in surrender as she stared at them.

"I can remove it."

Ronan had given in easily about letting Jamie get near to him. His decision had been made for him when the smoke began billowing overhead.

Jamie, with Artemis's knife in hand, had been working on

the wire for some time. Artemis had heard her hissing every so often but couldn't look away from Ronan to check on her. He was skittish with Jamie being so close with a weapon that she had to hold him tight to stop him moving. Artemis tried not to let the images of her attack on Fenris slip into her mind as she did.

When Jamie reached a hand out to touch his leg, a snarl vibrated within him as he attempted to buck Artemis off. It was the one thing a wolf couldn't stand. A stranger being so close. She knew she had to calm him down to help Jamie get him free.

You can trust her, Ronan, she said quietly. **I know her well.**

Artemis could feel his eyes on her at this. She just wasn't brave enough to meet them. Instead, she watched as Jamie worked, her eyes crinkled slightly as she frowned deeply over what she was doing, occasionally flinching at something Artemis couldn't see.

Oak is the girl who saved me from the humans when I was young. She offered him a small smile. **I have spent the last few passes of the sun at her side and...** Artemis sighed. **I was hurt by her recently, but I am finding it difficult to still feel that hurt. I think...** She met Ronan's gaze. **I think it hurts more to not be around her.**

Ronan did not speak. It was rare that he did anyway. He'd always been the silent type. His words were not important; it was his actions that showed his thoughts. As Jamie worked to free his leg, Ronan stayed perfectly still. That was how Artemis knew he trusted in her.

"Done!"

The sudden voice from Jamie had both Artemis and Ronan jumping in place. Turning to look at Jamie, she saw her blood-soaked hands held up high in surrender again, the knife discarded in snow.

"He's free," Jamie said with a smile as she turned to Artemis. "Tell him he can try walking."

Artemis didn't have the chance; Ronan was already twisting himself out of her grasp and taking careful steps around her. He may be more relaxed with Jamie, but he still wanted a comfortable distance between them.

He turned his head to look at his leg and huffed in frustration. While he could walk on it with relative ease, the leg was cut up badly. Blood openly oozed from below his knee and down to his paw. Pieces of his fur had been ripped off and now lay in the bloody pile of loose wires.

It will take time, but I will be fine, he said as he turned to Jamie. In a move that surprised both women, he bowed his head to her.

"Says thank you." Artemis smiled.

Jamie grinned back and went to push herself up from the ground with her hands when she cried out in pain. She fell back to her knees and pulled her hands close to her chest, cradling them.

Ronan skittered backwards. **What is wrong?**

I think she is hurt, Artemis said as she walked towards the girl. "Jamie?"

"It's..." Jamie winced. "...I'm fin—"

"Lie."

Jamie exhaled shakily. "Yeah, I deserve that."

Artemis watched as Jamie uncradled her hands from her chest. When Artemis caught a look of her hands, she had to hold back a gasp of horror at her torn up palms. Blood coated her hands, dripping down her wrists and forearms in a gory picture. Multiple cuts criss-crossed each other, making the scene even more horrifying.

Gently reaching forward, she placed her hands underneath Jamie's. Unable to look away from the wounds, she asked in a shaky voice, "Why?"

"He ... free," Jamie said in a tight voice filled with pain. "Only way."

"But you—"

"I'll be fine," Jamie interrupted.

Artemis turned away from both the injured hands and Jamie. Only when a shaky finger drew across her cheek did she look back.

"I'm sorry, Artemis…" Tears formed in Jamie's eyes. "I'm sorry for—"

Artemis shook her head. She didn't need to hear the apology. Not because she didn't believe Jamie's words or because she had already forgiven her. No, it was because she was not sure she had even been angry at Jamie in the first place. Hearing her side would make what had to happen next complicated. And her pack didn't need complicated.

"No." Artemis pushed Jamie's hands towards her chest. She hoped that by keeping them close, they would be sheltered from the cold. Artemis knew too well how the cold could hurt more than the cuts themselves. "Look after self."

Artemis… Ronan said nervously. **Something is coming.**

"I—" Jamie started but stopped when Artemis raised a finger to her lips.

Artemis turned towards Ronan who was facing away from them. His ears were twitching in the direction of the nearby mountains. **What is it?**

Something … loud. A deep roar of a beast, just past the mountains. No. Ronan's ears flattened against his head. **There is more than one.** He turned to her. **And they are coming closer.**

Her heart pounded in her chest. *Jamie said the humans were coming, could this be them?*

"What does he hear?" Jamie asked in earnest.

Artemis didn't have the chance to answer when a terrifying roar shrieked into the air, echoing all around them. The ground beneath their feet vibrated from whatever was happening in the distance. New lines of smoke trailed into the sky.

Jamie's shaky intake of breath drew Artemis's attention. Her tanned cheeks had lost their colour. Her lips trembled, whether from the pain of her hands or from fear, she wasn't sure. Her eyes didn't look away from the smoke-covered sky as she whispered: "They've begun."

40

JAMIE

They'd run out of time, and Jamie was all out of options.

"I have to find my dad," she heard herself saying.

When Artemis turned to her, her green eyes frightened in a way that Jamie hadn't seen since they were children, there was a tug at her heart. She didn't want to leave her. But she had to give it one last shot at saving this forest. At saving Artemis.

Reaching forward with her hand again, even though it hurt, she pressed the back of her knuckles gently against Artemis's cheek, grateful that she let her do so even after what she did.

"Go to your family," she said tightly. "Get somewhere safe outside the forest. Cross the mountains if you have to. Just get out."

"You—"

"I'll find a way to give you time."

"Jamie…" Artemis's voice wobbled. "I—"

She leant forward and rested her forehead against Artemis's. It had become their thing when they were kids, and again after they'd reunited. It helped Jamie feel stronger, so she could only hope it'd do the same for Artemis.

"Go, Artemis," she said. "I'll be OK."

Artemis only hesitated a second. Only a nudge from the wolf at her side got her up and moving towards the bushes.

"Go," Jamie repeated. "Get to safety. Go."

It felt too much like what had happened only a day and a half ago, but this time the roles were reversed. Jamie shook her head trying to undo the image in her mind and watched as the two headed towards the very place Artemis had emerged from not long ago.

Jamie stood and prepared to leave when she found Artemis still at the bush line. "Artemis, don't worry. It'll be fine. I promis—"

A pair of soft, rough lips pressed against hers. Jamie felt as if the world had stopped moving at the feel of Artemis against her lips. Just as quickly as the kiss happened, it was over. And Artemis was gone.

Reinvigorated and pissed beyond belief about what Materia and the Talbot group were doing, Jamie stormed in the opposite direction of the two wolves and towards camp.

She had to get back and warn her dad. She just had to hope that he wouldn't stop her from what she had planned next.

IT DIDN'T TAKE LONG to get back. Though that could be the adrenaline stopping her from freaking out about the blood on her hands and the echoing noise of an explosion in her ears. When she stumbled into the open land of the camp, her dad was the first to see her and came running.

"Jamie, did you— oh, God, your hands." He took her hands roughly into his and called out to the others, "Alicaster, get the medical bag!"

"Dad, I'll be fine, we need—"

"Hush! Of course you aren't fine, your hands are cut up and

bleeding, what even—" He pressed gently at the edge of the wounds. "A wire trap?"

"You're scary good at that, Dad." She laughed before wincing as he removed his hand from hers. Alicaster appeared beside them with the first aid kit. "We don't have time for this. We have to go stop—"

"No, we are going to treat these hands," he said firmly. "I will not have you getting an infection when we're so far from a hospital."

"I'll go let the Environmental Impact Agency know what's happening," Alicaster said before running back to the tents.

Her dad ripped open the kit and began pulling out antiseptic wipes, wraps of bandage, and tape. He glanced up at her. "This is going to hurt like a bitch."

Jamie laughed nervously. "Wow, Dad, didn't know you had such a— AH!" she yelled as he brushed a wipe across one of her wounds. "Son of God, you could have warned me!"

"I did." He brushed the wipe across another line. "Now, tell me what happened."

"I seriously doubt— ah, you moth—" She smothered that particular curse word, though the little smirk on her dad's lips when she did was enough for her to want to say it anyway. "Not funny."

"No, not funny. It's just … well, you reminded me of your mother." He smiled slightly as he moved to her other hand, wincing when Jamie grunted in pain. "On one of our last trips together before she got sick, she got into a one-sided fight with a barbed wire fence. It was silly really; there was definitely a safer way to go about it, but things were going too slowly for her liking, and she knew that if that fence didn't come down soon, the bison that were being herded toward it by hunters would be trapped. So, she took the knife I gave you and started cutting the wires, cutting her hands up in the process on the barbs."

Jamie let out a small gasp of pain as he went over the last of the cuts, closing her eyes to hold back the cry. "You … you never told me that story," she gritted out.

Her dad sighed heavily, which had Jamie opening her eyes to look at him. He sprinkled the blood clotting powder on her hands before putting on the non-stick dressing. Only when he finished that did he start talking again.

"I should have talked about her more with you," he said as he began wrapping her left hand in bandage. "I told you when you were young that I would be more present with you. I promised that when I took the job at the school that I'd be better." He looked up to her as he smoothed out the padding. "I didn't really keep that promise, did I?"

"Dad, no, you…" She wasn't too sure what to say next. "You did the best you could, I know that. I never resented you for that. I do" – she winced as another dressing was put atop her other hand – "I do wish you'd been more open with me but" – she smiled awkwardly – "better late and in the middle of a forest than never."

He laughed loudly at that. It was as he began wrapping her other injured hand in bandage that he said something that surprised her.

"You're going to confront the demolition crew, aren't you?"

Jamie glanced at him, expecting a look of disappointment, but he was still focused on her hands.

"Well, I…" Jamie stuttered out, considering lying to him. She let out a sigh. "I have to do something, Dad. Artemis is still out there. I have to give her time to get her family out of here."

He tied the knot on the last of the bandage. "You never cease to amaze me, Jamie."

"Dad, what do you—"

"We'll talk when you get back." He brushed tears from his eyes.

"What about you guys?" She looked back at the camp behind

them where Alicaster and Ritchie were talking to each other. Ritchie's camera lay atop their fold-up table. "Will you come?"

She met her dad's gaze, and he smiled. "Oh, don't worry, we'll be there soon. Ritchie has something up his sleeve."

"Of course he does," Jamie laughed.

"Now go," her dad said with a nudge to her shoulder. "Go save the forest for your girl."

Without another glance at her dad and camp, she turned and ran. The smoke had risen higher in the sky now. She could still hear the rumbling of the machines all around her. They had come to destroy this forest for their own greed and vengeance, but Jamie wasn't going to let them.

You won't get this forest, Materia, Jamie thought to herself as her feet pounded against the solid ground beneath her. *Not while I'm here. Not ever.*

PART III

FOR THE BETTER

41

ARTEMIS

$\mathcal{A}$rtemis could feel the panic rising the closer she got to the river and the further she got from Jamie. She had no idea what Jamie was planning, but in her gut, she knew something was going to go wrong.

Concentrate, Artemis, Ronan barked at her from ahead, **not far now.**

She shook her head and carried on running after Ronan. His limp had become more pronounced the more they had run through the Forest, but he didn't complain. He never did.

The river appeared ahead of them and Artemis watched as Ronan leapt across the thinnest part between the banks. As Artemis jumped across the water after Ronan, she found herself being knocked heavily to the ground. An open-clawed paw pressed heavily down on her chest as teeth were bared in her face.

As quickly as the wolf was on top of her, they were dragged off by Ronan, who stood snarling in front of her. Sitting up, Artemis found the two of them surrounded by the growling faces of the River pack. She had thought it may have just been them retaliating for her actions, but she recognised some familiar faces.

Back off! Ronan snarled. **No one touches her.**

Ronan? a disbelieving voice said from within the ranks. Artemis knew it was Mai before she'd even appeared from the crowd, her golden eyes falling on Ronan as if he were the only one there. **You ... you are OK?**

I am. He bowed his head. **I am sorry to have worried you.**

Your leg! Mai exclaimed and rushed to his side. His injury looked worse after their run to get here. Blood matted his fur and trickled down the whole limb, staining the snow-covered grass. **How did this happen?**

I was caught in a trap, he said gently. He turned towards the other wolves and growled, anger flashing in his eyes. **I would have died there if it were not for Artemis...** His eyes fell on her. **...and her human.**

A hush fell over the wolves. They glanced between each other, unsure how to take in this new information. That was until Fenris stepped forward.

While we are all pleased to see you have survived, Ronan, Fenris began with a nod at the younger wolf. When he turned towards Artemis, he exposed his teeth. **You have missed much of what has happened with this traitor.** Artemis dropped her gaze. **After all you did to us, to _me_,** he snarled, digging his claws into the ground, **you dare to reconnect with this human? Have you not shamed us—**

Enough!

Fenris and Artemis turned towards Mai in surprise. Her maw was covered in blood from where she had been tending to Ronan's wound, and as she bared her teeth at her father, she made a ferocious sight.

This has gone far enough, Father, Mai snapped. **Your hatred of humans has turned you against your own. What does that say about you?**

She is right, Ronan continued, his words strong and commanding alongside Mai. **You have allowed this vendetta to spread without looking at the reality.** Ronan raised his injured back paw to show off his slashed-up leg. **The human you so dearly hate, the one who caused you to turn against Artemis, saved me from a trap that may have cost me my leg. Or even my life. Does that not show you that you may have been wrong about some of them?**

Fenris snorted in irritation. **But was it not humans that laid the trap?**

Not this human. Ronan looked briefly at Artemis. **Not Oak. She was the one to warn us about the others. It is why we are still here.** Ronan turned to Artemis properly, his eyes silently telling her to speak.

Taking a breath, Artemis stepped forward. **The humans from beyond the mountain are coming to destroy the Forest.** The wolves watched her silently. **You felt the shake beneath your paws, yes?** A few of them nodded. **That was only the beginning. Now they are to bring with them beasts that we have never seen before, that cannot be stopped.**

You have led them—

Fenris, silence! Yue snapped as she emerged from the crowd. **Listen to Artemis, and for once in your life, focus on what she is telling you.**

Artemis could see how badly Fenris wanted to push back. His golden eyes flickering from his soul's to her own in quick succession. Artemis knew he was conflicted, and she couldn't blame him. She still remembered how she held him down to save Jamie. It was no wonder he was fighting back so much.

Eventually, Fenris begrudgingly lowered his head to listen in silence.

Oak, the girl who saved me all those years ago, came here to save us, Artemis said in as loud a voice she could. **She took it too far, that cannot be denied, but that does not negate the**

fact that she warned us of the danger. Ronan saw the beasts at our borders and, just as Oak had set him free, the humans tore apart the grove between the mountains. Artemis turned to Fenris. **They are here.**

We have to run. Ronan stepped forward and raised his head. **Oak has told us that if we travel beyond this Forest, over the mountains we once lived in, and to the other side, we may just make it.**

Artemis held herself higher at Ronan's support and continued. **Oak has shown me time and time again that she will do whatever it takes to protect us. She risked her own safety to free Ronan, causing herself harm to do so.** Artemis's voice shook slightly. **Now she faces these beasts alone to give our pack time to get to safety. I trust in her, and so should we all.**

I trust in Oak, Ronan echoed.

I too trust in Oak's words, Mai stood tall at Ronan's side. **Poor judgement aside, she has shown to me that her love for the Forest and** – she paused for a moment – **and for the beings within it is true.**

Fenris did not speak. He barely even looked at them. The muscles in his back tensed and untensed as if he were holding himself back. He glanced at Artemis for only a moment before he turned to Yue and had that silent conversation only souls could have. After they were done, Fenris stepped back to observe. With a smile, Yue spoke. **What would you have us do?**

Both Ronan and Mai paused at that, turning to one another in mild confusion before looking back to the white wolf.

Us? Mai asked, tilting her head.

Yue snorted in amusement. **Look around you, my darling pup, the pack is with you both.**

Artemis saw what Yue meant. Unlike when they had arrived, the wolves that had once been aggressive had now become docile, their focus solely on Ronan and Mai. Waiting for their guidance. A small smile grew on her face. This moment reminded her of the day Rae accepted her role as leader.

There was only one thing missing.

Stepping past the two wolves, Artemis turned to face them. In unison with the pack, she bowed low to the ground in respect. She could feel a warm presence at her side when she did. Artemis made sure not to move as Fenris lowered himself beside her. She could feel his eyes on her, but she did not turn to meet them.

The strength of the wolf is that of its pack, Ronan said with only a hint of hesitation. **We stick together beyond here. No wolf shall be left behind.**

We will send a signal to the other packs and animals across the Forest and let them know what is coming, Mai said with the commanding tone she had always had. **Once that is done, we leave. Only when we receive the signal from Oak shall we return.**

Artemis frowned and lifted her head to look at Mai. **Oak did not mention a signal. How will we know to come back?**

Ronan stepped forward first and lapped his tongue against her cheek. With a small bow, he turned to the wolves and called for them to follow. All but Fenris did. Artemis could feel her old friend watching her.

What do you mean, Mai? Artemis got to her feet. **What is going on?**

Mai didn't get the chance to answer.

Join the others, Mai, Fenris said. **I believe it is time that Artemis and I talked.**

Artemis's heart thudded in her chest, and to her dismay, Mai didn't argue back. He was still her father after all. She only offered a look of sympathy before she ran off to join her pack.

Walk with me? Fenris asked though with how quickly he moved, it did not seem like much of a request.

Without a word, she came to his side. She made sure to keep a comfortable distance between them to not push past his limits.

They walked in silence alongside the riverbank for some time. Artemis knew they should get a move on with this conversation; they didn't have much time to waste. Yet, neither of them was willing to make the first move to speak. In their silence, a chorus of howls echoed around the Forest. The pack was signalling to the Forest the danger that was coming. It didn't take long for Artemis to hear the pounding of paws, the chorus of bird song, and the cries of despair as the animals of her home fled.

I do not understand your fascination with this human.

Artemis nearly jumped in surprise at Fenris's voice. She looked down to Fenris who was gazing across the river, his ears twitching this way and that as he listened to the chaos around them.

I am unsure if I will ever understand it, he said with a sigh. He glanced up to Artemis, and her heart almost broke seeing him. He looked … defeated. His once bright-golden eyes had dulled, and he no longer held himself high. **But I do understand you.**

What do you mean? she asked.

He turned away. **I smelt the fear on you the moment you arrived.**

Of course, our family is in danger—

No. Fenris shook his head. **This fear was different. You may feel anxiety for our family, but you feel it for your human...** He paused, unsure of what he was about to say. **For your Oak, as much as you do your pack.** He slowed to a stop. **You must go to her.**

Artemis held back tears. **You … you do not want me?**

That is not what I meant, and I know you know that. Fenris stepped closer to her and waited for her to crouch down so he could look her in the eye. **But you cannot come with us.**

Why?

He dropped her gaze. **Because I cannot let you hurt yourself any longer.**

I don't—

You must go to her, he said, firmly, turning back to her with a sad determination in his eyes. **It is what you need. It is what you deserve. No ultimatums. No hiding. You can go.**

Fenris, I—

Go and be safe. He stepped towards her, nuzzling her cheek. **Send us a sign when we can return. Though there will be distance, I swear we will not be apart again.** He pushed his paw against her chest. **Now go, go to ... go to your soul.**

Artemis was stunned. None of what Fenris was saying made sense. And yet it did at the same time. It is why she listened to him. She would help save their home. She would help save Jamie. She would make her family proud. As she got to her feet, she knew in her bones that she would see them again soon. There was no chance that she would ever be without her family again.

For now, as she leapt across the river just as she had the day before, her feet hitting the ground hard as she charged ahead, she had one thing on her mind:

Finding Jamie.

JAMIE

Jamie had absolutely no plan whatsoever. She'd put on a brave face for her dad back at the camp, but as she marched out towards the mountains, hands and wrists bandaged and anger in her bones, she realised how stupid of an idea this was.

The closer she got to the split mountain, the faster her breathing became until she was borderline hyperventilating.

Of course this is when I have a panic attack, Jamie thought incredulously as she straightened her shoulders and kept walking.

It was as she rounded an oak tree that she finally saw the grove of trees between the mountains, or at least what had once been the grove. Now all that was left was sawdust, cracked rocks, and layers of bark splinters from where the trees had been blown up.

In their place was a row of trucks in all sizes. Some were at work already. Two were tearing out the stumps of the trees while others lifted the fallen tree logs onto another truck for removal.

If Jamie had been angry before at the mere idea of what these people would be doing, now she was feral.

"Hey!" she shouted.

The grinding growl of the machines drowned her out and, from the looks of it, the nearest driver had his headphones in.

"Goddammit," Jamie muttered as she thought of a plan.

When she threw the stone at the truck window, she thought it was a great idea. It was small and wouldn't do any damage. It would just grab their attention. Then the stone went through the window that wasn't a window and hit the driver in the side of the head.

She could see him yell something but couldn't hear it over the machine. When he turned in the direction the stone came from, Jamie knew she was in trouble. This was confirmed when he pointed at her angrily.

"Crap."

He turned his truck off, climbed out, and dropped to the ground. Pulling out a clip-on radio, he sent a call out to his friends. Jamie watched as one by one they turned in her direction.

Only a few more turned off their machines. The two in the largest trucks, one of which was intended to dig up the ground, stayed inside with the engines still on. The rest headed for her.

"Uh … hi, guys, uh, sorry about the stone, I thought you had a window," Jamie stuttered out as four large men came towards her. "I just wanted to get your attention cause, you know, I'm here and you're breaking things. I don't want to die or anything."

The one she'd hit with the stone gave her an odd look, like he was trying to decipher if she were lying or just plain idiotic. Naturally, like every man who'd ever given her that expression, he decided on the latter.

"C'mon, love, this is a work site. Not exactly a safe location for you." He went to reach out to her, but she sidestepped his touch. He frowned in annoyance. "Look, let's get you back down to the town—"

"No," Jamie said quickly. "My … my family is still here. We're camping, you see. No one told us what was happening. We have all our supplies and everything. What are we going to do?"

"Yous were camping here?" he asked, baffled, and turned to the other men. As he spoke, he lifted up his hard hat to brush back his thinning brown hair. "We weren't told anyone was here, were we?"

One of the stump cutters rubbed the back of his neck. "Naw, Matty, I don't think…" He trailed off and stared at Jamie with a frown. Then a light of realisation bloomed in his eyes. "You're one of those environmentalist lot, aren't ya?"

"You can't destroy this forest," Jamie said, giving up the façade easily. "You weren't meant to be here for another week."

The men collectively laughed.

"Look, kid, I don't know what hippie bull you're into" – the stump cutter reached out to her grab her arm – "but we've got a job to do so—"

Jamie slapped it away. "Don't touch me. And you aren't touching this forest."

She turned and ran towards the nearest tree. Before the truckers even realised what she was doing and planning, she was already on the first tree branch. When they caught on, they came charging after her.

"Oi!" Matty yelled. "C'mon kid, we aren't pissin' about. Get down from there before we knock it down."

"Then enjoy prison, dickwad!" she yelled back as she awkwardly climbed.

Jamie had never been the best at things like this. The occasional hike and bike ride? That she could do. Climbing a tree, however? Near impossible. It definitely didn't help that a lot of her climbing was relying on the strength of her legs instead of her hands which, with the bandage, looked like giant cotton buds.

Her hope was just to get high enough to not be easily grabbed by the truckers, and seeing as they weren't even attempting to follow her up the tree, she took it as a victory. Until she heard Matty talking into the walkie talkie.

"Hey, Ralph, bring the digger over."

Shit.

"Look, hey, Matty, Matty, hey," she shouted, grabbing the man's attention from up in the tree. Stopping on the current branch, she sat down and held tightly onto the tree trunk. "Matty, I swear I'm not a hippie."

"Tree hugging would say otherwise, sweetheart."

"I'm a little low on options, so just listen, OK?" Jamie said irritably. "Look, this isn't just about the animals here, alright? If Materia didn't tell you we were here, then I bet they didn't tell you about the wild-woman who lives with the wolves?"

Matty and his men laughed at that. "Do you think we're eejits, love?" the stump cutter said, stepping forward. "This isn't Tarzan. People don't live in forests with animals."

"It's true! Artemis lives here with one of the multiple packs in this eight-thousand-acre wood. She's been here since she was a kid!" Jamie pointed one of her bandaged hands towards the town. "They even kidnapped her when she younger and practically experimented on her, I—"

"Knock it off, kid," Matty said as the digger drew closer. "This ain't the movies. Now get down."

"Wait, wait, wait," she cried. "We have footage. I can prove it."

"Look, lady," he shouted, his patience clearly having run out. "I'm not getting paid enough for this bull. Either you get down or we bring you down."

Jamie gulped. "Y-you can't do that."

"Don't say I didn't warn you," he yelled over the growling

machine as he and his team stepped back and to the sides of the digger. Jamie watched as it moved slowly towards the tree.

Jamie closed her eyes and clenched her thighs around the trunk, ready for impact. When nothing happened except the continued roar of the engine, Jamie opened her eyes and felt her stomach clench painfully as she took in the sight below her.

The digger had stopped only a few inches in front of the tree, but there was no longer a driver inside it. Instead, the group of men that had surrounded her were backing away incredulously from the brave and stupidly beautiful Artemis who stood in front of Jamie's tree, knife in hand.

"No one hurt Jamie."

ARTEMIS

There was a part of her that wanted to tear these humans limb from limb. It could be simple enough, a slash of her knife to their calves to disable, using their size against them to topple them to the ground. The only reason she didn't was because she thought Jamie may not appreciate it.

She'd arrived just as the men were nearing the tree with the machine, and the sight had filled her with rage. A rage that had consumed her. How dare they cause harm to her home. But when she heard a familiar deep voice yelling from within the branches, she was ready to kill.

"No one hurt Jamie."

The five male humans stumbled away from her and Jamie's tree, their eyes trained on the knife in her hand.

One of the men, a short, large male with a lack of hair, was the first to speak. His deep voice sounded scratchy to her ears as he stammered out something that didn't make sense.

Before she could even try to translate it in her mind, the men backed off and rushed towards their purring beasts. Artemis wanted to charge after them, but the roar from their monsters kept her from going.

Artemis didn't move from her spot in front of the tree until all the men and their humongous beasts had fled. She watched as they ran, the carcasses of the trees they had harmed being crushed underfoot as they went, cracking so loudly that it reminded Artemis of the sound the smoking sticks made.

Even though they were gone, Artemis knew this was not the last she would see of these men. No monster as deadly as them gave in so easily.

For now, she lowered her weapon and turned towards Jamie. Just as she was about to call out that it was safe, she found a pair of legs dangling in front of her face. Jamie had gotten herself stuck on the last branch; her large coat caught among the tree.

"May need—" Jamie grunted, "some— AH!"

Dropping the knife entirely, Artemis threw open her arms to grab Jamie as she suddenly slipped out of her coat and fell from the tree, but she didn't grab her in time. The two of them went crashing to the floor.

Artemis let out a mewl of pain from how hard she hit her back on the ground. Her inability to catch her breath wasn't helped by the fact Jamie had fallen on top of her. Thankfully, Jamie realised where she'd fallen and quickly sat up, allowing Artemis the chance to breathe.

Inhaling deeply, Artemis glanced up to check on Jamie. Her hair had gone wild, curled up in various positions and strewn across her face until she pushed it back. Her strangely covered hands, though uncomfortable looking, didn't seem to be causing her pain. Artemis also couldn't see any scratches on her, which had her sighing in relief. Her only concern was the dark half-moons beneath her eyes which made Jamie look tired, but that was something to think about later.

"Are you OK?" Jamie asked in concern. Artemis smiled in amusement seeing as she wasn't the one who had fallen out of the tree. Her smile only faltered when she heard: "...pack get out?"

Pushing herself up to a sitting position, she looked into Jamie's eyes and nodded. "They gone."

"Why..." Jamie started but didn't finish her question. She didn't need to. Artemis knew what she was asking.

She reached out gingerly with her own hand to brush a gentle touch against Jamie's cheek. "Be here."

Just like they had been in the cave not so long ago, the two of them seemed to be drawn into each other. Yet, just as before, it seemed fate was not on their side because Artemis heard a growling from behind.

Jamie's eyes flickered with fear as she looked over her shoulder to the mountains behind them. In an instant, Jamie was off her lap and on her feet. Artemis followed suit and grabbed her knife, turning to face whatever danger was coming. When she saw the red-furred figure in the distance, she almost dropped the blade.

"...behind me." Jamie tugged at her hand, but Artemis wouldn't move. Couldn't move.

Atop the growling beasts Jamie called "quad-byks" rode three monsters. At their sides ran multiple false wolves, who stared directly at Artemis, snarling.

Even with all this danger coming, there was only one that Artemis saw. In the centre of the group, a smile on her face, was the woman who had haunted her sleep ever since she'd returned to the Forest. She had prayed that she would never see those cold blue eyes again. Her prayers had not been answered.

Tall Fox looked older. The fox-red of her head fur had faded, streaked with arctic white, and her pale skin had creases across her face and hands. But her eyes were the same. Cruel and unforgiving.

Her gaze followed Artemis's every move, seeking out any imperfection to punish her for. It was like being back in the prison all over again. Artemis could feel her hands shaking, but she wouldn't give in. Not this time.

She raised the knife in her hand.

Sliding from the beast's back, Tall Fox bared her teeth. "Now, now," she said coldly. "We only … talk."

Over my dead body, Artemis snarled, gripping her knife tighter.

At her side, she saw Jamie step in line with Artemis and, though her hands were injured, she raised her bandaged fists in the air. Their threat was clear.

"Call … dogs, Cora." Jamie snapped. "You… not … Artemis."

Tall Fox, or "Cora" as it seemed she was known in the human tongue, laughed harshly. Her cool blue eyes turned on Jamie and she clicked her tongue.

One of the false wolves at her side charged forward, snapping its jaws in Jamie's direction. Artemis leapt in front of her and knocked the animal aside. The creature let out a whimper that sounded too much like one of the pups, but Artemis wouldn't let that deter her. She snarled at the false wolf and watched it return to its master with their tail between its legs.

"You … a lot of trouble." Cora sighed, massaging her temple. She turned to one of the men beside her and said something to him in a low voice. Artemis couldn't catch it, but as he headed back to the four-legged machine, she was sure she didn't like where this was going. "What am … with you?"

"Leave," Jamie yelled as she came to stand beside Artemis. Anger burned in her eyes as she stared down the woman in front of them. "Last chance."

Artemis watched as the man Cora had sent off returned. She noticed Jamie tensing beside her at the sight of a strange red box with an oddly shaped black head in the man's hands. Artemis could only guess it was trouble from her reaction.

"Leave," Artemis repeated Jamie's words in a clear and deliberate voice. "Artemis home here. You leave."

Cora smiled, and though she tried to fight it, a shiver of fear ran down Artemis's back. She knew what followed that smile. And it always hurt.

"You kept the name I gave you, how precious—"

"No!" Artemis snapped. "I gave me. Jamie gave me. You nothing."

That cruel smile turned into a baring of teeth as Cora took a step towards them, the false wolves at her heel following her. The two men with sun-coloured fur stepped away from her, though not in fear, but in a coordinated move. Artemis followed them with her eyes, but thankfully Jamie had it under control.

"Hey!" she yelled at them. "Don't … try it."

The men looked at each other before turning to Cora. Clearly she was the leader of this group. Fortunately, Cora wasn't paying any attention to them. Her focus was solely on Artemis.

"Let us see," Cora said, her voice dripping with venom as she reached for something behind her. "...remember this."

From behind her came a familiar pure black stick with a softened end. Artemis's heart began to pound in her chest. She remembered that stick. Remembered its weight against her hands when she ate her food the wrong way. Remembered the smack it made against the bars when she was being forced into isolation for acting out.

Artemis took a step backwards. She barely noticed Jamie beside her. All she wanted to do was run. Run as fast and as far away as she could from those blue eyes and that black stick.

The dogs growled at her, though their ears flickered briefly in the direction of the nearby tree-line, as if they were distracted. Artemis watched as the men returned back to Cora's side, ready to help her if the smirk on their faces was anything to go by. Artemis was going to end up in a cage once more.

Her breath came in short, sharp bursts as panic filled her.

I can't go back there … not again.

JAMIE

rtemis was spiralling. She could feel it.

From how her body shook and her legs tensed, Jamie could tell she was about to bolt. Artemis was, justifiably, terrified of Cora. But running wasn't an option.

When Jamie was trying to figure out how to calm Artemis down, she caught movement along the tree-line. And from the flickering ears of the menacing dogs at Cora's side, she knew she wasn't the only one who sensed another presence. They were just too focused on the task their master had given them to investigate it. It was a familiar flash of blonde that had her biting back a smile.

This is the moment, Jamie thought, as she stepped closer to Artemis and rested a hand on her lower back.

"Artemis," she whispered into her hair, keeping her lips hidden from view of Cora. "You never have to be afraid of her again. She can't hurt you. I won't let her. We're stronger together."

The wild-woman didn't respond. Only the tightening of her grip on her knife showed Jamie that she'd heard her. Or at least, that's what she hoped it meant.

Jamie turned towards Cora. "You had no right to Artemis then, and I sure as hell won't let you near her now," Jamie snapped loudly enough for her voice to carry across the clearing. She needed it to be clear. "What kind of a monster kidnaps a child?"

"Kidnapped her?" Cora's eye twitched. She didn't seem to like the idea of being called what she was. "I saved her! She's human. She belongs with us."

"This is her home," Jamie retorted. "You want to destroy her home because, what? You're mad your little experiment didn't work?" Her eyes darted to the blonde with the gasoline canister. "Pretty sure deliberately starting a forest fire is arson. Demolition order or not. I'd just *hate* for you to go to prison."

Both Cora and her dogs snarled in unison. Her pale face turned red with rage as she stepped towards them. "You insolent little—"

A knife landed in the snow by her foot. Cora jumped backwards in shock as one of her dogs yelped in pain, their hind leg lightly bleeding.

Artemis growled, "No hurt Jamie. No hurt Artemis. Go."

Cora looked down at the knife and then back to the two of them. Her eyes flashing in defiance. "Why should I?"

Jamie smiled. "Because we have something you don't."

"Really?" Cora snarked. "And what would that be?"

"Ritchie."

A crack of a twig nearby was enough for the smile on Jamie's face to become a full-on beam. She could see Artemis turn to the noise, surprise in her expression as the hidden figures stepped out from the trees.

Ritchie, her dad, and Alicaster appeared from the shadows. Ritchie had his camera pointed towards them. Alicaster was holding an insanely large microphone that was directed at them too. And her dad was throwing her a thumbs-up.

"Say hello to your global audience, Dr Evil," Ritchie said with a smile. "I'm sure they'll be interested to hear more about your ideas on *saving* Artemis."

"Probably the police too," Alicaster piped up. "You know, for kidnapping and child abuse."

"Ah, yes, can't forget them," Ritchie agreed.

Cora's face was quite the picture. Jamie was grateful Ritchie was still filming, she'd want to look back at her expression whenever she felt sad. With the mention of police, the two hunters at Cora's side stepped away from her. Loyalty only went so far, Jamie guessed. Even the dogs seemed unsure of what to do now. Only when the tallest blonde put down the gasoline canister did Jamie start to breathe a little easier.

"I think it's time you leave, Dr Marcus," her dad said, his voice holding a dangerous tone that Jamie had never heard from him before. "Unless you want your admission of a child endangerment and threat of physical assault to be blasted across the internet."

Cora clenched her jaw. "Playing the same games as always, Mr Gander-Yoon." She glanced at Artemis. "Unfortunately for you, you're out of Hail Marys. The forest is done for."

"We'll see," Jamie snapped back. "We're pretty persistent as you may remember." Her eyes fell to the gasoline tank once more. "And if we catch even a whiff of foul play, or I guess I should say, a whiff of smoke, none of you will ever see the light of day again. I'll make sure of it."

The red-headed woman didn't say another word; instead, with her men and dogs in tow, she left the forest the same way her truckers had done. No one from the group relaxed until they were sure she was gone. When minutes had passed, eventually the silence was broken by Ritchie.

"Can we get Artemis a shirt now?"

ARTEMIS STAYED CLOSE by her side all the way back to camp. She didn't seem able to admit it but, even after her bravery in the knife throwing, Cora had still frightened her. When they returned to the camp and sat around the relit fire, Jamie made sure to stay near Artemis as best she could.

"As much as I hate to admit it," her dad began, "that woman isn't wrong. We're out of Hail Marys. All we have left is the hope that the EIA or Ritchie's film made some kind of progress with persuading the governor."

"Yeah, how's that gone views-wise, by the way?" Jamie asked Ritchie who was sitting next to Artemis, showing her things on his computer.

"Oh yeah, pretty good actually," he said, shifting in his chair. "It managed to find the right demographic, I guess you'd say. They've been blowing it up since. Think last time I checked it was at one hundred thousand views. The comments we have been getting have been pretty positive, which is a good sign."

"And the government petition?"

He shook his head. "No-go unfortunately. Doesn't seem people are checking the description box after watching the video, so it hasn't gained many signatures to get a response."

"Crap." Jamie dropped back into her chair in frustration.

"It could be fine." Alicaster leant forward to rest her arms on her knees. "We're waiting to hear back from the EIA on their progress, so hopefully, with the social media thing and our video of Cora, we could have enough incentive."

"Yeah, because us showing the people of Materia's abusive behaviours did so much before."

"I know you're irritated, Jamie," Alicaster replied somewhat frustratedly. "But this is the best we can do. You've got Artemis here; the packs have been warned and are moved out. We've done what we can."

"This is Artemis's home, we can't just—"

A hand rested against her shoulder, cutting her off. Jamie found Artemis looking at her, her green eyes light and warm.

"You try good." Artemis offered her a light smile before turning to the others. She bowed her head. "Th-ANK you."

No one said anything in response. All either too stunned by Artemis's words or too taken aback by her kindness. Jamie couldn't stop looking at her.

"And with that..." Alicaster clapped her hands together, making Artemis flinch. "I think it is time to sleep. We can't do anything until tomorrow anyway."

"You're right." Her dad pushed himself up to his feet. "I may give a final call to Fred with the EIA before I settle in, but you're right, sleep will do us good." He went to head for his tent before pausing. "Jamie?" She turned to him. "Try not to worry too much in the meantime. We'll work something out."

Jamie offered him a weak smile in response.

As everyone headed towards their tents for the night, Artemis tugged at Jamie's coat to stop her. They were the only ones left outside.

"Are you OK?" She rested her bandaged hand atop Artemis's.

Artemis tilted her head, conflicted. "Will be."

"Can I do anything?" Jamie asked.

"Walk?" Artemis's voice was so quiet that for a second, Jamie thought she'd imagined her saying that.

"Of course," Jamie said with a gentle smile. "Anywhere you want to go?"

"Yes," Artemis said, though she didn't elaborate after that. With Artemis holding Jamie's wrist, they began walking.

They didn't go in any particular direction at first. Artemis took them to the nearby trees but instead of walking into them, they walked along the border. Jamie watched her as she stared into the growing darkness and wondered what she was searching for.

Jamie was unsure how long they had been walking, more focused on Artemis's face than the world around them that she didn't realise they had stopped until a hand tugged at her wrist.

Blinking, Jamie refocused and realised where they were.

"Oak."

A soft blush bloomed on her cheeks at the name. She'd never been able to look at that type of tree again without thinking about it. When she realised they were walking towards the giant oak tree, Jamie started to feel the flutter of butterflies in her stomach. Artemis pulled them to a stop in front of it and turned to face Jamie. The butterflies intensified.

"Are you feeling better after—" Jamie's words were cut off by the feel of fingers against her cheek.

Her lips stayed parted in an embarrassing O shape in her surprise. She shouldn't have been as taken aback as she was. It wasn't uncommon for Artemis to be touching her face. But there was something in those breath-taking eyes that held hers so intensely that had Jamie wondering if she could ever look away again.

"Th-ANK you," Artemis said carefully, sounding out her words. Jamie dared not speak in fear of interrupting whatever was coming next. "For ev-ry-thi-ng. You..." she frowned. "I..." Artemis shook her head in frustration.

"It's OK," Jamie said at the rising look of irritation on the woman's face. "I understand—"

Artemis moved closer. Jamie stopped talking altogether. She'd have forgotten how to breathe too if she weren't almost hyperventilating when Artemis reached up with her other hand and drew her fingers across her lips. Just like she had at the cave.

Jamie didn't move. Whatever happened next, it had to be Artemis's decision first. She stared intently into the green eyes in front of her and watched as Artemis leant in closer.

A shaky breath escaped her as Artemis paused just a hair's breadth away from her lips, waiting for Jamie's permission. She didn't hesitate to give it.

Then their lips came together.

45

ARTEMIS

*J*amie's lips were like nothing she had ever tasted. Everything that she felt was heightened. The heat of Jamie's arms against her neck, the pounding of her heartbeat against her chest. Jamie pulled her closer and Artemis moved with her. She didn't want any part of her body to not be touching Jamie.

Artemis had never felt need like this before. It was as if she had been running for miles. Her body thrummed with life, she struggled to catch her breath, and her legs felt weak beneath her. Artemis wondered if this was what being driven mad was like because when the two of them parted for breath, it wasn't long before their lips were on each other again. They were drawn to each other like a moth to light.

The moon had risen above them when they finally separated. Their breathing was heavy, and their chests heaved with the need to catch their breath. Artemis looked into the oak-coloured eyes of the woman she … well, she was not fully sure what she was feeling right now. Her mind would not slow down.

Jamie stared back at her, searching her eyes. "…you OK?"

Artemis didn't answer for some time. As her heartbeat finally slowed in her chest, her mind began to replay every moment they'd had since she fought the cougar to save Jamie all those suns ago. She reached up her hand to Jamie's cheek and brushed a stray piece of hair behind her ear.

I think I have found my soul, Artemis said in her own tongue. Jamie frowned at her words, so with a smile, she said: "Yes."

She pulled Jamie in for another kiss.

WHEN THE TWO of them finally returned to the camp, the moon was in the height of the sky. They ducked into their tent as quietly as could be and slept curled up together until Ritchie came to wake them with an obnoxious banging.

"Let's go, lesbians, let's go."

Artemis, sitting up groggily, had no idea what that word meant. She'd heard it a lot from Ritchie, but no one explained what the word was. Jamie seemed to know because she shouted back, "Shut up, Ritchie!"

The distinct laugh of the boy was all she got in response.

Eventually all that could be heard was the small pattering of conversation between the three humans outside the tent alongside the crackling of the fire. Artemis smiled. It reminded her of the soft buzz she would hear with the pack as the elders prepared for the day ahead and the pups lounged around until she forced them awake. She was considering sleeping in when a soft hand on her back ushered her up.

"Let's go," Jamie whispered, "...work to do."

Artemis didn't say anything in response. She didn't want to admit she was still afraid that Cora would come back. But Jamie always knew. Her hands were still wrapped in "bandage" as she'd called it, but that didn't stop her reaching out her hand for Artemis to hold.

Paw-in-hand, they left the tent and made their way to the others who sat eating. Ritchie offered them both a plate of food, and with only a pause to make sure Jamie could feed herself without help, Artemis tucked in.

As she ate, the elders spoke in deep tones. Artemis may be able to understand a little more of what they were saying, but she still didn't pick up everything. Every so often in the breaks of conversation, Jamie would lean over and quietly and concisely explain. That was why Artemis knew they were talking about how to save the Forest.

Listening to the four of them, part of Artemis felt useless at being unable to offer guidance or thought on how to help her own home. These people had come here to protect her, and she could do nothing to support them except offer her gratitude.

She squeezed Jamie's wrist for her attention, wanting to contribute something. When Jamie turned, Artemis opened her mouth to speak when a sudden bang echoed in the air around them, cutting her off. All of them were on their feet instantly. Artemis drew her weapon and stepped in front of Jamie, ready to fight.

Her eyes darted this way and that, seeking out any sign of what the noise was and where it was coming from. She could feel a hand on her back, but she couldn't be distracted right now. They were in danger.

Then a bright glow of red lit up the land around them, illuminating them in an eerie shadow that reminded Artemis of the blood-red sunrise they used to have before a storm. But the sun had already risen.

Artemis looked up into the sky and saw the image of a falling red spark that left a trail of smoke behind it.

Sun's fever. Artemis stepped backwards, nearly tripping

over Jamie's feet in her terrified state. She turned and grabbed Jamie's wrist. **Sun's fever. We have to go!**

Artemis had only seen the destruction of sun's fever once in the Forest. While it never reached her and the pack, she had seen the rising smoke in the distance and the screams of the animals that were caught up in it. When she and the pack eventually left the safety of the caves, all they had found were the remains of far too many creatures and trees to count. Artemis hadn't been able to get the smell out of her nose for an entire moon cycle.

She desperately cried out to her new pack, "Run. Not sayfe."

Artemis tugged at Jamie's hand to follow her. She even knocked over a chair in her haste as she searched for a way to safety. Only when Jamie pulled back against her touch did Artemis turn towards her.

"It's OK. Not bad." Jamie pointed to herself and then to the others. "....sign."

Artemis's heart was still racing. Jamie seemed to realise and came closer. Resting her covered hands against her cheeks, she stared into Artemis's eyes. "You're OK. The Forest is OK."

She could feel treacherous tears in her eyes as she glanced towards the red glow. "Forest OK?"

When Jamie nodded, she almost collapsed from relief. Thankfully, Jamie pulled her into her arms and held her for a moment. She whispered gently into her ear, "...go to it, OK?" Jamie pulled back. "Stay with me."

Artemis didn't respond. She just took Jamie's hand in hers and held on, ready to follow closely. The team headed out with Not So Angry Lady carrying a smoking stick in hand – "just in case," she'd said. Artemis stuck close to Jamie, practically becoming her shadow. She had no idea what it was they were going towards, but as long as she had Jamie nearby, she would be safe.

46

JAMIE

*J*amie could see how frightened Artemis was of the flare gun flash, though she was trying not to show it. Jamie watched her closely for any sign of fear or hesitation to make sure she could comfort her instantly.

As they all headed towards the falling red light, Jamie noticed Artemis place her hand in the pocket that held her knife. She may not be fully relaxed, but Jamie hoped her presence was enough to keep her from spiralling. It helped Jamie too, knowing that Artemis was close by. They didn't know what they were heading towards, but with Alicaster's gun and her dad's strength in verbal fights, they felt it was a risk worth taking to investigate.

Her dad had suggested that she and Artemis stay further back just in case Cora and her lackey's had returned. Jamie was not against this plan. She wouldn't let Artemis see that woman again unless she was behind bars. Jamie could hardly imagine the amount of trauma the supposed doctor had caused Artemis if one sighting of her could freeze her in fear.

As she thought on how to help Artemis through these traumatic experiences, a cruel voice in the back of her mind spoke to her.

What is the point in making her so dependent on you? You're just going to abandon her anyway when the job is done, the voice told her. *She'll be all alone, left to pick up the pieces without you.*

Much as she didn't want to admit it, this worry had been on her mind ever since she and Artemis had kissed last night. This morning, Jamie had woken up with her arms around Artemis, a sensation and warmth she never wanted to be without. Yet, sooner rather than later, she would be.

Artemis belonged here with her family. What could Jamie offer her? A university flat in a big city with a small, crappy forest about fifty miles away from her. What kind of life would that be for her? Jamie wondered about the possibility of living in the wild with Artemis. Though she'd probably have to get a log house to stay in, which would defeat the purpose of being with Artemis and the pack. Jamie shook her head.

Each new scenario Jamie tried to draw up in her head just ended in disappointment and someone resenting someone. It wasn't her choice anyway. Artemis had lived here her whole life in the forest. Knew only this world. Yes, they had kissed. Yes, they had become attached to each other. But like any romance, after being away from each other for a few weeks, they'd move on with their lives.

Jamie didn't even realise she'd become lost in her thoughts until she was being tugged sideways after nearly walking into a tree.

Turning towards Artemis who stared at her in worry, Jamie tried to dispel her concern with a smile. Artemis's all-knowing eyes bored deeply into hers, seeking the truth. Jamie had to look away.

Saying goodbye is going to be so much harder than I realised, she thought, her heart clenching at the mere idea.

They walked on in silence until the ground began to glow

bright red and all thoughts of the future flew out of her head. Looking up, Jamie realised they were at the split mountain. Remembering her dad's words, she quickly tugged Artemis to a stop. When the girl glanced at her, she signalled for them to duck behind one of the trees. Artemis followed her lead.

The appearance of the flare's glare hadn't just got Jamie moving; it had always ignited her dad's rage.

"Seriously, what kind of fool risks a potential fire by using a flare gun?" Jamie heard her dad snap, his anger having grown the longer they'd travelled.

Jamie leant out from around the tree at his tone. She wondered if maybe it was coupled with seeing this place again. The randomly abandoned trucks weren't exactly the happiest reminder of what they had failed to protect this natural world against.

She heard one such truck roaring to life and felt Artemis startle behind her. Jamie watched as it began to drag one of the fallen trees away. Anxiety over the return of Cora and her goonies seized her heart, until the truck revealed the commotion behind it.

In the opening between the mountains stood a large group of people. Most of them didn't look like truck drivers if their suits and out-of-place hardhats on their heads was anything to go by. As Jamie stepped out from behind the tree, Artemis followed her; she made her way towards the others carefully.

"They're moving out," Ritchie said in confusion as he held up his camera to film. "I wonder why."

Still unsure of Artemis's safety, Jamie kept her tucked behind her back. "Dad, do you know—"

Before she could finish her question, her dad was stepping towards the open field. He was squinting at the group of men in the centre who, unlike the suits and occasional drivers, looked eccentrically out of place if the brightly coloured sweater vests and suede jackets was anything to go by. It was in the snow, by their feet, did Jamie see the slowly dying-out flare.

Alicaster lowered her rifle. "William, is that who I think it is?"

"I…" He took another step. "I think it— Johnson! Professor Johnson?!"

One of the men in the centre turned in their direction, and almost instantly, he was waving at them.

"William! You saw the flare? Lovely!" Professor Johnson said with an almost mad-scientist-like grin as they approached. "I thought it may be a little dramatic, but seeing as we had no other way to reach you, this seemed the best option."

"We do have a satellite phone," Jamie said in frustration. The use of the flare had unnecessarily frightened Artemis.

"You do?" he replied in surprise. Turning to the men behind him, he said, "Did anyone know that?"

"Fred, you had been speaking to—"

"Ah, no matter, you're here!" He turned back to them with a smile. It seemed the professor was a little prone to falling into his own world, a little like her dad, Jamie thought. "Professor Johnson, at your service. Young Jamie here may remember me from the first try at gaining protection for Swen."

"That was you?" Jamie asked, trying to hide the surprise in her voice. It had been over ten years after all, but she didn't remember him being as eccentric. "I mean, lovely to see you again."

"Of course, of course. Things have changed. Last time you saw me, I was a government liaison. Now I'm an EIA consultant. Fresh air does a lot for a man." He took a deep breath suddenly, as if to emphasise his point.

"And this must be the famous Artemis!" Fred beamed and stepped towards the wolf-woman who growled at him. "Of course, boundaries. Understood. Big fan. I saw you on film, my dear. Quite the experience." He turned to Jamie. "You as well, dear. The journey you both went on, well, it was quite persuasive."

Jamie frowned. "The journey we went on? What do you—" The film. Ritchie's film. She turned towards Ritchie who, camera in hand pointed at her, slowly lowered it as he stepped back. "What did you post, Ritchie?"

"Something for the cause, that's all." He gulped. "We just needed to capture the right audience and, well, there was a lot of footage of you with Artemis, so you know, I went with the story…"

Ritchie was lucky they were with company, otherwise Jamie would have demanded a lot more information. For now, though, with Artemis at her side and a rather bizarre professor nearby, she bottled it up for later.

"We'll talk at the camp," she said and turned to the professor just as he began talking with her dad.

"You were right, William. The film had created enough of a discussion both domestically and internationally that the governor couldn't ignore it," he said, practically vibrating with excitement. "That's why I love the youth of today. They know how to get things done on the largest of scales."

To Jamie's surprise, Artemis stepped closer to the professor, as if wanting to investigate him. Jamie supposed his open body language and generally pleasant and expressive tone was enough to spark her interest. She was still on guard, her hand still by her pocket, but the camaraderie between the men here and Jamie's dad seemed to help ease her anxiety.

"What does 'the governor couldn't ignore it' mean, professor?" Jamie asked as she followed Artemis's movements.

"You've got yourself an injunction, Miss Gander-Yoon." He beamed. "Local government will be sitting next week to determine the permanent protection status of Swen Forest."

"How?" Alicaster said with a frown. "The petition we had on the government website had hardly any signatures."

"A new organisation came in with their own petition," Fred replied. "Practically identical in its messaging and call to action, but it used young Ritchie here's film as their advertisement. That seemed to do the trick."

Ritchie smiled wildly. "For real?"

"Real indeed." Fred nodded before running a hand through his hair. "Though they had a rather interesting organisation name. It took some convincing and a few thousand more signatures for the governor to accept it."

"What was the organisation?" Jamie asked curiously.

"I believe it was, the, uh" – there was a brief awkward pause from Fred – "the Lesbians for the Environment."

All Jamie could hear after that was Ritchie's hysterical laughter.

47

ARTEMIS

Artemis didn't understand much of what was happening. After Excited Male and his strange pack had left, she and hers returned to the camp. The last that she'd seen of the split mountains was the sight of men pulling out a line of silver material to stretch between the rocks. Jamie had called it a "fence". Artemis called it odd.

Everything was moving at lighting speed, even the way Elder Will and Not So Angry Female spoke. It was all rather over-whelming. Until Jamie laid a hand on her back.

"Walk?" Jamie asked, a gentle smile on her face.

Artemis nodded.

The two of them left the camp and headed towards their tree. Artemis couldn't help but let her heart flutter as she thought of last night. She reached up to brush her fingers over her lips before turning to Jamie.

That was when Jamie told her everything.

Artemis couldn't lie to herself and say she understood every word, her understanding of the language still needed work after all. But she understood enough.

Excited Man and his pack had come to help them. In a

week's time, they would find out if their hard work, as well as Ritchie's and the Lesbians', had worked. If it did, Artemis's home and her family would be safe forever. They would never have to worry about another Cora or cruel traps again.

"If we fail…" Jamie looked down at her newly bandaged hands. They were no longer huge puffs of white that covered her whole hand and made them difficult to hold, they were now a patchwork of small white pockets. Artemis reached out to touch them, but Jamie pulled away. "If we fail. You run."

Artemis frowned. "Run?"

Jamie nodded. "Find…family and stay away…. Safe away. Not safe here."

"How come back?" Artemis asked.

"If we fail," Jamie said quietly, "you don't."

Artemis shook her head. That was not an option she was willing to accept. "You signal. When sayfe, you signal." Artemis moved closer. "I teach you wolf to do."

Thankfully, Jamie hadn't opposed her decision. Even if she hadn't been thrilled at Artemis's refusal if the frown that formed between her eyes meant anything. Whatever the case, as they waited for answers, Artemis taught Jamie her tongue just as Jamie had done with hers.

The first thing Jamie learnt was Artemis's name.

Days passed as they worked together like this. Each of them sharing their language with the other to grow closer. Neither of them broached the subject of what would happen when this "guv-i-nor" Jamie talked about gave his answer on the Forest. Artemis especially didn't want to talk about it. The more she thought of the outcomes of the decision, the more unfair they seemed.

If her home was safe, Jamie would leave. If her home was not safe, Artemis would have to leave. Either way, they would be without each other once again.

While she knew the saving of the Forest was the only option

she could accept, the safety of her pack and home had to be won at all costs after all. When she looked at Jamie, she couldn't imagine a home without her.

On the fourth day of their wait, Artemis took Jamie further into the Forest and to her favourite bathing stream.

As she stripped off her layers, a smile slipping across her lips at the flush that spread across Jamie's cheeks as she did, she stepped into the cool water and released a breath of relief. It had been too long since she had been here. The world has been far too chaotic for her to gain a chance to find peace within the waters.

A wolf must always make time for peace, her mother had once told her. One of the last lessons she had given Artemis at the riverside. **Life can be a heavy burden, but if you find your peace, then you can finally live.**

Jamie's shriek of surprise drew her out of the memory, and she turned quickly to find the girl throwing her coat back on, shivering, after seemingly dipping a single foot into the water. Artemis threw her head back and laughed.

"Oh, shut up," Jamie said irritably, though the smile on her face told another story.

After Artemis had finished bathing and redressed, the two of them spent the rest of the day by the water.

Jamie told her stories about her home and what her life had been like before she came here. Most of it involved her talking about meeting Ritchie, which Artemis smiled about. She liked Ritchie. He made Jamie happy.

Artemis had told her about her mother, Larka. A fierce wolf who had taken her in as a child and fought to protect and love her till the end. She may not have been able to communicate all her love for her mother, but Jamie understood her enough.

"She'd be proud of you," Jamie said.

Artemis met Jamie's gaze, and the two of them fell into a calm silence. When her eyes dropped to Jamie's lips, she found herself wondering what it would be like to kiss them again. They hadn't kissed again since the night by the tree. There had been moments where they could have, but there was a part of Artemis that held her back from doing so. A part that told her that soon the two of them would have to say goodbye.

The red of the evening sky flickered above them, signalling to them both that it was time to head back.

As they began walking home, Jamie's hand holding hers, Artemis wondered how on Mother Wolf's Earth she would ever be able to say goodbye to the woman she loved.

JAMIE

One more night until they had their answer, and Jamie was restless. She'd attempted to read her book at one point after Alicaster had refused to let her go to check on the mountains with her. "You make me anxious just being around you these days," she'd said before dragging Ritchie with her. She'd given up on the story pretty quickly and had taken to watching Artemis and her dad play a game of catch.

Her dad had always been a sports fanatic. He didn't always have time to go to the local American football games, but when he could, he was there, screaming and cheering in the front row. He'd tried to get Jamie into it, but she was never a fan, though that didn't stop her from going to the games with him. It was one of the few times she got to have some alone time with her dad.

Luckily for him, Artemis was a natural athlete.

He was teaching her how to catch in a makeshift game. They were both sporting huge grins as they formed a scrum ... or huddle – Jamie could never remember the term – before the game started. Artemis went off running and, after catching a particularly long throw, she and her dad cheered loudly.

Jamie cheered and clapped for them both as they restarted the game. She cheered each time Artemis caught the ball, almost falling out of her chair when Artemis bounced off a nearby tree trunk to catch a particularly high throw. That was around the same time Alicaster and Ritchie appeared and clapped alongside Jamie.

"Yes, get it, Artemis!" she whooped as Ritchie dropped down in the chair beside her, exhausted.

As Artemis and her dad continued playing, she could feel Ritchie's eyes on her the whole time. Eventually she gave in and asked: "What?"

"You don't know what you're going to do, do you?" he asked quietly, leaning his arm on the armrest of the chair.

"Do about wha—"

"C'mon, Jay, this is me."

Jamie bit her tongue and turned away. Honestly, she'd hoped no one would ask her because, if she were honest, she had no idea. Stupidly she'd thought that a resolution to her problem would just fall into her lap. Of course, like most things, this wasn't a movie.

"Her pack is waiting for her. If we get the forest its protection, I'll help bring them back and" – Jamie could feel the knot in her throat – "and I'll let her live the life she's meant to with her family. This is where she belongs."

"And if she'd be happier with you?"

Jamie sighed and looked at Ritchie. "I can't have her leave everything she knows just for me."

"What if she was the one to choose?" he asked.

"Ritchie, we've been living in our own bubble here. The real world is far different from what she's experienced here with us. She'd hate it." Jamie heard her dad and Artemis cheering again at what she could guess was an excellent catch. "She'd hate me, eventually."

That was Jamie's biggest fear. Having the person she … well, she couldn't quite put it into words yet. But the thought of Artemis resenting or even hating her broke her at the mere idea.

"Alright, now I'm mad." Ritchie stood up and grabbed Jamie's arm. "Come with me."

"Ow, hey," Jamie whined as she was pulled towards the boys tent. "What is wrong with you?"

Ritchie let go when they were inside and reached for his laptop. "You need to get your head out of your arse and see what's right in front of you." The laptop slowly booted up. "I think you're ready to see this now. I probably should have shown you sooner, but I thought you'd figure it out yourself."

"What is it— wait, is this the film?"

"Yup." Ritchie opened his movie folders and scrolled down to the one labelled "Artemie" and clicked on it. "Now sit and watch. I'll be outside."

"Hold on, wait!"

He disappeared out the tent and zipped it up just as the film loaded. Jamie rolled her eyes but checked the length of the video for how long she'd have to watch. She nearly baulked at the thirty-minute length.

How have hundreds of thousands of people watched a thirty-minute animal documentary?

And then the film started. Right away there was Jamie, front and centre. She'd almost forgotten that Ritchie had interviewed her. Jamie didn't even remember what she'd been asked about until she heard herself talking.

"Swen Forest is home to multiple wolf packs that, as we have seen with such experiments like Yellowstone, have helped bring versatility and growth to the ecosystem here. However, what makes Swen special is that, among the wolves here, there is one pack that has a human woman living among them. Her name is Artemis. She's been here since she was a child and knows no other life than being with the wolves."

Film Jamie was rattling off a few more facts about the forest when Artemis came into focus. Artemis rested her hand on Jamie's shoulder, her voice quiet, almost nervous as she said her name aloud. Jamie remembered this moment fondly. Artemis had wanted her attention and, though she couldn't stop filming, Jamie hadn't let go of her hand.

To her surprise though, her voice faded out as the camera focused on Jamie and Artemis holding hands.

"I never knew much about the wild," Ritchie's voice said in the narration. "I only came on this journey because I knew how important it was to my best friend, Jamie. She and her dad, Dr William Gander-Yoon, have been passionate about saving animals from humans since … well, since forever, I'd say. But it was Jamie who brought us here. And it was Artemis who helped me understand why."

On the screen, Jamie watched as the footage she had recorded of herself and Artemis meeting properly for the first time came on. Jamie laughed slightly at the blur across Artemis's chest, until she heard herself speaking.

"Trap…" she said in a shakier voice than she remembered. "Trap everywhere."

Jamie remembered showing Artemis in movements the danger that was coming, but seeing it on film was different. The way Artemis reacted and the reappearance of the wolf when she made the wrong choice.

It was the moment after the she-wolf had left that had Jamie holding her breath. She watched as Artemis pressed a hand to her lips and ushered for her to speak again. The silence in the film, beyond the sounds of the birds in the trees, made the intensity of the moment come back to her. When she watched Artemis pull her into an embrace, Jamie felt the tears start to rise.

"Seeing Jamie and Artemis together, for the first time like this, helped me understand why Jamie was so determined," Ritchie said as the image of her and Artemis by the fire was shown. Jamie was talking while Artemis watched her, her eyes so intensely focused on Jamie that she felt herself shiver. "That's not to say Jamie wouldn't fight so hard for a forest regardless of her personal connection, but when it came to Artemis, I knew she'd do anything. The same could be said for Artemis."

The camera focused on a solo scene with Artemis, something Jamie didn't remember happening. Artemis was sitting in a chair, her knife in hand, and the knitted jumper hugging her in the best ways. She was smiling at the knife in her hand when Ritchie spoke.

"What does being in this forest mean to you?"

Artemis frowned slightly, seemingly processing and translating what Ritchie had asked her when she finally spoke.

"Home," she said before laying her hand on her throat, checking her words. "Home and Jamie."

Ritchie spoke again, sounding confused. "But Jamie doesn't live here with you?"

"Jamie always here." Artemis looked up at the camera and placed the hand with the knife towards her heart. "Got Artemis home. Gave safety." She wiggled the knife. "Never gone. Even when gone."

"What did it mean when you found her here again?"

There was a pause from Artemis as she glanced away from the camera, seemingly to something in the distance. Jamie heard her own voice calling out for Artemis.

The look on the woman's face at just hearing Jamie's voice was everything. The bright light in her eyes, the tensing of her muscles as she pushed herself to her feet and went running off to where Jamie was. The camera followed Artemis as she went. The moment wasn't like that scene in romantic movies when a partner jumps into the other's arms. There wasn't anything romantic about it. Yet Jamie remembered that day.

She'd come back from a long day of documenting and removing the traps and had found a young dead fox in one of them. It was heartbreaking to see. When she'd arrived at the camp, she'd only wanted to see Artemis, even if she didn't know why.

Artemis had come running, and as if sensing something off about her, she had come to a slow stop and carefully reached out to take her hand and held it in hers.

"You OK."

It hadn't been a question but a simple statement which had Jamie smiling, just as she was now, watching the footage on screen.

"Many would describe Artemis as an empath," Ritchie's voice came again. "Professor Katie Alicaster explained that, having grown up around wolves, Artemis would have become more attuned to a person's emotions through their body language and chemical scent." The scene focused on another moment of Artemis passing Jamie a slice of toast. Jamie didn't even remember that happening. "Now I'm not one to disagree with science or whatever, but when I see Artemis and Jamie together, I don't know if I'd call Artemis an empath. She's a wolf-girl who, human or animal, knows what they need. She's a wolf who just also happens to be a Jamie-path."

Jamie scoff-laughed. "So cheesy."

A collection of scenes played in front of her with ambient music playing behind them. It showed just her and Artemis. Whether it was them talking together, out exploring the forest, or even just playing games together. One scene was of Jamie teaching Artemis how to speak and, each time she succeeded, the elation on both of their faces as they drew closer and closer to one another was as clear as day. There was no denying the story in front of her.

It was when Jamie watched one video of both her and Artemis falling asleep against each other by the fireside, their hands entwined and Jamie's head tucked into Artemis's neck, did the tears freely start to flow down her cheeks.

"Jamie and Artemis have been apart for over a decade. What was a chance meeting as kids that saved a young wolf-girl's life led to a love of a forest that one of them had never been in. Yet, what brought them together again is not something to be celebrated." Ritchie spoke again, the images changing from the two women to the horrors they'd found in the forest. "Swen Forest is in danger of being destroyed. From animal traps that kill, to the threat of deforestation, and even the fear that the nearby people will kidnap Artemis." The human-sized cage came into focus with the dying wolf beside it. "Swen is in danger. And Jamie has come to its rescue."

Footage of Jamie staring out into the forest that was glowing white from the rising moon above. It was the first night that they arrived at Swen. She'd been taking a break from the camp set-up and found herself watching the moon above. Jamie had been thinking about how she'd never seen the moon look as clear before. She didn't know Ritchie had been filming her.

"Jamie came to this forest to protect it, just as she would for any forest," Ritchie said in voiceover. "The wolves here, among many of the other species of animal that live in Swen, have had a complicated history with the town of Materia. Just like Jamie. But it was Artemis who brought her back here, even if she isn't ready to admit that to herself."

Ritchie appeared on screen, his expression serious in a way that Jamie didn't often see. "Swen Forest needs your help. If you wish to help save the wolves, the wood, and especially Artemis, follow the link below to our petition for the governor to bring in an emergency injunction and give the forest an official and permanent protection status. Or you can email them through their website also linked below. The animals of Swen need you."

Ritchie's face faded and more footage appeared showing the wolves, the forest itself, and even a final image of Jamie and Artemis playing in the snow together.

"Jamie and Artemis need you. Thank you all for watching. #Artemieforever."

As the makeshift credits rolled, Jamie didn't turn it off. She could barely move. When the film eventually cut to black, and Ritchie's desktop screen reappeared, she blinked back into reality.

Her heart was racing as thoughts that she'd been trying desperately to hold back finally broke free.

Maybe there is a way to be together, a voice told her. A voice that sounded so much like her mother. *Don't give up hope, uli aegiya.*

And then they got the call.

ARTEMIS

The camp was alive with an electricity that would have made Artemis's fur stand on end – if she had fur, that is.

Elder Will had been speaking into this device named a "fone" when the atmosphere had changed. He'd barely put it down before he was shouting out to the others, ecstatic glee in his voice as everyone began to shout and cheer wildly.

Artemis made eye contact with Jamie who was being lifted into the air by Ritchie. When Jamie was finally set down on the ground again, she came rushing to Artemis's side. Those beautiful oak-coloured eyes looked deep into her own, and a smile spread across her face. "The Forest is safe."

Artemis's heart skipped a beat.

"Your family is sa—"

Jamie didn't finish her sentence as Artemis pulled her into her arms with such force that they nearly tumbled backwards. Tucking her face into the side of Jamie's head, her nose burying into her soft, pine-scented hair, Artemis took a shaky breath. Arms wrapped around her and pulled her closer.

Quietly, so quiet Artemis wasn't sure she was hearing it at

first, Jamie whispered words against her neck that made her heart swell.

"I've got you."

A tear slipped down her cheek.

AFTER THE EXCITEMENT OF THE "FONE" call, things progressed quickly. Artemis had asked after they had all calmed down when she could call her family home. Thankfully for her, she wouldn't have to wait long.

To her surprise, Elder Alicaster was the one who stepped forward to help. Artemis had always assumed that the older woman hadn't liked her. They'd never spent much time together and, when they had, it had been in silence. Yet, here they were, at the centre of the camp surrounded by a strange collection of equipment that Elder Alicaster was putting together.

As Artemis sat waiting for the elder to finish their work with what she had called a "specker", she found herself watching Jamie. Since the news, Jamie and her father had been working together closely. Artemis was thrilled to see the two of them together, remembering Elder Will's words of trying to reconnect.

Their bond is repairing, Artemis thought with a smile. Of course, the cruel voice in the back of her mind had to finish this happy image with something less so. *Just as your bond is breaking.*

Since their hug the day of the call, they had not been as close. Artemis had felt the tension in the air for some time. A foreboding feeling that everything was coming to an end. Artemis never liked endings. For something to end, it meant that there was nothing to follow.

Artemis felt relief at being able to bring her family back. She had felt like something was missing within her when they had been apart. She often found herself wondering how Mai and

Ronan were doing in leading the pack. Wondered what it would be like to follow their lead, to see the two of them in action when guiding a hunt. She even thought about what their pups may look like and what it would be like to help raise them as she had done so for Fenris and Yue for so many seasons.

But, whenever she thought of returning to her pack, her mind went to Jamie. How long would they have left once the pack returned? Would Jamie come visit her? Would she have to lose her again? Artemis's heart hurt at the mere thought of being without her.

I suppose this is what Kiba felt like after he lost Rae, she thought. Elder Alicaster gestured her towards the strange metal that she called a "mike". *Will I look as lost as he did when she leaves?*

Artemis released her howl into the mike, sending out her signal. **Safe. We are safe.**

She repeated it, once, twice, and a third time before stepping away from the machine and nodding her head towards the elder. With her job done, Artemis turned towards Jamie and found her sitting alone.

Heading her way, Artemis reached out to ask if she was OK when Jamie looked up. Artemis was sure her heart stopped beating right then as she took in the unshed tears that glowed in Jamie's eyes. Everything that Artemis had been feeling – grief, frustration, loss, love, longing – was reflected back to her in those beautiful oak-coloured eyes.

Artemis had no idea what to do. Her chest ached as if it were being pulled in two different directions. One towards her pack, the other to Jamie. She just needed a chance to figure out what that meant and what to do about it.

As if the Forest were playing a cruel trick on her, in the wind that whipped the tents and swayed the trees, a chorus of howls echoed across the camp. The sound was faint and distant, but Artemis could still understand them.

We are coming home.

"Was that…?" Jamie started to ask but was seemingly unable to finish.

Artemis turned away. "They come." She swallowed. "I … I go."

"Your family is safe." Artemis looked back to Jamie as she stood from her seat. She offered her a small smile. "Go to them."

Artemis wanted her to say more but nothing came. She didn't get the chance to ask her when Elder Alicaster was putting a hand on her shoulder, patting it in camaraderie. Artemis turned to find her newfound pack holding back tears of their own.

"…after your-shelf, OK?" Elder Alicaster said with a raised eyebrow.

Artemis nodded and mimicked her motion by patting Alicaster's shoulder in return. When Elder Will came, she should have expected the tight hug, but it still surprised her to find the older man holding her close.

"Find your hap-i-ness," he whispered to her, though she didn't understand what he meant.

Before he'd even stepped away, Ritchie was jumping in and lifting her high off the ground in a tight hug that was followed by spinning them in a circle. Putting her down, he grasped her shoulders and looked her straight in the eye. "…howl when back." He smiled. Ritchie lent in closer to say something only she could hear. "Speak … the heart."

Artemis frowned.

When she went to say goodbye to Jamie, she found that she had walked away from the camp, her big coat on and her hands in its pockets. She nodded her head towards the trees. "I'll walk you," she said.

There was no arguing from Artemis. Waving goodbye to the others, she jogged towards Jamie and followed her as she walked ahead and into the Forest. At first Artemis had been happy that Jamie was with her. They wouldn't have to say goodbye just yet. But as Jamie walked in sullen silence, Artemis started to feel worried.

There was little distance between them, their shoulders brushing against one another. Jamie had kept her hands in her pockets for a lot of this, seemingly lost in thought from the frown that formed between her eyes. Then, without any change in expression or movement, Artemis felt Jamie's fingers interlock with hers. She didn't make a big deal of it, not wanting to risk losing her touch.

They didn't look at one another as they walked. Artemis didn't trust herself to stop the tears if they made eye contact, and from the shaky breathing that came from Jamie, she figured the case was the same with her.

Artemis wanted to say something. Anything. But she was afraid. Afraid that she'd make things harder than they already were going to be. Afraid that she was wrong. Afraid that Mai had been wrong.

Why would Mother Wolf curse me to have a soul that couldn't stay with me? Artemis thought bitterly, her grip tightening on Jamie's hand so much that it made Jamie turn to look at her. Artemis wouldn't meet her gaze.

They were walking slowly. Their natural paces were much faster than this, but both of them were fighting against it. Almost walking as if they were injured which, Artemis supposed, they were in a way.

Another chorus of howls echoed in the wind. They were calling for Artemis to come home.

"… they say?" Jamie asked quietly.

Artemis looped her spare arm through Jamie's and pulled her closer. She didn't answer her question. Instead, she asked one. "I see you?"

Jamie glanced towards her in surprise. "I-I hope so," she said before a frown formed across her forehead. "I far away… be hard."

"Can I go see you?" Artemis had no idea how she'd be able to do it, but if she could find a way to see her Jamie in her world, she would. "I go see you too."

Jamie pulled them to a stop. For a beat, they stood in silence. Their hands still clasped together, and Artemis's arms locked around Jamie's. Oak-coloured eyes searched hers as if she were trying to find an answer for a question she hadn't asked.

Then Jamie was leaning in to kiss her. Artemis met her halfway, and just as they had by the oak tree, the whole world disappeared around them. Arms wrapped around her waist as she looped hers around Jamie's shoulders, pulling her closer.

Artemis could feel the tears on her lips as they kissed, but she couldn't tell whose tears they were. All she could focus on was Jamie.

It was all over far quicker than Artemis wanted, and as her eyes fluttered open, the wetness on them letting her know that the tears had been hers, she took in Jamie's own tear-streaked face.

"I'm sorry." Jamie reached up to cup Artemis's face. Then, in a language Artemis had never heard before, she said something that Artemis didn't understand. From the freely flowing tears that fell down Jamie's cheeks, she wondered if that was the intention.

As quick as the wind, Jamie turned and ran. Artemis watched her go, her eyes never leaving her until she was gone from sight. And just like Artemis had all those years ago when her Oak had helped her escape, Jamie didn't look back.

JAMIE

She was a coward.

The moment she kissed Artemis, she knew that was all she was going to end up being. She couldn't even work up the courage to say what she'd been feeling ever since the day Artemis had protected her from Mrs Hammond. Instead, she hid herself behind the protective layer of her mum's native language.

"I'm sorry," she'd told Artemis, unable to look away from her, as she held her face in her hands. "Saranghae."

Then she'd run away.

She didn't even look back, so afraid that if she did she'd just turn right around and beg Artemis to come with her.

Her tears eventually stopped, practically freezing to her face as she kept running, trying desperately to put as much space between herself and Artemis as she could. It was only when she saw the campsite in the distance that she came to a stop, unable to bear the idea of seeing anyone right now.

Sticking to the tree-line, she sank herself down into the snow and closed her eyes, trying to calm down her racing heart. But with her eyes closed, all she could see was Artemis.

Her smile, her eyes, the way she walked, the warmth of her embrace, how she looked at her. Jamie wanted to push all these thoughts away, but she couldn't. Not anymore.

She was in love with Artemis. Had been since the day they first met as kids, though she'd not understood the feeling until years later. And she'd denied it ever since. Only now could she admit it to herself, and it just made everything so much more painful. Something about Artemis had always drawn her in. It was like the Greek myth of finding your whole, but different. Jamie had always been whole, and Artemis wasn't her missing piece. Artemis was like the moon. Vital, important, and always with Jamie's Earth.

And always out of reach, Jamie thought, fighting back tears.

Jamie wasn't sure how long she sat there in the snow with her back resting against a tree. With the sunlight fading, she knew it had been longer than was healthy. Still, she didn't move. Her eyes stayed on the forest behind her.

A desperate and pathetic part of her prayed that, maybe, just maybe, Artemis would come running through the trees to be with her. As Jamie expected, the forest stayed still.

More time had passed when she felt the presence at her side. When a blanket was laid across her legs, she finally looked up to find her dad.

She burst into tears.

Pulled into the warmth of her dad's embrace, his arms around her shoulders, Jamie let it all out. She couldn't stop herself. Didn't want to. He kissed the top of her head and held her closer. Burying herself deeper into his chest, her tears soaking into his jumper, she let him be her rock.

"I've got you," he whispered into her hair. "I'm here. I'm here. I'm not going anywhere. I've got you."

Her throat hurt, her eyes stung from the tears, and she was shivering. Yet her dad didn't move them from the cold, letting her cry as he laid his hand on her back to pat her softly there, just like her mum used to. Only then did the tears slowly stop.

She may have stopped crying, but she wasn't ready to leave her dad's embrace. And he didn't seem like he was willing to let go of her either if the squeeze he gave her was anything to go by.

"You're OK, you'll be OK." He placed another kiss on the top of her head. "I'm sorry it didn't work out like you wanted. You'll be OK."

"I love her, Dad," Jamie said so quietly she wasn't sure he heard her.

"I know." He placed his chin on her head and continued to pat her back. "You know, your mother told me a story about wolves once. She'd watched this family of wolves, but particularly focused on this female wolf who randomly broke off from the pack one day."

Jamie pulled back from her dad's chest and looked up at him; she'd not heard this story before.

"Your mum was fascinated by the idea of following a lone wolf, so she did." He smiled lovingly at the memory, his blue eyes sparkling as he spoke of her mum. He always looked like that when he did. "She followed the female for miles and miles. Rested when she rested, ate when she ate. They were practically companions, even if the she-wolf didn't know your mother was there. Or acted like she didn't, you know how smart wolves are."

Jamie smiled and nodded, thinking of Artemis's awareness of her surroundings. She always knew whenever she was coming and would wait for her.

"Anyway, Seon-mi followed the wolf to this new pack. Now this pack, as your mum discovered, had recently lost one of their leaders. They were in a state of flux as they waited for the next leader to step forward." Her dad paused to wrap the blanket tightly around her. Jamie didn't even realise how much she was shivering.

"Your mum watched as this she-wolf studied the pack, trying to determine if they were friendly to her arrival, when a male wolf appeared. They almost broke out into a fight when he attempted to chase her off. Your mum said, 'And like any woman, she wasn't having any of his bullshit.' That seemed to impress the male wolf.

"For the next few days, your mum watched as the two wolves kept meeting with one another. The time apart from one another became shorter and shorter until, eventually, they couldn't be without each other." He laughed. "'They were smitten,' she said. The two went on to become the leaders of this pack, their bond the very thing that kept the pack strong. Your mum called them soulmates. Said that a bond that deep was something that could never be kept apart, even if the universe throws in a few roadblocks here and there." Her dad looked at her and smiled. "Do you understand?"

Jamie frowned. "It's a nice story, Dad, it is. You know I love hearing about Mum. But what does the story have to do with me?"

To her surprise, her dad rolled his eyes. "Ritchie was right when he said lesbians are oblivious."

"Hey!" Jamie said. "We were having a great father-daughter moment here, why are you—"

"You and Artemis found your way back to each other after thirteen years," he interrupted her, his voice earnest. "You kept finding ways to be with each other. Whether it be Artemis saving you from a cougar when she didn't even know who you were, or you running off more than once to find her and always managing it. No matter what happens, the universe will always bring you two back together."

Jamie looked away. "You don't know that."

"You're right, I don't," he agreed. "But your mum believed in these things, so I'm going to put faith in her and hope that the universe proves me right."

The two of them fell quiet. This had been the longest

they'd spent with each other in a long time, especially when it came to talking about Mum. It had taken thirteen years, but they were finally at a stage where they were open with each other.

"Do you..." Jamie began nervously. "Do you think Mum would have approved of me and Artemis? Or, you know, me being gay?"

She'd never broached this subject with her dad. It had been hard enough telling him when she was nineteen and gaining no reaction. But she'd always wondered, or in reality, always feared, that maybe her mum would have been disappointed in her too. Not that she believed her dad was disappointed in her now, she just knew who she was was not what he expected or planned for.

"Your mum loves you," her dad said, placing a hand on her shoulder. "You should never doubt that. Your mum loves you and would never love you any less." He sighed and looked away. "And she definitely would have had words with me about how I reacted. Or didn't react I suppose."

"Dad, it's OK—"

"No, it wasn't. But know this" – he turned back to her – "your mum and I love you. And we both love Artemis. You never have to get any permission or approval from us. Ever."

"God, don't make me cry again," Jamie laughed tearfully.

"Deal," he said as a tear trickled down his own cheek. "Now come on, my arse is frozen, and I bet you can't even feel yours."

Jamie tried to get to her feet but had to have her dad help due to her wobbly and numb legs. "You're right."

"Let's get to the fire," he said. "We'll figure out what to do tomorrow."

The two of them walked back towards the camp, the glow of the fire visible. Jamie could just make out the image of Ritchie and Alicaster by the flames and, in seeing them, she knew what she wanted.

"We should go home, Dad," she said quietly. "Artemis belongs here with her family. I won't take her away from it."

"But what if she wants to be?" he asked.

Jamie didn't answer, and her dad didn't push. As they arrived back at camp, Alicaster and Ritchie glanced her way. Thankfully they didn't question her appearance.

Situated in front of the fire, a flask of tea in hand given to her by Alicaster, one thought came to mind.

Tomorrow, I will call for her. If she comes, I'll know. If she doesn't, we'll go. She stared up to the starry night sky. *I hope you were right about the universe, Mum.*

ARTEMIS

Mai was the first to find her.

When Artemis had gone out to find her family, she hadn't exactly known where to look for them. Should she go to the Riverside wolves? Would they come back to the caves? She was figuring out where to go when Mai appeared.

Artemis! She jumped up at her and knocked her to the ground. **You are OK. I was so worried.**

Laughing, she pushed back at the she-wolf, starting a playful fight with her. **I am offended. Me? In danger? Never.**

Pushing Mai off her properly, Artemis looked up to find the rest of the pack filing into the grounds. A few seemed nervous around her, shame in their eyes when they glanced her way. Even Fenris couldn't look at her. She understood though. A lot had changed after all.

Only when the pups came running to her, their cries echoing around them as they jumped up in her lap, scratching and tugging at her hair, desperate for her attention, did the rest of the pack relax.

You were gone so long, Kai said with a whimper. **We missed you.**

Silly pup. She scratched behind his ear. **I always come home.**

Artemis schooled her features as best she could, trying not to let her pack know the pain in her heart. She was with them again. That was all that should matter. Leaning forward, she bumped her nose against Solar and playfully nipped at Rickon's ear before looking at Mai.

Where to? she asked.

Mai turned towards the mountains in the distance where the cave resided. **Home.**

SMELLS FUNNY, Solar said, her nose twitching as the pups ran into the cave. She sniffed at Artemis. **Smells like you but not you. Why? And why do you have a strange coat? You did not have it before. Why?**

Ronan barked a laugh beside her as he followed the pups in, knocking his side against Artemis in play. He'd never been this playful with Artemis before. It seemed leadership had brought out a new side in him, though if that side meant teasing Artemis, she wasn't sure she liked it.

Now, Solar, you know better than to ask personal questions, Yue said, stepping forward and tapping her nose against the pup. **Come now, time to sleep.**

But Elder Artemis—

Has other duties to attend to, Yue interrupted. **Off you go, I will be right with you.**

Artemis shot Yue a grateful look as the pups grumbled their way into the cave. Yue leant forward and pushed her forehead against Artemis's side. **I am glad you are here,** she said quietly. When she pulled back, her bright-golden eyes looked into

Artemis's with the wisdom of the years she had lived. **Know that we are always here with you.**

Artemis tilted her head. **What do you—**

Fenris is waiting for you by the stream. Yue gestured behind them. **He has much to tell you.**

Artemis watched in confusion as Yue turned away to join her pups and Ronan. Night may be fast approaching, but they had travelled far to return. They could return to sleeping during the day tomorrow.

As the other wolves filed into the cave, each one passing her with a tender touch to her side or bow of the head, Artemis started to get a strange feeling in the pit of her stomach.

Is something wrong? The last time the pack had acted this way towards her, overly affectionate and calming, she had been coming down with a terrible illness that ailed her for a full moon cycle. The only other time before that had been after her mother's death. And Artemis prayed that was not the reason for this behaviour.

Stepping out from the cave, Artemis looked down at the stream and found both Fenris and Mai at the bank in deep conversation. The two turned towards her as she made her approach. Artemis was too far away to hear what they had been saying, but from their body language, it seemed to be a delicate topic for Fenris with how low he held his head in comparison to Mai's raised stance.

She hadn't even made it to the stream when Mai left her father behind. Artemis stopped in place and dropped to a crouch as she came to her.

Thank you for believing in me, Mai said, surprising Artemis. **Now it is time to believe in yourself and choose. Think of yourself for once, do you understand?**

Not particularly, Artemis said bluntly.

Ha! Mai barked with laughter. **Sounds about right. Go on, Father is waiting for you. It is time you two talked.**

With that, Mai ran off towards the cave. Artemis watched her go and couldn't help but smile as she saw Ronan meet her at the cave entrance. The two shared a gentle touch of the head that reminded her of Rae and Kiba all those seasons ago.

And of Jamie and I, she thought but quickly shook her head free of the image. Turning away, she walked over to the stream and sat beside Fenris.

They sat in silence for some time – Artemis unsure if she should begin or if Fenris should. She followed his gaze to the darkening horizon in front of them, noticing the reflection of the half moon and stars twinkling in the stream. Artemis wondered if he was waiting for something, but when he continued to stare out towards the split mountains, Artemis finally spoke.

Yue said you wished to see me?

Did my father ever tell you the story about when he was in human territory?

Well, I wasn't expecting that, Artemis thought. **No, he did not.**

It was long before he met Mother. Fenris took a heavy breath. **He had been born among the domesticated wolves. His mother was a human pet while his father had been a roaming wolf who was later killed by the human whose pet he had impregnated. Kiba had been cast out by the human owner when he was a youngling. He would have died if the mother from his old pack had not found him and took him in.**

I never knew... Artemis said, ashamed that she had never asked Kiba.

Most do not. He only confided in me in the days leading up to his passing, Fenris said. **Father had said that he hoped my knowing of his heritage would help inform my leadership choices. He believed that his understanding of humans had helped him, and in turn, it would help me.**

You have been a strong leader, Fenris. Artemis reached out a hand to his side. **Do not ever doubt that.**

Yet, I have not made the best of choices when it comes to you.

Artemis frowned and turned to face him. **What do you mean?**

Since I was a pup, I have looked up to your strength, he continued, turning towards her at last. **Yet unlike your willingness to understand and love unconditionally, I have allowed my fear of losing you and our family to control me.**

Fenris, you cannot blame yourself, Artemis argued. **It was understandable for you—**

No. He shook his head. **I was blind to the reality. I can only hope you will forgive me for what I have done.**

Without question, Fenris. She leant forward to press her forehead against his. **You were always my favourite.**

Artemis heard the whines from the nearby pups which made both her and Fenris bark a laugh. The heavy air around them fading, Artemis tried to move them onto another topic.

How has it been? Relinquishing your leadership, she asked. **Have Mai and Ronan been doing well?**

The stress of protecting the pack is one thing. He glanced over his shoulder and towards the cave where Mai and the others were settling in to rest. **The stress as a father is an entirely different one, though I know she will make me proud as she always has.** Fenris faced Artemis. **She has become very protective of you, you know.**

Artemis smiled. **I know. She has been an incredible sister.**

She would be honoured to know that. Her protection of you could even rival that of my mother's, your sister, Rae. Fenris's ears flattened against his head as he looked towards the split mountains once more. **Mai has made me see the selfishness I have held when it came to you.**

You haven't been—

Yes, I have, he said, his tail flicking in frustration behind him. **For that I can only say I am sorry.**

Artemis rested her hand on his side in an attempt to draw his gaze towards her. **Fenris, I do not understand.**

I found my soul, as did Mai, Rae, and Larka. Golden eyes found and held hers with an intensity Artemis hadn't been expecting. She didn't look away. **Nature gives us all the chance to find the one that compliments us, that balances us in a world not often in balance. Yue is the moon to my Earth, and I could not be without her since the day I found her.**

As it should always be, Artemis replied in agreement.

And yet I tried to stop you from being with yours. His voice began to waver. **I shamed you, even harmed you, all because I feared what it meant. I have selfishly led you to losing your soul out of this sense of duty to our family. Burdening you to—**

This family has never, Artemis interrupted, her voice dangerously low, **and *will never* be a burden to me.**

Yet, you give up everything – your soul and the happiness you find with her – to be forever alone with us.

I will not be alone, she argued back. **I have my family, I have my duties, I have—**

You have love in your heart for your Oak.

Artemis froze. The words were out in the open now. The very words she had been too afraid to say out loud in fear of what they may do to her.

I love her. Tears began to spill down her cheeks as she knelt in front of Fenris, pressing her head into the soft mud beneath her. **I am so sorry. I did not mean—**

No, no, Artemis. Fenris leapt to his feet and used his head to lift her up from the ground. **This is not something to be sorry for. It is I who must be sorry.**

But I—

Love is a blessing, he said gently. **Whether it be my love for**

you, your love for my pups, or our joint love for Rae and Kiba. Love is something to never be ignored or forgotten.

Fenris, she is not from here, she cried. **What am I meant to do?**

The pup she had helped raise into the incredible leader he had been and the loving father he is smiled at her as he leant forward to press his forehead to hers.

You know.

A sob tore itself from her throat as Artemis wrapped her arms tightly around Fenris's neck. Tucking her head into his fur, she cried openly as he stood strong within her embrace without complaint. When he lowered his head to rest on her shoulder, she held on tighter.

I will wait till the morning, she whispered into his neck. **For now, I will be with my family.**

JAMIE

*J*amie woke up at the crack of dawn to the sound of an echoing drill. Jumping up in her sleeping bag, she reached for Artemis, only to find her no longer there. Ignoring the ache in her heart, Jamie rushed out of her tent to find out what was going on.

Outside, all three of her camp mates were dismantling the site. Ritchie muttered under his breath as he worked to unpeg the boys tent while Alicaster put the repacked bags on the sled. When she found the source of her noise, her dad with an electric drill, she went to the firepit to see if he wanted help.

He looked up at her from his place in the snow and offered her a smile. "Sorry, Jamie-bear, didn't mean to wake you."

"It's okay, I'd just forgotten this was our last day, that's all." With a frown, her dad got to his feet, concern written all over his face. "I'll pack away my stuff for the sled," she said quickly, ducking back into the tent before he could say anything.

Taking a deep, shaky breath, Jamie began to pack away her belongings. As she grabbed her clothes, she came across the jumper she had given Artemis after the confrontation at the mountains. Jamie didn't pack it. Couldn't. Instead, she wrapped it around her waist.

All packed, she left the tent and took her case to Alicaster and the sled. As if the woman had been expecting her, she was leaning against the quadbike by the sled, watching her approach.

"Have you packed the microphone and speaker yet? I, uhm" – Jamie rubbed at her neck – "I may need them."

"I'd hoped you'd come and ask for it." Alicaster grabbed the strap of a big, black bag and passed it to Jamie. "Your father is great at motivational speeches, and Ritchie is good for teasing you into acting, but I was prepared to threaten you with a failing grade if you didn't get your act together."

Jamie couldn't stop the laugh that slipped past her lips. "Thanks, Alicaster," she said with a smile. "Maybe you can get me an interview for that internship with you—"

"Oh, God no, we can never work together again." Alicaster mounted the bags onto the sled. "There's only so much drama I can take."

Dismissed with the wave of a hand, Jamie left the woman to her work and headed back to help pack up the rest of the camp. They had a few hours before the EIA would begin securing the forest with new fences. They were even going to install cameras so they could keep an eye on the animals within and make sure no one from Materia trespasses. Her dad had heard from Fred last night, not long after she'd left with Artemis, and he had let him know the plan.

It was a comfort to Jamie to know that, even if Artemis didn't respond to her call, she and her family would be kept safe. She'd maybe see her on the video feeds sometime if she wasn't able to travel back to visit.

I wonder if I could get a grant or something to be an ambassador for Swen? Jamie thought as she worked to pack up the girls tent. *That sounds like a thing ... or I could make it a thing.*

It took an hour before the whole camp had been broken down and piled onto the sled or into the backpacks they'd be carrying. It had been sad to see the place they'd been calling home this last month returned to its natural state. Or natural enough, minus the dead grass where their tents had been.

"The forest will regrow quickly enough," her dad had said when he caught her staring. "It'll be OK."

Jamie just nodded as she slung her bag onto her back and the microphone around her shoulders.

"Let's head out, team." Alicaster grabbed hold of one of the ropes for the sled. "Grab a rein." She gestured to Jamie's still-bandaged hands. "Or in your case, wrap one around your waist; this sleigh isn't going to pull itself."

"Wait," Ritchie said, his voice going high. "We're going to have to pull this ourselves? There's, like, a team of people coming," Ritchie pointed out. "Couldn't they loan us a second quad bike or something?"

"The EIA won't be here for" – her dad looked at his watch – "another few hours. A little after midday is when they're due to arrive. Unless you want to wait here in the cold till then, we'll get moving."

Ritchie looked up to the sky and sighed. "This is what I get for helping lesbians."

"Hey!" Jamie said, smacking his arm playfully. "What happened to the gay/bi solidarity, hm?"

He picked up a rein and pulled it over his back, sending her a gentle glare. "It ended the moment I put this on."

Jamie threw her head back and laughed.

JAMIE HAD MADE her dad and Alicaster go on ahead on the quad bike together. Her dad may still be strong, but at his age, Jamie would rather he wasn't overexerting himself unnecessarily.

She'd helped justify her reasoning by saying the sooner they got to the mountains, the sooner he could call and check in with Fred and their car. Jamie had a bad feeling it had been vandalised since they'd been in. Ritchie had pitched in to say they'd need petrol and a quick drive around to get it working after a month of inactivity. Thankfully, her dad hadn't protested after that.

That had been an hour ago, and she and Ritchie had been making slow progress ever since. Some of that was intentional, and the other part was Ritchie's constant moaning.

"Why is it that when you're being a good daughter, I'm the one who suffers?" he asked in a breathless voice.

"Because friends stick together," she replied.

"We aren't friends anymore."

Jamie laughed. "I'll remember that next time I'm getting milkshakes."

"We're friends again when you get them," Ritchie said matter-of-factly. "But when it comes to physical adventures – get your head out the gutter," he said at her quiet giggle, "count me OUT."

"Deal," Jamie said. "Now pull this sleigh, not long now."

"You said that an hour ago!"

An hour after that, the two of them collapsed into the snow by the mountain in exhaustion. Jamie rolled over to stare up at the sky and managed to catch sight of the partially constructed fence from the other week. She smiled at the image of a proper fence in its place to keep the forest safe.

"I think I may actually be dead," Ritchie said into the snow he had buried his face into.

Jamie punched his arm, and when he whined, she said, "Not yet."

"Child abuse."

"You're older than me."

"Elder abuse."

"Come on, get up," Jamie groaned, trying to ignore the shaking in her legs. "We still have to take this across the barrier and to the car."

"Wait," Ritchie rolled over. "I thought you were gonna do your call thing?" He gestured to the bag with the microphone and speaker, that which Jamie had made the poor decision to carry on her back.

"I can do that after we take this across the border and to the car," she said. "A few more minutes won't kill me."

Ritchie pushed himself to his feet. "I can't believe I'm going to say this but…" He put his hands on his hips and scowled at her. "You aren't touching this sled."

"What? But you can't—"

"I can and I will," he said, though his wobbly legs said otherwise. "You don't get to be a coward about this, Jamie, not now." Ritchie stepped towards her and rested his hands on her arms. "You'll regret it if you don't give yourself this chance to see if Artemis will choose you. Hell, you'll regret it if you don't show Artemis that you want her."

"But what if—"

"What-ifs are a curse. If you don't try, you'll never know."

Jamie sighed. "When did you get to be so wise?"

"Trauma, but that's a conversation for my therapist," he said with a smile. "Now stop trying to deflect. I get it, I do, but—"

"You get being in love with a wild-woman raised by wolves that you have to leave behind?" Jamie said. "Wow, if I had a penny for every time I'd heard that, I'd have two, which isn't much—"

"But it's strange it happened twice," Ritchie said with her before flicking her on the forehead. "Shut up. Look, what I was trying to say is, I get being stuck between a rock and a hard place when it comes to someone you care about. You don't want to make her choose. But you'll regret it if you don't at least try."

"I know," Jamie whispered. "I just … I don't know. My mind keeps going to the worst-case scenario."

"Well." Ritchie took the bag off her back. "Only way to confirm or deny that scenario is to howl for your lady—"

"I'm not howling."

"—and see if she responds to your lover's call—"

"You're a dick."

"—or if she doesn't." He set the bag down on the ground and unzipped it. "Get it set up and give it a go. If you don't" – he grabbed hold of the sled – "I'm telling your dad you're a wimp."

Ritchie started running, dragging the sled behind him.

"Traitor!" she yelled after him.

"Loser!" he yelled back with a laugh as he disappeared unnervingly quick through the split mountains.

How the heck is he faster by himself? Jamie wondered only to shake her head from pondering on the thought too long. She had work to do.

Setting up the microphone and speaker didn't take as long as she wanted it to. She'd even been able to shape the bag into a stand for the machine to stand on. With her hands noticeably shaking, she switched on the two machines. As the feedback sounded from the speaker, Jamie thought of what to say. She hadn't learnt much of Artemis's language which, right now, was an annoying fact. But there was one word she had practised over and over again just like Artemis had.

Closing her eyes, she spoke into the universe, praying that it would work.

Artemis.

53

ARTEMIS

She'd slept in late. The whole pack had. Being back at the cave had been a soothing experience. Add in the relief that they were safe from the humans, and the wolves found themselves sleeping peacefully for the first time in a moon cycle. Even the knowledge that Artemis had made her choice had helped them rest easily. Their happiness for her and her love for them brought them closer.

They'd all slept in a tight-knit group. Neither the pups or her nieces and nephews wished to be apart from her on their last night. She guessed that was why she'd woken up with a paw digging into her chest.

Artemis.

I am sleeping, she murmured trying to ignore the anxious paws scratching at her chest.

Wake up, Artemis, Mai's voice demanded.

Groggily, she opened her eyes and found every wolf stood to attention, their ears pointed outside the cave, noses twitching as if they were trying to catch a scent.

Artemis jumped to her feet, on guard. **What is it?**

Artemis.

The voice came again, making every wolf react. The voice was unfamiliar which, seeing as it called Artemis by name, had them on edge.

Mai came to her side, her black-white patchwork fur standing on edge. **Do you know of any lone wolf in the area?**

No, I have not seen another— Artemis's heart thudded heavily in her chest. **...Oak.**

Mai turned to her confused. **Your soul? What does she have to do with this?**

I taught her... Artemis continued, stepping out into the beaming sun above. **I taught her my name.**

You did? Mai tilted her head in surprise.

And now she is calling for you, Fenris said as he stepped out from among the pack, his golden eyes warm in the risen sun. **Go to her, Artemis. Your soul is waiting.**

Nodding, Artemis went to run, but she couldn't bring herself to do it. She swallowed back the tears. **What ... What will I do when I miss home?**

Fenris came to her side and stared up at her. **You can never miss something that is always with you. The strength of the wolf is that of its pack. And you will always** – he pushed himself up onto his back legs, his two forelegs resting against her chest – *always* **be part of this pack. No matter where you are, we are with you.**

The tears she'd tried to hold back pricked at the corners of her eyes as she gently pressed her forehead to his. This tender moment was needed even if it was brief. Fenris dropped back down to all fours and tilted his head to the mountain.

Now go.

Artemis didn't have to be told twice.

THE FOREST WAS GUIDING her home.

As her feet pounded against the ground and her arms swung high up to her chest, the wind whipped up from behind her, pushing her faster through the Forest at a speed she never knew she could reach. As she ran, birds flew overhead in formation, guiding her towards the mountains. Each squawk a signal to the small mammals to keep out of her path.

Once, when she felt her chest tighten from pain, a blood-red fox appeared at her side. It ran in line with her until it sped off ahead, its golden eyes turning back to catch hers. It didn't say a word, but she knew what he was saying: *Catch me if you can.*

She smiled and turned up the speed, practically flying with each leap and bound through the groves. The mountain was still far away, but with the Forest guiding her, she could make it. She knew it.

I'm coming, Jamie. Wait for me.

54

ARTEMIE

Jamie hated waiting. Yet, here she was, sitting on one of the stumps of trees that had been cut, waiting.

It felt cruel that she could see both the mountains and the tall tree-line by the river in the distance. She could picture exactly where the cave was. Could imagine where Artemis was with her family once more. And she imagined Artemis and the pack curled together comfortably as the sounds of water rushed past them at the line of tall trees. In each image though, the reoccurring thought was that Artemis wasn't thinking about Jamie. She was forgetting her and all the human drama that had come to the forest.

Still, even with that niggling doubt playing with her mind, she stayed. Waiting.

Please, Artemis, she begged. *Find me.*

❄

ARTEMIS HAD BEEN PUSHING herself hard and fast, the mountain growing closer and closer the more she ran. Her muscles were stretched to the limit, and she had not drunk enough to sustain this pace. But she was doing it. Whether it was through sheer will or intense bullheadedness, she wasn't sure, she just knew not to question it.

She had never been as fast as her family. Never would be. But that didn't stop her from running until her lungs felt like they were burning and her legs felt as weak as a newborn fawn's.

In the distance, more than half a span a way, stood the split mountains. It was almost cruel how they stood there, looking closer than they actually were. Artemis growled and pushed herself faster.

Jamie, I'm coming. Wait for me, please.

IT WAS the sound of roaring engines that finally broke the camel's back. Turning from her spot by the microphone and towards the split in the mountains, she saw them.

Builders, business suits, and chatter. When Professor Fred stepped out of the car in a new colourful sweater vest, Jamie knew she was too late.

With a sigh, she began packing up the microphone and speaker. She'd had her shot, no point keeping the expensive equipment in the open. She heard her dad approach just as she zipped up the bag.

"Don't pack it away yet," he said earnestly. "Fred said he'll give us another half an hour before the team gets to work—"

"It's alright." She slung the bag onto her shoulder. "It's been three hours since we packed up the camp and an hour since I sent out the call." Jamie looked over her shoulder and back towards the distant mountain. "If she wanted to, she'd have come."

"Maybe she didn't know—"

"Dad, it's OK. She's where she needs to be. This is her home. Just because…" She swallowed. "Just because something happened between us doesn't mean she can give all this up." She glanced once more at the mountains. "Let's go."

His hand reached out for hers and squeezed it. "OK, Jamie-bear."

Hand-in-hand, they walked away, leaving the forest behind.

❅

ARTEMIS WASN'T GOING to make it in time. She'd left too late. Left Jamie waiting too long. Frustration built in her chest. Her legs began to slow down.

No, she snapped at herself in her mind. *I won't give up. Not now.*

So, sending all the prayers she ever could make towards the Mother Wolf, Artemis took a deep breath and let out an almighty howl.

❅

JAMIE PULLED her dad to a stop between the split mountains.

"Did you hear that?" She turned to look towards the trees behind them. "Was that… a howl?"

He frowned. "I don't know, I didn't hear it well enough."

Letting go of her dad's hand, Jamie headed back towards the forest, hoping to hear it again. But nothing happened.

"I definitely heard something…"

"Jamie, there are lots of noises in a forest," her dad said gently. "I know you want it to be her but—"

"Wait, wait, let me try something."

Her dad fell silent, letting her have her moment. She was grateful for that.

Reaching up, she cupped her hands around her mouth, took a breath, and let out her own howl.

ARTEMIS!

Artemis's heart pounded in her chest. She knew that broken wolf-tongue voice. The sound echoed around her, carried toward her by the winds, as if the Forest were trying to coax her forward.

The howl came again.

Artemis!

As pained as her legs were, she kept going, ignoring the pain that shot up her aching feet as she went.

"Jamie!" Artemis cried, her voice hoarse from thirst and exhaustion. "Jamie!"

She kept going and going until, eventually, she rounded a grove of trees. There, just ahead, with Elder Will at her side, stood the one who owned her heart. Artemis could barely catch her breath as she ran towards Jamie.

Her soul.

THE FIRST THING Jamie noticed was how exhausted Artemis looked. Her face red from exertion, her chest heaved as she ran, and even her legs moved awkwardly as if they would give out at any moment.

Jamie ran towards her, determined to reach Artemis so she wouldn't have to run anymore. But, like most things in her life, that didn't go according to plan as she slid on a particularly slippery piece of snow and went tumbling onto the ground, falling at Artemis's feet.

Artemis didn't even think. She dropped down to the ground atop Jamie and cupped her face in her hands.

"Why did you come?" Jamie asked, tears slipping down her cheeks.

Leaning down, Artemis let her nose brush against Jamie's. Her fingers brushed away the tears as she felt her own start to fall. As Jamie looked up at her, her eyes filled with question and love, Artemis finally spoke aloud the words she'd somehow always known.

"I love you."

Jamie let out a quiet sob as she reached up to hold Artemis's face in her own hands. She stared deeply into those beautiful, green eyes.

"I love you too."

And their lips came together, not for the last time, and never again as a goodbye. As their lips melded and their tears came together, mixing as one until neither could tell whose tears were whose, the Forest gave its blessing, and each of the packs across its land let out a chorus of howls to the sky.

Their daughter Artemis had found her soul in Jamie. That is all they could have ever asked for.

EPILOGUE

MAI

The winter was harsher than the pack had expected it to be. Their usual warnings that come ahead of a dreary and dangerous winter never came, so they were left unprepared.

Her first litter was going to have to show nature that they were not so easily taken. Mai could only pray that the protection and warmth of the cave they called home would save them from the cold. But being without food still plagued her mind.

As she lay on her side, allowing her pups to feed for the third time that day, the pack returned from a hunt. Ronan entered and came to her side first, licking the backs of the heads of their pups one by one after he gave her the attention she needed.

Much has been lost during the cold but— He turned towards Taki, who came forward with a small hare in his teeth. **We caught something for you and the pups. You will all need your strength to survive this bitter season.**

After she ate her own portion and her pups theirs from her milk, she stood up and moved to curl around the pups, guarding them from the cave's cool entrance.

Ronan curled up behind her and whispered gently into her

ear, **They will grow strong, I am sure of it. Do not fear, my soul.**

You sound like Artemis, Mai said with a smile. **When she helped raise me, she often was the one chastising me for my nervous habits. "You show them who is in charge and you will never be afraid," she had said.**

Artemis was always the smart one, Ronan said, barking a laugh at the disgruntled disagreement among the others. **Do not try to deny it, my friends. You know as well as I that we would not have thrived without her.**

I wish she were here, Mai confessed. **She would know what to do.**

You know exactly what she would say. Ronan licked the top of her head. **She would tell you that you are stronger than you believe, and when you do not, I will believe for you.**

Mai smiled. **Your impression of her is quite accurate.**

Thank you, Ronan said proudly. **I have been practising.**

Who Artemis? Young Oak asked from among the pups.

Oak was their firstborn, a wolf of mixed brown and grey. Her inquisitive golden eyes looked up as she wagged her tail, whacking her siblings with it as she did.

Ronan knocked Mai's side before standing to join the nearby wolves. **I believe this is a story you should tell. We will try for another hunt in the meantime.**

As the rest of the pups huddled around Mai, she shook her head in amusement as her soul led the pack back out into the storm. *Of course he would leave me with the storytelling responsibilities. He knows how terrible I am with them.*

Who Artemis? Little One asked, her grey-white coat jiggling as she shook in excitement for a story. Little One always enjoyed a story.

Mai looked at her six pups' faces and smiled.

Before you were born, there was a great wolf who went by the name of Artemis. The pups sat in silent and unmoving awe, enraptured in the story instantly. **She was no ordinary wolf, though. Artemis is the great wolf-human who helped protect this pack from harm and raised young like me.**

Where she go? Oak asked.

Mai felt a heaviness in her heart at that question. One that was a mixture of joy and sadness that could never be eased.

Like any great wolf, Artemis found her soul, a human who helped save our home named Oak.

Me! Oak barked. **I Oak.**

Yes, we named you after the woman who saved your father's life once, Mai smiled. **Artemis and Oak found each other when they were young, but lost each other just as quickly after. It took a great danger to us for them to meet again. It was the will of the Forest for them to find each other again. So, when they did, their love could not be ignored.**

Do you miss them, Mother? Little One asked, wriggling forward towards her as if to offer comfort.

Yes and no, my love, she responded, turning to look out to the blizzard beyond their cave doors. **You see, we are never truly without each other. What is it we always say?**

The strength of the wolf is that of its pack, the pups recited.

Wherever our Artemis and Oak may be, they will always be part of this pack. She turned back to her pups, her wise eyes telling them that this is a story they could never forget. **And the pack will always be part of them.**

How does the world look to someone who has never lived in it? Complicated, to say the least.

The story will continue with *Finding Home*, a short story that follows Artemis and Jamie into the world of the humans. After Artemis leaves with her soul at the end of *Way of the Wild*, she must learn to adapt to this human world. But can she do it?

Head over to www.francescamcmahon.com to find out when their journey continues.

ACKNOWLEDGMENTS

A huge thank-you to my incredible beta readers, Andrea S. U., Darrien Smartt, Eli Q-L, Katie Mack, Laurel Fredericks, Megs Peterson, Michael Griswold, Nicole Gill, and Robert Gaymer.

To my editor, Carly Catt, for being the most incredible editor and supporter. I'm sorry I made you cry while working. Thank you for making this pack of wolves stronger.

Special acknowledgement to the lovely Alexia Dahlin for her help and support in making sure that Jamie and her mum's Korean heritage was presented with love and respect.

ALSO BY FRANCESCA MCMAHON

INTO THE WILD

Home to the Wild

Way of the Wild

INTO THE WILD SHORTS

Echoes of the Past

Before I Go

Finding Home

EILEAN IN THE OTHERWORLD

The Spiral of Life

TALES OF TUATHE DÉ

The Green Man Falls

The Phantom Queen Listens

ANTHOLOGIES

Tales of Cthulu Invictus

Terror of Octobernomicon

Tales from the Otherworlds

ABOUT THE AUTHOR

Francesca McMahon was born in Oxford, England, to a Scottish father and an Essex mother. They gained a B.A. in Creative Writing at Edge Hill University and was shortlisted for the university's Dame Janet Suzman Playwriting Award in 2019. Since graduating, Francesca has worked consistently in publishing while working on her writing of fantasy, horror and romance fiction, as well as various tabletop RPGs and screenplays. As a queer person, her work is dedicated to the LGBTQIA+ community, and she hopes that anyone who needs it will find a home in her imaginary worlds.

You can learn more over at www.francescamcmahon.com or follow Francesca on social media, via Twitter, Instagram, and TikTok (@adoseoffran).

www.ingramcontent.com/pod-product-compliance
Lightning Source LLC
Chambersburg PA
CBHW032149190726
48290CB00005BB/1483